NORA ROBERTS

PROTECTING THE HEART

MILLS & BOON®

First Published 1991
Fifth Australian Paperback Edition 2016
ISBN 978 148921038 8

First Published 1984
Fifth Australian Paperback Edition 2016
ISBN 978 148921038 8

First Published 1993
Fifth Australian Paperback Edition 2016
ISBN 978 148921038 8

Published by
Mills & Boon
An imprint of Harlequin Enterprises (Australia) Pty Ltd
Level 13
201 Elizabeth Street
SYDNEY NSW 2000
AUSTRALIA

Printed and bound in Australia by McPherson's Printing Group

MIX
Paper from responsible sources
FSC® C001695
FSC www.fsc.org

CONTENTS

OPPOSITES ATTRACT

For Joan Schulhafer,
leader of tours, handler of details and good friend

Chapter 1

"Advantage, Starbuck."

Isn't it always? Asher mused. For a moment the large arena held that humming silence peculiar to indoor sports events. There was an aroma of roasted peanuts and sweat. The overhead lights heated the scent somewhat pleasantly while the crush of bodies added enforced camaraderie. A small child sent up a babbling complaint and was hushed.

Seated several rows back at mid-court, Asher Wolfe watched Ty Starbuck—tennis master, Gypsy, eternal boy of summer and former lover. She thought again, as she had several times during more than two hours of play, that he'd changed. Just how wasn't yet completely clear. More than three years had passed since she'd seen him in the flesh. But he hadn't aged, or thickened, or lost any of his characteristic verve.

Rarely over the years had she watched a televised match—it was too painful. Too many faces were familiar, with his the most strictly avoided. If Asher had chanced to come across a write-up or picture of him in the sports pages or in a gossip column, she had immediately put it aside. Ty Starbuck was out of her life. Her decision. Asher was a very decisive woman.

Even her decision to come to the U.S. Indoor Tennis Championship had been a cool-headed one. Before making this trip, she had carefully weighed the pros and cons. In the end logic had won. She was getting back into the game herself. On the circuit, meetings with Ty would be unavoidable. She would see him now, letting the press, her colleagues and fans see clearly that there was nothing left of what had been three years before. Ty would see too, and, she hoped fervently, so would she.

Ty stood behind the baseline, preparing to serve. His stance was the same, she mused, as was his sizzling concentration. He tossed the ball up, coming back and over with the wicked left-handed serve that had become synonymous with his name, a Starbuck.

Asher heard the explosion of his breath that forced the power into it. She held her own. A lesser player than the Frenchman, Grimalier, would never have gotten a racket on the ball. His return was quick—force meeting force—and the rally began.

The crowd grew noisier as the ball smashed and thudded. Echoes bounced crazily. There were cries of encouragement, shouts of appreciation for the prowess of the two players. Ty's basic entertainment value hadn't decreased since Asher had been out of the game. Fans adored or detested him, but they never, never ignored him. Nor could she, though she was no longer certain which category she fell into. Every muscle of his body was familiar to her, every move, every expression. Her feelings were a confused jumble of respect, admiration and longing, which swirled to reach a vortex of pain, sharply remembered. Still, she was caught up in him again. Ty Starbuck demanded every last emotion and didn't really give a damn if it was love or hate.

Both men moved quickly, their eyes riveted on the small white sphere. Backhand, forehand, drop shot. Sweat poured down unheeded. Both the game and the fans demanded it. A tennis buff wanted to see the effort, the strain, wanted to hear the grunts and whistling breaths, wanted to smell the sweat. Despite her determination to remain dispassionate, Asher found herself watching Ty with the undiluted admiration she'd held for him for more than ten years.

He played with nonchalant flash—contradictory terms, but there it was. Strength, agility, form—he had them all. He had a long, limber body, seemingly elastic until the muscles flowed and bunched. His six-two height gave him an advantage of reach, and he could twist and turn on a dime. He played like a fencer—Asher had always thought a swashbuckler. Graceful sweeps, lunges, parries, with an almost demonic glint in his dusk-gray eyes. His face was that of the adventurer—narrow, rakish, with a hint of strong bone vying with an oddly tender mouth. As always, his hair was a bit too long, flowing wild and black around a white sweatband.

He was a set-up, and held advantage, but he played as though his life depended on this one point. That hadn't changed, Asher thought, as her heart pounded at double time. She was as involved in the match as if she were the one with the racket in her hand and the sweat rolling over her skin. Her palms were slick, her own muscles tight. Tennis involved its onlookers. Starbuck absorbed them. That hadn't changed either.

Ty smashed the ball crosscourt at the sideline. It careened away even as the Frenchman dove toward it. Asher sucked in her breath at the speed and placement of the ball.

"Wide," the line judge said dispassionately. A loud complaint poured out of the crowd. Asher fixed her eyes on Ty and waited for the explosion.

He stood, breathing hard from the punishing rally, his eyes fixed on the judge. The crowd continued to roar disapproval as deuce was called. Slowly, his eyes still on the judge, Ty swiped his wristband over his brow. His face was inscrutable but for his eyes, and his eyes spoke volumes. The crowd quieted to a murmur of speculation. Asher bit hard on her bottom lip. Ty walked back to the baseline without having uttered a sound.

This was the change, Asher realized with a jolt. Control. Her breath came out slowly as the tension in her shoulders diminished. In years past, Ty Starbuck would have hurled abuse—and an occasional racket—snarled, implored the crowd for support or berated them. Now he walked silently across the service court with temper smoldering in his eyes. But he held it in check. This was something new.

Behind the baseline Ty took his time, took his stance, then cracked an ace, like a bullet from a gun. The crowd screamed for him. With a quiet, insolent patience he waited while the scoring was announced. Again, he held advantage. Knowing him, and others like him, Asher was aware that his mind was occupied with his next move. The ace was already a memory, to be taken out and savored later. He still had a game to win.

The Frenchman connected with the next serve with a blazing forehand smash. The volley was sweating, furious and blatantly male. It was all speed and fire, two pirates blasting at each other across a sea of hardwood. There was the sound of the ball hitting the heart of the racket, the skid of rubber soles on wood, the grunts of the competitors as they drew out more force, all drowned beneath the echoes of cheers. The crowd was on its feet. Asher was on hers without even being aware of it. Neither man gave quarter as the seconds jumped to a minute, and a minute to more.

With a swing of the wrist the Frenchman returned a nearly impossible lob that drove him behind the baseline. The ball landed deep in the right court. With a forceful backhand Ty sent the ball low and away from his opponent, ending the two-and-a-half-hour match, three sets to one.

Starbuck was the U.S. Indoor Tennis champion, and the crowd's hero.

Asher let the enthusiasm pour around her as Ty walked to the net for the traditional handshake. The match had affected her more than she'd anticipated, but she passed this off as professional admiration. Now she allowed herself to wonder what his reaction would be when he saw her again.

Had she hurt him? His heart? His pride? The pride, she mused. That she could believe. The heart was a different matter. He would be angry, she concluded. She would be cool. Asher knew how to maintain a cool exterior as well as she knew how to smash an overhead lob. She'd learned it all as a child. When they met, she would simply deploy his temper. She had been preparing for the first encounter almost as religiously as she had been preparing to pick up her profession again. Asher was going to win at both. After he had finished with the showers and the press, she would make it a point to seek him out. To congratulate him—and to present the next test. It was much wiser for her to make the first move, for her to be the one prepared. Confident, she watched Ty exchange words with Grimalier at the net.

Then Ty turned his head very slowly, very deliberately. With no searching through the crowd, no hesitation, his eyes locked on hers. The strength of the contact had her drawing in a sharp, unwilling breath. His eyes held, no wavering. Her mouth went dry. Then he smiled, an unpleasant, direct challenge. Asher met it, more from shock than temerity as the crowd bellowed his name. *Starbuck* echoed from the walls like a litany. Ten seconds—fifteen—he neither blinked nor moved. For a man of action he had an uncanny ability for stillness. Boring into hers, his eyes made the distance between them vanish. The smile remained fixed. Just as Asher's palms began to sweat, he turned a full circle for the crowd, his racket above his head like a lance. They adored him.

He'd known, Asher thought furiously as people swarmed around her. He had known all along that she was there. Her anger wasn't the hot, logical result of being outmaneuvered, but small, silver slices of cold fury. Ty had let her know in ten seconds, without words, that the game was still on. And he always won.

Not this time though, she told herself. She had changed too. But she stood where she was, rooted, staring out at the now empty court. Her thoughts were whirling with memories, emotions, remembered sensations. People brushed by her, already debating the match.

She was a tall, reed-slim figure tanned gold from hours in the sun. Her hair was short, sculptured and misty-blond. The style flattered, while remaining practical for her profession. Over three years of retirement, Asher hadn't altered it. Her face seemed more suited to the glossy pages of a fashion magazine than the heat and frenzy of a tennis court. A weekender, one might think, looking at her elegant cheekbones in an oval face. Not a pro. The nose was small and straight above a delicately molded mouth she rarely thought to tint. Makeup on the courts was a waste of time, as sweat would wash it away. Her eyes were large and round, a shade of blue that hinted at violet. One of her few concessions to vanity was to darken the thick pale lashes that surrounded them. While other women competitors added jewelry or ribbons and bows to the court dress, Asher had never thought of it. Even off the court her attire leaned toward the simple and muted.

An enterprising reporter had dubbed her "The Face" when she had been eighteen. She'd been nearly twenty-three when she had retired from professional play, but the name had stuck. Hers was a face of great beauty and rigid control. On court, not a flicker of expression gave her opponent or the crowd a hint of what she was thinking or feeling. One of her greatest defenses in the game was her ability to remain unruffled under stress. The standard seeped into her personal life.

Asher had lived and breathed tennis for so long that the line of demarcation between woman and athlete was smudged. The hard, unbendable rule, imposed by her father, was ingrained into her—privacy, first and last. Only one person had ever been able to cross the boundary. Asher was determined he would not do so again.

As she stood staring down at the empty court, her face told nothing of her anger or turmoil—or the pain she hadn't been prepared for. It was calm and aloof. Her concentration was so deep that the leader of the small packet of people that approached her had to speak her name twice to get her attention.

She'd been recognized, she discovered. Though Asher had known it was inevitable, it still gave her a twist of pleasure to sign the papers and programs thrust at her. She hadn't been forgotten.

The questions were easy to parry, even when they skirted close to her relationship with Ty. A smile and double-talk worked well with fans. Asher wasn't naïve enough to think it would work with reporters. That, she hoped, was for another day.

As she signed, and edged her way back, Asher spotted a few colleagues—an old foe, a former doubles partner, a smattering of faces from the past. Her eyes met Chuck Prince's. Ty's closest friend was an affable player with a wrist of steel and beautiful footwork. Though the silent exchange was brief, even friendly, Asher saw the question in his eyes before she gave her attention to the next fan.

The word's out, she thought almost grimly as she smiled at a teenage tennis buff. Asher Wolfe's picking up her racket again. And they'd wonder, and eventually ask, if she was picking up Ty Starbuck too.

"Asher!" Chuck moved to her with the same bouncy stride he used to cross a court. In his typical outgoing style he seized her by the shoulders and kissed her full on the mouth. "Hey, you look terrific!"

With a laugh Asher drew back the breath his greeting had stolen from her. "So do you." It was inevitably true. Chuck was average in almost every way—height, build, coloring. But his inner spark added appeal and a puckish sort of sexuality. He'd never hesitated to exploit it—good-naturedly.

"No one knew you were coming," Chuck complained, easing her gently through the thinning crowd. "I didn't know you were here until..." His voice trailed off so that Asher knew he referred to the ten seconds of potent contact with Ty. "Until after the match," he finished. He gave her shoulder a quick squeeze. "Why didn't you give someone a call?"

"I wasn't entirely sure I'd make it." Asher allowed herself to be negotiated to a clear spot in a rear hallway. "Then I thought I'd just melt into the crowd. It didn't seem fair to disrupt the match with any the-prodigal-returns business."

"It was a hell of a match." The flash of teeth gleamed with enthusiasm. "I don't know if I've ever seen Ty play better than he did in the last set. Three aces."

"He always had a deadly serve," Asher murmured.

"Have you seen him?"

From anyone else the blunt question would have earned a cold stare. Chuck earned a quick grimace. "No. I will, of course, but I didn't want to distract him before the match." Asher linked her fingers—an old nervous habit. "I didn't realize he knew I was here."

Distract Starbuck, she thought with an inner laugh. No one and nothing distracted him once he picked up his game racket.

"He went crazy when you left."

Chuck's quiet statement brought her back. Deliberately she unlaced her fingers. "I'm sure he recovered quickly." Because the retort was sharper than she had intended, Asher shook her head as if to take back the words. "How have you been? I saw an ad with you touting the virtues of a new line of tennis shoes."

"How'd I look?"

"Sincere," she told him with a quick grin. "I nearly went out and bought a pair."

He sighed. "I was shooting for macho."

As the tension seeped out of her, Asher laughed. "With that face?" She cupped his chin with her hand and moved it from side to side. "It's a face a mother could trust—foolishly," she added.

"Shh!" He glanced around in mock alarm. "Not so loud, my reputation."

"Your reputation suffered a few dents in Sydney," she recalled. "What was that—three seasons ago? The stripper."

"Exotic dancer," Chuck corrected righteously. "It was merely an exchange of cultures."

"You did look kind of cute wearing those feathers." With another laugh she kissed his cheek. "Fuchsia becomes you."

"We all missed you, Asher." He patted her slim, strong shoulder.

The humor fled from her eyes. "Oh, Chuck, I missed you. Everyone, all of it. I don't think I realized just how much until I walked in here today." Asher looked into space at her own thoughts, her own memories. "Three years," she said softly.

"Now you're back."

Her eyes drifted to his. "Now I'm back," she agreed. "Or will be in two weeks."

"The Foro Italico."

Asher gave him a brief smile that was more determination than joy. "I've never won on that damn Italian clay. I'm going to this time."

"It was your pacing."

The voice from behind her had Asher's shoulders stiffening. As she faced Chuck her eyes showed only the merest flicker of some secret emotion before they calmed. When she turned to Ty he saw first that his memory of her beauty hadn't been exaggerated with time, and second that her layer of control was as tough as ever.

"So you always told me," she said calmly. The jolt was over, she reasoned, with the shock of eye contact in the auditorium. But her stomach muscles tightened. "You played beautifully, Ty...after the first set."

They were no more than a foot apart now. Neither could find any changes in the other. Three years, it seemed, was barely any time at all. It occurred to Asher abruptly that twenty years wouldn't have mattered. Her heart would still thud, her blood would still swim. For him. It had always, would always be for him. Quickly she pushed those thoughts aside. If she were to remain calm under his gaze, she couldn't afford to remember.

The press were still tossing questions at him, and now at her as well. They began to crowd in, nudging Asher closer to Ty. Without a word he took her arm and drew her through the door at his side. That it happened to be a woman's rest room didn't faze him as he turned the lock. He faced her, leaning lazily back against the door while Asher stood straight and tense.

As he had thirty minutes before, Ty took his time studying her. His eyes weren't calm, they rarely were, but the emotion in them was impossible to decipher. Even in his relaxed stance there was a sense of force, a storm brewing. Asher met his gaze levelly, as he expected. And she moved him. Her power of serenity always moved him. He could have strangled her for it.

"You haven't changed, Asher."

"You're wrong." Why could she no longer breathe easily or control the furious pace of her heart?

"Am I?" His brows disappeared under his tousled hair for a moment. "We'll see."

He was a very physical man. When he spoke, he gestured. When he held a conversation, he touched. Asher could remember the brush of his hand—on her arm, her hair, her shoulder. It had been his casualness that had drawn her to him. And had driven her away. Now, as they stood close, she was surprised that Ty did not touch her in any way. He simply watched and studied her.

"I noticed a change," she countered. "You didn't argue with the referees or shout at the line judge. Not once." Her lips curved slightly. "Not even after a bad call."

He gave her a lightly quizzical smile. "I turned over that leaf some time ago."

"Really?" She was uncomfortable now, but merely moved her shoulders. "I haven't been keeping up."

"Total amputation, Asher?" he asked softly.

"Yes." She would have turned away, but there was nowhere to go. Over the line of sinks to her left the mirrors tossed back her reflection…and his. Deliberately she shifted so that her back was to them. "Yes," she repeated, "it's the cleanest way."

"And now?"

"I'm going to play again," Asher responded simply. His scent was reaching out for her, that familiar, somehow heady fragrance that was sweat and victory and sex all tangled together. Beneath the placid expression her thoughts shot off in a tangent.

Nights, afternoons, rainy mornings. He'd shown her everything a man and woman could be together, opened doors she had never realized existed. He had knocked down every guard until he had found her.

Oh God, dear God, she thought frantically. Don't let him touch me now. Asher linked her fingers together. Though his eyes never left hers, Ty noted the gesture. And recognized it. He smiled.

"In Rome?"

Asher controlled the urge to swallow. "In Rome," she agreed. "To start. I'll go in unseeded. It has been three years."

"How's your backhand?"

"Good." Automatically she lifted her chin. "Better than ever."

Very deliberately Ty circled her arm with his fingers. Asher's palms became damp. "It was always a surprise," he commented, "the power in that slender arm. Still lifting weights?"

"Yes."

His fingers slid down until they circled the inside of her elbow. It gave him bitter pleasure to feel the tiny pulse jump erratically. "So," he murmured softly, "Lady Wickerton graces the courts again."

"Ms. Wolfe," Asher corrected him stiffly. "I've taken my maiden name back."

His glance touched on her ringless hands. "The divorce is final?"

"Quite final. Three months ago."

"Pity." His eyes had darkened with anger when he lifted them back to hers. "A title suits you so well. I imagine you fit into an English manor as easily as a piece of Wedgwood. Drawing rooms and butlers," he murmured, then scanned her face as if he would memorize it all over again. "You have the looks for them."

"The reporters are waiting for you." Asher made a move to her left in an attempt to brush by him. Ty's fingers clamped down.

"Why, Asher?" He'd promised himself if he ever saw her again, he wouldn't ask. It was a matter of pride. But pride was overwhelmed by temper as the question whipped out, stinging them both. "Why did you leave that way? Why did you run off and marry that damn English jerk without a word to me?"

She didn't wince at the pressure of his fingers, nor did she make any attempt to pull away. "That's my business."

"*Your* business?" The words were hardly out of her mouth before he grabbed both her arms. "*Your* business? We'd been together for months, the whole damn circuit that year. One night you're in my bed, and the next thing I know you've run off with some English lord." His control slipped another notch as he shook her. "I had to find out from my sister. You didn't even have the decency to dump me in person."

"Decency?" she tossed back. "I won't discuss decency with you, Ty." She swallowed the words, the accusations she'd promised herself never to utter. "I made my choice," she said levelly, "I don't have to justify it to you."

"We were lovers," he reminded her tightly. "We lived together for nearly six months."

"I wasn't the first woman in your bed."

"You knew that right from the start."

"Yes, I knew." She fought the urge to beat at him with the hopeless rage that was building inside her. "I made my choice then, just as I made one later. Now, let me go."

Her cool, cultured control had always fascinated and infuriated him. Ty knew her, better than anyone, even her own father—certainly better than her ex-husband. Inside, she was jelly, shuddering convulsively, but outwardly she was composed and lightly disdainful. Ty wanted to shake her until she rattled. More, much more, he wanted to taste her again—obliterate three years with one long greedy kiss. Desire and fury hammered at him. He knew that if he gave in to either, he'd never be able to stop. The wound was still raw.

"We're not finished, Asher." But his grip relaxed. "You still owe me."

"No." Defensive, outraged, she jerked free. "No, I don't owe you anything."

"Three years," he answered, and smiled. The smile was the same biting challenge as before. "You owe me three years, and by God, you're going to pay."

He unlocked the door and opened it, stepping back so that Asher had no choice but to meet the huddle of reporters head-on.

"Asher, how does it feel to be back in the States?"

"It's good to be home."

"What about the rumors that you're going to play professionally again?"

"I intend to play professionally beginning with the opening of the European circuit in Rome."

More questions, more answers. The harsh glare of a flash causing light to dance in front of her eyes. The press always terrified her. She could remember her father's constant instructions: Don't say any more than absolutely necessary. Don't let them see what you're feeling. They'll devour you.

Churning inside, Asher faced the pack of avid reporters with apparent ease. Her voice was quiet and assured. Her fingers were locked tightly together. With a smile she glanced quickly down the hall, searching for an escape route. Ty leaned negligently against the wall and gave her no assistance.

"Will your father be in Rome to watch you play?"

"Possibly." An ache, a sadness, carefully concealed.

"Did you divorce Lord Wickerton so you could play again?"

"My divorce has nothing to do with my profession." A half-truth, a lingering anger, smoothly disguised.

"Are you nervous about facing young rackets like Kingston and old foes like Martinelli?"

"I'm looking forward to it." A terror, a well of doubt, easily masked.

"Will you and Starbuck pair up again?"

Fury, briefly exposed.

"Starbuck's a singles player," she managed after a moment.

"You guys'll have to keep your eyes open to see if that changes." With his own brand of nonchalance, Ty slipped an arm around

Asher's rigid shoulders. "There's no telling what might happen, is there, Asher?"

Her answer was an icy smile. "You've always been more unpredictable than I have, Ty."

He met the smile with one of his own. "Have I?" Leaning down, he brushed her lips lightly. Flashbulbs popped in a blaze of excitement. Even as their lips met, so did their eyes. Hers were twin slits of fury, his grimly laughing and ripe with purpose. Lazily he straightened. "The Face and I have some catching up to do."

"In Rome?" a reporter cracked.

Ty grinned and quite deliberately drew Asher closer. "That's where it started."

Chapter 2

Rome. The Colosseum. The Trevi fountain. The Vatican. Ancient history, tragedy and triumphs. Gladiators and competition. In the Foro Italico the steaming Italian sun beat down on the modern-day competitors just as it had on those of the Empire. To play in this arena was a theatrical experience. It was sun and space. There were lush umbrella pines and massive statues to set the forum apart from any other on the circuit. Beyond the stadium, wooded hills rose from the Tiber. Within its hedge trimmings, ten thousand people could chant, shout and whistle. Italian tennis fans were an emotional, enthusiastic and blatantly patriotic lot. Asher hadn't forgotten.

Nor had she forgotten that the Foro Italico had been the setting for the two biggest revelations in her life: her consuming love for tennis, her overwhelming love for Ty Starbuck.

She had been seven the first time she had watched her father win the Italian championship in the famed *campo central.* Of course she had seen him play before. One of her earliest memories was of watching her tall, tanned father dash around a court in blazing white. Jim

Wolfe had been a champion before Asher had been born, and a force to be reckoned with long after.

Her own lessons had begun at the age of three. With her shortened racket she had hit balls to some of the greatest players of her father's generation. Her looks and her poise had made her a pet among the athletes. She grew up finding nothing unusual about seeing her picture in the paper or bouncing on the knee of a Davis Cup champion. Tennis and travel ruled her world. She had napped in the rear of limousines and walked across the pampered grass of Wimbledon. She had curtsied to heads of state and had her cheek pinched by a president. Before she began attending school she had already crossed the Atlantic a half dozen times.

But it had been in Rome, a year after the death of her mother, that Asher Wolfe had found a life's love and ambition.

Her father had still been wet and glowing from his victory, his white shorts splattered with the red dust of the court, when she had told him she would play in the *campo central* one day. And win.

Perhaps it had been a father's indulgence for his only child, or his ambition. Or perhaps it had been the quietly firm determination he saw in seven-year-old eyes. But Asher's journey had begun that day, with her father as her guide and her mentor.

Fourteen years later, after her own defeat in the semi-finals, Asher had watched Starbuck's victory. There had been nothing similar in the style of her father and the style of the new champion. Jim Wolfe had played a meticulous game—cold control with the accent on form. Starbuck played like a fireball—all emotion and muscle. Often, Asher had speculated on what the results would be if the two men were to meet across a net. Where her father brought her pride, Ty brought her excitement. Watching him, she could understand the sense of sexuality onlookers experienced during a bullfight. Indeed, there was a thirst for blood in his style that both alarmed and fascinated.

Ty had pursued her doggedly for months, but she had held him off. His reputation with women, his temper, his flamboyance and nonconformity had both attracted and repulsed her. Though the attraction was strong, and her heart was already lost, Asher had sensibly listened to her head. Until that day in May.

He'd been like a god, a powerful, mythological warrior with a strength and power that even the biased Italian crowd couldn't resist. Some cheered him, some cheerfully cursed him. He'd given them the sweat they had come to see. And the show.

Ty had taken the championship in seven frenzied sets. That night Asher had given him both her innocence and her love. For the first time in her life she had allowed her heart complete freedom. Like a blossom kept in the sheltered, controlled climate of a hothouse, she took to the sun and storm wildly. Days were steamier and more passionate—nights both turbulent and tender. Then the season had ended.

Now, as Asher practiced in the early morning lull on court five, the memories stirred, sweet and bitter as old wine. Fast rides on back roads, hot beaches, dim hotel rooms, foolish laughter, crazy loving. Betrayal.

"If you dream like that this afternoon, Kingston's going to wipe you out of the quarter-finals."

At the admonishment, Asher snapped back. "Sorry."

"You should be, when an old lady drags herself out of bed at six to hit to you."

Asher laughed. At thirty-three, Madge Haverbeck was still a force to be reckoned with across a net. Small and stocky, with flyaway brown hair and comfortably attractive features, she looked like an ad for home-baked cookies. She was, in fact, a world-class player with two Wimbledon championships, a decade of other victories that included the Wightman Cup and a wicked forehand smash. For two years Asher had been her doubles partner to their mutual satisfaction and success. Her husband was a sociology professor at Yale whom Madge affectionately termed "The Dean."

"Maybe you should sit down and have a nice cup of tea," Asher suggested while tucking her tongue in her cheek. "This game's rough on middle-aged matrons."

After saying something short and rude, Madge sent a bullet over the net. Light and agile, Asher sprang after it. Her concentration focused. Her muscles went to work. In the drowsy morning hum the ball thudded on clay and twanged off strings. Madge wasn't a woman to consider a practice workout incidental. She hustled over the court, driving Asher back to the baseline, luring her to the net, hammering at her by mixing her shots while Asher concentrated on adjusting her pace to the slow, frustrating clay.

For a fast, aggressive player, the surface could be deadly. It took strength and endurance rather than speed. Asher thanked the endless hours of weight lifting as she swung the racket again and again. The muscles in the slender arm were firm.

After watching one of Asher's returns scream past, Madge shifted her racket to her left hand. "You're pretty sharp for three years off, Face."

Asher filled her lungs with air. "I've kept my hand in."

Though Madge wondered avidly about Asher's marriage and years of self-imposed retirement, she knew her former partner too well to question. "Kingston hates to play the net. It's her biggest weakness."

"I know." Asher slipped the spare ball in her pocket. "I've studied her. Today she's going to play my game."

"She's better on clay than grass."

It was a roundabout way of reminding Asher of her own weakness. She gave Madge one of her rare, open smiles. "It won't matter. Next week I'm playing center court."

Slipping on a warm-up jacket, Madge gave a hoot of laughter. "Haven't changed much, have you?"

"Bits and pieces." Asher dabbed at sweat with her wristband. "What about you? How're you going to play Fortini?"

"My dear." Madge fluffed at her hair. "I'll simply overpower her."

Asher snorted as they strolled off the court. "You haven't changed either."

"If you'd told me you were coming back," Madge put in, "we'd be playing doubles. Fisher's good, and I like her, but…"

"I couldn't make the decision until I was sure I wouldn't make a fool of myself." Slowly Asher flexed her racket arm. "Three years, Madge. I ache." She sighed with the admission. "I don't remember if I ached like this before."

"We can trade legs any time you say, Face."

Remembering, Asher turned with a look of concern. "How's the knee?"

"Better since the surgery last year." Madge shrugged. "I can still forecast rain though. Here's to a sunny season."

"I'm sorry I wasn't there for you."

Madge hooked her arm through Asher's in easy comradeship. "Naturally I expected you to travel six thousand miles to hold my hand."

"I would have if…" Asher trailed off, remembering the state of her marriage at the time of Madge's surgery.

Recognizing guilt, Madge gave Asher a friendly nudge with her elbow. "It wasn't as big a deal as the press made out. Of course," she added with a grin, "I milked it for a lot of sympathy. The Dean brought me breakfast in bed for two months. Bless his heart."

"Then you came back and demolished Rayski in New York."

"Yeah." Madge laughed with pleasure. "I enjoyed that."

Asher let her gaze wander over the serene arena, quiet but for the thud of balls and hum of bees. "I have to win this one, Madge. I need it. There's so much to prove."

"To whom?"

"Myself first." Asher moved her shoulders restlessly, shifting her bag to her left hand. "And a few others."

"Starbuck? No, don't answer," Madge continued, seeing Asher's expression out of the corner of her eye. "It just sort of slipped out."

"What was between Ty and me was finished three years ago," Asher stated, deliberately relaxing her muscles.

"Too bad." Madge weathered Asher's glare easily. "I like him."

"Why?"

Stopping, Madge met the direct look. "He's one of the most alive people I know. Ever since he learned to control his temper, he brings so such emotion to the courts. It's good for the game. You don't have a stale tournament when Starbuck's around. He also brings that same emotion into his friendships."

"Yes," Asher agreed. "It can be overwhelming."

"I didn't say he was easy," Madge countered. "I said I liked him. He is exactly who he is. There isn't a lot of phony business to cut through to get to Starbuck." Madge squinted up at the sun. "I suppose some of it comes from the fact that we turned pro the same year, did our first circuit together. Anyway, I've watched him grow from a cocky kid with a smart mouth to a cocky man who manages to keep that wicked temper just under the surface."

"You like him for his temper?"

"Partly." The mild, homey-looking woman smiled. "Starbuck's just plain strung right, Asher. He's not a man you can be ambivalent about. You're either for him or against him."

It was as much inquiry as statement. Saying nothing, Asher began to walk again. Ambivalence had never entered into her feeling for Ty.

On his way home from his own practice court Ty watched them. More accurately he watched Asher. While she remained unaware of him, he could take in every detail. The morning sun glinted down on her hair. Her shoulders were strong and slender, her gait long, leggy and confident. He was grateful he could study her now with some dispassion.

When he had looked out and had seen her in the stands two weeks before, it had been like catching a fast ball with his stomach. Shimmering waves of pain, shock, anger, one sensation had raced after the other. He had blown the first set.

Then he had done more than pull himself together. He had used the emotions against his opponent. The Frenchman hadn't had a chance against Ty's skill combined with three years of pent-up fury. Always, he played his best under pressure and stress. It fed him.

With Asher in the audience the match had become a matter of life and death. When she had left him she'd stolen something from him. Somehow, the victory had helped him regain a portion of it.

Damn her that she could still get to him. Ty's thoughts darkened as the distance between them decreased. Just looking at her made him want.

He had wanted her when she had been seventeen. The sharp, sudden desire for a teenager had astonished the then twenty-three-year-old Ty. He had kept a careful distance from her all that season. But he hadn't stopped wanting her. He had done his best to burn the desire out by romancing women he considered more his style—flamboyant, reckless, knowledgeable.

When Asher had turned twenty-one Ty had abandoned common sense and had begun a determined, almost obsessive pursuit. The more she had evaded him, the firmer she refused, the stronger his desire had grown. Even the victory, tasted first in Rome, hadn't lessened his need.

His life, which previously had had one focus, then had realigned with two dominating forces. Tennis and Asher. At the time he wouldn't have said he loved tennis, but simply that it was what and who he was. He wouldn't have said he loved Asher, but merely that he couldn't live without her.

Yet he had had to—when she'd left him to take another man's name. A title and a feather bed, Ty thought grimly. He was determined to make Asher Wolfe pay for bringing him a pain he had never expected to feel.

By turning left and altering his pace Ty cut across her path, apparently by chance. "Hi, Madge." He gave the brunette a quick grin, flicking his finger down her arm before turning his attention fully to Asher.

"Hiya, Starbuck." Madge glanced from the man to the woman and decided she wasn't needed. "Hey, I'm late," she said by way of explanation, then trotted off. Neither Asher nor Ty commented.

From somewhere in the surrounding trees Asher heard the high clear call of a bird. Nearer at hand was the slumberous buzz of bees and dull thud of balls. On court three, someone cursed fluently. But Asher was conscious only of Ty beside her.

"Just like old times," he murmured, then grinned at her expression. "You and Madge," he added.

Asher struggled not to be affected. The setting had too many memories. "She hit to me this morning. I hope I don't have to face her in the tournament."

"You go against Kingston today."

"Yes."

He took a step closer. In her mind's eye Asher saw the hedge beside her. With Ty directly in her path, dignified retreat was impossible. For all her delicacy of looks, Asher didn't run from a battle. She linked her fingers, then dragged them apart, annoyed.

"And you play Devereux."

His acknowledgment was a nod. "Is your father coming?"

"No." The answer was flat and brief. Ty had never been one to be put off by a subtle warning.

"Why?"

"He's busy." She started to move by him, but succeeded only in closing the rest of the distance between them. Maneuvering was one of the best aspects of Ty's game.

"I've never known him to miss one of your major tournaments." In an old habit he couldn't resist nor she prevent, he reached for her hair. "You were always his first order of business."

"Things change," she responded stiffly. "People change."

"So it seems." His grin was sharp and cocky. "Will your husband be here?"

"Ex-husband." Asher tossed her head to dislodge his hand. "And no."

"Funny, as I recall he was very fond of tennis." Casually he set down his bag. "Has that changed too?"

"I need to shower." Asher had drawn nearly alongside of him before Ty stopped her. His hand slipped to her waist too quickly and too easily.

"How about a quick set for old times' sake?"

His eyes were intense—that oddly compelling color that was half night and half day. Asher remembered how they seemed to darken from the pupils out when he was aroused. The hand at her waist was wide-palmed and long-fingered—a concert pianist's hand, but it was rough and worked. The strength in it would have satisfied a prizefighter.

"I don't have time." Asher pushed to free herself and connected with the rock-hard muscles of his forearm. She pulled her fingers back as though she'd been burned.

"Afraid?" There was mockery and a light threat with the overtones of sex. Her blood heated to the force she had never been able to fully resist.

"I've never been afraid of you." And it was true enough. She had been fascinated.

"No?" He spread his fingers, drawing her an inch closer. "Fear's one of the popular reasons for running away."

"I didn't run," she corrected him. "I left." *Before you did,* she added silently. For once, she had outmaneuvered him.

"You still have some questions to answer, Asher." His arm slid around her before she could step back. "I've waited a long time for the answers."

"You'll go on waiting."

"For some," he murmured in agreement. "But I'll have the answer to one now."

She saw it coming and did nothing. Later she would curse herself for her passivity. But when he lowered his mouth to hers, she met it without resistance. Time melted away.

He had kissed her like this the first time—slowly, thoroughly, gently. It was another part of the enigma that a man so full of energy and turbulence could show such sensitivity. His mouth was exactly as Asher remembered. Warm, soft, full. Perhaps she had been lost the first time he had kissed her—drawn to the fury—captured by the tenderness. Even when he brought her closer, deepening the kiss with a low-throated groan, the sweetness never diminished.

As a lover he excelled because beneath the brash exterior was an underlying and deep-rooted respect for femininity. He enjoyed the softness, tastes and textures of women, and instinctively sought to bring them pleasure in lovemaking. As an inherent loner, it was another contradiction that Ty saw a lover as a partner, never a means to an end. Asher had sensed this from the first touch so many years ago. Now she let herself drown in the kiss with one final coherent thought. It had been so long.

Her arm, which should have pushed him away, curved up his back instead until her hand reached his shoulders. Her fingers grasped at him. Unhesitatingly she pressed her body to his. He was the one man who could touch off the passion she had so carefully locked inside. The only man who had ever reached her core and gained true intimacy—the meeting of minds as well as of bodies. Starved for the glimpses of joy she remembered, Asher clung while her mouth moved avidly on his. Her greed for more drove away all her reserve, and all her promises.

Oh, to be loved again, truly loved, with none of the emptiness that had haunted her life for too long! To give herself, to take, to know the pure, searing joy of belonging! The thoughts danced in her mind like dreams suddenly remembered. With a moan, a sigh, she pressed against him, hungry for what had been.

The purpose of the kiss had been to punish, but he'd forgotten. The hot-blooded passion that could spring from the cool, contained woman had forced all else from his mind but need. He needed her, still needed her, and was infuriated. If they had been alone, he would have taken her and then faced the consequences. His impulses were still difficult to control. But they weren't alone. Some small part of his mind clung to reality even while his body pulsed. She was soft and eager. Everything he had ever wanted. All he had done without. Ty discovered he had gotten more answers than he'd bargained for.

Drawing her away, he took his time studying her face. Who could resist the dangerous power of a hurricane? The wicked, primitive rumblings of a volcano? She stared at him, teetering between sanity and desire.

Her eyes were huge and aware, her lips parted breathlessly. It was a look he remembered. Long nights in her bed, hurried afternoons or lazy mornings, she would look at him so just before loving. Hot and insistent, desire spread, then closed like a fist in his stomach. He stepped back so that they were no longer touching.

"Some things change," he remarked. "And some things don't," he added before turning to walk away.

There was time for deep breathing before Asher took her position for the first serve. It wasn't the thousand pairs of eyes watching around the court that had her nerves jumping. It was one pair, dark brown and intense, seventy-eight feet away. Stacie Kingston, age twenty, hottest newcomer to the game in two years. She had energy, force and drive, along with a fierce will to win. Asher recognized her very well. The red clay spread out before her, waiting.

Because she knew the importance of mastering the skittish nerves and flood of doubts, she continued to take long, deep breaths. Squeezing the small white ball, Asher discovered the true meaning of trial by fire. If she won, here where she had never won before, three years after she had last lifted a racket professionally, she would have passed the test. Rome, it seemed, would always be her turning point.

Because it was the only way, she blocked out the past, blocked out tomorrow and focused wholly on the contest. Tossing the ball up, she watched the ascent, then struck home. Her breath came out in a hiss of effort.

Kingston played a strong, offensive game. A studied, meticulous player, she understood and used the personality of clay to her advantage, forcing Asher to the baseline again and again. Asher found the dirt frustrating. It cut down on her speed. She was hurrying, defending herself. The awareness of this only made her rush more. The ball eluded her, bouncing high over her head when she raced to the net, dropping lazily into the forecourt when she hugged the baseline. Unnerved by her own demons, she double-faulted. Kingston won the first game, breaking Asher's serve and allowing her only one point.

The crowd was vocal, the sun ferocious. The air was thick with humidity. From the other side of the hedge Asher could hear the games and laughter of schoolchildren. She wanted to throw aside her racket and walk off the court. It was a mistake, a mistake, her mind repeated, to have come back. Why had she subjected herself to this again? To the effort and pain and humiliation?

Her face was utterly passive, showing none of the turmoil. Gripping the racket tightly, she fought off the weakness. She had played badly, she knew, because she had permitted Kingston to set the pace. It had taken Asher less than six minutes from first service to defeat. Her skin wasn't even damp. She hadn't come back to give up after one game, nor had she come back to be humiliated. The stands were thick with people watching, waiting. She had only herself.

Flicking a hand at the short skirt of her tennis dress, she walked back to the baseline. Crouched, she shifted her weight to the balls of her feet. Anger with herself was forced back. Fear was conquered. A cool head was one of her greatest weapons, and one she hadn't used in the first game. This time, she was determined. This time, the game would be played her way.

She returned the serve with a drop shot over the net that caught Kingston off balance. The crowd roared its approval as the ball boy scurried across the court to scoop up the dead ball.

Love-fifteen. Asher translated the scoring in her head with grim satisfaction. Fear had cost her the first game. Now, in her own precise way, she was out for blood. Kingston became more symbol than opponent.

Asher continued to draw her opponent into the net, inciting fierce volleys that brought the crowd to its feet. The roar and babble of languages did not register with her. She saw only the ball, heard only the effortful breathing that was hers. She ended that volley with a neatly placed ball that smacked clean at the edge of the baseline.

Something stirred in her—the hot, bubbling juice of victory. Asher tasted it, reveled in it as she walked coolly back to position. Her face was wet now, so she brushed her wristband over her brow before she cupped the two service balls in her hand. Only the beginning, she told herself. Each game was its own beginning.

By the end of the first set the court surface was zigzagged with skid marks. Red dust streaked the snowy material of her dress and marked her shoes. Sweat rolled down her sides after thirty-two minutes of ferocious play. But she'd taken the first set six-three.

Adrenaline was pumping madly, though Asher looked no more flustered than a woman about to hostess a dinner party. The competitive drives she had buried were in complete control. Part of her sensed Starbuck was watching. She no longer cared. At that moment Asher felt that if she had faced him across the net, she could have beaten him handily. When Kingston returned her serve deep, Asher met it with a topspin backhand that brushed the top of the net. Charging after the ball, she met the next return with a powerful lob.

The sportswriters would say that it was at that moment, when the two women were eye to eye, that Asher won the match. They remained that way for seconds only, without words, but communication had been made. From then Asher dominated, forcing Kingston into a defensive game. She set a merciless pace. When she lost a point she came back to take two. The aggressiveness was back, the cold-blooded warfare the sportswriters remembered with pleasure from her early years on the court.

Where Starbuck was fire and flash, she was ice and control. Never once during a professional match had Asher lost her iron grip on her temper. It had once been a game among the sportswriters—waiting for The Face to cut loose.

Only twice during the match did she come close to giving them satisfaction, once on a bad call and once on her own poor judgment of a shot. Both times she stared down at her racket until the urge to stomp and swear had passed. When she had again taken her position, there had been nothing but cool determination in her eyes.

She took the match six-one, six-two in an hour and forty-nine minutes. Twice she had held Kingston's service to love. Three times she had served aces—something Kingston with her touted superserve had been unable to accomplish. Asher Wolfe would go on to the semi-finals. She had made her comeback.

Madge dropped a towel over Asher's shoulders as she collapsed on her chair. "Good God, you were terrific! You destroyed her." Asher said nothing, covering her face with the towel a moment to absorb sweat. "I swear, you're better than you were before."

"She wanted to win," Asher murmured, letting the towel drop limply again. "I *had* to win."

"It showed," Madge agreed, giving her shoulder a quick rub. "Nobody'd believe you haven't played pro in three years. I hardly believe it myself."

Slowly Asher lifted her face to her old partner. "I'm not in shape yet, Madge," she said beneath the din of the still-cheering crowd. "My calves are knotted. I don't even know if I can stand up again."

Madge skimmed a critical glance over Asher's features. She couldn't detect a flicker of pain. Bending, she scooped up Asher's warm-up jacket, then draped it over Asher's shoulders. "I'll help you to the showers. I don't play for a half hour. You just need a few minutes on the massage table."

Exhausted, hurting, Asher started to agree, then spotted Ty watching her. His grin might have been acknowledgment of her victory. But he knew her, Asher reflected, knew her inside as no one else did.

"No thanks, I'll manage." Effortfully she rose to zip the cover around her racket. "I'll see you after you beat Fortini."

"Asher—"

"No, really, I'm fine now." Head high, muscles screaming, she walked toward the tunnel that led to the locker rooms.

Alone in the steam of the showers, Asher let herself empty, weeping bitterly for no reason she could name.

Chapter 3

It was the night after her victory in the semi-finals that Asher confronted Ty again. She had kept herself to a rigorous schedule of practice, exercise, press, and play. Her pacing purposely left her little time for recreation. Practice was a religion. Morning hours were spent in the peaceful tree-shaded court five, grooving in, polishing her footwork, honing her reflexes.

Exercise was a law. Push-ups and weight lifting, stretching and hardening the muscles. Good press was more than a balm for the ego. Press was important to the game as a whole as well as the individual player. And the press loved a winner.

Play was what the athlete lived for. Pure competition—the testing of the skills of the body, the use of the skills of the mind. The best played as the best dancers danced—for the love of it. During the days of her second debut, Asher rediscovered love.

In her one brief morning meeting with Ty she had rediscovered passion. Only her fierce concentration on her profession kept her from dwelling on a need that had never died. Rome was a city for lovers—it had been once for her. Asher knew that this time she must think of it only as a city for competition if she was to survive the first hurdle of regaining her identity. Lady Wickerton was a woman she hardly recognized. She had nearly lost Asher Wolfe trying to fit an image. How could she recapture herself if she once again became Starbuck's lady?

In a small club in the Via Sistina where the music was loud and the wine was abundant, Asher sat at a table crowded with bodies. Elbows nudged as glasses were reached for. Liquor spilled and was cheerfully cursed. In the second and final week of the Italian Open, the tension grew, but the pace mercifully slowed.

Rome was noise, fruit stands, traffic, outdoor cafés. Rome was serenity, cathedrals, antiquity. For the athletes it was days of grueling competition and nights of celebration or commiseration. The next match was a persistent shadow over the thoughts of the winners and the losers. As the music blared and the drinks were poured, they discussed every serve, every smash and error and every bad call. Rome was blissfully indolent over its reputation for bad calls.

"Long!" A dark, lanky Australian brooded into his wine. "That ball was inside by two inches. Two bloody inches."

"You won the game, Michael," Madge reminded him philosophically. "And in the second game of the fifth set, you had a wide ball that wasn't called."

The Australian grinned and shrugged. "It was only a little wide." He brought his thumb and forefinger close together at the good-natured razzing of his peers. "What about this one?" His gesture was necessarily shortened by the close quarters as he lifted a drink toward Asher. "She beats an Italian in the Foro Italico, and the crowd still cheers her."

"Breeding," Asher returned with a mild smile. "The fans always recognize good breeding."

Michael snorted before he swallowed the heavy red wine. "Since when does a bloody steamroller need breeding?" he countered. "You flattened her." To emphasize his point he slammed a palm down on the table and ground it in.

"Yeah." Her smile widened in reminiscent pleasure. "I did, didn't I?" She sipped her dry, cool wine. The match had been longer and more demanding than her first with Kingston, but her body had rebelled a bit less afterward. Asher considered it a double victory.

"Tia Conway will go for your jugular," he said pleasantly, then called to his countrywoman at a nearby table. "Hey, Tia, you gonna beat this nasty American?"

A dark, compact woman with striking black eyes glanced over. The two women measured each other slowly before Tia lifted her glass in salute. Asher responded in kind before the group fell back to its individual conversations. With the music at high volume, they shouted to be heard, but words carried only a foot.

"A nice woman," Michael began, "off the court. On it, she's a devil. Off, she grows petunias and rosemary. Her husband sells swimming pools."

Madge chuckled. "You make that sound like a misdemeanor."

"I bought one," he said ruefully, then looked back at Asher. She was listening with half an ear to the differing opinions on either side of her of a match by two players. "Still, if I played mixed doubles, I'd want Face for a partner." Asher acknowledged this with a curious lift of a brow. "Tia plays like a demon, but you have better court sense. And," he added as he downed more wine, "better legs."

For this Madge punched him in the shoulder. "What about me?"

"You have perhaps the best court sense of any female world-class player," Michael decided slowly. "But," he continued as Madge accepted her due with a regal nod, "you have legs like a shotputter."

A roar of laughter rose up over Madge's indignation. Asher leaned back in her chair, enjoying the loosening freedom of mirth as Madge challenged Michael to show his own and be judged. At that moment Asher's eyes locked with Ty's. Her laughter died unnoticed by her companions.

He'd come in late and alone. His hair was unruly, as though he had ridden in a fast car with the top down. Even completely relaxed, dressed in jeans, his hands in his pockets, some aura of excitement swirled around him. In the dim light his face was shadowed, all hollows and planes, with his eyes dark and knowing. No woman could be immune to him. A former lover was helpless not to remember what magic his mouth could perform.

Asher sat still as a stone—marble, pale and elegant in the rowdy, smoke-curtained bar. She couldn't forget any more than she could stop wanting. All she could do was refuse, as she had three years before.

Without taking his eyes from hers Ty crossed the room, skirted crowded tables. He had Asher by the arm, drawing her to her feet before the rest of the group had greeted him.

"We'll dance." It was a command formed in the most casual tones. As on court, Asher's decision had to be made in a tenth of a second. To refuse would have incited speculative gossip. To agree meant she had her own demons to deal with.

"I'd love to," she said coolly, and went with him.

The band played a slow ballad at ear-splitting volume. The vocalist was flat, and tried to make up for it by being loud. Someone knocked a glass off a table with a splintering crash. There was a pungent scent of spilled wine. A bricklayer argued with a Mexican tennis champion on the proper way to handle a topspin lob. Someone was smoking a pipe filled with richly sweet cherry tobacco. The floorboards were slightly warped.

Ty gathered her into his arms as though she had never been away. "The last time we were here," he murmured in her ear, "we sat at that corner table and drank a bottle of Valpolicella."

"I remember."

"You wore the same perfume you're wearing now." His lips grazed her temple as he drew her closer. Asher felt the bones in her legs liquefy, the muscles in her thighs loosen. "Like sun-warmed petals." Her heartbeat was a light, uncertain flutter against his. "Do you remember what we did afterward?"

"We walked."

The two hoarsely spoken words seemed to shiver along his skin. It was impossible to keep his mouth from seeking small tastes of her. "Until sunrise." His breath feathered intimately at her ear. "The city was all rose and gold, and I wanted you so badly, I nearly exploded. You wouldn't let me love you then."

"I don't want to go back." Asher tried to push away, but his arms kept her pressed tight against him. It seemed every line of his body knew every curve of hers.

"Why? Because you might remember how good we were together?"

"Ty, stop it." She jerked her head back—a mistake as his lips cruised lazily over hers.

"We'll be together again, Asher." He spoke quietly. The words seemed to sear into the tender flesh of her lips. "Even if it's only once...for old times' sake."

"It's over, Ty." The claim was a whisper, the whisper unsteady.

"Is it?" His eyes darkened as he pressed her against him almost painfully. "Remember, Asher, I know you, inside out. Did your husband ever find out who you really are? Did he know how to make you laugh? How," he added in a low murmur, "to make you moan?"

She stiffened. The music whirled around them, fast now with an insistent bass beat. Ty held her firmly against him, barely swaying at all. "I won't discuss my marriage with you."

"I damn well don't want to know about your *marriage.*" He said the word as if it were an obscenity as his fingers dug into the small of her back. Fury was taking over though he'd sworn he wouldn't let it. He could still get to her. Yes, yes, that was a fact, he knew, but no more than she could still get to him. "Why did you come back?" he demanded. "Why the hell did you come back?"

"To play tennis." Her fingers tightened on his shoulder. "To win." Anger was growing in her as well. It appeared he was the only man who could make her forget herself enough to relinquish control. "I have every right to be here, every right to do what I was trained to do. I don't owe you explanations."

"You owe me a hell of a lot more." It gave him a certain grim satisfaction to see the fury in her eyes. He wanted to push. Wanted to see her anger. "You're going to pay for the three years you played lady of the manor."

"You don't know anything about it." Her breath came short and fast. Her eyes were nearly cobalt. "I paid, Starbuck, I paid more than you can imagine. Now I've finished, do you understand?" To his surprise, her voice broke on a sob. Quickly she shook her head and fought back tears. "I've finished paying for my mistakes."

"What mistakes?" he demanded. Frustrated, he took her by the shoulders. "What mistakes, Asher?"

"You." She drew in her breath sharply, as if stepping back from a steep edge. "Oh, God, you."

Turning, she fought her way through the swarm of enthusiastic dancers. Even as she sprang out into the sultry night Ty whirled her around. "Let me go!" She struck out blindly, but he grabbed her wrist.

"You're not going to walk out on me again." His voice was dangerously low. "Not ever again."

"Did it hurt your pride, Ty?" Emotion erupted from her, blazing as it could only from one who constantly denied it. "Did it hurt your ego that a woman could turn her back on you and choose someone else?"

Pain ripped through him and took over. "I never had your kind of pride, Asher." He dragged her against him, needing to prove he had some kind of power over her, even if it was only physical. "The kind you wear so that no one can see you're human. Did you run because I knew you? Because in bed I could make you forget to be the perfect lady?"

"I left because I didn't want you!" Completely unstrung, she shouted, pounding with her free hand. "I didn't want—"

He cut her off with a furious kiss. Their tempers soared with vivid passion. Anger sizzled in two pairs of lips that clung because they were helpless to do otherwise. There was never any choice when they were together. It had been so almost from the first, and the years had changed nothing. She could resist him, resist herself, for only so long. The outcome was inevitable.

Suddenly greedy, Asher pressed against him. Here was the sound and the speed. Here was the storm. Here was home. His hair was thick and soft between her questing fingers, his body rock-hard against the firmness of hers. His scent was his "off-court" fragrance—something sharp and bracing that she'd always liked.

The first taste was never enough to satisfy her, so she probed deeper into his mouth, tongue demanding, teeth nipping in the way he himself had taught her. A loud crash of brass from the band rattled the windows behind them. Asher heard only Ty's moan of quiet desperation. Between the shadows and the moonlight they clung, passion building, old needs merging with new.

Her breath trembled into the night as he took a crazed journey of her face. His hands slid up until his thumbs hooked gently under her chin. It was a familiar habit, one of his more disarming. Asher whispered his name half in plea, half in acceptance before his mouth found hers again. He drew her into him, slowly, inevitably, while his fingers skimmed along her cheekbones. The more tempestuous the kiss, the more tender his touch. Asher fretted for the strong, sure stroke of his hands on her body.

Full circle, she thought dizzily. She had come full circle. But if once before in Rome she had been frightened when his kisses had drained and exhilarated her, now she was terrified.

"Please, Ty." Asher turned her head until her brow rested on his shoulder. "Please, don't do this."

"I didn't do it alone," he muttered.

Slowly she lifted her head. "I know."

It was the vulnerability in her eyes that kept him from dragging her back to him. Just as it had been her vulnerability all those years before that had prevented him taking her. He had waited for her to come to him. The same would hold true this time, he realized. Cursing potently under his breath, Ty released her.

"You've always known how to hold me off, haven't you, Asher?"

Knowing the danger had passed, she let out an unsteady breath. "Self-preservation."

Ty gave an unexpected laugh as his hands dove for his pockets. "It might have been easier if you'd managed to get fat and ugly over the last three years. I wanted to think you had."

A hint of a smile played on her mouth. So his moods could change, she thought, just as quickly as ever. "Should I apologize for not accommodating you?"

"Probably wouldn't have made any difference if you had." His eyes met hers again, then roamed her face. "Just looking at you—it still takes my breath away." His hands itched to touch. He balled them into fists inside his pockets. "You haven't even changed your hair."

This time the smile bloomed. "Neither have you. You still need a trim."

He grinned. "You were always conservative."

"You were always unconventional."

He gave a low appreciative laugh, one she hadn't heard in much too long. "You've mellowed," he decided. "You used to say radical."

"*You've* mellowed," Asher corrected him. "It used to be true."

With a shrug he glanced off into the night. "I used to be twenty."

"Age, Starbuck?" Sensing a disturbance, Asher automatically sought to soothe it.

"Inevitably." He brought his eyes back to hers. "It's a young game."

"Ready for your rocking chair?" Asher laughed, forgetting caution as she reached up to touch his cheek. Though she snatched her hand away instantly, his eyes had darkened. "I—" She searched for a way to ease the fresh tension. "You didn't seem to have any problem smashing Bigelow in the semi-finals. He's what, twenty-four?"

"It went to seven sets." His hand came out of his pocket. Casually he ran the back of it up her throat.

"You like it best that way."

He felt her swallow quickly, nervously, though her eyes remained level. "Come back with me, Asher," he murmured. "Come with me now." It cost him to ask, but only he was aware of how much.

"I can't."

"Won't," he countered.

From down the street came a high-pitched stream of Italian followed by a bellow of laughter. Inside the club the band murdered a popular American tune. She could smell the heat-soaked fragrance of the window-box geraniums above their heads. And she could remember, remember too well, the sweetness that could be hers if she crossed the line. And the pain.

"Ty." Asher hesitated, then reached up to grasp the hand that lingered at her throat. "A truce, please. For our mutual benefit," she added when his fingers interlaced possessively with hers. "With us both going into the finals, we don't need this kind of tension right now."

"Save it for later?" He brought her reluctant hand to his lips, watching her over it. "Then we pick this up in Paris."

"I didn't mean—"

"We deal now or later, Face, but we deal." He grinned again, tasting challenge, tasting victory. "Take it or leave it."

"You're just as infuriating as ever."

"Yeah." The grin only widened. "That's what keeps me number one."

On an exasperated laugh, Asher let her hand relax in his. "Truce, Starbuck?"

He let his thumb glide back and forth over her knuckles. "Agreed, on one condition." Sensing her withdrawal, he continued. "One question, Asher. Answer one question."

She tried to wrest her hand away and failed. "What question?" she demanded impatiently.

"Were you happy?"

She became very still as quick flashes of the past raced through her head. "You have no right—"

"I have every right," he interrupted. "I'm going to know that, Asher. The truth."

She stared at him, wanting to pit her will against his. Abruptly she found she had no energy for it. "No," she said wearily. "No."

He should have felt triumph, and instead felt misery. Releasing her hand, he stared out at the street. "I'll get you a cab."

"No. No, I'll walk. I want to walk."

Ty watched her move into the flood of a streetlight and back into the dark. Then she was a shadow, disappearing.

The streets were far from empty. Traffic whizzed by at the pace that seemed the pride of European cities. Small, fast cars and daredevil taxis. People scattered on the sidewalks, rushing toward some oasis of nightlife. Still, Ty thought he could hear the echo of his own footsteps.

Perhaps it was because so many feet had walked the Roman streets for so many centuries. Ty didn't care much for history or tradition. Tennis history perhaps—Gonzales, Gibson, Perry, these names meant more to him than Caesar, Cicero or Caligula. He rarely thought of his own past, much less of antiquity. Ty was a man who focused on the present. Until Asher had come back into his life, he had thought little about tomorrow.

In his youth he had concentrated fiercely on the future, and what he would do if… Now that he had done it, Ty had come to savor each day at a time. Still, the future was closing in on him, and the past was never far behind.

At ten he had been a hustler. Skinny and streetwise, he had talked his way out of trouble when it was possible, and slugged his way out when it wasn't. Growing up in the tough South Side of Chicago, Ty had been introduced to the seamier side of life early. He'd tasted his first beer when he should have been studying rudimentary math. What had saved him from succumbing to the streets was his dislike and distrust of organized groups. Gangs had held no appeal for Ty. He had no desire to lead or to follow. Still, he might have chosen a less honorable road had it not been for his unquestioning love for his family.

His mother, a quiet, determined woman who worked nights cleaning office buildings, was precious to him. His sister, four years his junior, was his pride and self-assumed responsibility. There was no father, and even the memory of him had faded before Ty reached mid-childhood. Always, he had considered himself the head of the family, with all the duties and rights that it entailed. No one corrected him. It was for his family that he studied and kept on the right side of the law—though he brushed the line occasionally. It was for them that he promised himself, when he was still too young to realize the full extent of his vow, to succeed. One day he would move them out, buy them a house, bring his mother up off her knees. The picture of how hadn't been clear, only the final result. The answer had been a ball and racket.

Ada Starbuck had given her son a cheap, nylon-stringed racket for his tenth birthday. The gift had been an impulse. She had been determined to give the boy something other than the necessary socks and underwear. The racket, such as it was, had been a gesture of hope. She could see too many of her neighbors' children fall into packs. Ty, she knew, was different. A loner. With the racket he could entertain himself. A baseball or football required someone to catch or pass. Now Ty could use a concrete wall as his partner. And so he did—at first for lack of something better to do. In the alley between apartment buildings he would smash the ball against a wall scrawled with spray paint. DIDI LOVES FRANK and other less romantic statements littered his playing field.

He enjoyed setting his own rhythm, enjoyed the steady thud, thump, smash he could make. When he became bored with the wall, he began haunting the neighborhood playground courts. There, he could watch teenagers or middle-aged weekenders scramble around the courts. He hustled pennies retrieving balls. Deciding he could do better than the people he watched, Ty badgered an older boy into a game.

His first experience on a court was a revelation. A human forced you to run, sent balls over your head or lined them at you with a speed a stationary wall couldn't match. Though he lost handily, Ty had discovered the challenge of competition. And the thirst to win.

He continued to haunt the courts, paying more attention to details. He began to select the players who took the game seriously. Possessing quite a bit of charm even at that age, Ty talked himself into more games. If someone took the time to teach, he listened and adjusted the advice to suit his own style. And he was developing a style. It was rough and untutored, with the flash the sportwriters would later rave about just a spark. His serve was a far cry from a grown Starbuck's, but it was strong and uncannily accurate. He was still awkward, as growing boys are, but his speed was excellent. More than anything else, his fierce desire to win had his game progressing.

When the cheap racket simply disintegrated under constant use, Ada raided the household budget and bought Ty another. Of the hundreds of rackets he had used in his career, some costing more than his mother had made in a week, Ty had never forgotten that first one. He had kept it, initially from childhood sentiment, then as a symbol.

He carved out a name for himself in the neighborhood. By the time he was thirteen it was a rare thing for anyone, child or adult, to beat Ty Starbuck on the courts. He knew his game. He had read everything he could get his hands on—tennis as a sport, its history, its great players. When his contemporaries were immersed in the progress of the White Sox or the Cubs, Ty watched the Wimbledon matches on the flickering black-and-white TV in his apartment. He had already made up his mind to be there one day. And to win. Again, it was Ada who helped the hand of fate.

One of the offices she cleaned belonged to Martin Derick, a lawyer and tennis enthusiast who patronized a local country club. He was an offhandedly friendly man whose late hours brought him in contact with the woman who scrubbed the hall outside his door. He called her Mrs. Starbuck because her dignity demanded it, and would exchange a word of greeting on his way in or out. Ada was careful to mention her son and his tennis abilities often enough to intrigue and not often enough to bore. Ty had come by his shrewdness naturally.

When Martin casually mentioned he would be interested in seeing the boy play, Ada told him there was an informal tournament set for that Saturday. Then she hurriedly arranged one. Whether curiosity or interest prompted Martin to drive to the battered South Side court, the results were exactly as Ada hoped.

Ty's style was still rough, but it was aggressive. His temper added to the spark, and his speed was phenomenal. At the end of a set, Martin was leaning against the chain-link fence. At the end of the match, he was openly cheering. Two hours on the manicured courts of his club had never brought him quite this degree of excitement. Ideas humming in his brain, he walked over to the sweaty, gangly teenager.

"You want to play tennis, kid?"

Ty spun the racket as he eyed the lawyer's pricey suit. "You ain't dressed for it." He gave the smooth leather shoes a mild sneer.

Martin caught the insolent grin, but focused on the intensity of the boy's eyes. Some instinct told him they were champion's eyes. The ideas solidified into a goal. "You want to play for pay?"

Ty kept spinning the racket, wary of a hustle, but the question had his pulse leaping. "Yeah. So?"

This time Martin smiled at the deliberate rudeness. He was going to like this kid, God knew why. "So, you need lessons and a decent court." He glanced at Ty's worn racket. "And equipment. What kind of power can you get out of plastic strings?"

Defensive, Ty tossed up a ball and smashed it into the opposing service court.

"Not bad," Martin decided mildly. "You'd do better with sheep gut."

"Tell me something I don't know."

Martin drew out a pack of cigarettes and offered one to Ty. He refused with a shake of his head. Taking his time, Martin lit one, then took a long drag.

"Those things'll mess up your lungs," Ty stated idly.

"Tell me something I don't know," the lawyer countered. "Think you can play on grass?"

Ty answered with a quick, crude expletive, then sliced another ball over the net.

"Pretty sure of yourself."

"I'm going to play Wimbledon," Ty told him matter-of-factly. "And I'm going to win."

Martin didn't smile, but reached into his pocket. He held out a discreet, expensively printed business card. "Call me Monday," he said simply, and walked away.

Ty had a patron.

The marriage wasn't made in heaven. Over the next seven years there were bitter arguments, bursts of temper and dashes of love. Ty worked hard because he understood that work and discipline were the means to the end. He remained in school and studied only because his mother and Martin had a conspiracy against him. Unless he completed high school with decent grades, the patronage would be removed. As to the patronage itself, Ty accepted it only because his needs demanded it. But he was never comfortable with it. The lessons polished his craft. Good equipment tightened his game. He played on manicured grass, well-tended clay and wood, learning the idiosyncrasies of each surface.

Every morning before school he practiced. Afternoons and weekends were dedicated to tennis. Summers, he worked part-time in the pro shop at Martin's club, then used the courts to hone his skill. By the time he was sixteen the club's tennis pro could beat him only if Ty had an off day.

His temper was accepted. It was a game of histrionics. Women found a certain appeal in his lawlessness. Ty learned of female pleasures young, and molded his talent there as carefully as he did his game.

The only break in his routine came when he injured his hand coming to the defense of his sister. Ty considered the two-week enforced vacation worth it, as the boy Jess had been struggling with had a broken nose.

He traveled to his first tournament unknown and unseeded. In a lengthy, gritty match heralded in the sports pages, he found his first professional victory. When he lost, Ty was rude, argumentative and brooding. When he won, he was precisely the same. The press tolerated him because he was young, brilliant and colorful. His rise from obscurity was appreciated in a world where champions were bred in the affluent, select atmosphere of country clubs.

Before his nineteenth birthday Ty put a down payment on a three-bedroom house in a Chicago suburb. He moved his family out. When he was twenty he won his first Wimbledon title. The dream was realized, but his intensity never slackened.

Now, walking along the dark streets of Rome, he thought of his roots. Asher made him think of them, perhaps because hers were so markedly different. There had been no back alleys or street gangs in her life. Her childhood had been sheltered, privileged and rich. With James Wolfe as a father, her introduction to tennis had come much earlier and much easier than Ty's. At four she had a custom-made racket and had hit balls on her father's private courts. Her mother had hired maids to scrub floors, not been hired out to scrub them.

At times Ty wondered if it was that very difference that had attracted him to her. Then he would remember the way she felt in his arms. Backgrounds were blown to hell. Yet there was something about her reserve that had drawn him. That and the passion he had sensed lay beneath.

The challenge. Yes, Ty admitted with a frown, he was a man who couldn't resist a challenge. Something about the cool, distant Asher Wolfe had stirred his blood even when she had been little more than a child. He'd waited for her to grow up. And to thaw out, he reminded himself ruefully. Turning a corner without direction, Ty found himself approaching one of Rome's many fountains. The water twinkled with light gaiety while he watched, wishing his blood were as cool.

God, how he wanted her still. The need grated against pride, infuriating and arousing him. He would have taken her back that night even knowing she had been another man's wife, shared another man's bed. It would have been less difficult to have thought about her with many lovers than with one husband—that damn titled Englishman whose arms she had run to straight from his own. *Why?* The question pounded at him.

How many times in those first few months had he relived their last few days together, looking for the key? Then he'd layered over the hurt and the fury. The wound had healed jaggedly, then callused. Ty had gone on because he was a survivor. He'd survived poverty, and the streets, and the odds. With an unsteady laugh he raked a hand through his thick mop of hair. But had he really survived Asher?

He knew he had taken more than one woman to bed because her hair was nearly the same shade, her voice nearly the same tone. Nearly, always nearly. Now, when he had all but convinced himself that what he remembered was an illusion, she was back. And free. Again, Ty laughed. Her divorce meant nothing to him. If she had still been legally tied to another man, it would have made no difference. He would still have taken her.

This time, he determined, he'd call the shots. He was out of patience. He would have her again, until he decided to walk away. Challenge, strategy, action. It was a course he had followed for half his life. Taking out a coin, he flipped it insolently into the rippling waters of a fountain, as if daring luck to evade him. It drifted down slowly until it nestled with a hundred other wishes.

His eyes skimmed the streets until he found the neon lights of a tiny bar. He wanted a drink.

Chapter 4

Asher had time to savor her title as Italian Woman's Champion on the flight between Rome and Paris. After the match she had been too exhausted from nearly two hours of unrelenting competition to react. She could remember Madge hugging her, the crowd cheering for her. She could remember the glare of flashbulbs in her face and the barrage of questions she had forced herself to answer before she all but collapsed on the massage table. Then the celebrations had run together in a blur of color and sound, interviews and champagne. Too many faces and handshakes and hugs. Too many reporters. Now, as the plane leveled, reaction set in. She'd done it.

For all of her professional career, the Italian clay had beaten her. Now—now her comeback was viable. She had proven herself. Every hour of strain, every moment of physical pain during the last six months of training had been worth it. At last Asher could rid herself of all the lingering doubts that she had made the right decision.

Though there had been no doubts about her choice to leave Eric, she mused, feeling little emotion at the dissolution of her marriage—

a marriage, Asher remembered, that had been no more than a polite play after the first two months. If she had ever made a truly unforgivable mistake, it had been in marrying Lord Eric Wickerton.

All the wrong reasons, Asher reflected as she leaned back in her seat with her eyes closed. Even with her bitter thoughts of Eric, she could never remove the feeling of responsibility for taking the step that had legally bound them. He had known she hadn't loved him. It hadn't mattered to him. She had known he wanted her to fit the title of Lady. She hadn't cared. At the time the need to escape had been too overpowering. Asher had given Eric what he had wanted—a groomed, attractive wife and hostess. She had thought he would give her what she needed in return. Love and understanding. The reality had been much, much different, and almost as painful as what she had sought to escape. Arguments were more difficult, she had discovered, when two people had no mutual ground. And when one felt the other had sinned…

She wouldn't think of it, wouldn't think of the time in her life that had brought such pain and disillusionment. Instead, she would think of victory.

Michael had been right in his assessment of Tia on the court. She was a small, vibrant demon who played hard and never seemed to tire. Her skill was in picking holes in her opponent's game, then ruthlessly exploiting them. On court she wore gold—a thin chain around her neck, swinging hoops at her ears and a thick clip to tame her raven hair. Her dress was pastel and frilled. She played like an enraged tigress. Both women had run miles during the match, taking it to a full five sets. The last one had consisted of ten long, volatile games with the lead shooting back and forth as quickly as the ball. Never had it been more true that the match wasn't over until it was over.

And when it was over, both women had limped off the court, sweaty, aching and exhausted. But Asher had limped off with a title. Nothing else mattered.

Looking back at it, Asher found herself pleased that the match had been hard won. She wanted something the press would chatter about, something they would remember for more than a day or two. It was always news when an unseeded player won a world title—even considering Asher's record. As it was, her past only made her hotter copy. She needed that now to help keep the momentum going.

With Italy behind her, Paris was next. The first leg of the Grand Slam. She had won there before, on clay, the year she had been Starbuck's lady. As she had with Eric, Asher tried to block Ty out of her mind. Characteristically he wasn't cooperative.

We pick this up in Paris.

The words echoed softly in her head, part threat, part promise. Asher knew him too well to believe either was idle. She would have to deal with him when the time came. But she wasn't naïve or innocent any longer. Life had taught her there weren't any easy answers or fairy-tale endings. She'd lost too much to believe happy-ever-after waited at the end of every love affair—as she had once believed it had waited for her and Ty. They were no longer the prince and princess of the courts, but older, and, Asher fervently hoped, wiser.

She was certain he would seek to soothe his ego by trying to win her again—her body if not her heart. Remembering the verve and depth of his lovemaking, Asher knew it wouldn't be easy to resist him. If she could have done so without risking her emotions, Asher would have given Ty what he wanted. For three colorless years she had endured without the passion he had brought to her life. For three empty years she had wondered and wanted and denied.

But her emotions weren't safe. On a sigh, Asher allowed herself to feel. She still cared. Not a woman to lie to herself, Asher admitted she loved Ty, had never once stopped loving him. It had never been over for her, and deep within she carried the memory of that love. It brought guilt.

What if he had known? she thought with the familiar stir of panic. How could she have told him? Asher opened her eyes and stared blindly through the sunlight. It was as harsh and unforgiving as the emotions that raged through her. Would he have believed? Would he have accepted? Before the questions were fully formed,

Asher shook her head in denial. He could never know that she had unwittingly married another man while she carried Ty's child. Or that through her own grief and despair she had lost that precious reminder of her love for him.

Closing her eyes, Asher willed herself to sleep. Paris was much too close.

"Ty! Ty!"

Pausing in the act of zipping the cover on his racket, Ty turned. Pleasure shot into his eyes. In a quick move he dropped his racket and grabbed the woman who had run to him. Holding her up, he whirled her in three dizzying circles before he crushed her against him. Her laughter bounced off the air in breathless gasps.

"You're breaking me!" she cried, but hugged him tighter.

Ty cut off her protest with a resounding kiss, then held her at arm's length. She was a small woman, nearly a foot shorter than he, nicely rounded without being plump. Her gray-green eyes were sparkling, her generous mouth curved in a dazzling smile. She was a beauty, he thought—had always been a beauty. Love surrounded him. He tousled her hair, dark as his own, but cut in a loose swinging style that brushed her shoulders. "Jess, what are you doing here?"

Grinning, she gave his ear a sisterly tug. "Being mauled by the world's top tennis player."

Ty slipped an arm around her shoulders, only then noticing the man who stood back watching them. "Mac." Keeping his arm around Jess, Ty extended a hand.

"Ty, how are you?"

"Fine. Just fine."

Mac accepted the handshake and careful greeting with light amusement. He knew how Ty felt about his little sister—the little sister who was now twenty-seven and the mother of his child. When he had married Jess, over two years before, Mac had understood that there was a bond between brother and sister that would not be severed. An only child, he both respected and envied it. Two years of being in-laws had lessened Ty's caution with him but hadn't alleviated it. Of course, Mac mused ruefully, it hadn't helped that he was fifteen years Jess's senior, or that he had moved her across the country to California, where he headed a successful research and development firm. And then, he preferred chess to tennis. He'd never have gotten within ten yards of Jessica Starbuck if he hadn't been Martin Derick's nephew.

Bless Uncle Martin, Mac thought with a glance at his lovely, adored wife. Ty caught the look and relaxed his grip on his sister. "Where's Pete?" he asked, making the overture by addressing Mac rather than his sister.

Mac acknowledged the gesture with a smile. "With Grandma. They're both pretty pleased with themselves."

Jess gave the bubbling laugh that both men loved. "Hardly more than a year old and he can move like lightning. Mom's thrilled to chase him around for a few weeks. She sends her love," she told Ty. "You know how she feels about long plane flights."

"Yeah." He released his sister to retrieve his bag and racket. "I talked to her just last night; she didn't say anything about your coming."

"We wanted to surprise you." Smug, Jess hooked her hand into Mac's. "Mac thought Paris was the perfect place for a second honeymoon." She sent her husband a brief but intimate look. Their fingers tightened.

"The trick was getting her away from Pete for two weeks." He gave Ty a grin. "You were a bigger incentive than Paris." Bending, he kissed the top of his wife's head. "She dotes on Pete."

"No, I don't," Jess disagreed, then grinned. "Well, I wouldn't if Pete weren't such a smart baby."

Mac began to unpack an old, favored pipe. "She's ready to enroll him in Harvard."

"Next year," Jess responded dryly. "So, you're going in as top seed," she continued, giving her full attention to her brother. Was there some strain around his eyes? she wondered, then quickly discounted it. "Martin's proud enough to bust."

"I was hoping he might make it out for the tournament." Ty glanced toward the empty stands. "Funny, I still have a habit of looking for him before a match."

"He wanted to be here. If there had been any way for him to postpone this trial, but..." Jess trailed off and smiled. "Mac and I will have to represent the family."

Ty slung the bag over his shoulder. "You'll do fine. Where are you staying?"

"At the—" Jess's words came to a stop as she spotted a slender blonde crossing an empty court a short distance away. Reaching up, she brushed at her brow as if pushing aside an errant strand of hair. "Asher," she murmured.

Ty twisted his head. Asher wasn't aware of them, as Chuck was keeping her involved in what appeared to be a long, detailed description of a match. "Yes," Ty said softly. "Asher." He kept his eyes on her, watching the movements of her body beneath the loosely fitting jogging suit. "Didn't you know she was here?"

"Yes, I—" Jess broke off helplessly. How could she explain the flurry of feelings that she experienced in seeing Asher Wolfe again. The years were winked away in an instant. Jess could see the cool blue eyes, hear the firmly controlled voice. At the time there'd been no doubt in her mind about right and wrong. Even the chain reaction that had begun on a hazy September afternoon had only served to cement Jess's certainty. Now there'd been a divorce, and Asher was back. She felt her husband's warm palm against hers. Right and wrong weren't so clearly defined any longer.

A bubble of nausea rose as she turned to her brother. He was still watching Asher. Had he loved her? Did he still? What would he do if he ever learned of his sister's part in what had happened three years before? Jess found the questions trembling on her tongue and was afraid of the answers. "Ty..."

His eyes were dark and stormy, a barometer of emotion. Something in them warned Jess to keep her questions to herself. Surely there would be a better time to bring up the past. She had both a sense of reprieve and a feeling of guilt.

"Beautiful, isn't she?" he asked lightly. "Where did you say you were staying?"

"And because he's eighteen and played like a rocket in the qualifying rounds, they're muttering about an upset." Chuck tossed a tennis ball idly, squeezing it when it returned to his palm. "I wouldn't mind if he weren't such a little twerp."

Asher laughed and snatched the ball as Chuck tossed it again. "And eighteen," she added.

He gave a snort. "He wears designer underwear, for God's sake. His mother has them dry cleaned."

"Down boy," Asher warned good-naturedly. "You'll feel better once you wipe him out in the quarter-finals. Youth versus experience," she added because she couldn't resist. Chuck twisted a lock of her hair around his finger and pulled.

"You meet Rayski," he commented. "I guess we could call that two old pros."

Asher winced. "Your point," she conceded. "So, what's your strategy for this afternoon?"

"To beat the tar out of him," Chuck responded instantly, then grinned as he flexed his racket arm. "But if he gets lucky, I'll leave it up to Ty to smash him in the semis or the finals."

Asher bounced the ball on the clay. Her fingers closed over it, then released it again. "You're so sure Ty will get to the finals?"

"Money in the bank," he claimed. "This is his year. I swear, I've never seen him play better." Pleasure for his friend with the light lacing of envy gave the statement more impact. "He's going to be piling up titles like dominoes."

Asher said nothing, not even nodding in agreement as Chuck sought to prove his point by giving her a replay of Ty's qualifying match. A breeze stirred, sending blossoms drifting to the court at her feet. It was early morning, and the Stade Roland Garros was still drowsily charming and quiet. The thump of balls was hardy noticeable. In a few hours the fourteen thousand seats around the single center court would be jammed with enthusiasts. The noise would be human and emotional, accented by the sounds of traffic and squealing brakes on the highway that separated the stadium from the Bois de Boulogne.

Asher watched the breeze tickle a weeping willow as Chuck continued his rundown. In this first week of the games, tennis would be played for perhaps eleven hours a day so that even the first-round losers used the courts enough to make the trip worthwhile. It was considered by most pros the toughest championship to win. Like Ty, Asher was after her second victory.

Paris. Ty. Was there nowhere she could go that wasn't so firmly tied in with memories of him? In Paris they'd sat in the back of a darkened theater, necking like teenagers while an Ingmar Bergman film had flickered on the screen unnoticed. In Paris he had doctored a strained muscle in her calf, pampering and bullying so that she had won despite the pain. In Paris they had made love, and made love, and made love until they were both weak and exhausted. In Paris Asher had still believed in happy endings.

Fighting off memories, Asher glanced around the stadium. Her eyes locked with Jess's. Separated by a hundred yards, both women endured a jolt of shock and distress. They stared, unable to communicate, unable to look away.

"Hey, it's Jess!" Chuck interrupted himself to make the announcement. He waved, then grabbed Asher's hand to drag her with him. "Let's go say hi."

Panicked, Asher dug in her heels. "No, I—I have to meet..." Her mind was devoid of excuses, but she snatched her hand from Chuck's. "You go ahead, I'll see you later." Over Chuck's protest, she dashed in the opposite direction.

Breathless, Asher found herself in the Jardin des Plantes with its sweet, mingling scents, little plaques and poetry. It seemed an odd setting for jangled nerves. Making an effort to calm herself, she slowed her pace.

Silly to run, she told herself. No, she corrected herself, stupid. But she hadn't been prepared to see Ty's sister, the one person who knew all the reasons. To have confronted Jess then, when her mind was already so crowded with Ty, would have been disastrous. Steadying, Asher told herself she just needed a little time to prepare. And it had been obvious Jess had been just as stunned as she. At the moment, Asher was too busy calming herself to wonder why.

She wouldn't, couldn't, think about the last time she'd seen Jessica Starbuck—that hot, close Indian summer afternoon. It would be too easy to remember each word spoken in the careless disorder of the hotel room Asher had shared with Ty. She would remember the hurt, the frantic packing, then her irrevocable decision to go to Eric.

Oh, Ty had been right, she had run away—but she hadn't escaped. So little had changed in three years, and so much. Her heart had remained constant. With a sigh Asher admitted it had been foolish to believe she could take back what she had given so long ago. Ty Starbuck was her first lover, and the only man she had ever loved.

A child had been conceived, then lost before it could be born. She'd never forgiven herself for the accident that had taken that precious, fragile life from her. Perhaps more than a lack of love and understanding, it had been the loss of Ty's child that had destroyed any hope for her marriage.

And if the child had lived? she asked herself wearily. What then? Could she have kept it from him? Could she have remained the wife of one man while bearing the child of another? Asher shook her head. No, she would no longer dwell on possibilities. She'd lost Ty, his child, and the support of her own father. There could be no greater punishments to face. She would make her own future.

The touch of a hand on her shoulder had her whirling around. Asher stared up at Ty, her mind a blank, her emotions in turmoil. A hush seemed to spread over the garden, so she could hear the whisper of air over leaves and blossoms. The scent that reached her was sweet and heady—like a first kiss. He said nothing, nor did she until his hand slid down her arm to link with hers.

"Worried about the match?"

Almost afraid he would sense them, Asher struggled to push all thoughts of the past aside. "Concerned," she amended, nearly managing a smile. "Rayski's top seed."

"You've beaten her before."

"And she's beaten me." It didn't occur to her to remove her hand from his or to mask her doubts. Slowly the tension seeped out of her. Through the link of hands Ty felt it. They had stood here before, and the memory was sweet.

"Play her like you played Conway," he advised. "Their styles are basically the same."

With a laugh Asher ran her free hand through her hair. "That's supposed to be a comfort?"

"You're better than she is," he said simply, and earned an astonished stare. Smiling, he brushed his fingers carelessly over her cheek. "More consistent," he explained. "She's faster, but you're stronger. That gives you an advantage on clay even though it isn't your best surface."

At a loss, Asher managed a surprised, "Well."

"You've improved," Ty stated as they began to walk. "Your backhand doesn't have the power it should have, but—"

"It worked pretty well on Conway," Asher interrupted testily.

"Could be better."

"It's perfect," she disagreed, rising to the bait before she caught his grin. Her lips curved before she could stop them. "You always knew how to get a rise out of me. You're playing Kilroy," she went on, "I've never heard of him."

"He's been around only two years. Surprised everyone in Melbourne last season." He slipped an arm around her shoulders in a gesture so familiar, neither of them noticed. "What's that flower?"

Asher glanced down. "Lady's slipper."

"Silly name."

"Cynic."

He shrugged. "I like roses."

"That's because it's the only flower you can identify." Without thinking, she leaned her head on his shoulder. "I remember going in to take a bath one night and finding you'd filled the tub with roses. Dozens of them."

The scent of her hair reminded him of much more. "By the time we got around to clearing them out, it took over an hour."

Her sigh was wistful. "It was wonderful. You could always surprise me by doing something absurd."

"A tub of lady's slippers is absurd," he corrected. "A tub of roses is classy."

Her laughter was quick and appreciative. Her head still rested on his shoulders. "We filled everything in the room that could pass for a vase, including a bottle of ginger ale. Sometimes when I—" She cut herself off, abruptly realizing she would say too much.

"When you what?" Ty demanded as he turned her to face him. When she only shook her head, he tightened his grip. "Would you remember sometimes, in the middle of the night? Would you wake up and hurt because you couldn't forget?"

Truth brought tension to the base of her neck. In defense, Asher pressed her palms against his chest. "Ty, please."

"I did." He gave her a frustrated shake that knocked her head back. "Oh, God, I did. I've never stopped wanting you. Even hating you I wanted you. Do you know what it's like to be awake at three o'clock in the morning and need someone, and know she's in another man's bed."

"No, no, don't." She was clinging to him, her cheek pressed against his, her eyes tightly shut. "Ty, don't."

"Don't what?" he demanded as he drew her head back. "Don't hate you? Don't want you? Hell, I can't do anything else."

His eyes blazed into her, dark with fury, hot with passion. She could feel the race of his heart compete with hers. Abandoning pride, she pressed her lips to his.

At the instant of contact he stood still, neither giving nor taking. On a moan she drew him closer, letting her lips have their way. A shudder coursed through him, an oath ripped out, then he was responding, demanding, exciting. Why had he tried to resist? Nothing was clear to him as her lips raced crazily over his face. Wasn't this what he wanted? To have her again, to prove he could, to purge his system of her once and for all. Motives dimmed in desire. There was only Asher—the sweet taste of her, her scent more heady, more seductive than the garden of flowers. He couldn't breathe and not fill himself on her. So he surrendered to the persuading lips and soft body that had haunted his dreams.

Dragging his lips from hers only a moment, Ty pulled her through the fragile branches of a willow. The sun filtered through the curtain of leaves, giving intermittent light. In the cool dimness his mouth sought hers again and found it yielding. The blood pounded in his veins.

He had to know if her body was the same, unchanged during the years he'd been denied her. As his hand took her breast he groaned. She was small and firm and familiar. Through the material of her jacket he felt the nipple harden in quick response. Impatient, he tugged the zipper down, then dove under her shirt until he found the smooth tender flesh that had always made him feel his hands were too rough. Yet she didn't draw away as his calluses met her. She pressed against him. Her moan was not one of discomfort, but of unmistakable pleasure.

Trembling, her fingers reached for his hair. He could feel the urgency in them just as he could taste it on her heated lips. He broke his kiss only to change angles, then deepened it, allowing his tongue to drink up all the dark flavors of her mouth. Against his palm her heart thudded wildly, but only his fingers moved to arouse her.

Slowly his other hand journeyed to her hip to mold the long, slender bone. He was lost somewhere between yesterday and today. The heavy fragrance of flowers still wet with morning dew was more seductive than perfume. Half dreaming, Ty took his mouth to her throat. He heard her sigh float off on the scented air. Was she dreaming too? Was the past overlapping this moment for her as well as for him? The thoughts drifted into his mind, then out again before they could be answered. Nothing mattered but that he was holding her again.

From far off came a ripple of laughter. Ty brought his mouth back to Asher's. A rapid smattering of French drifted to him. Ty drew her closer until their bodies seemed fused. Footsteps and a giggle. Like a dreamer, he sensed the intrusion and swore against it. For another moment he clung, drawing on her lingering passion.

When he released her, Asher was breathless and swaying. Wordlessly he stared down at her with eyes nearly black with emotion. Her lips were parted, swollen from his, and he gave in to need and kissed her one long last time. Gently now, slowly, to store up every dram of sweetness. This time she trembled, her breath coming harsh and fast like a diver's who breaks surface after a long submersion. Disoriented, she gripped his arms.

How long had they been there? she wondered. It could have been seconds or days. All she was sure of was that the longing had intensified almost beyond control. Her blood was racing in her veins, her heart pounding desperately. She was alive. So alive. And no longer certain which path she would take.

"Tonight," Ty murmured, bringing her palm to his lips.

The vibration shot up her arm and into her core. "Ty…" Asher shook her head as she tried to draw her hand away. His fingers tightened.

"Tonight," he repeated.

"I can't." Seeing the temper shoot into his eyes, Asher covered their joined hands with her free one. "Ty, I'm frightened."

The quiet admission killed his anger. He let out a weary sigh. "Damn you, Asher."

Saying nothing, she wrapped her arms around his waist, pressing her cheek to his chest. Automatically Ty reached to smooth her hair. His eyes closed. "I'm sorry," she whispered. "I was frightened of you once before. It seems to be happening again." And I love you, she told him silently. As much as ever. More, she realized. More, because of the years of famine.

"Asher." He held her away from him. She felt the passion swirling around him. "I won't promise to wait for you to come to me this time. I won't promise to be gentle and patient. Things aren't the same."

She shook her head, but in agreement. "No, things aren't the same. It might be better, much better for both of us if we just stayed away from each other."

Ty laughed shortly. "We won't."

"If we tried," Asher began.

"*I* won't."

She let out a breath of exasperation. "You're pressuring me."

"Damn right." Before she could decide whether to laugh or to scream, she was in his arms again. "Do you think I don't feel pressured too?" he demanded with a sudden intensity that kept Asher from answering. "Every time I look at you I remember the way things were for us and drive myself crazy trying to figure out why you left me. Do you know what that does to me?"

She gripped his upper arms with strong hands. "You have to understand, I won't go back. Whatever happens to us now begins now. No questions, no whys." She saw the anger boiling in his eyes, but kept hers level. "I mean that, Ty. I can't give you explanations. I won't dig up the past."

"You expect me to live with that?"

"I expect nothing," she said quietly. The tone caused him to look deeper for the answers she refused to give. "And I've agreed to nothing. Not yet."

"You ask for too much," he bit off as he released her. "Too damn much."

She wanted to go to him, go back to his arms and beg him to forget the past. Perhaps it was possible to live for the moment if one wanted to badly enough. It might have been pride that stopped her, or the deeply ingrained survival instinct she had developed since that long-ago September afternoon when she had fled from him and the prospect of pain. Asher laced her fingers together and stared down at them. "Yes, I know. I'm sorry, Ty, we'll only hurt each other."

Tense and tormented, he turned back. "I've never wanted to hurt you, Asher. Not even when I thought I did."

The ache spread so quickly, she almost gasped from it. Isn't that what Jess had said that day? *He'd never want to hurt you...never want to hurt you.* Asher could hear the words echoing inside her head. "Neither of us wanted to," she murmured. "Both of us did. Isn't it foolish to do it again?"

"Look at me." The command was quiet and firm. Bracing herself, Asher obeyed. His eyes were locked on hers—those dark, penetrating eyes that conveyed such raw feeling. Gently he touched her cheek. Without hesitation her hand rose to cover his. "Now," he whispered, "ask me again."

A long, shuddering breath escaped. "Oh, Ty, I was so sure I could prevent this. So sure I could resist you this time."

"And now?"

"Now I'm not sure of anything." She shook her head before he could speak again. "Don't ask now. Give us both some time."

He started to protest, then managed to restrain it. He'd waited three years, a bit longer wouldn't matter. "Some time," he agreed, lowering his hand. But as she started to relax, he took her wrist. The grip was neither gentle nor patient. "The next time, Asher, I won't ask."

She nodded, accepting. "Then we understand each other."

His smile was a trifle grim. "That we do. I'll walk you back." He drew her through the curtain of leaves.

Chapter 5

Fifth set. Seventh game. At the baseline Ty crouched, ready to spring for Michael's serve. The air was heavy, the sky thick with rain-threatening clouds so that the light was dreary. Ty didn't notice. He didn't notice the stadium full of people, some dangling through the railing, some hanging from the scoreboard. He didn't notice the shouts and whistles that were either for or against him.

Tennis was a game of the individual. That was what had drawn him to it. There was no one to blame for a loss, no one to praise for a win but yourself. It was a game of motion and emotion, both of which he excelled in.

He had looked forward to meeting Michael in the semis. The Australian played a hot, passionate game full of dramatic gestures, furious mutters and pizzazz. There were perhaps five competitors Ty fully respected, Michael being one of them. Wanting to win was only a step below wanting a challenge. A fight. He'd grown up scrapping. Now the racket was merely an extension of his arm. The match was a bout. The bout was one on one. It had never—would never—be only a game.

The Australian was a set up, with his momentum still flowing. Ty's only thought at the moment was to break his serve and even the match. Thus far he had spotted no weaknesses in his opponent's game. Like a boxer, he watched for the opening.

He heard the sound of the ball hitting the sweet spot of the racket before it rocketed toward him. It landed deep in the corner of the service court, beautifully placed. Ty's mind and body moved as one as he sprang for the return. Defense, offense, strategy all had to be formulated in a fraction of a second. Strength had to be balanced with form. Both men sprinted over the court for the rally, faces glowing with concentration and sweat. The roar of the crowd rose to meet the distant thunder.

Thus far, the ratio had been nearly ten to one in favor of ground strokes. Ty decided to alter the pace and go with power. Using a vicious left-to-right slice, he shook Michael's balance. Ty blasted away at the attempted passing shot, barely shortening his backswing. Michael couldn't reach the backhand volley, let alone return it. Love-fifteen.

Shaking the damp hair back from his face, Ty returned to the baseline. A woman in the crowd called out what could have been a congratulations or a proposition. Ty's French wasn't strong enough to decipher the phrase. Michael's serve sent up a puff of smoke. Before his return was over the net, Ty was at mid-court and waiting. A testing ground stroke, a sharp return. A tricky topspin, a slice. Michael's decision to try to lob over Ty was a mistake. The smoking smash careened off the court and into the grandstands. Love-thirty.

Michael walked a complete circle, cursing himself before he took his position again. Casting off impatience, Ty waited. Crouched, swaying side to side, unblinking, he was ready. Both players exploited angles and depths with ground strokes. There was a long, patient rally as each watched for the chance to smash a winner. It might have been pure showmanship if it hadn't been for the sounds of exertion coming from the two players.

A UPI photographer had his motor drive humming as he recorded the game. He framed Ty, arms extended for balance, legs spread for the stretch, face fierce. It crossed his mind as he continued to snap that he wouldn't want to face that American on any playing field.

Gracefully, with an elegance belied by his expression, Ty executed a backhand with a touch of underspin. Michael's return thudded against the net. Love-forty.

Angry and shaken, Michael punched his first serve into the net. Having no choice at game point, he placed his next serve carefully. Ty went straight for the volley and took the net. The exchange was fast and furious, the players moving on instinct, the crowd screaming in a mixture of languages. Ty's wrist was locked. The ball whipped from racket to racket at terrifying speed. There were bare seconds between contact, making both men anticipate flight rather than see it. Changing tactics in the wink of an instant, Ty brought the racket face under at the moment of impact. With a flick of a wrist he dropped a dump shot over the net. Risky, experts would say. Gutsy, fans would claim. Ty would ignore both. Game and set.

"Oh, Mac!" Jess leaned back and expelled a long breath. "I'd nearly forgotten what it was like to watch Ty play."

"You watched him just a few weeks ago," he pointed out, using a damp handkerchief to wipe his neck. The wish for his air-conditioned office flitted only briefly into his mind.

"On television," Jess returned. "That's different. Being here… can't you feel it?"

"I thought it was the humidity."

Laughing, Jess shook her head. "Always down to earth, Mac. That's why I love you."

Her smile seemed to open just for him. It could still make his blood sing. "Then I intend to stay there," he murmured, kissing her knuckles. Feeling her hand tense, he looked up, puzzled. Her eyes were aimed over his shoulder. Curious, he turned, spotting a few tennis faces he recognized. Among them was Asher Wolfe. It was on her that his wife's gaze was locked.

"That's the former Lady Wickerton, isn't it?" he asked casually. "She's stunning."

"Yes." Jess tore her eyes away, but the tension in her fingers remained. "Yes, she is."

"She won her match this morning. We'll have an American going into the women's finals." Jess said nothing as Mac stuffed the handkerchief back into his pocket. "She was away from the game for a while, wasn't she?"

"Yes."

Intrigued by his wife's flat answer, Mac probed. "Didn't she and Ty have something going a few years back?"

"It was nothing." With a nervous swallow Jess prayed she spoke the truth. "Just a passing thing. She's not Ty's type. Asher's very cool, much more suited to Wickerton than to Ty. He was attracted to that for a while, that's all." She moistened her lips. "And it was obvious she wasn't serious about him, otherwise she'd never have married Wickerton so quickly. She was making Ty unhappy, very unhappy."

"I see," Mac murmured after a moment. Jess had spoken too quickly and too defensively. Studying his wife's profile, he wondered. "I suppose Ty's too involved in his career to be serious about a woman?"

"Yes." The look Jess gave him was almost pleading. "Yes, he'd never have let her go if he'd been in love with her. Ty's too possessive."

"And proud," he reminded her quietly. "I don't think he'd run after any woman, no matter how he felt about her."

Feeling her stomach roll, Jess said nothing. She turned to watch her brother take the position for his first serve.

Instead of the hazy afternoon she saw a brilliant morning. Instead of the clay of Roland Garros she saw the newly empty grass courts of Forest Hills. Ty was leaning over the rail, staring out at center court. She had a fanciful thought that he looked like the captain of a ship with his eyes on the open, endless sea. In her world she loved no one more than him, could conceive of loving no one more. He was brother and father and hero. He'd provided her with a home, clothes and an education, asking nothing in return. As a result, she would have given him anything.

Crossing to him, she slipped her arm around him, nestling her head in the crook of his shoulder.

"Thinking about this afternoon?" she murmured. He was slated to face Chuck Prince in the finals of the U.S. Open.

"Hmm?" Distracted, Ty shrugged. "No, not really."

"It must feel odd to compete against your closest friend."

"You must forget you're friends for a couple hours," Ty returned.

He was brooding; she sensed it. And unhappy. There was no one, including her mother, Jess felt more loyalty to. Her grip around him tightened. "Ty, what is it?"

"Just restless."

"Have you fought with Asher?"

Absently he tousled her hair. "No, I haven't fought with Asher."

He lapsed into silence for so long that Jess began to suspect he wasn't telling the entire truth. She was already worried about him and Asher. The relationship had lasted longer than was habitual for Ty. Jess saw Asher's reserve as coldness, her independence as indifference. She didn't hang on Ty as other women did. She didn't listen raptly to every word he spoke. She didn't adore him.

"Do you ever think back, Jess?" he asked suddenly.

"Think back?"

"To when we were kids." His eyes skimmed over the manicured courts, but didn't see them. "That crummy apartment with the paper walls. The DeMarcos next door screaming at each other in the middle of the night. The stairwell always smelled of old garbage and stale sweat."

The tone of his voice disturbed her. Seeking comfort as much as to comfort, she turned her face into his chest. "Not often. I guess I don't remember it as well as you. I hadn't turned fifteen when you got us out."

"I wonder sometimes if you can ever escape that, if you can ever really turn your back on it." His eyes were focused on something Jess couldn't see. She strained to share the vision. "Old garbage and stale sweat," he repeated quietly. "I can't forget that. I asked Asher once what smell she remembered most from her childhood. She said the wisteria that hung over her bedroom window."

"Ty, I don't understand."

He swore softly. "Neither do I."

"You left all that behind," she began.

"I left it," he corrected her. "That doesn't mean I left it behind. We were having dinner last night. Wickerton stopped by the table and started a conversation about French Impressionists. After five minutes I didn't know what the hell they were talking about."

Jess bristled. She knew because Ty had sent her to college. She knew because he had provided the opportunity. "You should have told him to get lost."

With a laugh Ty kissed her cheek. "That was my first thought." Abruptly he sobered. "Then I watched them. They understand each other, speak the same language. It made me realize there are some fences you just can't climb."

"You could if you wanted to."

"Maybe. I don't." He let out a long breath. "I don't really give a damn about French Impressionists. I don't give a damn about the mutual friends they have that are distant cousins of the Queen of England, or who won at Ascot last month." Storm warnings were in his eyes, but he shrugged. "Even if I did, I wouldn't fit into that kind of life because I'd always remember the garbage and sweat."

"Asher has no business encouraging that man," Jess stated heatedly. "He's been following her around since Paris."

Ty gave a grim laugh. "She doesn't encourage or discourage. Drawing room conversation," he murmured. "Ingrained manners. She's different from us, Jess, I've known that all along."

"If *she'd* tell him to get lost—"

"She couldn't tell anyone to get lost any more than she could sprout wings and fly."

"She's cold."

"She's different," Ty returned immediately but without heart. He cupped his sister's chin in his hand. "You and me, we're the same. Everything's up front. If we want to shout, we shout. If we want to throw something, we throw it. Some people can't."

"Then they're stupid."

This time his laugh was warm and genuine. "I love you, Jess."

Throwing her arms around him, she hugged him fiercely. "I can't bear to see you unhappy. Why do you let her do this to you?"

Frowning, Ty stroked her hair. "I've been trying to figure that out. Maybe…maybe I just need a shove in the right direction."

Jess held him tighter, searching her mind for the answer.

Seventh set. Tenth game. The crowd was as vocal, as enthusiastic and as hungry as it had been an hour before. Leaning forward in his seat, his eyes glued to the ball, Chuck sat between Asher and Madge.

"You've got something riding on this one, don't you, cowboy?" Madge commented dryly though her own heart was pumping. Chuck would face the winner in the finals.

"It's the best match I've seen in two years." His own face was damp, his own muscles tense. The ball traveled at such speeds, it was often only a white blur.

Asher spoke to neither of them. Her objectivity had been long since destroyed. Ty enthralled her. Both men possessed the raw athletic ability competitors admired and envied. Both were draining the other's resources without mercy. But it was Ty, always Ty, who ripped the emotion from her.

She could admire Michael, admit his brilliance, but he didn't cause that slow, churning ache in her stomach. Had she not once been Ty's lover, had she not even known him, would she still be so drawn? Controlled rage. How was it a woman raised in such an ordered, sheltered existence would be pulled irresistibly to a man with such turbulent passion? Opposites attract? she wondered. No, that was much too simple.

Sitting in the crowded stadium, Asher felt the thrill of desire as clearly as though she had been naked in his arms. She felt no shame. It was natural. She felt no fear. It was inevitable. Years made up of long, unending days vanished. What a waste of time, she thought suddenly. No, a loss, she corrected herself. A loss of time—nothing's ever wasted. *Tonight.* The decision came to her as effortlessly as it had the first time. Tonight they would be together. And if it was only once—if once was all he wanted—it would have to be enough. The long wait was over. She laughed out loud in relief and joy. Chuck sent her an odd look.

"He's going to win," Asher said on a second laugh. Leaning on the rail, she rested her chin on her folded hands. "Oh, yes, he's going to win."

There was a dull ache in his racket arm that Ty ignored. The muscles in his legs promised to cramp the moment he stopped moving. He wouldn't give in to them any more than he would give in to the man across the net. One thing hadn't changed in twenty years. He still hated to lose.

A point away from the match, he played no less tigerishly than he had in the first game. The rallies had been long and punishing. The ball whistled. Sweat dripped. For the last twenty minutes Ty had forsaken artistry for cunning. It was working.

Power for power, they were in a dead heat, so that Ty chose to outmaneuver the Australian. He worked him over the court, pacing him, some might say stalking him. The game went to deuce three times while the crowd grew frantic. An ace gave him advantage—a screeching bullet that brought Ty the final impetus he needed. Then Ty played him hot-bloodedly. The men drove from side to side, their faces masks of effort and fury. The shot came that he'd been waiting for. Michael's awesome backhand drove crosscourt to his southpaw forehand. The ball came to Ty at waist level. Michael didn't even have to see the return to know it was over.

Game, set and match.

The heat hit him then, and the fatigue. It took an effort not to stagger. Simply to have fallen to his knees would have been a relief. He walked to the net.

Michael took his hand, then draped his free arm around Ty's shoulder. "Damn you, Starbuck," he managed breathlessly. "You nearly killed me."

Ty laughed, using his opponent for balance a moment. "You too."

"I need a bloody drink." Michael straightened, giving Ty a glazed grin. "Let's go get drunk."

"You're on."

Turning, they separated, victor and vanquished, to face the press, the showers and the massage tables. Ty grabbed the towel someone handed him, nodding at the questions and congratulations being hurled at him. Behind the cloth he could hear the click and whir of cameras. He was too weary to curse them. Someone was gathering his rackets. He could hear the clatter of wood on wood. The strength that had flowed freely through him only moments before drained. Exhausted, he let the drenched towel fall. His eyes met Asher's.

So blue, he thought. Her eyes are so blue. And cool, and deep. He could drown in them blissfully. The unbearable heat vanished, as though someone had opened a window to a fresh spring breeze.

"Congratulations." When she smiled, his fatigue slid away. Strangely it wasn't desire that replaced it, but comfort, sweet simple comfort.

"Thanks." He took the racket bag from her. Their hands barely brushed.

"I suppose the press is waiting for you inside."

The short retort Ty made was both agreement and opinion. On a low laugh she stepped closer.

"Can I buy you dinner?"

The quirk of his brow was the only indication of surprise. "Sure."

"I'll meet you at seven in the lobby of the hotel."

"All right."

"Starbuck, what do you feel was the turning point of the match?"

"What strategy will you use playing Prince in the finals?"

Ty didn't answer the reporters, didn't even hear them as he watched Asher weave her way through the crowd. From overhead Jess watched with a small, fluttering sensation of déjà vu.

Ty got under the stream of the shower fully dressed. He let the cool water sluice over him while he stripped. A reporter from *World of Sports* leaned against a tiled wall, scribbling notes and tossing questions. Naked, with his clothes in a soggy heap at his feet, Ty answered. Always, he handled the press naturally because he didn't give a damn what they printed. He knew his mother kept a scrapbook, but he never read the articles or interviews. Lathering the soap over his face with both hands, he washed the sticky sweat away. Someone passed him a plastic jug of fruit juice. With the water streaming over him, he guzzled it down, replacing lost fluid. The weakness was seeping back, and with it the pain. He made his way to the massage table by instinct, then collapsed onto it.

Strong fingers began to work on him. Questions still hammered in his ear, but now he ignored them. Ty simply closed his eyes and shut them out. A line of pain ran up his calf as the muscles were kneaded. He winced and held on, knowing relief would follow. For ten agonizing minutes he lay still while his body was rubbed and pounded. He began to drift. Like a mother's memory of the pain of childbirth, his memory of the pain began to dim. He could remember winning. And he could remember dark blue eyes. With those two visions tangling in his mind, he slept.

The floor of the lobby was marble. White marble veined with pink. Madge had commented that it would be the devil to keep clean. Her husband had dryly commented that she wouldn't know one end of the mop from the other. Asher sat, listening to their comfortable banter while she told herself she wasn't nervous. It was six-fifty.

She'd dressed carefully, choosing a simple crêpe de Chine as pale as the inside of a peach. Her hair fluffed back from her face, exposing the tiny pearl and coral drops at her ears. Her ringless fingers were interlaced.

"Where are you eating?"

Asher brought her attention back to Madge. "A little place on the Left Bank." There was an enthusiastic violinist, she remembered. Ty had once passed him twenty American dollars and cheerfully told him to get lost.

At the bellow of thunder Madge glanced toward the lobby doors. "You're going to play hell getting a cab tonight." She leaned back. "Have you seen Ty since the match?"

"No."

"Chuck said both he and Michael were sleeping on the tables like babies." A chuckle escaped as she crossed strong, short legs. "Some industrious stringer for a French paper got a couple of classic shots."

"Athletes in repose," her husband mused.

"It kind of blows the tough-guy image."

Asher smiled, thinking how young and vulnerable Ty looked in sleep. When the lids closed over those dramatic eyes, he reminded her of an exhausted little boy. It was the only time the frenetic energy stilled. Something stirred in her. If the child had lived… Hurriedly she censored the thought.

"Hey, isn't that Ty's sister?"

Asher turned her head to see Jess and Mac crossing the lobby. "Yes." Their eyes met, leaving no choice. Gripping her husband's hand, Jess walked across the white marble.

"Hello, Asher."

"Jess."

A quick moistening of lips betrayed nerves. "I don't think you know my husband. Mackenzie Derick, Lady Wickerton."

"Asher Wolfe," she replied smoothly, taking Mac's hand. "Are you related to Martin?"

"My uncle," Mac informed her. "Do you know him?"

The smile brought warmth to her eyes. "Very well." She made the rest of the introductions with a natural poise Mac approved of.

Cool, yes, he mused, remembering his wife's description. But with an underlying vibrancy perhaps a man would discern more quickly than another woman. He began to wonder if Jess's opinion of Ty's feelings was accurate.

"Are you a tennis fan, Mr. Derick?" Asher asked him.

"Mac," he supplied. "Only by marriage. And no, I don't play, much to Uncle Martin's disgust."

Asher laughed, appreciating the humor in his eyes. A strong man, she thought instantly. His own man. He wouldn't take second place to Ty in his wife's life. "Martin should be satisfied having cultivated one champion." Her eyes drifted to Jess, who was sitting straight and tense beside Madge. "Is your mother well?"

"Yes, yes, Mom's fine." Though she met the cool, clear gaze, her fingers began to pleat the material of her skirt. "She's at home with Pete."

"Pete?"

"Our son."

Asher's throat constricted. Mac noticed with some surprise that her knuckles whitened briefly on the arm of her chair. "I didn't know you'd had a baby. Ada must be thrilled to have a grandchild." The pressure on her heart was unbearable. Her smile was casual. "How old is he?" she made herself ask.

"Fourteen months." As the tension built in one woman, it flowed out of the other. Jess was already reaching into her purse for her wallet. "I swear he never walked, he started out running. Mom says he's like Ty. He has his coloring too." She was offering a picture. Asher had no choice but to accept it.

There was some of his father in him—the shape of the face. But the Starbuck genes were strong. The baby's hair was dark and thick, like his mother's. Like Ty's. The eyes were large and gray. Asher wondered if she could actually feel the air of perpetual motion around the child, or if she imagined it. Another baby would have had dark hair and gray eyes. Hadn't she pictured the face countless times?

"He's beautiful," she heard herself say in a calm voice. "You must be very proud of him." When she handed the snapshot back her hands were perfectly steady.

"Jess thinks he should wait until he's twelve before he runs for president."

Asher smiled, but this time Mac didn't find the reflected warmth in her eyes. "Has Ty bought him a racket yet?"

"You know him very well," Mac observed.

"Yes." She looked back at Jess steadily. "Tennis and his family come first, always."

"I hate to admit it," Madge put in with a sigh, "but I can remember a dozen years ago when this one was a skinny teenager, chewing her fingernails at every one of Ty's matches. Now you're a mother."

Jess grinned, holding out her hands for inspection. "And I still bite my nails at Ty's matches."

It was Asher who saw him first. But then, her senses were tuned for him. Ty stepped off the elevator dressed in slim black slacks and a smoke-gray shirt. He wouldn't have chosen the shirt because it matched his eyes so perfectly. Asher knew he wore it because it would have been the first thing his hand had grabbed from the closet. He wore clothes with the casual style of one who gave no thought to them and still looked marvelous. A disciplined body and trained grace made it inevitable. His hair had been combed, but defied order. He paused briefly, even in stillness communicating motion. Asher's heartbeat was a dull, quick thud.

"Oh, there's Ty!" Jess sprang up, hurrying across the lobby to meet him. "I didn't get to congratulate you. You were absolutely wonderful."

Though his arm slipped around her, Jess saw that his eyes had drifted over her head. Without turning, she knew who they focused on.

Asher didn't see, nor did she speak.

"Well, Starbuck, you earned your pay today," Madge commented. "The Dean and I are going to the Lido to hold Michael's hand."

"Tell him I lost three pounds on the court today." He spoke to her, lightly enough, but his eyes never left Asher's.

"I don't think that's going to make him feel a hell of a lot better," she returned, giving her husband a nudge as she rose. "Well, we're off to fight for a taxi. Anyone going our way?"

"As a matter of fact," Mac began, picking up the hint easily, "Jess and I were on our way out too."

"Want a lift, Ty?" Madge's husband gave her an offended look as she ground her heel into his foot. But he shut his mouth firmly when Madge shot him a deadly glance.

Even to a man who rarely comprehended subtleties, it became obvious there were things being said without words. The little group had simply ceased to exist for Ty and Asher. After a hard look at the silent couple The Dean straightened his glasses and grinned at his wife.

"I guess not, huh?"

"You're so quick, babe." Madge began shepherding the rest toward the doors. "Anyone know some French obscenities? It's the best way to get a cab in the rain."

Asher rose slowly. From behind her she could hear the ding of a bell on the desk and the whoosh of the storm as the doors were opened then quickly closed. For a moment Ty thought she looked like something that should be enclosed in glass. Not to be touched, not to be soiled. She reached out her hand.

When he took it, it was warm. Flesh and blood.

In unspoken agreement they turned away from the doors and walked to the elevator.

Chapter 6

They didn't speak, but then they didn't need to. With one hand still holding hers, Ty pushed the button for his floor. The elevator began its silent rise. Once, the hand in his trembled lightly. He found it unbearably exciting. The numbers above their heads flashed ponderously until at last the car stopped. When the doors slid open they stepped into the carpeted hall together.

Asher heard the key jingle against loose change as Ty reached into his pocket. She heard the click of the lock before he released her hand. The choice was still hers. She stepped out of the light into the dimness of the room.

It smelled of him. That was her first thought. The air carried Ty's lingering fragrance. Something sharp, something vital. Something she had never forgotten. All at once her nerves began to jump. The poise that had carried her this far fell away. Searching for something to say, she wandered the room. It was untidy, with a shirt thrown here, shoes tossed there. She knew if she opened the closet, she would find a neat stack of rackets, the only semblance of order. Instead, she moved to the window. Rain ran like tears down the glass.

"It's going to storm all night."

As if to accent her words, lightning split the sky. Asher counted to five, then heard the thunder answer. Hundreds of lights spread through the darkness. The city was there, crowded, moving—distant. Staring through the wet glass, she waited for Ty to speak.

Silence. The patter of rain on the window. The distant hum of traffic. Another moan of thunder. Unable to bear it, Asher turned.

He was watching her. The small bedside lamp threw both light and shadow into the room. His stance was neither relaxed nor threatening, and she understood. He had given her a choice before she entered. Now he wouldn't let her go. A bridge had been burned. Asher felt nothing but relief that the decision was already made. But her fingers were numb as she reached to loosen the thin belt at her waist.

Crossing to her, Ty laid his hands over hers, stopping the movement. Asher stared up at him, unsure, as nervous as the first time. Without speaking he took her face in his hands to study her. He wanted to remember her this way—in shadowed light with the fury of a storm at her back. Her eyes were dark with traces of fear, traces of desire. In a gesture of surrender her arms had dropped to her sides. But he didn't want surrender—perhaps she had forgotten.

As he lowered his head Ty watched her lids shut, her lips part in anticipation. Gently he kissed her temple, then the other, then the delicate curve of an eyebrow. Without haste, his eyes closed. He reacquainted himself with her face through taste and touch. Her lips beckoned, but he nibbled along the line of her jaw, on the hollow of her cheek.

His thumb brushed her bottom lip as he whispered kisses over her face. He remembered every curve. Her breath shuddered out as he kissed the corners of her mouth. He brushed his over it, retreating when Asher sought more pressure. There was only the fleeting promise of more. With a moan she gripped his forearms. He'd waited for the strength. He'd waited for the demands. Again he touched his lips to hers, allowing his tongue a brief taste. Now her arms wrapped possessively around him. Now passion exploded, mouth against mouth. Lightning flashed, illuminating them as one form in the ageless wonder of lovers.

"Undress me," she whispered breathlessly, hardly able to speak as her lips fused again and again with his. "I want you to undress me."

In answer, he lowered the zipper slowly, allowing his fingers to trail along her bare skin. He found more silk, something thin and fragile. The dress slithered down her body to lie at her feet. Growing impatient, Asher worked her hands between them to deal with the buttons of his shirt while her mouth continued to cling to his. She felt the hard muscle, the line of ribs, the mat of hair. A moan wrenched from her out of deep, desperate need.

The thigh-length chemise was too much of a barrier. Longing for the intimacy of flesh against flesh, Asher reached to draw down the strap. Again Ty stopped her.

"Don't rush," he murmured, then tore at her control with a deep, lingering kiss. The pressure was hard and demanding, the lips soft and heated. "Come to bed."

In a haze she let him lead her, felt the mattress give under her weight, then his. Anticipation shivered along her skin. "The light," she whispered.

As he circled her throat with his hand, Ty's eyes met hers. "I need to see you." Thunder exploded as his mouth crushed down on hers.

When she would have hurried, he set the pace. Languorous, sleepy, enervating. It seemed her lips alone would pleasure him enough for a lifetime. She was so soft, so moist. Far from pliant, Asher moved against him, inviting, insisting. Her urgency excited him, but Ty chose to savor. Over the silk his hands roamed to trace her shape from thigh to breast. The peaks strained against the sheer material.

He took his mouth to her shoulder, catching the narrow strap of the silk with his teeth. Inch by inch he lowered it until her flesh was exposed to him. She was firm and creamy-white in contrast to the tan of her arms and shoulders.

"So lovely," he whispered while his fingertip brought down the second strap.

When she was naked to the waist, his mouth ranged down slowly, though with her hands in his hair she urged him down. With lips parted, Ty sought the peak of her breast. Asher arched, pressing him down. She wanted him to be greedy, wanted to feel the rough scrape of his tongue. When she did she could no longer be still. Her body vibrated with the beat of a hundred tiny pulses. Desire, raw and primitive, tore through her with the power to obliterate all but one thought. She was woman; he was man. Seeking pleasure, Asher moved under him, letting her hands roam.

He abandoned gentleness because she wanted none. It had always driven him wild when her passion was unleashed. She had no inhibitions, no shame. When they came together like this she was all fire, and as dangerous as the lightning in the night sky. Ty wasn't even aware of his control slipping away. Hard-palmed hands ran bruisingly over tender skin. Short, manicured nails dug into strong shoulders.

His breathing was ragged when he tore the garment from her. She gave him no time to view her nakedness. Her fingers were busy, struggling to remove the last barrier of his clothing. Their frantic movements took them over the bed, tangling in the sheets. Her skin was damp and trembling, but her hands were so strong, and so certain. There could be no more waiting.

A pain stabbed into him as he entered her. It was sharp, then sweet. He thought he heard her cry out as she had that first night when he had taken her innocence. Then she was wrapped around him—legs, arms. Her mouth fastened on his. The storm crashed directly overhead. They rose with it.

His hand lay lightly on her breast. Asher sighed. Had she ever known such pure contentment? she wondered. No, not even when they had been together before. Then she hadn't known what it would be like to do without him. She shuddered, then moved closer.

"Cold?" Ty drew her to him until her head rested on the curve of his shoulder.

"A little. Where's my chemise?"

"Devoured."

She laughed, flinging her arms around him as though she would never let go. Free, she thought. How wonderful to be free—to love, to laugh. Supporting herself on his chest, she stared down into his face. For once his eyes were calm. A faint smile curved his lips. Beneath her his breathing was even and slow, to match hers. To match, her mind repeated. They had always been like two halves of the same whole.

"Oh, God, I missed you, Ty." On those words she buried her face against his throat. Empty, empty, she thought. It seemed like a lifetime of emptiness had been wiped away with an hour of fulfillment.

"Asher—"

"No, no questions. No questions." Wildly she rained kisses over his face. "Just feel, just be with me. I need to laugh tonight, the way we used to."

He stopped her hurried movements by taking her head in his hands. There was a plea in her eyes and a light trace of desperation. No, he didn't want to see that now. Pushing away the questions that drummed in his head, he smiled at her.

"I thought you were going to buy me dinner."

Relief washed over her before she grinned. "I have no idea what you're talking about."

"You asked me for a date."

Tossing her head back, she arched an elegant brow. "*I* asked you? You've been out in the heat too long, Starbuck."

"Dinner," he repeated, rolling her over until he loomed above her.

"As far as I can tell, you've already eaten a sixty-dollar silk chemise. Are you still hungry?"

For an answer, he lowered his mouth to her neck and bit, none too gently. Laughing, she tried to twist away. "Food," he muttered. "I have to eat."

Remembering a weakness, she found the spot on his ribs and squeezed. His body jerked, giving her the opportunity to slither away. She was giggling like a girl when he grabbed her and pulled her back. "How many people know the indomitable Starbuck is ticklish?" she demanded when he pinned her arms over her head. "What would the press pay to find out?"

"About the same as they'd pay to find out elegant Asher Wolfe has a heart-shaped birthmark on her very attractive bottom."

Asher considered this a moment. "Even," she decided. Her smile slanted seductively. "Do you really want to go out to eat?"

Desire fluttered lightly in the pit of his stomach as he looked down at her. The light angled across her face, accenting the smooth, glowing skin and darkened eyes. The thunder was a distant rumble now, but he felt it vibrate in his head.

"There's always room service," he murmured, tasting her lips. He kept her arms pinned as he dropped light, teasing kisses over her face. Nestling in the vulnerable curve of her neck, he used his tongue to stir and arouse.

"Ty," she moaned, unable to struggle against the captivity. "Make love to me."

His chuckle was low and he was pleased. "Oh, I am. This time," he whispered into her ear, "we won't hurry. Hours, love." His tongue darted to her ear, making her squirm in agonized delight. "Hours and hours." Then he shifted, bringing her close to his side. Cradling her, he felt her heart pounding against him. When he reached for the phone, Asher glanced up, puzzled. "Food," he reminded her.

She gave a weak laugh. "I should have remembered your stomach comes first."

His hand grazed over her breast. "Not necessarily." Her nipple was already taut. He flicked his thumb over it lazily.

"Ty—" With a kiss he silenced her.

"Champagne," he said into the phone while driving Asher mad with careless strokes and fondling. "Dom Pérignon. Caviar," he went on, sending her a questioning look that she was powerless to answer.

"Beluga." He gave her a light kiss, running his hand down to the flat of her stomach. She quivered, turning into him. Legs tangled as he brushed his lips over her shoulder. "Cold shrimp." He bit her tender bottom lip. "Mmm, that'll do. Yes, for two." As he dropped the phone back on its cradle, Asher found his mouth in a desperate, yearning kiss. "Food excites you?" he mumbled against the hungry lips. Struggling not to take her instantly, he ran his hand to her hip, kneading warm flesh.

"I want you." Her voice was low and throaty, her hands questing. "I want you now."

"Shh." Slow, patient, his stroking aroused rather than subdued. "Relax. There's time. I want to see you again." He drew away from her. "Really see you."

She was burning for him. Now she lay naked and vulnerable under his gaze. As she watched, his eyes darkened, grew stormy. Her breathing quickened. When she reached out he took her hand, burying his lips in the palm.

"You're more beautiful than ever," he said huskily. "It shouldn't be possible. I've looked at you so many times and have been afraid to touch."

"No." Asher pulled him to her until they were heart to heart. "I'm never more alive than when you touch me." With a sigh Ty nestled down until his head rested between her breasts. Asher combed her fingers through his hair as contentment layered over desire. "Today, when I watched you playing Michael, I wanted you. Sitting there, surrounded by thousands of people in the middle of the afternoon, all I could think about was being with you like this." She gave a gurgle of laughter. "Wicked thoughts, such wonderfully wicked thoughts."

"So your invitation to dinner carried an ulterior motive."

"In your weakened condition I knew you'd be a pushover, though I had thought I'd have to take you out and ply you with food and wine first."

"And if I'd refused?"

"I'd have come up with something else."

Grinning, he lifted his head. "What?"

Asher shrugged. "I could have come up here and seduced you before you'd gotten your strength back."

"Hmm…I almost wish I'd said no."

"Too late. I have you now."

"I could get stubborn."

Slowly she smiled. "I know your weaknesses," she whispered, running a fingertip up the nape of his neck. His shudder was quick and uncontrollable. Leaning up, she took his face in her hands. Lazily she rubbed her lips over his, then deepened the touch into a kiss—a long, draining taste that left him weak. Her tongue glided over his, then retreated.

"Asher." On an oath he crushed her beneath him, savaging her mouth with a need that had risen so quickly, it left him dazed. He didn't hear the discreet knock on the door, nor did he understand her murmurs.

"The door," she managed. "Ty, it's room service."

"What?"

"The door."

Laying his forehead on hers, he struggled to recapture his control. "They're awful damn quick," he muttered. He found he was trembling. How could he have forgotten that she could make him tremble? After letting out a long breath, he rose. Asher pulled the sheets up to her chin and watched him cross to the closet.

A beautiful body, she thought, both proud and admiring. Long and lean, with a network of muscle. She looked her fill as he rummaged through his closet for a robe. Strong shoulders, trim waist, narrow hips and long legs. An athlete's body, or a dancer's. He was made to compete.

He shrugged into the robe, belting it carelessly. Grinning, he turned to her. Asher's heart lodged in her throat. "Ty, you're so beautiful."

His eyes widened in astonishment. Torn between amusement and masculine discomfort, he headed for the door. "Good God," he said, making Asher smother a giggle. She brought her knees up to her chest as he signed the check at the door. In some ways, she mused, he was a little boy. To his way of thinking, the word *beautiful* applied only to a woman—or to an ace. He'd be more insulted than complimented having it applied to himself. Yet she saw him that way—not only physically. He was a man capable of lovely gestures, a man unashamed of his deep love for his mother, unafraid to show tenderness. He had no cruelty in him, though on the court he was unmerciful. His temper was explosive, but he was incapable of holding a grudge. Asher realized that it was his basic capacity for feeling that she had missed most of all. And still he had never, in all their closeness, in all the months of intimacy, told her that he loved her. If he had once said the words, she would never have left him.

"Where have you gone?"

Asher turned her head to see him standing beside a tray, a bottle of champagne in his hands. Quickly she shook her head and smiled again. "Nowhere." She cocked her head at the bottle. "All that just for us?"

He walked to the bed and sat on the edge. "Did you want some too?" The cork came off with a resounding pop as she cuffed his shoulder. With an easy stretch he rolled the tray toward them. "Here, hold the glasses." Without ceremony he poured champagne until it nearly ran over the rims.

"Ty, it'll spill on the bed."

"Better be careful then," he advised as he set the bottle back in the ice. He grinned as she sat cross-legged, balancing two glasses in her hands. The sheet was held in place over her breasts by arms pressed tightly to her sides.

She returned the grin with a glance of exasperation. "Aren't you going to take one?"

"Oh, I don't know." Hooking a finger under the sheet, he nudged it downward, exposing creamy flesh.

"Ty, cut it out, I'll spill it!"

"Better not, we have to sleep here." He urged the sheet a trifle lower. Frustrated, Asher looked from glass to glass. Wine swayed dangerously.

"This is a dirty trick, Starbuck."

"Yeah, I like it."

Asher narrowed her eyes. "I'm going to pour both glasses into your lap."

"Terrible waste," he decided, kissing her. "It's good stuff. I always found it strange," he began, lazily kissing her face as he spoke, "that I was bred for beer and you were bred for champagne, but you haven't any head for it."

"I have a perfectly good head for champagne."

Chuckling, he brushed his lips over her throat. "I remember one very memorable night when we shared a bottle. Three glasses make you crazy. I like you crazy."

"That's absurd." The lift of brow challenged him. Without hesitation Asher brought a glass to her lips, losing the sheet as she drank it. Ty watched the linen pool into her lap before she drained the last drop. "That's one," Asher announced, lifting the second glass. Ty plucked it from her fingers.

"Let's spread it out a little," he advised, amused. He drank, more conservatively, then reached for the tray of caviar. "You like this stuff."

"Mmm." Suddenly hungry, Asher spread a generous amount on a toast point. Ty settled down to the bowl of cold shrimp and spicy sauce. "Here, it's good." Though he allowed her to feed him a bite, he wrinkled his nose.

"Overrated," he stated. "This is better." He popped a shrimp into Asher's mouth.

"'S wonderful," she agreed with a full mouth, then chose another. "I didn't know I was so hungry."

Ty filled her glass again. Could anyone else imagine her, he wondered, sitting naked in bed, licking sauce from her finger? Did anyone else know how totally open she could be? She was talking now, in fits and starts as she ate, replaying her match. Ty let her ramble, pleased just to hear her voice, to see her animation. She was satisfied with her serve, worried about her backhand volley.

Publicly she chose her words with care, and made certain there were few of them. If a reporter could see her now, Ty mused, he'd wear a pencil down to the nub. She was full of joy and doubt, fear and self-congratulation. Words tumbled out without discretion. Her face was animated, her hands gestured. By the time she had slowed down, her second glass was empty. Perhaps she was completely happy, because she wasn't even aware of the sensation. She was simply at ease, completely herself. Comfortably full, she toyed with the last of the caviar.

"Are you worried about playing Chuck in the finals?"

Ty bit into a shrimp. "Why?"

"He was always good," Asher began, frowning a bit. "But he's developed over the past few years."

Grinning, Ty tilted more wine into her glass. "Don't you think I can beat him?"

She sent him a long, considering look. "You were always good too."

"Thanks." After setting the caviar on the tray, he stretched lengthwise on the bed.

"Chuck plays a bit like my father did," Asher mused. "Very clean, very precise. His talent's polished rather than raw."

"Like mine."

"Yes. That raw athletic ability is something every competitor envies. My father used to say that you had more natural talent than any player he'd seen in his career." Over the rim of her glass she smiled down at him. "Yet he always wanted to smooth out your form. Then there were your…antics on the court."

Ty laughed, kissing her knee through the sheet. "It used to drive him crazy."

"I imagine he'd be more pleased if he saw you play now."

"And you?" Ty countered. "How would he feel if he saw you play now?"

Asher shifted her eyes from his to stare into her glass. "He won't."

"Why?"

As if to erase the question, she lifted her hand. "Ty, please."

"Asher," he said quietly, grasping her fingers. "You're hurting."

If she could have held it back, she would have. But the words tumbled out. "I let him down. He won't forgive me."

"He's your father."

"And he was my coach."

Unable to comprehend, Ty shook his head. "What difference does that make?"

"All the difference." The pain slipped out. As if to numb it, she swallowed more wine. "Please, not tonight. I don't want anything to spoil tonight."

Her fingers had tightened on his. One by one Ty kissed them until he felt the tension relax. "Nothing could." Over their joined hands, dark, intense eyes met hers. Spontaneously her pulse began to race. "I never got you completely out of my mind," he confessed. "Too many things reminded me—a phrase, a song. Silence. There were times alone at night I would have sworn I heard you breathing in the quiet beside me."

The words moved her…hurt her. "Ty, those were yesterdays. We can start now."

"Now," he agreed. "But we'll have to deal with yesterday sooner or later."

Though she opened her mouth to disagree, she knew. "Later then. Right now I don't want to think about anything but being with you."

He grinned, brushing a stray curl from her cheek. "It's difficult to argue with that."

"Don't get cocky," she told him, then tossed off the rest of her champagne. "That was three," Asher said haughtily. "And I'm not the least affected."

Ty had no trouble recognizing the signs—the flushed cheeks, the glowing eyes and misty smile. Whatever she might say, he knew the champagne was swimming in her head. And when they loved again, she would be soft and strong and passionate. He found himself wanting to simply look at her for a few minutes more. Once they touched, the fire would take them.

"Want another?" he offered.

"Sure."

Wisely he filled her glass only halfway before he replaced the bottle. "I caught your interview today," Ty commented. "It was on while I was changing."

"Oh?" Asher shifted to lie on her stomach, propping herself on her elbows. "How'd I do?"

"Hard to say. It was all in French."

She laughed, adjusting her position so that she could take another sip. "I'd forgotten."

"How about a translation?"

"He asked things like—Mademoiselle Wolfe, do you find any changes in your style after your temporary retirement? And I said something like I feel I've tightened my serve." She chuckled into her wine. "I didn't mention that my muscles beg for me to give them a break after two sets. He asked how I felt about playing the *young* Miss Kingston in the finals and I refrained from punching him in the mouth."

"That was diplomatic," Ty answered, slipping the glass from her fingers.

"I'm a hell of a diplomat," Asher agreed. Rolling over on her back, she looked up at him. He lounged just behind her so that she had to tilt her head at an odd angle to make eye contact. "You stole my glass."

"Yes, I did." After setting it on the tray, Ty gave the wheeled table a slight shove.

"Did we finish dinner?" Reaching up and back, she locked her arms around his neck.

"We've definitely finished dinner." He allowed her to urge him down until his mouth hovered above hers.

"Got any suggestions about what we should do now?" She liked the strangeness of having his face upside down over hers. Playfully she nipped at his lip.

"No. Do you?"

"Got a deck of cards?"

"Uh-uh."

"Then I guess we'll have to make love." She gave a rich, low laugh before she kissed him again. "All night—just to pass the time."

"It's something to do. Rainy nights are so boring."

Eyes dancing, she nodded. "Mmm, yes. Let's make the best of it."

Her lips were curved in a smile as his met them, but they parted eagerly. She found it strangely seductive to have his tongue meet hers this way. On a gurgle of laughter, she closed her teeth gently, capturing him. In response, he trailed his fingers over her breast until her moan freed him.

"I get dizzy kissing you upside down," Asher murmured.

"I like you dizzy." Leaning forward, he trailed moist kisses over her throat. The tip of his tongue picked up her flavor, then lingered over it. He could feel pulse beats both with his hand and his lips. Finding the curve of his neck vulnerable, Asher began to give him the same pleasure he was bringing her.

"I want to touch you," she complained. "I can't touch you this way."

But he continued to explore from where he was, enjoying the freedom his hands had over her body. The scent of the rich sauce still lingering in the air, and the zing of champagne clung to two tongues as they joined. The mattress groaned quietly as she shifted. Then she was on her knees, pressed body to body. In a quick move she had stripped the robe from him so he was as naked as she. With a half laugh, half sigh, she ran her palms up his strong back.

Entwined, enchanted, neither noticed that the rain had ceased. Inside the quiet room, pleasure built. Strong thigh pressed against strong thigh, hungry lips sought hungry lips. Their passion was equal, their needs the same. Together, they lay down.

Soft sighs became moans. Before long, gentle caresses became demanding. Both seemed desperate to touch and be touched, to have their own weaknesses exploited. With instinctive understanding they held back the final gift. The inner fire built, dampening their flesh, but still they lingered over each other. There was so much to make up for, so much time to recapture. Though passion was flaring, this thought hovered in the back of both their minds. Tonight was a fresh beginning. They wanted all of it.

Asher thought her lungs would burst. The combination of wine and passion buzzed in her head. A laugh, smoky with desire, floated from her as he gasped her name. She wanted to tempt him, torment him, give to him. His stomach was hard and flat with muscle, yet the touch of her fingertip could make it quiver. Asher had forgotten this sense of power and exulted in it. Her small hands could make him weak. Her shapely, serious mouth could drive him wild.

The power shifted so abruptly, she was helpless. He found her greatest vulnerability and used his tongue to destroy her last vestige of control. Half wild, she called for him, struggling to have more, desperate to have all. Arching, she pressed him closer, cresting on a wave of delight that had no chance to recede. She thrashed as if in protest, yet arched again in invitation. As she built toward a higher peak, Ty slid up her body. Greedy, she drew him inside of her, hearing his gasp for breath before there was only feeling.

Later, they still clung together, damp, spent, fulfilled. He shifted only to turn out the light. In the midnight darkness they molded to each other, drifting toward sleep.

"You'll move in with me."

The murmur was a statement rather than a question. Asher opened her eyes before she answered. She could just see the outline of his face. "Yes, if you want me."

"I never stopped wanting you."

Without the light he didn't see the flicker of doubt in her eyes before he slept.

Chapter 7

She was afraid of London. Lady Wickerton had lived there—hostessing parties in the elegant three-story house in Grosvenor Square, attending the ballet at the Royal Opera House, the theater in Drury Lane, shopping in the West End. Lady Wickerton had played bridge with members of Parliament and had sipped tea at Buckingham Palace. Lady Wickerton had been a quiet, dutiful wife, a woman of intelligence, breeding and control. She had nearly suffocated in London.

Perhaps if Ty hadn't come between Jim Wolfe's daughter and Eric Wickerton's wife, Asher would have accepted her role with ease. She'd wanted to, had struggled to. Too much passion simmered inside her. It had been there all of her life, but the months with Ty had liberated it. Controlling something dormant was entirely different from harnessing something that pulsed with life. There had not even been her profession as an outlet for the energy that drove her.

Coming back to London was the most difficult step yet. There she would not only have to face memories of Ty, but the ghost of a woman she had pretended to be. It was all so familiar—Westminster

Abbey, Trafalgar Square, the smells, the voices. Even the anticipation of Wimbledon couldn't block them out. There would be faces here that would remember the coolly elegant Lady Wickerton. And there would be questions.

Publicly she would remain aloof, distant and uninformative. Asher felt she owed Eric that much. She would simply refuse to discuss her marriage or its demise. Her early training, her years of following her father's rules, would serve her now more than ever.

She would give them tennis. With two straight championships now under her belt, Asher would have been spotlighted in any case. It was up to her to sway the press away from her personal life toward her professional resurgence. What was growing between her and Ty was still too fragile to be shared.

Happiness. She had nearly forgotten how simple and overwhelming the feeling was. Lazy midnight talks, crazy loving, quiet walks. They shared a hotel room and made it home for the days and nights they were there. She felt as much a gypsy as he, and was content to be so. Once she had looked for roots, stability, commitment. She'd learned that they meant nothing without the fullness of love. His spontaneity had always fascinated her. This time Asher would resolve the lingering fear of it and enjoy.

"Aren't you dressed yet?"

At the question Asher stopped tying her tennis shoe and glanced up. Ty stood in the doorway between the small parlor and bedroom. Fully dressed, impatient, he frowned at her. His hair fell over his forehead as unruly as ever and still slightly damp from his shower. Waves of love radiated through her.

"Nearly," Asher tossed back. "Not everyone can move quickly in the morning, you know—especially on six hours sleep."

The frown became a grin. "Something keep you up?" He caught the shoe she hurled at him in one hand, his eyes never leaving her face. Apparently the late night hadn't affected him. He looked well rested and full of barely controlled energy. "You can always take a nap after morning practice."

"Awfully pleased with yourself this morning, aren't you?"

"Am I?" Still grinning, he came toward her, tossing her shoe lightly. "It probably has something to do with trouncing that British kid in the quarter-finals yesterday."

"Oh?" Lifting a brow, Asher looked up at him. "Is that all you're pleased about?"

"What else?"

"Let me have my shoe," she demanded. "So I can throw it at you again."

"Did you know you have a poor morning attitude?" he asked, holding the shoe out of reach.

"Did you know you've been insufferable ever since you won the French?" she countered sweetly. "Remember, it's only one quarter of the Grand Slam."

He moved the shoe farther out of reach as she made a grab for it. "For you too, Face," he reminded her.

"The rest's on grass." In an attempt to hold him still, Asher grabbed the waistband of his warm-up pants.

"The woman's insatiable," he sighed. Diving, he pinned her beneath him on the bed.

"Ty! Stop!" Laughing, Asher pushed against him as he nuzzled at her neck. "We'll be late for practice."

"Oh. You're right." Giving her a quick kiss, he rolled away from her.

"Well," Asher muttered as she sat up, "you didn't take much persuading." Even as she started to tidy her hair, she was spun back into his arms. Her startled exclamation was smothered by his lips.

Long, deep, infinitely tender, smolderingly passionate. His arms circled her. Asher felt her bones soften, then dissolve. Her head fell back, inviting him to take more. Cradling her, Ty went on a slow exploration of her mouth. For the moment he enjoyed the sense of total domination. If they continued, he knew she would begin her own demands. Then it would be power for power. The knowledge excited him. Still, he laughed against her lips. There was time. A lifetime.

"You awake yet?" he asked her as he ran a hand lightly over her breast.

"Mmm-hmm."

"Good. Let's go." After setting her on her feet, he gave Asher's bottom a friendly pat.

"I'll get you for that," she promised. Needs stirred inside her, not quite under control.

"I certainly hope so." With an easy smile Ty slipped an arm around her shoulders. "You need to work on your backhand volley," he began as they walked from the room.

Insulted, Asher tossed her head back. "What are you talking about?"

"If you'd shorten your swing a bit more—"

"Shorten your own swing," she retorted. "And while you're at it," she continued, "you weren't exactly Mr. Speed yesterday."

"Gotta save something for the finals."

Asher snorted as she punched the elevator button. "Your conceit never wavers."

"Confidence," Ty contradicted. He liked seeing her this way—relaxed, but ready to laugh or to slap back. Briefly he wondered if she realized she was even more beautiful when she forgot caution. "What about breakfast?"

"What about it?"

"Want to grab some eggs after practice?"

She slid her eyes to his as the doors opened. "Is that your best offer?"

Ty lifted a brow as he followed her into the elevator. Asher exchanged a polite nod with a middle-aged couple in tweed. "Maybe you'd like to take up where we left off last night?" Ty lounged against an elevator wall as Asher gaped at him. "What did you say your name was again?"

Asher could feel two pairs of shocked and interested eyes boring into her back. "Misty," she replied, allowing a trace of cockney to color her voice. "Will you spring for champagne again, Mr. Starbuck? It was ever so good."

He recognized the light of challenge in her eyes and grinned. "So were you, sweetie."

When the doors opened to the lobby, the older couple moved out reluctantly. Asher punched Ty in the arm before she followed.

In less than an hour they were both concentrating on form and speed and the capricious bounces a ball could take on grass. Was she playing better? Asher wondered as she sprang for Madge's slice. She felt looser, less encumbered. Indeed, she felt as though losing were not even a possibility. At Wimbledon she could forget the city of London.

Instead, she could remember the qualifying games at Roehampton, with their anything-goes attitude. Both bad language and rackets had flown. It was a contrast to the elegance and glamour of Wimbledon. Here both the players and the crowd were steeped in tradition. Hydrangeas against a backdrop of rich green grass, ivy-covered walls, limos and chauffeurs. Colors were soothing, mauve and green, as if time itself had sobered them.

Here spectators would be well-mannered, quiet between points, applauding after them. Even those in standing room would behave, or the chair judge would tell them politely to quiet down. No one hung from the scoreboards at Wimbledon. It was as revered as the changing of the guards, as English as double-decker buses.

There was no doubt, as one gazed around the immaculately tended velvet lawns, the pampered roses, the dollhouse kiosks and the stands that could accommodate more than twenty-five thousand, that Wimbledon *was* tennis. It was here former players migrated to. It was here future players aspired to. Asher remembered Ty telling her about watching the matches one long-ago July Fourth and making a vow. He had kept it, not once, but four times. More than anything she had wanted before, Asher wanted them to both walk away from Centre Court as champions.

Behind the baseline, Asher stood with a racket and a ball, staring off into space.

"Had enough?" Madge called out.

"Hmm...what?" Asher's head snapped around. Seeing Madge standing with her legs spread, hand on hips, had her laughing. "I suppose I have, I was daydreaming."

From opposite ends of the court, they walked toward their bags and jackets. "No sense asking if you're happy," Madge began conversationally. "You look absolutely miserable floating two inches off the ground."

"That obvious, huh?"

"I won't pretend not to be pleased," Madge added smugly. "I've always thought you two made a great team. Going to make it official?"

"I— No, we're just taking it one day at a time." Asher kept her eyes lowered as she packed her racket. "Marriage is just a formality, after all."

"And pigs fly," Madge countered calmly. When Asher glanced up with a cautious smile, she went on. "For some, yes, you're right. Not for you, Face. Why did you stay in an unhappy marriage for three years?" When Asher started to speak, Madge lifted a hand. "Because to you marriage is a promise, and you don't break promises."

"I failed once," she began.

"Oh, all by yourself? Isn't that being a bit self-absorbed?" Impatient, Madge settled her hands on her hips again. "Listen, you aren't going to let one mistake keep you from being happy, are you?"

"I am happy," Asher assured her, punctuating the statement by touching Madge's shoulder. "Ty's all I've ever wanted, Madge. I can't risk losing him again."

Her brow puckered in confusion. "But you left him, Asher, not the other way around."

"I'd already lost him," she said flatly.

"Asher, I don't—"

"It's a new day," she interrupted, then took a deep breath of scented morning air. "A fresh start. I know what mistakes I made and have no intention of repeating them. There was a time in my life that I thought I had to come first, before this." Holding up the small white ball, Asher examined it. "Before anything. I looked on tennis as a competitor, his family as a rival. That was stupid." Dropping the ball into a can, Asher closed it.

"That's funny," Madge mused. "There was a time in my life I thought The Dean's work came first. He thought the same about me. It wasn't true in either case."

With a smile Asher slung her bag over her shoulder. "Ty won't ever forget that tennis took him out of that tenement. Maybe he shouldn't. That's the thing that brings fire to his game."

She knows him so well in some ways, Madge thought, and not at all in others. "And what brings the ice to yours?"

"Fear," Asher answered before she thought. For a moment she gave Madge a blank look, then shrugged. Saying it aloud made it seem rather unimportant. "Fear of failure, or exposure." Laughing, she began to walk. "Thank God you're not a reporter."

The gravel crunched underfoot as they moved down the path. It was a sound Asher associated with the tidiness of English courts. "Remind me to tell you sometime what goes through my head five minutes before a match."

With a sigh Asher hooked her arm through her old partner's. "Let's hit the showers."

There was no dream. Asher slept as deeply as a child, with no worries, no nagging fears. The curtains were drawn closed so that the afternoon sun filtered through lazily. Traffic sounds muffled through it, coming as a quiet drone. She wore only a short terry robe and lay on top of the spread. Ty would come back to wake her so that they could spend some time sight-seeing before nightfall. Because they were both scheduled to play the following day, they would go to bed early.

The knock on the door wakened her. Sitting up, Asher ran a hand through her tousled hair. He'd forgotten his key, she thought groggily. She stepped from the dim bedroom into the brighter parlor, wincing against the change of light. Absently she wondered what time it was as she opened the door. Shock took a moment to penetrate.

"Eric," she whispered.

"Asher." He gave her what was nearly a bow before he elbowed his way into the room. "Did I wake you?'

"I was napping." She closed the door, trying to recover her scattered wits. He looked the same, she thought. Naturally he would. Eric would see no reason to change. He was tall, slim, with a military carriage. He had a sharp-featured European face, a bit haughty and remote. Dark blond hair was cut and groomed to indicate wealth and conservatism. Light eyes in a pale face—both romantic, yet intelligent and cold. Asher knew that his mouth could twist into a hard line when he was crossed. As a suitor he had been charming, as a lover, meticulous. As a husband he'd been unbearable. She drew herself straight. He was no longer her husband.

"I didn't expect to see you, Eric."

"No?" He smiled. "Did you think I wouldn't drop by while you were in town? Lost a bit of weight, Asher."

"Competition tends to do that." Years of training had her gesturing toward a chair. "Please, sit down. I'll get you a drink."

There was no reason to be upset by him now, she told herself. No need to feel fear or guilt. Divorced couples managed to be civilized more often than not. Eric, Asher thought with a grim smile, was a very civilized man.

"Have you been well?" She poured his scotch neat, then added ice to Perrier for herself.

"Quite well. And you?"

"Yes. Your family?"

"Doing wonderfully." Eric accepted the glass she offered, then eyed her over the rim. "And your father?" He watched for the flash of pain, and was satisfied.

"As far as I know, he's fine." Quite consciously Asher drew on the mask as she sat.

"Still hasn't forgiven you for giving up your career."

Her eyes were level now and expressionless. "I'm sure you're aware he hasn't."

Mindful of the crease in his pants, Eric crossed his legs. "I thought perhaps now that you're competing again…" He allowed the sentence to die.

Asher watched the bubbles rise in her glass, but left them untasted. "He no longer acknowledges me," she said flatly. "I'm still paying, Eric." She lifted her eyes again. "Does that satisfy you?"

He drank leisurely for a moment. "It was your choice, my dear. Your career for my name."

"For your silence," Asher corrected. "I already had your name."

"And another man's child in your belly."

Ice clinked against ice as her hands shook. Quickly she controlled the tremor. "One would have thought it would have been enough that I lost the child," she murmured. "Did you come all this way to remind me?"

"I came," Eric said as he leaned back, "to see how my ex-wife was adjusting. You're victorious on the courts, Asher, and as lovely as ever." She didn't speak as his eyes roamed the room. "Apparently you didn't waste too much time picking up with your old lover."

"My mistake was in leaving him, Eric. We both know that. I'm very, very sorry."

He sent her an icy look. "Your mistake was in trying to pass his bastard off on me."

Furious and trembling, Asher sprang to her feet. "I never lied to you. And by God, I'll never apologize again."

He remained seated, swirling liquor. "Does he know yet?"

Her color drained dramatically enough to make him smile genuinely. Hate ate at him. "No, I see he doesn't. How interesting."

"I kept my word, Eric." Though her hands were laced tightly together, Asher's voice was strong. "As long as I was your wife, I did everything you asked of me."

He acknowledged this with a slight nod. Her honesty hadn't been enough—nor had her three years of penance. "But you're not my wife any longer."

"We agreed. The marriage was intolerable for both of us."

"What are you afraid he'd do?" Eric mused, frowning up at the ceiling. "He's a very physical man as I remember, with a primitive sort of temper." Lowering his eyes, he smiled again. "Do you think he'd beat you?"

Asher gave a short laugh. "No."

"You're very confident," he murmured. "What exactly are you afraid of?"

Wearily she dropped her hands to her sides. "He wouldn't forgive me, Eric, any more than you have. I lost the child, I lost my father. My self-esteem. I'll never lose the guilt. I hurt nothing but your pride, Eric, haven't I suffered enough for that?"

"Perhaps…perhaps not." Rising, he stepped toward her. She remembered the scent of his crisp, dignified cologne very well. "Perhaps the most perfect punishment might be in never knowing your secret is safe. I'll make you no promises, Asher."

"It astonishes me that I was ever naïve enough to think of you as a kind man, Eric," she said softly.

"Justice," he returned, toasting her.

"Revenge has little to do with justice."

He shrugged an elegant shoulder. "All in your viewpoint, my dear."

She wouldn't give him the satisfaction of breaking down—of weeping, of screaming or begging. Instead, Asher stood perfectly still. "If you've said all you've come to say, I'd like you to go."

"Of course." After finishing off the liquor, he set down the glass. "Sleep well, darling. Don't bother, I'll let myself out." Eric turned the doorknob and found himself face-to-face with Ty. Nothing could have pleased him more.

Ty noted his cold, satisfied smile before his gaze shifted to Asher.

Standing in the center of the room, she seemed frozen. There was anguish, and, he thought, fear in her eyes. Her face was dead-white and still. Even as he wondered what it was she feared, Ty took in the rest of her appearance. The tousled hair, the brief robe and exposed skin had rage boiling in him. Asher could feel it from where she stood.

His eyes whipped back to Eric's. There was murder in them. "Get the hell out of here."

"Just on my way," Eric said equably, though he had inched back against the door in instinctive defense. His last thought as he shut it behind him was that Asher would bear the brunt of the fury in Ty's eyes. That alone had made it worth the trip.

The room vibrated with the silent storm. Asher didn't move. It seemed Ty would stare at her for eternity. The trembling was difficult to control, but she forced herself. If she made light of the incident, perhaps so would he.

"What the hell was he doing here?"

"He just dropped by...I suppose to wish me luck." The lie sliced at her.

"Cozy." Crossing to her, Ty caught the lapel of her robe in his hand. "Don't you usually dress for visitors, Asher? Then again, I suppose it isn't necessary for ex-husbands."

"Ty, don't."

"Don't what?" he demanded. Though he struggled against the words, the accusations, the feelings, he knew it was a losing battle. Against the unknown he would always attack. "Wouldn't it be better form to meet him somewhere else? It's a little sticky here, isn't it?"

The cold sarcasm hurt more than his fury would have. With so much to hide, she could only shake her head. "Ty, you know there's nothing between us. You know—"

"What the hell do I know?" he shouted, grasping the other lapel. "Don't ask, don't question. Then I walk in and find you entertaining the bastard you left me for."

"I didn't know he was coming." She gripped his arms for balance as he nearly lifted her off her feet. "If he had called, I would have told him to stay away."

"You let him in." Enraged, he shook her. "Why?'

Despair rather than fear clutched at her. "Would you be happier if I had slammed the door in his face?"

"Yes, damn it."

"I didn't." She pushed at him now, as furious as he. "I let him in, I gave him a drink. Make what you like of it. I can't stop you."

"Did he want you back?" he demanded, ignoring her struggles. "Is that why he came?"

"What does it matter?" Impotently she slammed her fists into his chest. "It's not what *I* want." She threw back her head, her eyes burning.

"Then tell me, tell me now why you married him." When she tried to pull away, he dragged her back. "I'll have that much, Asher, and I'll have it now."

"Because I thought he was what I needed," she cried out. Roaring in her ears was the anger, the fear she had felt for Eric.

"And was he?" To prevent her from striking out, Ty grasped her wrist.

"No!" She jerked but couldn't free herself. Frustration added to an almost unreasonable fury. "No, I was miserable. I was trapped." Her voice was both strong and harsh. "I paid in ways you can't imagine. There wasn't a day I was happy. Does that satisfy you?"

She did something he had never seen her do before. She wept. His grip on her wrists loosened as he watched tears flood her eyes and spill onto her cheeks. Never in all the years he'd known her had he seen that kind of torment on her face. Tearing herself from his grip, Asher fled into the bedroom, slamming the door at her back.

She wanted peace. She wanted privacy. The grief had hit her unexpectedly. If the tears hadn't clogged her throat, she would have told him about the baby. The words had been there, ready to spill out in anger. Then speech had been impossible. Now she needed to weep it out.

Ty stared at the closed door for a long time. The wrenching sound of sobbing came to him. It was a reaction he hadn't expected. His anger was justified, as were his questions. Anger for anger he could have comprehended, but the pain he heard was altogether different. Having come from a family of women, he understood a woman's tears. Over the years he'd done his share of comforting and soothing. But these sobs were hot and bitter—and Asher never wept.

Jess cried easily, quiet, feminine tears. His mother wept with joy or silent sadness. These he could handle. A shoulder could be offered, a few sympathetic words, a teasing comment. Instinctively he knew none of those were the prescription for raw grief.

He still had questions. He still had anger. But the sounds from the bedroom forced him to put them aside. Ty recognized when tears were used as a weapon or a defense. These were being torn from her unwillingly. Dragging a hand through his hair, he wondered if it was Eric or himself who was responsible for them. Or something he knew nothing about. Cursing softly, he went to the door and opened it.

She lay curled on the bed in a ball of misery. Her body shook. When he touched her she jerked away. Saying nothing, Ty lay down beside her, gathering her close. For another moment she fought him. *Alone.* Her tears were not to be observed, not to be shared. *Private.* Ty dealt with her struggles by merely holding her tighter in arms that were both strong and gentle.

"I'm not going anywhere," he murmured.

With no more protest, Asher clung to his comfort and let her grief run its course.

It had grown dark and her body was weak. There were no more tears left in her. Ty's arms were strong around her. Beneath her damp cheek she could hear the steady beat of his heart. Gently, almost absently, his fingers stroked the base of her neck.

She'd nearly told him. Asher closed her eyes, too weary to feel fear or regret. If she could have summoned up the energy, she would have been grateful for the tears that had prevented her confession.

I lost your baby. Would he be holding her now if those words had spilled out? What good would it do to tell him? she asked herself. Why make him grieve for something he had never known? And grieve he would, she knew, after the anger passed. It came to her suddenly that it wasn't only fear that kept the secret locked inside her. She couldn't bear to see Ty hurt as she had hurt.

How could she explain to him about Eric without dragging up old bitterness, opening old wounds? Ty hadn't wanted her any longer—Jess had made that abundantly clear. But Eric had. It had been her pride that had turned to Eric, then her sense of duty that had kept her with him. Perhaps if she had been stronger after the accident she would never have made those promises to him....

Asher had floated to consciousness on a wave of pain. What reason was there to wake up and hurt? she thought groggily. Sleep, sleep was so peaceful.

She remembered the shouting, the fall, the swimming darkness. The baby...Ty's baby. Panic—the panic pierced by lethargy. Her eyelids seemed weighted with lead, but she forced them open even as she reached a protective hand to her stomach. Stern and cold, Eric's face floated in front of her eyes.

"The baby," she managed through dry lips.

"Dead."

Tearing, burning grief replaced the pain. "No." Moaning, she closed her eyes again. "Oh, God, no. My baby, not my baby. Ty—"

"Listen to me, Asher." Eric spoke briskly. For three days he had waited while Asher drifted in and out of consciousness. She had lost the baby and a great deal of blood. Once she had nearly slipped away, but he had willed her to live. The love he had once felt had turned to resentment that bordered on hate. She had deceived him, made a fool of him. Now he would have his payment.

"My baby..."

"The baby's dead," he said flatly, then gripped her hand. "Look at me." She obeyed with eyes glazed with sorrow. "You're in a private clinic. The reason for your being here will never be known beyond the front doors. If you do what I say."

"Eric…" A spark of hope flickered. With what strength she had, Asher tightened her fingers on his. "Are they sure? Couldn't there be a mistake? Please—"

"You miscarried. The servants will be discreet. As far as anyone knows, we've slipped away for a few days."

"I don't understand." She pressed her hand against her stomach as if to make the truth a lie. "The fall…I fell down the stairs. But—"

"An accident," he stated, making the loss of the child sound like a broken glass.

Insidiously the pain slipped through. "Ty," Asher moaned, shutting her eyes.

"You're my wife, and will remain so until I say differently." Eric waited until her eyes focused on him again. "Would you have me call your lover and tell him you married me while carrying his child?"

"No." She could only whisper the word. *Ty.* She ached for him. He was lost to her—as lost as the child they'd made together.

"Then you'll do as I say. You'll retire from professional tennis. I won't have the press speculating about the two of you and dragging my name through the mud. You'll behave as I expect Lady Wickerton to behave. I will not touch you," he continued with a trace of disgust. "Any physical desire I felt for you is gone. We will live in the manner I designate or your lover will hear from me about this game you played. Is this understood?"

What did it matter how she lived? Asher asked herself. She was already dead. "Yes. I'll do whatever you want. Please, leave me alone now."

"As you wish." He rose. "When you're stronger, you'll give an official press release on your retirement. Your reason will be that you have no more time for tennis or any desire for a career that would take you away from your husband and your adopted country."

"Do you think it matters to me?" she whispered. "Just let me alone, let me sleep."

"Your word, Asher."

She gave him a long last look before she wearily closed her eyes. "My word, Eric."

And she had kept it. She had tolerated Eric's pleasure when her father had turned away from her. She had ignored his discreet but frequent affairs. For months she had lived like a zombie, doing as she was bid. When the layers of grief began to peel away, his hold remained through guilt and threats. When she had begun to come to life again, Asher had bargained for her freedom. Nothing was more important to Eric than his reputation. She held his many women in one hand, he held the knowledge of Ty's child in the other. They'd made an uneasy agreement.

Now he was back, Asher mused. Perhaps because she was making a success of her life again. Still, she felt he would keep his silence, if only to ensure a hold over her. Once he spoke, all ties were severed. Or if she spoke…

She remembered the look on Ty's face when he had seen her with Eric. Explanations would never be accepted now. Perhaps the day would come when they fully trusted each other, when the memory of betrayal would be dimmed.

She'd been silent for some time. By the steadiness of her breathing she might have been sleeping. Ty knew she was awake and thinking. What secrets was she holding from him? he wondered. And how long would it be before the air between them was finally cleared? He wanted to demand, but her vulnerability prevented him. More than anything else, he didn't want to risk her slipping behind the wall she could so easily erect.

"Better?" he murmured.

She sighed before he felt the faint movement of her head as she nodded. There was one thing she could settle between them, one thing she could make him understand. "Ty, he means nothing to me. Do you believe that?"

"I want to."

"Believe it." Suddenly intense, she sat up and leaned against his chest. If she could give him nothing else, she could give him this.

"I feel nothing for Eric, not even hate. The marriage was a mistake. From the start it was nothing more than a façade."

"Then why—"

"It's always been you," she said before she crushed her mouth to his. "Always you." She pressed her lips to his throat, passion erupting in her as swiftly as the tears. "I stopped living for so long and now..." Her mouth ran wildly over his face. "I need you now, only you."

Her mouth met his fervently, saying more than words. Her ardor touched off his own. There was no need for questions now, or for answers. She pulled the shirt from him, eager to touch. Pressing her lips to heated flesh, she heard him groan. Though her hands moved swiftly to undress him, her lips loitered, lingering to arouse. With her tongue she left a moist trail of fire.

His body was a pleasure to her—hard muscle, long bones, taut flesh. Delighting in him, she sought new secrets. If she nibbled at his waist, his breathing grew shallow, his fingers gripped her hair. If she moved her palm along his thigh, his moan vibrated with need. Giddy with power, she ran a crazed trail from stomach to chest, her lips hungry and seeking.

He struggled to pull the robe from her as she caught his earlobe between her teeth. Low, sultry laughter drove him wild. Neither heard the seam rip as he tugged the terry cloth from her. Limber and quick, she made it impossible for him to grant them both the final relief. Her lovemaking tormented and thrilled him while her agility held him off.

"Now," he demanded, grasping her hips. "Asher, for God's sake."

"No, no, no," she murmured, then cut off his oath with a searing kiss. She found the torture exquisite. Though her own body begged for fulfillment, she wanted to prolong it. As his hands slid over her damp skin, she arched back, reveling in his touch. She belonged, and always would, to the man who could release her fires.

Neither was in control, each a slave to the other. She wanted nothing more than to be bound to him—here, in a dark room with the sound of her own breathing raging in her ears, in the sunlight with the secrets of the night still humming between them. For always.

Beneath her, his body was hot and moist and moving. The rhythm seduced her. Everything warm, everything giving, flowed through her. Thoughts vanished, memories dimmed. Now—there was only now—the all-powerful, greedy present.

This time when he gripped her hips she made no attempt to stop him. Her head fell back in complete abandonment as they joined. The moan was rich and deep, and from both of them. As one, they were catapulted up, beyond pleasure, into ecstasy.

Chapter 8

Asher had driven in limousines all her life. As a child she'd ridden behind a chauffeur named George in a shiny maroon car with smoked glass and a built-in bar. George had remained the family driver though the cars had changed—an elegant white Rolls, a sturdy blue Mercedes.

Lady Wickerton's driver had been Peter and the car had been an old discreet gray Daimler. Peter had been as silent and as efficient as the car. Asher felt no thrill at being driven in the long black limo toward Wimbledon.

As they passed through Roehampton, she watched the scenery. Tidy, healthy trees, trimmed shrubs, orderly flowers. In a few hours, she would be in Centre Court. Aching, sweating...and winning. This was the big prize. Credibility, prestige, press. They were all at Wimbledon.

Once before she and Ty had taken the championships and led the dancing at the Wimbledon Ball—in that year of her life that had brought complete joy and complete misery. Now she would play her old foe Maria Rayski with all the verve and all the cunning she had at her disposal.

Though she'd thought her life had begun to come to order with her first win, Asher now realized she'd been wrong. The turning point was today, here in the arena that was synonymous with her profession. She would play her best here, on the surface she knew best, in the country in which she had lived like a prisoner. Perhaps true confidence would begin after this match was over.

She thought of Ty, the young boy who had once vowed to play and win. Now, in the lush interior of the limo, Asher made a similar vow. She would have a championship season. Reestablish Asher Wolfe *for* Asher Wolfe. Then she would be ready to face the woman. The woman would face the only man who mattered.

The crowds waited for her and other arriving players. The greetings were enthusiastic. Roaming spectators sipped champagne and nibbled on strawberries and cream. Signing autographs, Asher felt light, confident, ready. Nothing, she thought, could mar such a day. The Fourth of July, the brilliant sunshine, the scent of garden flowers.

She remembered other Wimbledons. So little had changed. Fans mingled with players, chatting, laughing. The atmosphere was one of an informal tea party with the promise of a spectacle. But she could feel the nerves. They were there, just under the bonhomie, in the young players, the veterans, doubles and singles finalists. Mixing among them were rock stars and celebrities, millionaires and landed gentry.

Asher saw faces from the past, players from her father's generation. For them it was a reunion, nostalgia, tradition. There were people she had entertained in Grosvenor Square. For them it was a social event. The dress was summer-garden-party chic—picture hats and pastels. Because yesterdays had to be faced, Asher greeted former acquaintances.

"Asher, how lovely to see you again…." "What a sweet little outfit…." "How strange it is not to see you at the club anymore…."

There was speculation, thinly veiled by stretched manners. She dealt with it calmly, as she had during her three years of marriage.

"Where's that old man of yours?"

Turning, Asher clasped two large hands warmly. "Stretch McBride, you haven't changed a bit."

Of course he had. When he'd first tickled Asher's chin, he'd been thirty. His face had been unlined, his hair untouched with gray. He'd won nearly every major championship there was to win twice around. Though he was still tall, and nearly as lean as he had been in his prime, the twenty years showed on his face.

"You always told a lie beautifully." Grinning, he kissed her cheek. "Where's Jim?"

"In the States," she answered, keeping her smile bright. "How have you been, Stretch?"

"Just fine. Got five grandchildren and a nice string of sporting goods stores on the East Coast." He patted her hand. "Don't tell me Jim isn't going to be here? He hasn't missed it in forty years."

It was a struggle not to show the pain, much less not to feel it. "As far as I know, he won't be. I'm awfully glad to see you again. I haven't forgotten that you taught me the dump shot."

Pleased, he laughed. "Use it on Maria today," he advised. "I love to see Americans win at Wimbledon. Tell your old man hello for me."

"Take care, Stretch." Her smile evaded the promise she couldn't give. With a parting kiss, he moved away.

Turning, Asher found herself face-to-face with Lady Daphne Evans. The striking brunette had been one of Eric's more discreet dalliances, and one of Asher's more difficult trials. Her eyes automatically cooled, though her voice was scrupulously polite.

"Daphne, you look exquisite."

"Asher." Daphne skimmed cool eyes over Asher's brief tennis dress, down long bare legs to her court shoes. "You look different. How odd to find you an athlete."

"Odd?" Asher countered. "I've always been an athlete. Tell me, how is your husband?"

The thrust was parried with a quick laugh. "Miles is in Spain on business. As it happens, Eric escorted me today."

Though her stomach churned, her face remained composed. "Eric's here?"

"Yes, of course." Meticulously Daphne adjusted the brim of her rose-pink hat. "You don't think he'd miss this Wimbledon, do you?" Long mink lashes swept down, then up again. "We're all very interested in the results. Will we see you at the ball, darling?"

"Naturally."

"Well, I must let you mingle, mustn't I? That's traditional. Best of luck." With a flash of a smile Daphne swirled her skirts and was gone.

Asher fought the nausea, but began to nudge her way through the crowd. All she wanted was the comparative peace of the A locker rooms. The day ahead promised to be enough of a fight without contending with ghosts. With a few smiles and mechanically gracious greetings, she made her way out of the main throng. A few moments to herself—that was what she needed before the stands began to fill, before her strength and abilities were put to the test.

She knew Eric well enough to be certain he had asked Daphne to seek her out. Yes, he would want to be sure she knew he was there—before the match. As she slipped into the locker room, Asher noticed her hands were shaking. She couldn't allow it. In thirty minutes she would have to be in complete control.

When she walked onto the court Asher was careful not to look into the crowd. It would be easier on her nerves if the people who watched and cheered remained anonymous. As she attempted to empty her mind of all but the first game, Asher watched Maria Rayski.

On her own side of the court, Rayski paced, gesturing occasionally to the crowd, tossing comments. Her nerves were undisguised. It was always so, Asher mused. Rayski chewed her nails, cracked her knuckles and said the first thing that came into her mind. In a wary sort of fashion Asher had always liked her. At five foot ten, she was tall for a woman and rangy, with a deadly stretch. Fatalistically Asher recalled she had a habit of badgering her opponent.

Well, she decided as she chose her game racket, Rayski's histrionics might just keep her mind off who was, and who was not, in the stands. She eyed the television camera dispassionately. With the wonder of technology, the match would be relayed to the States with only a brief delay. Would her father even bother to watch? she wondered. Silently she walked to the baseline for the first serve.

There was no cautious testing in the first games. Rayski went straight for the jugular. Both were fast players, and while Rayski was more aggressive, Asher was a better strategist. A ball could take ungodly bounces on grass, particularly the lush grass of Wimbledon's Centre Court. To defend, to attack, required instinct and timing. It also required complete concentration.

The lead jockeyed back and forth during the first set as the players gave the fourteen thousand spectators the show they'd come to see. Over the elegant, century-old court, they sweated, gritted their teeth and scrambled, not for the enjoyment of those who paid to see, but for the game. Rayski tossed an occasional taunt over the net between rallies. Asher might have been deaf for all the response she gave. She had her rhythm—nothing was going to interfere with it. She placed her ground strokes with deadly precision, charged the net for short angling volleys. Both her form and her energy seemed at perfect peak.

Everything changed when the women took their seats for the towel-off before the third set.

Because she had forgotten about everything but the game, Asher's defenses were lowered. An inadvertent glance up in the stands had her eyes locking with Eric's. A slow, icy smile spread over his face as he lifted a hand in salute—or reminder.

What the devil's wrong with her? Ty asked himself. He shifted closer to the edge of his seat and studied Asher with narrowed eyes. She'd just dropped two games straight, the second one on a double fault. True, Rayski was playing superbly, but so had Asher—until the third set. She was playing mechanically now, as if the life had gone out of her. Too often she was missing basic shots or failing to put anything extra on a return. Rayski's serve was not her strongest weapon, yet she was repeatedly breezing service winners past Asher.

If he didn't know her better, he would have sworn Asher was tanking the match. But Asher wasn't capable of deliberately losing.

Carefully Ty watched for signs of an injury. A strained muscle or twisted ankle would explain the change in her. She gave no sign of favoring a leg. The composure on her face was as perfect as a mask. Too perfect, Ty reflected as the third game went to fifteen-love. Something was definitely wrong, but it wasn't physical. Disturbed, he quickly scanned the crowd.

There were dozens of faces he knew, some by name, some by reputation. There was an award-winning actor he'd once played a celebrity tourney with. Ty had found him an earthy man with a credible forehand. He recognized the ballet star because Asher had once dragged him to see *The Firebird.* Beside the ballerina was a country-western singer with a crossover hit. Ty passed over them, looking for an answer. He found it sitting near the Royal Box.

There was a cool, satisfied smile on Eric's face as he watched his ex-wife. Beside him, a thin, flashy woman in a rose-colored hat looked bored. Rage rose in Ty instantly. His first instinct was to yank Eric up by his five-hundred-dollar lapels and rearrange the expression on his face with his fists.

"Son of a bitch," he muttered, already rising. The hand that grasped his wrist was strong.

"Where are you going?" Madge demanded.

"To do something I should've done three years ago."

Still clinging to his arm, Madge twisted her head to follow the direction of his eyes. "Oh, boy," she said under her breath. Through her fingertips she could feel Ty's temper. Only briefly did she consider the personal satisfaction she would gain from letting Ty do what he wanted. "Hold on," she snapped between her teeth. "Listen to me. Punching him out isn't going to do anything for Asher."

"The hell it won't," he retorted. "You know why he's here."

"To upset her," Madge managed calmly enough. "Obviously he's succeeding. Go talk to her." A strong man might have cringed from the blazing look Ty turned on her. Madge merely arched a brow. "You want to start a fight, Starbuck, do it after the match. I'll referee. Right now, use your head."

His control didn't come easily. Madge watched him struggle for it, lose it, then finally win. Though his eyes were still stormy, the hand under hers relaxed. "If talking doesn't work," he said flatly, "I'm going to break him in half."

"I'll hold your coat," she promised before Ty slipped away.

Knowing he'd have only a moment, Ty decided to use words sparingly—and make them count. After losing the game without making a point, Asher slumped into her chair. She didn't see Ty waiting for her.

"What the hell's wrong with you?"

Her head jerked up at the harsh tone. "Nothing." She was tired, already defeated as she mopped at the sweat on her face.

"You're handing the match to Rayski on a platter."

"Leave me alone, Ty."

"Going to give him the satisfaction of watching you fall apart in front of fourteen thousand people, Face?" There was sarcasm without a trace of sympathy in his voice. He noted the quick, almost indiscernible flash in her eyes. He'd wanted to see it. Always, she played better if there was anger beneath the ice.

"I never thought I'd see you tank a match."

"Go to hell." Whirling, she stalked back to the baseline. Nobody, she thought as she waited for Rayski to take position, nobody accused Asher Wolfe of tanking. Rayski crouched in her pendulum receiving stance while Asher gave the ball a few testing bounces. Tossing it, she drew back her racket and lunged. The effort of the serve came out in a force of breath. The finely pulverized chalk at the baseline rose on contact. Without giving the ace a thought, Asher took her stance for the next serve.

Her anger had teeth. She could feel it gnawing at her. A photographer zoomed in on her face and captured the contradictory placid expression and frosted eyes. Temper was energy. Asher flew across the court, striking the ball as if it were the enemy. Yet her battle was sternly controlled. No one watching her would realize that she cursed Ty with each stroke. No one but Ty himself. Satisfied, he watched her turn her fury on her opponent.

Oh, she was fabulous to see, he thought. Those long, slim legs, the strong shoulders. Her form was so smooth, so precise, yet beneath was that excitement, that smoldering passion. She was as she played, he mused, and wanted her. No one but he knew just how reckless she could be, just how abandoned. The thought had desire moving through him. She was the woman all men fantasized about—part lady, part wanton. And his, Ty told himself fiercely. Only his.

After watching Asher fire a backhand volley past Rayski, he glanced up. Eric's smile was gone. As if sensing the scrutiny, the Englishman looked down. The two men studied each other as the crowd applauded Asher's game. Ty laughed, softly, insolently, then walked away.

Though the match held close to the last point, the impetus Ty had instilled in her carried Asher to the win. She was polite, even charming as she accepted the Wimbledon plate. Inside she was raging. The joy of victory couldn't penetrate the fury and resentment she was feeling. Ty had turned the tide of her emotions away from Eric and onto himself.

She wanted to shout. She smiled and raised her trophy for the crowd to see. She wanted to scream. Politely she allowed the army of cameras to snap her. Fatigue didn't touch her. The ache in her arm might not have existed.

At last freeing herself from the press and well-wishers, she simmered under the shower and changed. Determination made her remain at Wimbledon to watch Ty's match. Stubbornness made her refuse to admire his game. Eric was forgotten. Asher's only thought was to vent her fury at the first possible moment. It took five hard sets and two and a half hours before Ty could claim his own trophy.

Asher left the stadium before the cheers had died.

* * *

He knew she'd be waiting for him. Even before Ty slipped the key in the lock, he knew what to expect. He looked forward to it. His adrenaline was still flowing. Neither the shower nor the massage had taken it from him. Wimbledon always affected him this way. As long as he played, winning there would be his first goal.

Now, the demanding games behind him, the win still sweet, he felt like a knight returning home victorious from the wars. His woman waited. But she wouldn't throw herself into his arms. She was going to scratch at him. Oh, yes, he was looking forward to it.

Grinning, Ty turned the knob. He had no more than shut the door behind him than Asher stormed out of the bedroom.

"Congratulations, Face," he said amiably. "Looks like I get first dance at the ball."

"How dare you say those things to me in the middle of the match?" she demanded. Eyes glittering, she advanced on him. "How dare you accuse me of tanking?"

Ty set his bag and rackets on a chair. "What do you call what you were doing?"

"Losing."

"Quitting," he corrected her. "You might as well have put up a sign."

"I've never quit!"

He lifted a brow. "Only for three years."

"Don't you dare throw that in my face." Raising both hands, she shoved him. Instead of being offended, he laughed. It pleased him enormously that he could rattle her control.

"You did good," he reminded her. "I couldn't take a chance on your losing." He gave her cheek an affectionate pinch. "I didn't want to open the ball with Maria."

"You conceited, overconfident louse!" She shoved him again. "Gramaldi almost took you. I wish he had." She shouted the lie at him. "You could use a good kick in the ego." With the intention of storming back into the bedroom, she whirled. Catching her wrist, Ty spun her back around.

"Aren't you going to congratulate me?"

"No."

"Aw, come on, Face." He grinned appealingly. "Give us a kiss."

For an answer Asher balled her hand into a fist. Ducking the blow, Ty gripped her waist and slung her over his shoulder. "I love it when you're violent," he said huskily as she pulled his hair.

To her own surprise—and annoyance—she had to choke back a laugh. "Then you're going to get a real charge out of this," she promised, kicking wildly as he threw her on the bed. Even though her reflexes were quick, Ty had her pinned beneath him in seconds. Breathless, she struggled to bring her knee up to his weakest point.

"Not that violent." Wisely he shifted to safety.

She twisted, squirmed and struggled. "You take your hands off me."

"Soon as I'm finished," he agreed, slipping a hand under the blouse that had come loose from her waistband.

Refusing to acknowledge the sensation of pleasure, Asher glared at him. "Don't you touch me."

"I have to touch you to make love to you." His smile was reasonable and friendly. "It's the only way I know how."

I will not laugh, she ordered herself as the gurgle rose in her throat. She was angry, furious, she reminded herself.

Ty recognized the weakening and capitalized on it. "Your eyes get purple when you're mad. I like it." He kissed her firmly shut mouth. "Why don't you yell at me some more?"

"I have nothing more to say to you," Asher claimed haughtily. "Please go away."

"But we haven't made love yet." Lightly he rubbed his nose against hers.

Refusing to be charmed, she turned her head away. "We aren't going to."

"Wanna bet?" With one swift move he ripped her blouse from neck to waist.

"Ty!" Shocked, Asher gaped at him, her mouth open.

"I nearly did that when you were on Centre Court today. You should be glad I waited." Before she could react he tore her shorts into ragged pieces. Thinking he might have gone mad, Asher stayed perfectly still. "Something wrong?" he asked as his hand moved to cup her breast.

"Ty, you can't tear my clothes."

"I already did." Soft as a feather, his hand roamed down to her stomach. "Want to tear mine?"

"No." Her skin was beginning to quiver. She tried to shift away and found herself held prisoner.

"I made you angry."

Her head cleared long enough for her to glare at him. "Yes, and—"

"Angry enough to win," he murmured, trailing his lips along her throat. "And when I watched you I nearly exploded from wanting you. All that passion simmering just under the surface. And only I know what it's like when it escapes."

She gave a little moan as his fingers stroked the point of her breast but tried to cling to reality. "You had no business saying I was tanking."

"I didn't say that, I only planted the idea." When he lifted his head, the look in his eyes had her drawing in a quick breath. "Did you think I'd stand by and watch him get to you like that? No man gets to you, Asher, no man but me."

With a savage kiss he cut off all words, all thoughts.

It always surprised Asher that Ty could project such raw sexuality in black tie. Conservative, formal dress could do nothing to alter his air of primitive masculinity. The material could cover the muscles, but it couldn't disguise the strength. There had been times Asher had wondered if it was his earthiness that had drawn her to him. Glimpsing him in a room filled with elegantly attired men and women, she knew it was more than that. It was all of him, every aspect, from temper to humor, that had made her his.

The Wimbledon Ball was as traditional as the tournament. The music, the lights, the people. It was always an evening to remember for its beauty and tastefulness. Asher counted the hours until it would be over. Scolding herself, she tuned back into the conversation of her dance partner. She'd always enjoyed a party, always found pleasure in quiet well-run affairs. But now she wished she and Ty could have shared a bottle of wine in their room.

She didn't want the spotlight this evening, but candlelight. Over the heads of the other dancers her eyes met Ty's. It took only one brief glance to know that his thoughts mirrored hers. Love threatened to drown her.

"You're a lovely dancer, Miss Wolfe."

As the music ended, Asher smiled at her partner. "Thank you." Her smile never wavered as it ran through her head that she had completely forgotten the man's name.

"I was a great fan of your father's, you know." The man cupped a hand under her elbow to lead her from the dance floor. "The Golden Boy of Tennis." With a sigh he patted Asher's hand. "Of course, I remember his early days, before you were born."

"Wimbledon has always been his favorite. Dad loved the tradition…and the pomp," Asher added with a smile.

"Seeing the second generation here is good for the soul." In a courtly gesture he lifted her hand to his lips. "My best to you, Miss Wolfe."

"Jerry, how are you?"

A stately woman in silk brocade swept up to them. Lady Mallow, Eric Wickerton's sister, was, as always, elegant. Asher's spine stiffened.

"Lucy, what a pleasure!"

She offered her fingers to be kissed, sending Asher a brief glance as she did so. "Jerry, Brian's been searching for you to say hello. He's just over there."

"Well then, if you ladies will excuse me."

Having dispatched him, Lucy turned to her former sister-in-law. "Asher, you're looking well."

"Thank you, Lucy."

She gave Asher's simple ivory sheath a brief survey, thinking that if she had worn something so basic, she would have blended in with the wallpaper. On Asher, the muted color and simple lines were stunning. Lucy gave her a candid stare. "And are you well?"

A bit surprised, Asher lifted a brow. "Yes, quite well. And you?"

"I meant that as more than small talk." Lucy's hesitation was brief, as was her glance to determine if they could be overheard. "There's something I've wanted to say to you for a long time." Stiffening, Asher waited. "I love my brother," Lucy began. "I know you didn't. I also know that throughout your marriage you did nothing to disgrace him, though he didn't return the favor."

The unexpected words had Asher staring. "Lucy—"

"Loving him doesn't blind me, Asher," she continued briskly. "My loyalty is with Eric, and always will be."

"Yes, I understand that."

Lucy studied Asher's face a moment, then she seemed to sigh. "I gave you no support when you were my brother's wife and I wanted to offer my apologies."

Touched, Asher took her hand. "There's no need. Eric and I were simply wrong for each other."

"I often wondered why you married him," Lucy mused, still searching Asher's face. "At first I thought it was the title, but that had nothing to do with it. Something seemed to change between you so soon after you were married, hardly two months." Asher's eyes clouded for only a moment under Lucy's direct gaze. "I wondered if you'd taken a lover. But it became very obvious in a short time that it was Eric, not you, who was…dallying. Just as it's become obvious that there's been only one man in your life." Her gaze shifted. Asher didn't have to follow it to know it rested on Ty.

"Knowing that hurt Eric."

"Knowing that, Eric should never have married you." Lucy sighed again, a bit indulgently. "But then, he's always wanted what belonged to someone else. I won't speak of that, but I'll tell you now what I should have told you long before—I wish you happiness."

On impulse, Asher kissed her cheek. "Thank you, Lucy."

Smiling, she glanced over at Ty again. "Your taste, Asher, has always been exquisite. I've envied it, though it's never been right for me. It's time I joined Brian."

As she turned away, Asher touched her hand. "If I wrote you, would you be uncomfortable?"

"I'd be very pleased." Lucy moved away, silks rustling.

Smiling, Asher realized she had been right. Wimbledon was her turning point. Another layer of guilt had been lifted. She was coming closer to discovering who she was, and what she needed. Feeling a hand on her arm, she turned to smile at Ty.

"Who was that?"

"An old friend." Asher lifted a hand to his cheek. "Dance with me? There's no other way I can hold you until we can be alone."

Chapter 9

Asher knew she had made great strides when pressure from the press no longer tightened her nerves. Her habitual terror of saying the wrong thing, or saying too much, faded. She still had secrets. Before coming to Australia she'd promised herself a moratorium. Whatever decisions had to be made would wait. For the moment she wanted to concentrate on happiness. Happiness was Ty—and tennis.

There were good memories in Australia—wins, losses. Good tennis. The people were relaxed, casual. The friendliness was exactly what Asher needed after the tension of England. Aussies remembered The Face, and welcomed her. For the first time since her comeback Asher found the winning taking second place to the enjoying.

The change in her was noticeable even during the early rounds. Her smiles came more frequently. Though her play was no less intense and concentrated, the air of being driven was fading.

From the first row of the stands Ty watched her in early morning practice. He'd just completed two hours of his own. Now, his legs stretched out, he studied her from behind the protection of tinted glasses. She'd improved, he mused…not only as an athlete. He remembered how important athletic ability was to her. The fact that she was a strategist and a craftsman had never been enough. Always, she had striven to be recognized as a good athlete. And so she would be, he thought, as she raced to the net to slap a return with her two-fisted backhand. Perhaps in some ways the years of retirement had toughened her.

His face clouded a moment. Consciously he smoothed the frown away. This wasn't the time to think of that or to dwell on the questions that still plagued him. Whys—so many whys hammered at him. Yet he recognized that she was grabbing this time to be carefree. He'd give her that. He would wait. But when the season was over, he'd have his answers.

When her laughter floated to him he forgot the doubts. It was a rich, warm sound, heard all too rarely. Leaning back, Ty chugged down cold fruit juice and looked around him.

If Wimbledon was his favorite stadium, the grass of Kooyong was his favorite surface. It was as hard as a roadbed and fast. A ball bounced true here, unlike other grass courts. Even at the end of the season, when the courts were worn and soiled, the surface remained even. Even after a deluge of rain, the Australian grass was resilient. Kooyong was a treasure for the fast, for the aggressive. Ty was ready for just such a match. Through half-closed eyes he watched Asher. She was ready, too, he decided. And ever more ready to enjoy it. A smile touched his mouth. Whatever questions there were, whatever answers, nothing could harm what was between them now.

Noting the practice session was winding up, Ty jumped lightly down to the court. "How about a quick game?"

Madge shot him a look and continued to pack up her rackets. "Forget it, hotshot."

He grabbed a racket from her, bouncing a ball lightly on the strings. "Spot you two points."

With a snort Madge snatched the ball, dropping it into the can. "Take him on, Asher," she suggested. "He needs a lesson."

Catching her tongue between her teeth, Asher studied him. "Head to head," she decided.

"You serve."

Asher waited until he had taken his receiving position. Cupping two balls in her hand, she sent him a smile. "Been a while, hasn't it, Starbuck?"

"Last time we played you never got to game point." He gave Madge a wink. "Sure you don't want that handicap?"

Her ace answered for her. As pleased as he was surprised, Ty sent her a long look. Removing the tinted glasses, he tossed them to Madge. "Not bad, Face." His eyes followed the trail of the next serve. He sent it to the far corner to brush the service line. Ty liked nothing better than to watch Asher run. The range of her backhand was limited, but perfectly placed. He was on it in a flash. The last time they had played he had beaten her handily even while holding back. Now he scented challenge.

Asher lined the ball straight at him, hard and fast. Pivoting, Ty slammed it back. The ball whistled on her return. With a powerful swing Ty sent her to the baseline, then nipped her return so that the ball brushed the net and died in the forecourt.

"Fifteen-all." Ty feigned a yawn as he went back to position.

Narrowing her eyes, Asher served. The rally was a study in speed and footwork. She knew he was playing with her, moving her all over the court. Aware that she was no match for his power, she chose to catch him off guard. The ball thudded. She raced. It soared. She followed. The sounds of rackets cutting air had a steady, almost musical sound. A rhythm was set. Patiently she adhered to it until she sensed Ty relaxing. Abruptly she altered the pacing and slapped the ball past him.

"Getting crafty," he muttered.

"Getting slow, old timer," she retorted sweetly.

Ty slammed her next serve crosscourt. After the bounce, it landed somewhere in the grandstands. Under her breath Asher swore pungently.

"Did you say something?"

"Not a thing." Disgusted, Asher shook her hair back. As she readied to serve, she caught the look in Ty's eyes. They rested not on her ball or racket, but on her mouth.

All's fair, she mused with a secret smile. Slowly and deliberately she moistened her lips with the tip of her tongue. Taking a long, preliminary stretch, she served. Distracted, Ty was slow to meet the ball. Asher had little trouble blowing the return past him.

"Game point," she said softly, sending him an intimate smile. Keeping her back to him, she bent to pick up a fresh ball, taking her time about it. She could almost feel Ty's eyes run up the long length of her legs. Smoothing a hand down her hip, she walked back to the baseline. "Ready?"

He nodded, dragging his eyes away from the subtle sweep of her breasts. When his eyes met hers, he read an invitation that had his pulse racing. His concentration broken, he barely returned her serve. The rally was very short.

Victorious, Asher let out a hoot of laughter before she walked to the net. "Your game seemed to be a bit off, Starbuck."

The gibe and the laughter in her eyes had him wanting to strangle her…and devour her. "Cheat," he murmured as he walked to meet her at the net.

Asher's look was guileless and she was faintly shocked. "I have no idea what you're talking about." The words were hardly out of her mouth when she was pulled against him, her lips crushed under his. Laughter and desire seemed to bubble in her simultaneously. Without being aware of it, she dropped her racket and clung to him.

"You're lucky I don't toss you on the ground here and now," he mumbled against her mouth.

"What's lucky about that?" Enchanted, Asher strained against him. How was it possible for one kiss to make her head swim?

Ty drew back, inches only. His whole body was throbbing for her. "Don't tempt me."

"Do I?" she asked huskily.

"Damn you, Asher. You know just how much."

His voice shook, delighting her. She found she needed him to be as vulnerable as she. "I'm never sure," she whispered, dropping her head to his chest.

His heart was beating too rapidly. Ty tried to fight down the impossible surge of need. Not the time, not the place, his sanity stated. Control was necessary. "You were sure enough to use a few tricks to distract me."

Lifting her head, Asher smiled at him. "Distract you? How?"

"Took your time picking up that ball, didn't you?"

She seemed to consider a moment. "Why, I've seen Chuck do the same thing playing against you. It never seemed to make any difference." She let out a whoop of surprise as he lifted her up and over the net.

"Next time I'll be ready for you, Face." After giving her a brief, bruising kiss, he dropped her to her feet. "You could play naked and I wouldn't blink an eye."

Catching her lip between her teeth, she sent him a teasing glance. "Wanna bet?" Before he could connect his racket with her bottom, she dashed away.

The locker room wasn't empty as Asher walked in, but the crowd was thinning. With the fifth rounds completed, there were fewer contenders, and therefore fewer bodies. She was looking forward to her match that afternoon with a hot newcomer who had hopped up in the rankings from one hundred and twentieth to forty-third in one year. Asher had no intention of strolling into the finals. Even the pressure of Grand Slam potential couldn't mar her mood. If ever there was a year she could win it, Asher felt it was this one.

She greeted a towel-clad Tia Conway as the Australian emerged from the showers. Both women knew they would face each other before the tournament was over. Asher could hear a laughing argument taking place over the sound of running water. As she started to remove her warm-up jacket, she spotted Madge in a corner.

The brunette sat with her head leaning back against the wall, her eyes shut. She was pale despite her tan, and there were beads of perspiration on her brow. Asher rushed over to kneel at her feet.

"Madge."

Opening her eyes slowly, Madge sighed. "Who won?"

For a moment Asher went blank. "Oh, I did. I cheated."

"Smart girl."

"Madge, what's wrong? God, your hands are like ice."

"No, it's nothing." She let out a breath as she leaned forward.

"You're sick, let me—"

"No, I've finished being sick." After a weak smile Madge swiped the sweat from her brow. "I'll be fine in a minute."

"You look terrible. You need a doctor." Asher sprang to her feet. "I'll call someone." Before she could move, Madge had her hand.

"I've seen a doctor."

Every sort of nightmare went through Asher's head. In stark terror she stared at her friend. "Oh, God, Madge, how bad?"

"I've got seven months." As Asher swayed, Madge caught her arm tightly. "Good grief, Asher, I'm pregnant, not dying."

Stunned, Asher sank to the bench. *"Pregnant!"*

"Shh." Quickly Madge glanced around. "I'd like to keep this quiet for a while. Damn morning sickness catches me off guard at the worst times." Letting out a shaky breath, she relaxed against the wall again. "The good news is it's not supposed to last long."

"I don't—Madge, I don't know what to say."

"How about congratulations?"

Shaking her head, Asher gripped both of Madge's hands in hers. "Is this what you want?"

"Are you kidding?" On a half laugh, Madge leaned against Asher's shoulder. "I might not look too happy at the moment, but inside I'm doing cartwheels. I've never wanted anything so badly in my life." She sat silently for a moment, her hand still in Asher's. "You know, during my twenties all I could think about was being number one. It was great being there. The Wrightman Cup, Wimbledon, Dallas—all of it. I was twenty-eight when I met The Dean, and still ambitious as hell. I didn't want to get married, but I couldn't live without him. As for kids, I thought, hell, there's plenty of time for that. Later, always later. Well, I woke up one morning in the hospital with my leg screaming at me and I realized I was thirty-two years old. I'd won just about everything I thought I had to win, and yet something was missing. For the better part of my life I've floated around this old world from court to court. Team tennis, pro-am tourneys, celebrity exhibitions, you name it. Until The Dean there was nothing but tennis for me. Even after him, it was the biggest slice of the pie."

"You're a champion," Asher said softly.

"Yeah." Madge laughed again. "Yeah, by God, I am, and I like it. But you know what? When I looked at the snapshot of Ty's nephew I realized that I wanted a baby, The Dean's baby, more than I'd ever wanted a Wimbledon plate. Isn't that wild?"

She let the statement hang in silence a moment as both women absorbed it. "This is going to be my last tournament, and even while that's hurting, I keep wishing it was over so I could go home and start knitting booties."

"You don't know how to knit," Asher murmured.

"Well, The Dean can knit them then. I'll just sit around and get fat." Twisting her head to grin at Asher, Madge saw the tears. "Hey, what's this?"

"I'm happy for you," Asher muttered. She could remember her own feelings on learning of her pregnancy—the fear, the joy, the nausea and elation. She'd wanted to learn to sew. Then it had been over so quickly.

"You look overjoyed," Madge commented, brushing a tear away.

"I am really." She caught Madge to her in a viselike hug. "You'll take care of yourself, won't you? Don't overdo or take any chances?"

"Sure." Something in the tone had the seed of a thought germinating. "Asher, did you… Did something happen when you were married to Eric?"

Asher held her tighter for a moment, then released her. "Not now.

Maybe someday we'll talk about it. How does The Dean feel about all this?"

Madge gave her a long, measuring look. The non-answer was answer enough, so she let it lay. "He was all set to take out a full-page ad in *World of Sports,*" she stated. "I've made him wait until I officially retire."

"There's no need to retire, Madge. You can take a year or two off, lots of women do."

"Not this one." Stretching her arms to the ceiling, Madge grinned. "I'm going out a winner, ranked fifth. When I get home, I'm going to learn how to use a vacuum cleaner."

"I'll believe that when I see it."

"You and Ty are invited to my first home-cooked dinner."

"Great." Asher kissed her cheek. "We'll bring the antacid."

"Not nice," Madge mused. "But wise. Hey, Face," she continued before Asher could rise. "I wouldn't want this to get around but—" her eyes were suddenly very young, and she looked very vulnerable "—I'm scared right out of my socks. I'll be almost thirty-four by the time this kid makes an appearance. I've never even changed a diaper."

Firmly Asher took Madge's shoulders and kissed both of her cheeks. "You're a champion, remember?"

"Yeah, but what do I know about chicken pox?" Madge demanded. "Kids get chicken pox, don't they? And braces, and corrective shoes, and—"

"And mothers who worry before there's anything to worry about," Asher finished. "You're already slipping right into the slot."

"Hey, you're right." Rather pleased with herself, Madge rose. "I'm going to be great."

"You're going to be terrific. Let's get a shower. You've got a doubles match this afternoon."

With feelings mixed and uncertain, Asher rode the elevator to her hotel room late that afternoon. She had won her round with the young upstart from Canada in straight sets. Six-two, six-love. There was little doubt that Asher had played some of the finest tennis in her career in court one. But she didn't think of that now. Her mind kept drifting back to her interlude with Madge, and from there back to her thoughts on learning of her own pregnancy.

Would Ty have wanted to take out full-page ads, or would he have cursed her? Like Eric, would he have accused her of deceit, of trickery? Now that they were being given a second chance, would he want marriage and children? What was it Jess had said that day? she wondered. *Ty will always be a gypsy, and no woman should ever expect to hold him.*

Yet Asher had expected to hold him, and, despite all her vows, was beginning to expect it again. Her love was so huge, so consuming, that when she was with him, it was simply impossible to conceive of doing without him. And perhaps because she had once, briefly, carried his child inside her, the need to do so again was overwhelming.

Could a woman tame a comet? she asked herself. Should she? For that's what he was—a star that flew, full of speed and light. He wasn't the prince at the end of the fairy tale who would calmly take up his kingdom and sit on a throne. Ty would always search for the next quest. And the next woman? Asher wondered, recalling Jess's words again.

Shaking her head, she told herself to think of today. Today they were together. Only a woman who had lived through change after change, hurt after hurt, could fully appreciate the perfection of a moment. Others might not recognize it, but Asher did. And the moment was hers.

She unlocked the door to their suite and was immediately disappointed. He wasn't there. Even had he been sleeping in the other room, she would have sensed him. The air was never still when Ty was around. Tossing her bag aside, she wandered to the window. The light was still full as the sun had only just began to set. Perhaps they would go out and explore Melbourne, find one of the tiny little clubs with loud music and laughter. She'd like to dance.

Twirling in a circle, Asher laughed. Yes, she would like to dance, to celebrate for Madge...and for herself. She was with the man she loved. A bath, she decided. A long, luxurious bath before she changed into something cool and sexy. When she opened the door to the bedroom, Asher stopped and stared in astonishment.

Balloons. Red, yellow, blue, pink and white. They floated throughout the room in a jamboree of color. Helium-filled, they rose to the ceiling, trailing long ribbons. There were dozens of them—round, oval, thin and fat. It was as if a circus had passed hurriedly through, leaving a few souvenirs. Grasping a ribbon, Asher drew one down to her while she continued to stare.

They were three layers deep, she saw in astonishment—at least a hundred of them bumping against one another. Her laughter came out in a quick burst that went on and on.

Who else would think of it? Who else would take the time? Not flowers or jewelry for Ty Starbuck. At that moment she could have floated to the ceiling to join the gift he had given her.

"Hi."

She turned to see him lounging in the doorway. In a flash Asher had launched herself into his arms, the single balloon still grasped in her hand. "Oh, you're crazy!" she cried before she found his lips with hers. With her arms wrapped around his neck, her legs around his waist, she kissed him again and again. "Absolutely insane."

"Me?" he countered. "You're the one standing here surrounded by balloons."

"It's the best surprise I've ever had."

"Better than roses in the bathtub?"

Tossing her head back, she laughed. "Even better than that."

"I thought about diamonds, but they didn't seem like as much fun." As he spoke he moved toward the bed.

"And they don't float," Asher put in, looking up at the ceiling of colorful shapes.

"Good point," Ty conceded as they fell together onto the bed. "Got any ideas how we should spend the evening?"

"One or two," Asher murmured. The balloon she held drifted up to join the others.

"Let's do both." He stopped her laugh with a soft kiss that became hungry quickly. "Oh, God, I've waited all day to be alone with you. When the season's over we'll find someplace—an island, another planet—anyplace where there's no one but us."

"Anyplace," she whispered in agreement while her hands tugged at his shirt.

Passion soared swiftly. Ty's needs doubled as he sensed hers. She was always soft, always eager for him. If the pounding of his blood would have allowed, he would have revered her. But the force of their joined desire wouldn't permit reverence. Clothes were hastily peeled away—a blouse flung aside, a shirt cast to the floor. Overhead, the balloons danced while they savored each other. The scent of victory seemed to cling to both of them, mixed with the faint fragrance of soap and shampoo from the post-game showers. Her lips tasted warm and moist, and somehow of himself as much as of her.

When there was nothing to separate them, they tangled together, their bodies hot and throbbing. With questing hands he moved over territory only more exciting in its familiarity. He could feel reason spin away into pure sensation. Soft here, firm there, her body was endless delight. The warmth of her breath along his skin could make him tremble. Her moan, as he slipped his fingers into her, made him ache. With open-mouthed kisses he trailed over her, seeking the hot heady flavor of her flesh. It seemed to melt into him, filling him to bursting.

When she arched, offering everything, Ty felt a surge of power so awesome he almost feared to take her. Too strong, he thought hazily. He was too strong and was bound to hurt her. He felt he could have lifted the world without effort. Yet she was drawing him to her with murmuring pleas.

There was no control in madness. She stole his sanity with her smooth skin and soft lips. There were no more pastel colors from frivolous balloons. Now there was gleaming silver and molten reds and pulsing blacks whirling and churning into a wild kaleidoscope that seemed to pull him into its vortex. Gasping her name, Ty thrust into her. The colors shattered, seeming to pierce his skin with a multitude of shards. And in the pain was indescribable pleasure.

When he was spent, nestled between her breasts, Asher gazed up at the darkening ceiling. How could it be, she wondered, that each time they were together it was different? Sometimes they loved in laughter, sometimes in tenderness. At other times with a smoldering passion. This time there had been a taste of madness in their loving. Did other lovers find this infinite variety, this insatiable delight in each other? Perhaps the two of them were unique. The thought was almost frightening.

"What are you thinking?" Ty asked. He knew he should shift his weight from her, but found no energy to do so.

"I was wondering if it should be so special each time I'm with you."

He laughed, kissing the side of her breast. "Of course it should, I'm a special person. Don't you read the sports section?"

She tugged his hair, but tenderly. "Don't let your press go to your head, Starbuck. You have to win a few more matches before you wrap up the Grand Slam."

He massaged the muscles of her thigh. "So do you, Face."

"I'm only thinking as far ahead as the next game," she said. She didn't want to think of Forest Hills, or the States—or the end of the season. "Madge is pregnant," she said half to herself.

"What!" Like a shot, Ty's head came up.

"Madge is pregnant," Asher repeated. "She wants to keep it quiet until the Australian Open is over."

"I'll be damned," he exclaimed. "Old Madge."

"She's only a year older than you," Asher stated defensively, causing him to laugh again.

"It's an expression, love." Absently he twined one of Asher's curls around a finger. "How does she feel about it?"

"She's thrilled—and scared." Her lashes lowered, shielding her expression a moment. "She's going to retire."

"We're going to have to throw her one hell of a party." Rolling onto his back, he drew Asher close to his side.

After a moment she moistened her lips and spoke casually. "Do you ever think about children? I mean, it would be difficult, wouldn't it, combining a family with a profession like this?"

"It's done all the time, depends on how you go about it."

"Yes, but all the traveling, the pressure."

He started to pass it off, then remembered how she had lived her childhood. Though he had never sensed any resentment in her, he wondered if she felt a family would be a hindrance to her career. Physically a baby would prevent her from playing for some time. And she'd already lost three years, he reflected with an inner sigh. Ty pushed the idea of their children out of his mind. There was time, after all.

"I imagine it's a hassle to worry about kids when you've got a tournament to think of," he said lightly. "A player's got enough trouble keeping track of his rackets."

With a murmured agreement, Asher stared into space.

In the thin light of dawn she shifted, brushing at a tickle on her arm. Something brushed over her cheek. Annoyed, Asher lifted her hand to knock it away. It came back. With a softly uttered complaint she opened her eyes.

In the gray light she could see dozens of shapes. Some hung halfway to the ceiling, others littered the bed and floor. Sleepy, she stared at them without comprehension. Irritated at having been disturbed, she knocked at the shape that rested on her hip. It floated lazily away.

Balloons, she realized. Turning her head, she saw that Ty was all but buried under them. She chuckled, muffling the sound with her hand as she sat up. He lay flat on his stomach, facedown in the pillow. She plucked a red balloon from the back of his head. He didn't budge. Leaning over, she outlined his ear with kisses. He muttered and stirred and shifted away. Asher lifted a brow. A challenge, she decided.

After brushing the hair from the nape of his neck, she began to nibble on the exposed flesh. "Ty," she whispered. "We have company."

Feeling a prickle of drowsy pleasure, Ty rolled to his side, reaching for her. Asher placed a balloon in his hand. Unfocused, his eyes opened.

"What the hell is this?"

"We're surrounded," Asher told him in a whisper. "They're everywhere."

A half dozen balloons tipped to the floor as he shifted to his back. After rubbing his face with his hands, he stared. "Good God." With that he shut his eyes again.

Not to be discouraged, Asher straddled him. "Ty, it's morning."

"Uh-uh."

"I have that talk show to do at nine."

He yawned and patted her bottom. "Good luck."

She planted a soft, nibbling kiss on his lips. "I have two hours before I have to leave."

"'S okay, you won't bother me."

Wanna bet? she asked silently. Reaching out, she trailed her fingers up his thigh. "Maybe I'll sleep a bit longer."

"Mmm-hmm."

Slowly she lay on top of him, nuzzling her lips at his throat. "I'm not bothering you, am I?"

"Hmm?"

She snuggled closer, feeling her breasts rub against his soft mat of hair. "Cold," she mumbled, and moved her thigh against his.

"Turn down the air-conditioning," Ty suggested.

Brows lowered, Asher lifted her head. Ty's eyes met hers, laughing, and not a bit sleepy. With a toss of her head Asher rolled from him and tugged on the blanket. Though her back was to him, she could all but see his grin.

"How's this?" Wrapping an arm around her waist, he fit his body to hers. She gave him a shrug as an answer. "Warmer?" he asked as he slid his hand up to cup her breast. The point was already taut, her pulse already racing. Ty moved sinuously against her.

"The air-conditioning's too high," she said plaintively. "I'm freezing."

Ty dropped a kiss at the base of her neck. "I'll get it." He rose, moving to the unit. It shut off with a dull mechanical thud. With a teasing remark on the tip of his tongue, he turned.

In the fragile morning light she lay naked in the tumbled bed, surrounded by gay balloons. Her hair rioted around a face dominated by dark, sleepy eyes. The faintest of smiles touched her lips, knowing, inviting, challenging. All thoughts of joking left him. Her skin was so smooth and touched with gold. Like a fist in the solar plexus, desire struck him and stole his breath.

As he went to her, Asher lifted her arms to welcome him.

Chapter 10

"Asher, how does it feel being only three matches away from the Grand Slam?"

"I'm trying not to think about it."

"You've drawn Stacie Kingston in the quarter-finals. She's got an oh-for-five record against you. Does that boost your confidence?"

"Stacie's a strong player, and very tough. I'd never go into a match with her overconfident."

Her hands folded loosely, Asher sat behind the table facing the lights and reporters. The microphone in front of her picked up her calm, steady voice and carried it to the rear of the room. She wore her old team tennis jacket with loose warm-up pants and court shoes. Around her face her hair curled damply. They'd barely given her time to shower after her most recent win at Forest Hills before scheduling the impromptu press conference. The cameras were rolling, taping her every movement, recording every expression. One of the print reporters quickly scribbled down that she wore no jewelry or lipstick.

"Did you expect your comeback to be this successful?"

Asher gave a lightning-fast grin—here then gone—something she would never have done for the press even two months before. "I trained hard," she said simply.

"Do you still lift weights?"

"Every day."

"Have you changed your style this time around?"

"I think I've tightened a few things up." She relaxed, considering. Of all the people in the room, only Asher was aware that her outlook toward the press had changed. There was no tightness in her throat as she spoke. No warning signals to take care flashing in her brain. "Improved my serve particularly," she continued. "My percentage of aces and service winners is much higher than it was three or four years ago."

"How often did you play during your retirement?"

"Not often enough."

"Will your father be coaching you again?"

Her hesitation was almost too brief to be measured. "Not officially," she replied evasively.

"Have you decided to accept the offer of a layout in *Elegance* magazine?"

Asher tucked a lock of hair behind her ear. "News travels fast." Laughter scattered around the room. "I haven't really decided," she continued. "At the moment I'm more concerned with the U.S. Open."

"Who do you pick to be your opponent in the finals?"

"I'd like to get through the quarters and semis first."

"Let's say, who do you think will be your strongest competition?"

"Tia Conway," Asher answered immediately. Their duel in Kooyong was still fresh in her mind. Three exhausting sets—three tie breakers—in two grueling hours. "She's the best all-around woman player today."

"What makes you say that?"

"Tia has court sense, speed, strength and a big serve."

"Yet you've beaten her consistently this season."

"But not easily."

"What about the men's competition? Would you predict the U.S. will have two Grand Slam winners this year?"

Asher fielded the question first with a smile. "I think someone mentioned that there were still three matches to go, but I believe it's safe to say that if Starbuck continues to play as he's played all season, no one will beat him, particularly on grass, as it's his best surface."

"Is your opinion influenced by personal feelings?"

"Statistics don't have any feelings," she countered. "Personal or otherwise." Asher rose, effectively curtailing further questioning. A few more were tossed out at random, but she merely leaned toward the mike and apologized for having to end the meeting. As she started to slip through a rear door, she spotted Chuck.

"Nicely done, Face."

"And over," she breathed. "What are you doing here?"

"Keeping an eye on my best friend's lady," he said glibly as he slipped an arm around her shoulders. "Ty thought it would be less confusing if he kept out of the way during your little tête-à-tête with the members of the working press."

"For heaven's sake," Asher mumbled, "I don't need a keeper."

"Don't tell me." Chuck flashed his boy-next-door smile. "Ty had it in his head the press might badger you."

Tilting her head, Asher studied his deceptively sweet face. "And what were you going to do if they had?"

"Strong-arm 'em," he claimed while flexing his muscle. "Though I might have been tempted to let them take a few bites out of you after that comment about nobody beating Ty. Didn't you hear they were naming a racket after me?"

Asher circled his waist with her arm. "Sorry, friend, I call 'em like I see 'em."

Stopping, he put both hands on Asher's shoulders and studied her. His look remained serious even when she gave him a quizzical smile. "You know, Face, you really look good."

She laughed. "Well, thanks…I think. Did I look bad before?"

"I don't mean you look beautiful, that never changes. I mean you look happy."

Lifting a hand to the one on her shoulder, Asher squeezed. "I am happy."

"It shows. In Ty too." Briefly he hesitated, then plunged ahead. "Listen, I don't know what happened between you two before, but—"

"Chuck…" Asher shook her head to ward off questions.

"But," he continued, "I want you to know I hope you make it this time."

"Oh, Chuck." Shutting her eyes, she went into his arms. "So do I," she sighed. "So do I."

"I asked you to keep an eye on her," Ty said from behind them. "I didn't say anything about touching."

"Oh, hell." Chuck tightened his hold. "Don't be so selfish. Second-seeds need love too." Glancing down at Asher, he grinned. "Can I interest you in lobster tails and champagne?"

"Sorry." She kissed his nose. "Somebody already offered me pizza and cheap wine."

"Outclassed again." With a sigh Chuck released her. "I need somebody to hit with tomorrow," he told Ty.

"Okay."

"Six o'clock, court three."

"You buy the coffee."

"We'll flip for it," Chuck countered before he sauntered away.

Alone, Asher and Ty stood for a moment in awkward silence while an airplane droned by overhead. The awkwardness had cropped up occasionally on their return to the States. It was always brief and never commented on. In the few seconds without words, each of them admitted that full truths would soon be necessary. Neither of them knew how to approach it.

"So," Ty began as the moment passed, "how did it go?"

"Easily," Asher returned, smiling as she stood on tiptoe to kiss him. "I didn't need the bodyguard."

"I know how you feel about press conferences."

"How?"

"Oh..." He combed her hair with his fingers. "*Terrified*'s a good word."

With a laugh she held out her hand as they started to walk. "*Was* a good word," Asher corrected him. "I'm amazed I ever let it get to me. There was one problem though."

"What?"

"I was afraid I'd faint from starvation." She sent him a pitiful look from under her lashes. "Someone did mention pizza, didn't they?"

"Yeah." He grinned, catching her close. "And cheap wine."

"You really know how to treat a woman, Starbuck," Asher told him in a breathless whisper.

"We'll go Dutch," he added before he pulled her toward the car.

Twenty minutes later they sat together at a tiny round table. There was the scent of rich sauce, spice and melted candles. From the jukebox in the corner poured an endless succession of popular rock tunes at a volume just below blaring. The waitresses wore bib aprons sporting pictures of grinning pizzas. Leaning her elbows on the scarred wooden table, Asher stared soulfully into Ty's eyes.

"You know how to pick a class joint, don't you?"

"Stick with me, Face," he advised. "I've got a hamburger palace picked out for tomorrow. You get your own individual plastic packs of ketchup." Her lips curved up, making him want to taste them. Leaning forward, he did. The table tilted dangerously.

"You two ready to order?" Snapping her wad of gum, the waitress shifted her weight to one hip.

"Pizza and a bottle of Chianti," Ty told her, kissing Asher again.

"Small, medium or large?"

"Small, medium or large what?"

"Pizza," the waitress said with exaggerated patience.

"Medium ought to do it." Twisting his head, Ty sent the waitress a smile that had her pulling back her shoulders. "Thanks."

"Well, that should improve the service," Asher considered as she watched the woman saunter away.

"What's that?"

Asher studied his laughing eyes. "Never mind," she decided. "Your ego doesn't need any oiling."

Ty bent his head closer to hers as a defense against the jukebox. "So what kind of questions did they toss at you?"

"The usual. They mentioned the business from *Elegance*."

"Are you going to do it?"

She moved her shoulders. "I don't know. It might be fun. And I don't suppose it would hurt the image of women's tennis for one of the players to be in a national fashion magazine."

"It's been done before."

Asher conquered a grin and arched her brows instead. "Do you read fashion magazines, Starbuck?"

"Sure. I like to look at pretty women."

"I always thought jocks tended to favor other sorts of magazines for that."

He gave her an innocent look. "What sorts of magazines?"

Ignoring him, Asher went back to his original question. "They're playing up this Grand Slam business for all it's worth."

"Bother you?" As he laced their fingers together, he studied them. There was an almost stunning difference in size and texture. Often he'd wondered how such an elegant little hand could be so strong... and why it should fit so perfectly with his.

"A bit," Asher admitted, enjoying the rough feel of his skin against hers. "It makes it difficult to go into a match thinking of just that match. What about you? I know you're getting the same kind of pressure."

The waitress brought the wine, giving Ty a slow smile as she set down the glasses. To Asher's amusement, he returned it. He's a devil, she thought. And he knows it.

"I always look at playing a game at a time, one point at a time." He poured a generous amount of wine in both glasses. "Three matches is a hell of a lot of points."

"But you'd like to win the Grand Slam?"

Raising his glass, he grinned. "Damn right." He laughed into her eyes as he drank. "Of course, Martin's already making book on it."

"I'm surprised he's not here," Asher commented, "analyzing every volley."

"He's coming in tomorrow with the rest of the family."

Asher's fingers tightened on the stem of her glass. "The rest of the family?"

"Yeah, Mom and Jess for sure. Mac and Pete if it can be arranged." The Chianti was heavy and mellow. Ty relaxed with it. "You'll like Pete; he's a cute kid."

She mumbled something into her wine before she swallowed. Martin had been there three years ago, along with Ty's mother and sister. Both she and Ty had gone into the U.S. Open as top seeds; both had been hounded by the press. The two of them had shared meals then, too, and a bed. So much was the same—terrifyingly so. But there had been so much in between.

There'd been no small boy with Ty's coloring then. No small boy with that air of perpetual energy to remind her of what was lost. Asher felt the emptiness inside her, then the ache, as she did each time she thought of the child.

Misinterpreting her silence, Ty reached over to take her hand. "Asher, you still haven't spoken to your father?"

"What?" Disoriented, she stared at him a moment. "No, no, not since… Not since I retired."

"Why don't you call him?"

"I can't."

"That's ridiculous. He's your father."

She sighed, wishing it were so simple. "Ty, you know him. He's a very stringent man, very certain of what's right and what's wrong. When I left tennis I did more than disappoint him, I…wasted what he'd given me."

Ty answered with a short, explicit word that made her smile. "From his viewpoint that's the way it was," she went on. "As Jim Wolfe's daughter I had certain responsibilities. In marrying Eric and giving up my career I shirked them. He hasn't forgiven me."

"How do you know that?" he demanded. His voice was low under the insistent music, but rich with annoyance. "If you haven't spoken to him, how can you be sure how he feels now?"

"Ty, if his feelings had changed, wouldn't he be here?" She shrugged, wishing they could have avoided the subject for a while longer. "I thought, at first, that when I started playing again it might make the difference. It hasn't."

"But you miss him."

Even that wasn't so simple. To Ty, family meant something warm and loving and eternal. He'd never understand that Asher looked not so much now for her father's presence or even his love, but simply his forgiveness. "I'd like him to be here," she said finally. "But I understand his reasons for not coming." Her brow clouded for a moment with a realization that had just come to her. "Before, I played for him, to please him, to justify the time and effort he put into my career. Now I play for myself."

"And you play better," Ty put in. "Perhaps that's one of the reasons."

With a smile she lifted his hand to her lips. "Perhaps that's one of them."

"Here's your pizza." The waitress plopped the steaming pan between them.

They ate amid noise and their own casual chatter. Even the pressure of the upcoming matches had no effect on Asher's mood. The cheese was hot and stringy, making Ty laugh as she struggled against it. The contents of the squat bottle of Chianti lowered as they drank leisurely, content to let the meal drag on. Tennis was forgotten while they spoke of everything and nothing at all. A group of teenagers poured in, laughing and rowdy, to feed another succession of quarters into the jukebox.

Why am I so happy to be in this loud, crowded room? she wondered. The cooling pizza and lukewarm wine were as appealing as the champagne and caviar they had shared in Paris. It was Ty. The place never mattered when she was with him. Abruptly it occurred to Asher that it was herself as well. She was being herself. There weren't any guards, or the need for any. Ty was the only man she'd ever been close to who required none from her.

Her father had wanted her to be perfect—his glass princess. All through her youth she had done everything in her power to please him. With Eric, she had been expected to be the cool, well-mannered Lady Wickerton, a woman who could discuss art and politics intelligently. She was to have been like crystal, many-faceted, elegant and cold.

All Ty had ever expected her to be was Asher. He accepted her flaws, even admired them. Because he had wanted her to be herself, she'd been able to be just that. Not once in all the time she had known him had he ever demanded that she fit a pattern or requested that she conform to any standards but her own. Impulsively she reached over to take his hand, then pressed it to her cheek. There was warmth against warmth, flesh against flesh.

"What's this for?" he asked, allowing his fingers to spread.

"For not wanting glass."

His brows drew together in confusion. "Am I supposed to know what that means?"

"No." Laughing, Asher leaned closer. "Have you drunk enough wine that your resistance is down and you'll be easily seduced?"

A slow smile spread. "More than enough."

"Then come with me," Asher ordered.

It was late when Ty lay sleepless beside Asher. Curled close, her hand caught loosely in his, she slept deeply, drugged with loving and fatigue. Her scent hung in the air so that even in the dark Ty could visualize her. A small alarm clock ticked monotonously at his left, its luminous dial glowing. Twelve twenty-seven.

His mind was far too active for sleep. He sensed, as he knew Asher did, that the idyll was nearly over. They were back where they had once ended, and questions would not be put off too much longer. Impatience gnawed at him. Unlike Asher, Ty looked for the end of the season. Only then would the time be right for answers and explanations. He was not used to biding his time, and the strain was beginning to tell. Even tonight under the laughter he had understood her wordless request that he not probe.

The question of her father, Ty mused, shifting the pillow to brace his back. She was more unhappy about the estrangement than she admitted. It showed in her eyes. It was incomprehensible to him that members of a family could turn away from one another. His thoughts drifted to his mother, to Jess. There was nothing either of them could do he wouldn't forgive. He'd never be able to bear the thought of being responsible for their unhappiness. Could a father feel any different about a daughter? An only daughter, a much-loved daughter, Ty reflected.

He could remember Jim Wolfe's pride in Asher. Ty had often sat beside him during one of Asher's matches in her early days as a pro, then consistently during her last year. Even in such a private man the adoration had showed. It wasn't possible to believe it had been only for the athlete and not for the woman.

Surprisingly Jim had accepted Ty's relationship with his daughter. No, Ty corrected, approved. He'd seemed to enjoy seeing them together. Once, Ty recalled, he had gone as far as outlining his expectations to Ty of their future. At the time Ty had been both amused and annoyed at the fatherly interference. What plans he had had for a future with Asher had still been vague. Then, when they had crystalized in his mind, it had been too late. Frowning, Ty glanced down at her.

In the pale shaft of moonlight her face seemed very fragile. Her hair was a silvery, insubstantial cloud around it. A wave of longing swamped him so that he had to fight the need to wake her and satisfy himself that she was there for him. His feelings for her had always been mixed—wild desire, unbearable tenderness, traces of fear. There had been no other woman who had ever brought him such sharp and conflicting emotions. Watching her sleep, he felt the need to protect. There should be no shadow of unhappiness in her eyes when they opened.

How many obstacles would they have to overcome before they were really together? he wondered. There was one he might remove himself. Perhaps the time had come to take the first step. On impulse, Ty slipped from the bed and into the sitting room.

It took only moments by phone to travel from coast to coast. Dropping into a chair, Ty listened to the faint crackling on the wire before it began to ring.

"Wolfe residence."

In the two words, Ty recognized the trained voice of a servant. "Jim Wolfe please. It's Ty Starbuck."

"One moment please."

Ty sat back, keeping one ear trained on the adjoining bedroom. He heard two distinct clicks as one extension was lifted and the other replaced.

"Starbuck."

The quiet, cautious voice was instantly recognizable. "Jim. How are you?"

"Well." A bit surprised by the late night call, Jim Wolfe settled behind his desk. "I've been reading quite a bit about you."

"It's been a good year. You were missed at Wimbledon."

"That makes five for you there."

"And three for Asher," he returned pointedly.

There was a moment of complete silence. "Your slice volley's cleaner than it once was."

"Jim, I called to talk about Asher."

"Then we have nothing to say."

For a moment the cool, calm statement left Ty speechless. In a flood, fury took over. "Just a damn minute. I have plenty to say. Your daughter's battled her way back to the top. She's done it without you."

"I'm aware of that. Do you have a point?"

"Yes, I have a point," Ty retorted. "I've never seen anyone work as hard as she has these past few months. And it hasn't been easy, dealing with the pressure, the press, the constant questions on why her father isn't in the stands while she wins championship after championship."

"Asher knows my feelings," Jim said flatly. "They're no concern of yours."

"Whatever concerns Asher concerns me."

"So..." Jim picked up a slim gold pen from the desk and carefully examined it. "We're back to that."

"Yes, we are."

"If you've decided to resume your relationship with Asher, it's your business, Ty." He flung the pen back onto the desk. "And it's my business if I don't."

"For God's sake, Jim," Ty began heatedly, "she's your daughter. You can't turn your back on your own child."

"Like father, like daughter," Jim murmured.

"What the hell does that mean?" Frustrated, Ty rose to pace, dragging the phone with him.

"Asher wiped her child out of existence. I've done the same."

All movement stopped. Ty felt something freeze in him as his knuckles turned white on the receiver. "What child?"

"She turned her back on everything I taught her," Jim went on, not hearing Ty's harshly whispered question. "The daughter I knew couldn't have done it." The words, and the anger that accompanied them, had been held in for years. Now they came bursting out. "I tried to understand why she married that pale excuse for a man, even tried to resign myself to her throwing away her career. But some things I won't forgive. If the life she chose to live was worth the price of my grandchild, she's welcome to it."

Enraged at letting his feelings pour out so openly, Jim slammed down the receiver.

Three thousand miles away Ty stood, staring at nothing. With infinite care he placed the phone back on the table. Too many thoughts were whirling in his head, too many questions and half-answers. He had to think, to take his time. Silently he walked back into the bedroom and dressed.

He wanted to shake her awake and demand an explanation; he wanted to wait until he had a grip on himself. Torn, Ty sat on a chair and stared at the still form in the bed. Asher slept so peacefully, her quiet breathing hardly stirred the air.

A child? Asher's child? But there was no child, Ty reasoned. If Lord and Lady Wickerton had produced an offspring, there would have been some mention of it in the press. An heir was never kept secret. Dragging a hand through his hair, Ty shifted. Besides, he reasoned, if Asher had had a child, where was it? Struggling to overcome the jealousy at imagining Asher's bearing another man's child, Ty went over his conversation with Jim Wolfe again.

Asher wiped her child out of existence....

His fingers tightened on the arms of the chair as he stared at her sleeping form. Abortion? Without warning, a storm of emotion took over that he had to systematically fight back until his pulse leveled. All attempts to think of the word with an open mind were futile. He couldn't rationalize it, not when it was Asher, not when the child was part of her. Could the woman he thought he knew have made that kind of choice? For what purpose? Was it possible that the social life she had sought had been more important than...

As bitterness filled him, Ty shook his head. He wouldn't believe it of her. Controlled, yes. There were times Asher could be infuriatingly controlled. But never calculating. Jim had been talking in riddles, he decided. There'd never been a child. There couldn't have been.

He watched Asher stir. With a soft murmur she shifted toward the emptiness beside her where Ty should have been. He sensed the moment she woke.

The moonlight gleamed on her arm as she lifted it, brushing her fingers at the hair that curled around her face. She placed her hand on his pillow, as if testing it for warmth.

"Ty?"

Not trusting himself, he said nothing. If only she would go back to sleep until he had resolved his feelings. He could still taste the bitterness at the back of his throat.

But she wouldn't sleep. Although groggy, Asher sensed tension in the air. Ty's emotions were always volatile enough to be felt tangibly. *Something's wrong, something's wrong,* hammered in her brain.

"Ty?" she called again, and a hint of fear touched the word. Asher had struggled to a sitting position before she saw him. The moonlight was enough to allow her to see that his eyes were dark and fixed on her face. It was also enough to let her see that they were cold. Her pulse began to race. "Couldn't you sleep?" she asked, struggling to convince herself it was all her imagination.

"No."

Asher laced her fingers together as she swallowed. "You should have woke me."

"Why?"

"We—we could have talked."

"Could we?" Cold anger filled him. "We can talk as long as I don't ask any questions you don't want to answer."

She'd been expecting the showdown, but not like this. His resentment was already wrapping around her. Still, he had a right, and she'd put him off too long. "Ty, if it's answers you want, I'll give them to you."

"Just like that?" he snapped, rising. "Just ask and you'll answer. Nothing more to hide, Asher?"

Stung by his tone, she stared up at him. "It wasn't a matter of hiding, Ty, not really. I needed time—we needed time."

"Why was that, Asher?" he asked in a tone that was uncharacteristically cool. She felt a shudder zip down her spine. "Why was time so important?"

"There were things I wasn't sure you'd understand."

"Like the baby?"

If he had slapped her, Asher couldn't have been more stunned. Even in the moonlight he could see her face go white. Her eyes grew huge and dark and desperate. "How..." The words wouldn't form.

Though they raced around in her mind, Asher seemed incapable of forcing any through her lips. How had he found out? Who had told him? How long had he known?

"Eric," she managed, though the name threatened to strangle her. "Eric told you."

Sharp disappointment cut through him. Somehow he had hoped it hadn't been true that she had conceived and rejected another man's child. "So it's true," he exclaimed. Turning from her, Ty stared through the window at the darkness. He found he couldn't be logical or objective. It was one thing to understand the concept of freedom of choice, and another to apply it to Asher.

"Ty, I…" She tried to speak. All of her worst fears were hurtling down on her. The gulf between them was already tangible and threatening to widen. If only she had been able to tell him in her own way, in her own time. "Ty, I wanted to tell you myself. There were reasons why I didn't at first, and then…" Asher shut her eyes. "Then I made excuses."

"I suppose you thought it was none of my business."

Her eyes flew open again. "How can you say that?"

"What you do with your life when you're married to one man isn't the concern of another, even when he loves you."

Simultaneous flashes of pain and joy rushed through her. "You didn't," she whispered.

"Didn't what?"

"You didn't love me."

He gave a brief laugh, but didn't turn back to her. "No, of course I didn't. That's why I couldn't stay away from you. That's why I thought of you every moment."

Asher pressed the heel of her hand between her eyes. Why now? she thought wildly. Why is it all happening now? "You never told me."

This time he turned. "Yes, I did."

Furiously she shook her head. "You never said it. Not once. Even once would have been enough."

In concentration, his brows drew together. She was right, he decided. He'd never said the words. He'd shown her in every way he knew how, but he'd never said the words. "Neither did you," he blurted, speaking his thoughts.

She let out a breath that was perilously close to a sob. "I was afraid to."

"Damn it, Asher, so was I."

For a long, tense moment they stared at each other. Had she been that blind? Had she needed words so badly that she hadn't seen what he'd been giving her? The words would never have come easily to him because they meant everything. For Ty, a declaration of love wasn't a casual phrase but a declaration of self.

Asher swallowed a tremor, wanting her voice to be strong. "I love you, Ty. I've always loved you. And I'm still afraid." As she held out a hand he glanced down at it, but made no move to accept it. "Don't turn away from me now." She thought of the child she had lost. "Please, don't hate me for what I did."

He couldn't understand, but he could feel. It seemed love for her justified anything. Crossing to her, Ty took the offered hand and brought it to his lips. "It'll be better when we've talked this out. We need to start clean, Asher."

"Yes." She closed her hand over their joined ones. "I want that too. Oh, Ty, I'm so sorry about the baby." Her free arm wrapped around his waist as she dropped her head on his chest. The relief, she thought. The relief of at last being able to share it with him. "I couldn't tell you before, when it happened. I didn't know what to do. I didn't know how you'd feel."

"I don't know either," he answered.

"I felt so guilty." She shut her eyes tight. "When Jess showed me that picture of your nephew, I could almost see how the baby would have looked. I always knew he would have had your hair, your eyes."

"Mine?" For a moment nothing seemed to function. His mind, his heart, his lungs. Then, in a torrent, everything came together. *"Mine?"* Asher gave an involuntary cry as he crushed her fingers in his. Before she could speak he had her by the shoulders, digging into her flesh. His eyes alone brought her ice-cold terror. "The baby was mine?"

Her mouth moved to form words, but nothing came out. Confusion and fear overtook her. But he'd already known, she thought desperately. No, no, he hadn't. Eric's baby, her mind flashed. He'd thought it was Eric's baby.

"Answer me, damn you!" He was shaking her now, violently. Limp as a rag doll, Asher made no protest and sought no defense. Both would have been futile. "Was it my baby? Was it mine?"

She nodded, too numb to feel the pain.

He wanted to strike her. Looking at her face, Ty could almost feel the sensation of his hand stinging against it. And he'd want to keep striking her until rage and grief could no longer be felt. Reading his thoughts in his eyes, Asher made no move to protect herself. For an instant his fingers tightened on her arms. With a violent oath he hurled her away. Hardly daring to breathe, she lay on the bed and waited.

"You bitch. You had my child in you when you married him." He flung the words at her, struggling not to use his fists. "Did he make you get rid of it when he found out? Or did you take care of it so you could play the lady without encumbrances?"

She wasn't aware that her breathing was ragged, or that she was trembling. Her mind was too numb to take in more than half of his words. All she understood was the fury of his feelings. "I didn't know. I didn't know I was pregnant when I married Eric."

"You had no right to keep this from me." Towering over her, he reached down to yank her to her knees. "You had no right to make a decision like that when the child was mine!"

"Ty—"

"Shut up. Damn you!" He shoved her away, knowing neither of them was safe if they remained together. "There's nothing you can say, nothing that could make me even want to look at you again."

He strode from the room without a second glance. The sound of the slamming door echoed over and over in Asher's mind.

Chapter 11

Ty took the quarter-finals in straight sets. Most said he played the finest tennis in his career on that hazy September afternoon. Ty knew he wasn't playing tennis. He was waging war. He'd gone onto the court full of vengeance and fury, almost pummeling his opponent with the ball. His swing was vicious, his aim deadly.

The violence showed in his face, in the grim set of his mouth, in the eyes that were nearly black with emotion. It wasn't the winning or losing that mattered to him, but the release of the physical aspect of the temper that he'd barely controlled the night before. When he struck, he struck brutally, always moving. The motion itself was a threat. He'd often been called a warrior, but the description had never been more true. As if scenting blood, he hounded his opponent, then ground him mercilessly into the ground.

Ty's only disappointment was that the match didn't last longer. There hadn't been enough time to sweat out all of his fury. He wondered if there would ever be enough time.

In the stands there were differing reactions as he stalked off the courts.

"Name of God, Ada, I've never seen the boy play better." Martin Derick beamed like a new father. His voice was hoarse from cheering and cigarettes. A pile of butts lay crushed at his feet. "Did you see how he massacred that Italian?"

"Yes."

"Oh-ho, two matches more and our boy's going to have a Grand Slam." Martin squeezed Ada's workworn hands between his two smooth ones. "Nothing's going to stop him now!"

In her quiet, steady way, Ada stared down at the court. She'd seen more than Ty's victory. There'd been fury in her son's eyes. Outrage, hurt. She recognized the combination too well. She'd seen it in a little boy who'd been teased because his father had deserted him. Then, he'd used his fists to compensate. Today, Ada mused, he'd used a racket. As Martin recounted every serve and smash, Ada sat silently and wondered what had put that look back in her son's eyes.

"Mom." Jess leaned close so that her voice wouldn't carry. "Something's wrong with Ty, isn't it?"

"I'd say something's very wrong with Ty."

Jess rubbed her cheek against Pete's, wishing his powdery scent would calm her. Giggling, he squirmed out of her arms and dove toward his father. "Asher wasn't in the stands today."

Ada lifted her eyes to her daughter's. Jess had mentioned, perhaps too casually, that Ty was seeing Asher Wolfe again. Ada had hardly needed the information. Once she had heard Asher was competing again, she'd known what the results would be.

The only time she had ever seen Ty truly devastated had been when Asher had married the polished British lord. His rage and threats had been expected. But they turned to a brooding that had concerned her a great deal more.

"Yes, I noticed," Ada replied. "Then, she's got a match of her own."

"On the next court, and not for a half hour." Jess cast another worried glance around at the people who filled the stands. "She should have been here."

"Since she wasn't, there must be a reason."

A fresh tremor of unease ran up Jess's back. "Mom, I've got to talk to you—alone. Can we go get a cup of coffee?"

Without question, Ada rose. "You fellas keep Pete entertained," she ordered, tousling her grandson's hair. "Jess and I'll be back in a few minutes."

"You're going to tell her?" Mac spoke softly as he touched his wife's hand.

"Yes. Yes, I need to."

Bouncing his son on his knee, he watched them melt into the crowd.

After they had settled at a table, Ada waited for her daughter to begin. She knew Jess was marking time, ordering coffee, speculating on the chances of rain. Ada let her ramble. An orderly, even-tempered woman, she had learned the best way to deal with her emotional offspring was to ride out the storm. Eventually Jess stopped stirring her coffee and lifted her eyes to her mother's.

"Mom, do you remember when we were here three years ago?"

How could she forget? Ada thought with a sigh. That was the year Ty had won the U.S. Open, then barely had time to savor it before the world had crumbled around his ears. "Yes, I remember."

"Asher left Ty and married Eric Wickerton." When Ada remained silent, Jess lifted her coffee cup and drank as if to fortify herself. "It was my fault," she blurted out.

Ada took the time to taste her own coffee, deciding it wasn't half bad for restaurant brew. "Your fault, Jess? How?"

"I went to see her." In quick jerks Jess began to shred her napkin. She'd thought it would be easier now that she had told Mac everything, but with her mother's gaze steady and patient on hers, she felt like a child again. "I went to her hotel room when I knew Ty wouldn't be there." After pressing her lips together, she let the confession come out in a burst. "I told her Ty was tired of her. I told her he—he was bored."

"I'm surprised she didn't laugh in your face," Ada commented.

Quickly Jess shook her head. "I was convincing," she went on. "Maybe because I was convinced it was the truth. And I—I was sympathetic." Remembering how well she had played the role of reluctant messenger tore at her. "Oh, God, Mom, when I look back and remember the things I told her, how I said them…" Anguished, her eyes met her mother's. "I told her Ty thought she and Eric were suited to each other. There was enough truth in that, but I turned it around to give her the impression that Ty was hoping Eric would take her off his hands. And I defended Ty, telling Asher he'd never want to hurt her, that he was really very concerned that she'd gotten in over her head. I—I made it seem as though Ty had asked my opinion on the best way to untangle himself from an affair he had no more interest in."

"Jess." Ada stopped the movement of her nervous daughter's hands with her own. "Why did you do such a thing?"

"Ty wasn't happy. I'd talked to him just the night before, and he was so down, so unsure of himself. I'd never seen Ty unsure of himself." Her fingers began to move restlessly under her mother's. "It seemed so clear to me that Asher was wrong for him, hurting him. I was convinced I had to save him from being hurt more."

Leaning back, Ada let her gaze drift. The West Side Tennis Club was respectfully dingy, very American. Perhaps that was why she'd always liked it. It was noisy. The Long Island Railroad ran alongside, competing with helicopters, planes and road traffic. Ada had never completely gotten used to the relative quiet of suburbia after a lifetime in the inner city. Now she sat back, absorbing the noise, trying to think of the right words. It occurred to her that parenting didn't stop when children became adults. Perhaps it never stopped at all.

"Ty loved Asher, Jess."

"I know." Jess stared down at the shredded paper napkin. "I didn't think he did. I thought if he'd loved her, he would have been happy. And if she had loved him, she would have…well, she would have acted like all the other women who hung around him."

"Do you think Ty would have loved her if she had been like all the other women?"

Jess flushed, amazing herself and amusing her mother. It was a bit disconcerting to think of the tiny, white-haired Ada Starbuck, mother, grandmother, knowing about passion. "It wasn't until after I met Mac that I realized love doesn't always make you smile and glow," Jess went on, keeping her eyes lowered. "There are times when I was miserable and confused over my feelings for Mac and I began to remember that last talk I had with Ty before I went to see Asher. I realized how alike Ty and I are, how the stronger our feelings are, the more moody we can become."

On a deep breath she met her mother's gaze levelly. "I tried to rationalize that Asher wouldn't have left Ty, that she wouldn't have married Eric if she had really cared. And that if he had, Ty wouldn't have let her go."

"Pride can be just as strong as love. The things you said to Asher made her feel unwanted, and betrayed, I imagine, that Ty would have spoken to you about it."

"If the situation had been reversed, I would have scratched her eyes out and told her to go to hell."

Ada's laugh was a warm, young sound. "Yes, you would. Then you'd have gone to the man you loved and used your claws on him. Asher's different."

"Yes." Miserable, Jess pushed her untouched coffee aside. "Ty always said so. Mom, when they got back together, I was so guilty and frightened. Then I was relieved. And now, I can tell something's gone wrong again." As she had as a child, Jess gave her mother a long, pleading look. "What should I do?"

Strange, Ada mused, that her children wanted to pamper her on one hand, thrusting dishwashers and fancy jewelry on her, while on the other, they still looked to her for all the answers. "You'll have to talk to both of them," Ada said briskly. "Then you'll have to back off and let the two of them work it out. You might be able to heal what you did three years ago, but you can do nothing about what's between them now."

"If they love each other—"

"You made a decision for them once," Ada pointed out. "Don't make the same mistake again."

She hadn't been able to sleep. She hadn't been able to eat. Only the promise she had made to herself never to quit again forced Asher onto the court. Purposely she remained in the dressing room until the last moment to avoid the fans who wandered the walkways and mingled with players. It would take more effort than she could have summoned to smile and make small talk.

When she came outside the humidity hit her like a fist. Shaking off the weakness, Asher went directly to her chair. She heard the applause, but didn't acknowledge it. She couldn't afford to. Even before she began, Asher knew her biggest problem would be concentration.

Her arms ached, her whole body ached and she felt bone-deep exhausted. Pain was something she could ignore once the match was under way, but she wasn't sure she could ignore the jellied weakness inside her, the feeling that someone had punched a yawning hole in the center of her life. Still wearing her warm-up jacket, she took a few experimental swings.

"Asher." Cursing the interruption, she glanced over at Chuck. Concern touched his eyes as he stepped toward her. "Hey, you don't look good. Are you sick?"

"I'm fine."

He studied the shadowed eyes and pale cheeks. "Like hell."

"If I come out on the court, I'm well enough to play," she returned, exchanging one racket for another. "I've got to warm up."

Baffled, Chuck watched her stalk onto the court. It took only a moment of study to see that she wasn't in top form. Chuck moved away to find Ty.

He was in the showers, his eyes closed under the spray. He'd been curt and brief with the press and even briefer with his colleagues. He wasn't in the mood for congratulations. Anger lay curled inside him, undiminished by the physical demands he had placed on himself. He needed more—a sparring match, a marathon run—anything to pump the poison out of his system. Though he heard Chuck call him, Ty remained silent and kept his eyes shut.

"Ty, will you listen to me? Something's wrong with Asher."

Taking his time, Ty stepped back so that the water beat on his chest. Slowly he opened his eyes. "So?"

"So?" Astonished, Chuck gaped at him. "I said something's wrong with Asher."

"I heard you."

"She looks sick," Chuck continued, certain that Ty didn't comprehend. "I just saw her. She shouldn't be playing today. She looks awful."

Ty fought the instinctive need to go to her. He could remember vividly the scene the night before. With a flick of the wrist he shut off the shower. "Asher knows what she's doing. She makes her own decisions."

Too stunned to be angry, Chuck stared at him. He'd never seen Ty look cold any more than he'd ever seen Asher look furious. Until today. "What the devil's going on here?" he demanded. "I just told you your woman's sick."

Ty felt the tightening in his belly and ignored it. "She's not my woman." Grabbing a towel, he secured it lightly around his waist.

After dragging a hand through his hair, Chuck followed Ty into the locker room. He'd known since that morning when he and Ty had practiced together that something was wrong. Accustomed to his friend's mercurial moods, he had dismissed it, assuming Ty and Asher had had a lover's quarrel. But no lover's quarrel would make Ty indifferent to Asher's health.

"Look, if you two have had a fight, that's no reason—"

"I said she's not my woman." Ty's voice was deadly calm as he pulled on jeans.

"Fine," Chuck snapped. "Then if the field's clear, I might just try my luck." He was slammed back against the lockers, feet dangling as Ty grabbed his shirt in both hands, jerking him up. Coolly, Chuck looked into the stormy eyes. "Not your woman, friend?" he said softly. "Tell that to somebody who doesn't know you."

Breathing hard, Ty struggled against the need to strike back. The hours of violent tennis hadn't drained the anger or the grief. Without a word he dropped Chuck to his feet, then snatched a shirt from his locker.

"Are you going out there?" Chuck demanded. "Somebody should stop her before she makes whatever's wrong with her worse. You know damn well she isn't going to listen to me."

"Don't push me." Ty dragged the shirt over his head before he slammed the locker door. This time Chuck kept his silence. He heard the tremor in Ty's voice and recognized that the emotion wasn't anger. Only once before had he seen his friend this torn apart. It had been Asher then, as it was obviously Asher now. With warring loyalties, he reached out.

"Okay, you want to talk about it?"

"No." Clenching his fists, Ty fought to regain his control. "No, just go on out…keep an eye on her."

She was fighting, and losing. Asher had used almost all her reserve of energy to take the first set to a tie breaker. The ultimate loss had taken its emotional toll. Kingston was a crafty enough player to sense her opponent's flagging stamina and capitalized on it. Precision was nothing without strength. Asher's strength was ebbing quickly.

The noise played havoc with her concentration. Already playing below par, she needed the sound of the ball hitting the racket. Engines drowned it out, denying her the sense of hearing. On the brittle grass the ball jumped, skidded and stopped. Top speed was necessary, and she didn't have it.

Unable to prevent himself, Ty came to the edge of the tunnel to watch. Immediately he could see that Chuck hadn't exaggerated. She was too pale, too slow. Instinctively he took a step forward. Restraining himself was more difficult than going on, but he stopped, cursing her even as he cursed himself. She'd made her own choice. She herself had cut off any right he had to influence her. From where he stood he could hear her labored breathing, see the strain she fought to keep from her face. At the twinge of fresh pain he turned away from the court.

With a blind determination that was more nerves than power, Asher had taken the second set to three-all. Her face shone with sweat. Weakened, Asher knew that she would have to find a hole in Kingston's game soon, and have the wit and stamina to exploit it. Grit was a weapon, but not weapon enough against power, precision and cunning.

At double break point Asher prepared to serve again. If she could pull this one out, she'd have a chance. If Kingston broke her serve, the match was as good as over. *Concentrate, concentrate,* she ordered herself as she gave the ball a few testing bounces. She counted each one, trying to calm herself. Ty's furious, accusing words hammered in her brain. His face, enraged and stricken, floated in front of her eyes. Tossing the ball, Asher drove at it with her racket.

"Fault."

She shut her eyes and cursed. Control, she ordered herself. If she lost control now, she lost everything. As she took an extra moment, the crowd began to hum in speculation.

"Come on, Face, let's see what you're made of!"

Gritting her teeth, Asher put everything she had left into the serve. The ace brought a roar of approval. She wasn't beaten yet.

But her next serve was soft. Slapping it back to her, Kingston incited a hard, punishing rally. Asher battled by instinct, all reserve depleted. Her eyes, her mind, were fixed on the ball and the ball only. Dodging after a slice, she skidded, barely meeting it with her racket as she stumbled. She went down to her knees, crumbling into a ball of exhaustion and pain.

Someone's hands hooked under her armpits, pulling her to her feet. Asher pushed them away blindly to stagger to her chair.

"Come on, Asher." Chuck toweled off her streaming face, talking to her as she drew in ragged, straining breaths. "Come on, babe, you're not in any shape to be out here today. I'll help you inside."

"No." She shook off his hand. "No, I won't forfeit." Rising, she dropped the towel to the ground. "I'm going to finish."

Helpless, Chuck watched her fight a losing battle.

Asher slept for almost twenty-four hours straight. Her body recharged as she lay motionless in the bed she had shared so recently with Ty. The loss of the match—and the Grand Slam—meant little. She'd finished. Her pride was whole because she had refused to give up, because she had managed to face the reporters after the match and give them a calm accounting. When they had speculated on the state of her health, she'd told them she'd been fit to play. She would give no excuses for losing. If there was blame, it lay within herself. That was the primary rule of the game.

On returning to her room, Asher only took time to strip to her underwear before falling exhausted onto the bed. Sleep came immediately. Hours later she didn't hear the door open or Ty's footsteps as he crossed to the bedroom to look at her.

Asher lay flat on her stomach across the spread—something he knew she did only when absolutely depleted. Her breathing was deep, a heavy sound of fatigue. The hands he had thrust in his pockets balled into fists.

His emotions were pulling in too many directions. She shouldn't be allowed to do this to him, he thought furiously. She shouldn't make him want to hurt and protect at the same time. Walking to the window, he remained silent for a quarter of an hour, listening to her breathe. Before he left her, Ty drew the drapes closed so that the sunlight wouldn't disturb her.

When Asher awoke, a full day had passed. The aches made themselves known.

Keeping her mind a blank, she ran a hot bath. As the water lapped over her, she slipped into a half doze. Asher heard the knock on the door, and ignored it. The phone rang, but she didn't open her eyes.

Disturbed, Jess replaced the receiver after ten full rings. Where could Asher be? she wondered. She knew Asher was still registered at the hotel, but she hadn't answered the phone or the door in more than a day. She'd tried to tell Ty, but he simply wouldn't listen. Any more than he'd listened to her attempts at confession.

Her conscience plagued her. She hadn't tried hard enough, Jess berated herself. She'd been so afraid of losing Ty's love, she had allowed him to brush her off when she tried to talk to him. Well, no more, she determined.

Checking her watch, Jess calculated that Ty would be preparing for the day's match. She cursed, then fretted, then made herself a promise. When it was over, win or lose, she was going to corner her brother and make him listen until she'd told him everything.

Now that the vow had been made, Jess discovered that the waiting wasn't easy. In the stands she marked time. Ty played with the same fierce anger she had observed in his quarter-final match. It was just as effective.

Beneath her pride in him was the constant thought that her brother might turn away from her after he'd heard her out. But Jess sat patiently through the match and through the press conference. She'd left it to her mother to persuade Martin to go back to the hotel instead of dragging Ty off for a replay of the match. Like a tennis groupie, Jess waited for Ty to emerge from the locker room, then pounced.

"Ty, I need to talk to you."

"I'm talked out, Jess." He patted her hand, then removed it from his arm. "I want to get out of here before the next sportswriter latches onto me."

"Fine, I'll drive. You'll listen."

"Look, Jess—"

"Now, Ty."

Annoyed, Ty stalked to the car. For the first time in his life he wished his family hadn't come. He'd managed to avoid them for the most part, using fatigue or practice as excuses. His mother knew him too well, and her silence questioned him constantly. Martin was ecstatic, wanting to analyze every volley and shower praise. And the hardest of all was watching Pete, darting here and there, babbling, laughing, reminding Ty of something that might have been.

"Look, Jess, I'm tired—"

"Just get in," she interrupted tersely. "I've already put this off for too long."

They slammed their doors simultaneously. Not a very auspicious start, she mused as she merged with traffic, but she'd never finish if she didn't begin. "Okay, I've got some things to tell you, and I'd like you to hear me out before you say anything."

"Unless I want to hitch a damn ride back, I don't have much choice, do I?"

She sent him a worried look. "Don't hate me, Ty."

"Oh, come on, Jess." Ashamed of wishing her away, he gave her hair a quick tousle. "I might be mad at being shanghaied, but I'm not going to hate you."

"Just listen," she started. Staring straight ahead, she began.

At first, Ty paid little attention. She was hopping back to the summer he had first been with Asher. He started once to interrupt, not wanting to be reminded. Jess shook her head fiercely and silenced him. With strained patience Ty sat back and watched the passing scenery.

When Jess told him that she had gone to see Asher, his brows lowered. His concentration focused. Listening to her pouring out the things she had said—*Ty's tired of you.... He doesn't know exactly how to end things without hurting you*—his rage built swiftly. Jess felt the fury swirling, and barely paused for breath.

"She seemed to have no reaction to anything I said. She was very cool, totally in control of herself. It just seemed to reinforce what I thought of her." Stopping for a light, Jess swallowed quickly. "I didn't understand how anyone could have strong feelings and not express them, not then. After I met Mac I realized..." When the light changed she gunned the motor with a jerk of her foot, then stalled the engine. On a frustrated oath she started the car again as Ty remained silent.

"When I look back on it," Jess continued after a shaky breath, "I remember how pale she got, how quiet. It wasn't indifference, but shock. She listened to everything I said, never raising her voice or shedding a tear. I must have hurt her terribly."

Her voice broke and she waited for him to speak, but there was nothing but thick, vibrant silence. "I had no right, Ty," Jess continued quickly. "I know that. I wanted—I wanted to help, to pay you back somehow for everything you'd done for me. At the time, I thought I was telling her the things you couldn't bring yourself to. I'd convinced myself... Oh, I don't know." Jess made a quick gesture with her hand before she gripped the gear shift. "Maybe I was even jealous, but I didn't think you loved her and I was so sure she didn't love you. Especially when she married so quickly."

Because tears were forming, she pulled over to the side of the road. "Ty, to tell you I'm sorry isn't enough, but I don't have anything else."

The silence in the car vibrated for the space of three heartbeats. "What made you think you could play God with my life?" Ty demanded in a sudden burst that had her jolting. "Who the hell put you in charge?"

Forcing herself to meet his eyes, Jess spoke quietly. "There's nothing you can say to me I haven't said to myself, but you're entitled."

"Do you have any idea what you did to my life?"

She shuddered involuntarily. "Yes."

"I was going to ask Asher to marry me that night, the night I got back and found you in our room. The night you told me she'd gone off with Wickerton."

"Oh, God, Ty." Choking back a sob, Jess laid her head on the steering wheel. "I never thought...I never realized she meant that much to you."

"She was everything I wanted, don't you understand? Everything! I was half crazy because I wasn't sure she'd say yes." He drummed his fist against the dash. "And, God, I'm still not sure. I'll never be sure." The anguish in his voice made Jess straighten.

"Ty, if you'd go see her. If you'd—"

"No." He thought again of the child. His child. "There are other reasons now."

"I'll go," Jess began. "I can—"

"No!" The word whipped out at her, causing Jess to swallow the rest of the sentence. "Stay away from her."

"All right," she agreed unsteadily. "If that's the way you want it."

"That's the way I want it."

"You still love her," Jess asked.

Ty turned his head so that his eyes met his sister's. "Yes, I love her. That isn't always enough, Jess. I don't think I'd ever be able to forget…"

"Forget?" she prompted when he trailed off. "Forget what?"

"Something she took from me…" Angry energy built up again, grinding at his nerves. "I've got to walk."

"Ty." Jess stopped him with a tentative hand on the arm as he jerked open the door of the car. "Do you want me to go away—back to California? I can make up an excuse, even leave Pete and Mac here for the rest of the tournament. I won't stay for the finals if it upsets you."

"Do what you want," he told her shortly. He started to slam the door of the car when he caught the look in her eyes. He'd protected her all of his life, too long to change now. Love was rooted in him. "It's history, Jess," he said in calmer tones. "Past history. Forget it."

Turning, Ty walked away, hoping he'd be able to believe his own words.

Chapter 12

Asher sat on the bed to watch the men's singles championship. The television commentary barely penetrated as she judged and dissected each stroke and volley for herself. She couldn't go to the stadium, but nothing would prevent her from watching Ty compete.

On the close-ups, she studied his face carefully. Yes, some strain showed, she noted, but his concentration was complete. His energy was as volatile as ever, perhaps more so. For that she could be grateful.

Each time they replayed a shot in slow motion, Asher could fully appreciate the beauty of his form. Muscles rippled as he stretched; feet left the turf in a leap for more power. He was a raw athlete with anger simmering just under the discipline. The graphite racket was no more than an extension of the arm that was whipping the ball harder and harder. As always, his hair flew around the sweatband, dramatic and unruly. His eyes were dark with a rage barely contained. Was it the game that drove him? she wondered. The insatiable thirst to win? Or were there other emotions pushing him this time?

If there were, it was easy to see that they added to the impetus. He was an explosion heating up, a storm rumbling just overhead. Asher knew him well enough to recognize that his control balanced on a very thin edge, but it made his game all the more exciting.

His topspin drove to Chuck's backhand and was returned, power for power. A slice, a lob, an overhead. Turned the wrong way, Chuck pivoted, sprinted, but had no chance to return. The call was late, judging Ty's ball long.

His head whipped around to the judge, his eyes deadly. Asher shuddered when the camera zoomed in so that the undisguised fury seemed aimed directly at her. For a moment they seemed to stare into each other's eyes. Disgust warred with temper before he turned to resume his receiving stance. Crouched like a cat, his eyes intense, he waited. Asher let out an unsteady breath.

Ty was judging the bounce with uncanny accuracy. If it threatened to die, he was under it. When it chose to soar, he got behind it. With unrelenting challenge he charged the net. He baited Chuck, dared him, and, time after time, outwitted him. His game was all aggression and power—Starbuck at his best, she thought with undiminished pride. He could demoralize even a seasoned pro like Chuck with a lightning-fast return that lifted chalk from the service line. With each swing she could hear the grunt of exertion and the swish of air. How she wanted to be there.

He wouldn't want her. She wouldn't soon forget that look of rage and disgust he had turned on her—too much like the one his video image had projected. A man like Starbuck had no ambivalent emotions. It was love or hate; she'd felt them both.

She'd been cut out of his life. She had to accept that. She had to… quit? Asher asked herself. Suddenly her chin rose. Was that what she was doing again? She looked back at the screen as the camera zoomed in on Ty's face. His eyes were opaque and dangerous before he went into a full stretch for his serve. The force of her feelings attacked her. She loved and wanted and needed.

No, damn it! Rising, Asher cursed him. No, if she was going to lose, she was going down fighting, just as she had on the courts. He wouldn't brush her out of his life so easily this time. Briefly she'd forgotten that she no longer aimed her actions at pleasing those around her. Perhaps he didn't want to see her, but that was just too bad. He would see her...and he would listen.

Just as she snapped off the set, a knock sounded on her door. Battling impatience, Asher went to answer. Her expression changed from grim determination to wonder.

"Dad!"

"Asher." Jim met her stunned expression with an unsmiling nod. "May I come in?"

He hadn't changed, she thought wildly. He hadn't changed at all. He was still tall and tanned and silvery-blond. He was still her father. Her eyes filled with love and tears. "Oh, Dad, I'm so glad to see you." Grasping his hand, she drew him into the room. Then the awkwardness set in. "Sit down, please." While gesturing to a chair, Asher sought something to fill the gap. "Shall I order up something to drink? Some coffee?"

"No." He sat as she suggested and looked at his daughter. She was thinner, he noted. And nervous, as nervous as he was himself. Since Ty's phone call, he'd done little but think of her. "Asher," he began, then sighed. "Please sit down." He waited until she settled across from him. "I want to tell you I'm proud of the way you've played this season."

His voice was stiff, but she expected little else. "Thank you."

"I'm most proud of the last match you played."

Asher gave him a small smile. How typical that it was tennis he spoke of first. "I lost."

"You played," he countered. "Right down to the last point, you played. I wonder how many people who watched knew that you were ill."

"I wasn't ill," Asher corrected him automatically. "If I came on court—"

"Then you were fit," he finished, before he shook his head. "I drummed that into you well, didn't I?"

"A matter of pride and sportsmanship," she said quietly, giving him back the words he had given her again and again during her training.

Jim lapsed into silence, frowning at the elegant hands that lay folded in her lap. She'd always been his princess, he thought, his beautiful, golden princess. He'd wanted to give her the world, and he'd wanted her to deserve it.

"I didn't intend to come here to see you."

If the statement hurt, she gave no sign. "What changed your mind?"

"A couple of things, most particularly, your last match."

Rising, Asher walked to the window. "So, I had to lose to have you speak to me again." The words came easily, as did the light trace of bitterness. Though love had remained constant, she found no need to give him unvarnished adulation any longer. "All those years I needed you so badly, I waited, hoping you'd forgive me."

"It was a hard thing to forgive, Asher."

He rose, too, realizing his daughter had grown stronger. He wasn't sure how to approach the woman she had become.

"It was a hard thing to accept," she countered in the calm voice he remembered. "That my father looked at me as athlete first and child second."

"That's not true."

"Isn't it?" Turning, she fixed him with a level stare. "You turned your back on me because I gave up my career. Not once when I was suffering did you hold out a hand to me. I had no one to go to but you, and because you said no, I had no one at all."

"I tried to deal with it. I tried to accept your decision to marry that man, though you knew how I felt about him." The unexpected guilt angered him and chilled his voice. "I tried to understand how you could give up what you were to play at being something else."

"I had no choice," she began furiously.

"No choice?" His derision was sharp as a blade. "You made your own decision, Asher—your career for a title—just as you made it about the child. My grandchild."

"Please." She lifted both hands to her temples as she turned away.

"Please don't. Have you any idea how much and how often I've paid for that moment of carelessness?"

"Carelessness?" Stunned into disbelief, Jim stared at the back of her head. "You call the conception of a child carelessness?"

"No, *no!*" Her voice trembled as it rose. "The loss. If I hadn't let myself get upset, if I had looked where I was going, I never would have fallen. I never would have lost Ty's child."

"What!" As the pain slammed into his stomach, Jim sank into the chair. "Fallen? Ty's child? *Ty's?*" He ran a hand over his eyes as he tried to sort it out. Suddenly he felt old and frail and frightened. "Asher, are you telling me you miscarried Ty's child?"

"Yes." Wearily she turned back to face him. "I wrote you, I told you."

"If you wrote, I never received the letter." Shaken, Jim held out a hand, waiting until she grasped it. "Asher, Eric told me you aborted his child." For an instant, the words, their meaning, failed to penetrate. Her look was blank and vulnerable enough to make him feel every year of his age. "A calculated abortion of your husband's child," he said deliberately. When she swayed he gripped her other hand. "He told me you'd done so without his knowledge or permission. He seemed devastated. I believed him, Asher." As she went limp, he drew her down to her knees in front of him. "I believed him."

"Oh, God." Her eyes were huge and dark with shock.

Her father's fingers trembled in hers. "He phoned me from London. He sounded half mad—I thought with grief. He said that you hadn't told him until after it was done. That you had told him you wanted no children to interfere with the life you intended to build as Lady Wickerton."

Too numb for anger, Asher shook her head. "I didn't know even Eric could be so vindictive, so cruel."

It all began to make horrid sense. Her letters to her father hadn't been answered. Eric had seen that they were never mailed. Then, when she had phoned him, Jim had been cold and brief. He'd told her that he could never resolve himself to her choice. Asher had assumed he meant her rejection of her career.

"He wanted me to pay," she explained as she dropped her head on her father's lap. "He never wanted me to stop paying."

Gently Jim cupped her face in his hands. "Tell me everything. I'll listen, as I should have a long time ago."

She started with Jess, leaving nothing out including her final stormy estrangement from Ty. Jim's mouth tightened at her recounting of the accident and the hospital scene with Eric. Listening, he cursed himself for being a fool.

"And now, Ty…" As realization struck her, she paled. "Ty thinks—Eric must have told him I'd had an abortion."

"No, I told him."

"You?" Confused, Asher pressed her fingers to the headache in her temple. "But how—"

"He called me a few nights ago. He wanted to convince me to see you. I told him enough to make him believe the lie just as I'd believed it."

"That night when I woke up," Asher remembered. "Oh, my God, when he realized it had been his baby… The things he was saying! I couldn't think at the time." She shut her eyes. "No wonder he hates me."

Color flooded back into her face. "I have to tell him the truth and make him believe it." Scrambling up, she dashed for the door. "I'll go to the club. I have to make him listen. I have to make him understand."

"The match must be nearly over." Jim rose on unsteady legs. His daughter had been through hell, and he had done nothing but add to it. "You'll never catch him there."

Frustrated, Asher looked at her watch. "I don't know where he's staying." Releasing the doorknob, she went to the phone. "I'll just have to find out."

"Asher…" Awkward, unsure, Jim held out his hand. "Forgive me."

Asher stared into his face as she replaced the receiver. Ignoring the hand, she went into his arms.

* * *

It was nearly midnight when Ty reached the door of his room. For the past two hours he'd been drinking steadily. Celebrating. It wasn't every day you won the Grand Slam, he reminded himself as he searched for his keys. And it wasn't every day a man had a half dozen women offering to share their beds with him. He gave a snort of laughter as he slid the key into the lock. And why the hell hadn't he taken one of them up on it?

None of them was Asher. He shook away the thought as he struggled to make the doorknob function. No, he simply hadn't wanted a woman, Ty told himself. It was because he was tired and had had too much to drink. Asher was yesterday.

The hotel room was dark as he stumbled inside. If he was right about nothing else, he was right about having too much to drink. Through glass after glass Ty had told himself the liquor was for celebrating, not for forgetting. The kid from the Chicago slum had made it to the top, in spades.

The hell with it, he decided, tossing his keys into the room. With a thud they landed on the carpet. Swaying a bit, he stripped off his shirt and threw it in the same direction. Now if he could just find his way to the bed without turning on a light, he'd sleep. Tonight he'd sleep—with enough liquor in his system to anesthetize him. There'd be no dreams of soft skin or dark blue eyes tonight.

As he fumbled toward the bedroom, a light switched on, blinding him. With a pungent curse Ty covered his eyes, balancing himself with one hand on the wall.

"Turn that damn thing off," he muttered.

"Well, the victor returns triumphant."

The quiet voice had him lowering the hand from his eyes. Asher sat primly in a chair, looking unruffled, soft and utterly tempting. Ty felt desire work its way through the alcohol.

"What the hell are you doing here?"

"And very drunk," she said as if he hadn't spoken. Rising, she went to him. "I suppose you deserve it after the way you played today. Should I add my congratulations to the host of others?"

"Get out." He pushed away from the wall. "I don't want you."

"I'll order up some coffee," she said calmly. "We'll talk."

"I said get out!" Catching her wrist, he whirled her around. "Before I lose my temper and hurt you."

Though her pulse jumped under his fingers, she stood firm. "I'll leave after we talk."

"Do you know what I want to do to you?" he demanded, shoving her back against the wall. "Do you know that I want to beat you senseless?"

"Yes." She didn't cringe as his fury raged down on her. "Ty, if you'll listen—"

"I don't want to listen to you." The image of her lying exhausted on the bed raced through his mind. "Get out while I can still stop myself from hurting you."

"I can't." She lifted a hand to his cheek. "Ty—"

Her words were cut off as he pressed her back into the wall. For an instant she thought he would strike her, then his mouth came down on hers, bruising, savage. He forced her lips apart, thrusting his tongue deep as she struggled. His teeth ground against hers as though to punish them both. There was the faint taste of liquor, reminding her he had drink as well as anger in his system. When she tried to turn her head, he caught her face in his hand—not gently, in the touch she remembered, but viselike.

He could smell her—the soft talc, the lightly sexy perfume. And the fear. She made a small, pleading sound before she stopped fighting him. Without being aware of what he did, he lightened the grip to a caress. His lips gentled on hers, tasting, savoring. Mumbling her name, he trailed kisses over her skin until he felt the essence of her flowing back into him. God, how he'd missed her.

"I can't do without you," he whispered. "I can't." He sank to the floor, drawing her down with him.

He was lost in her—the feel, the taste, the fragrance. His mind was too full of Asher to allow him to think. Sensation ruled him, trembling along his skin to follow the path of her fingers. It was as if she sought to soothe and arouse him at once. He was helpless to resist her—or his need for her. As if in a trance, he took his lips over her, missing nothing as his hunger seemed insatiable. Her quickening breaths were like music, setting his rhythm.

The air grew steamier as his hands homed in on secrets that made her moan. Her body shuddered into life. No longer gentle, but demanding, she tangled her fingers in his hair and guided him to sweet spaces he'd neglected. Then ever greedy, ever giving, she drew him back to her mouth. Her tongue toyed with his lips, then slid inside to drink up all the flavors. His head swimming, he answered the kiss.

The need for her was unreasonable, but Ty was beyond reason. Without her there'd been an emptiness that even his fury couldn't fill. Now the void was closing. She was in his blood, in his bone, so essential a part of him he had been able to find no place of separation. Now there was no will to do so.

Under him, she was moving, inviting, entreating. He whispered a denial against her mouth, but his pounding blood took control. He was inside her without being aware of it. Then all sensations spiraled together in an intensity that made him cry out. And it was her name he spoke, in both ecstasy and in despair.

Drained, Ty rolled from her to stare at the ceiling. How could he have let that happen? he demanded. How could he have felt such love, found such pleasure in a woman he had vowed to amputate from his life? He wondered now if he'd ever find the strength to stay away from her. Life with her, and life without her, would be two kinds of hell.

"Ty." Reaching over, Asher touched his shoulder.

"Don't." Without looking at her he rose. "Get dressed, for God's sake," he muttered as he tugged on his own jeans with trembling hands. Who had used whom? he wondered. "Do you have a car?"

Sitting up, Asher pushed her hair out of her face. Hair, she remembered, that only moments before he had been kissing. "No."

"I'll call you a cab."

"That won't be necessary." In silence she began to dress. "I realize you're sorry that this happened."

"I'm damned if I'll apologize," he snapped.

"I wasn't asking you to," she told him quietly. "I was going to say that I'm not sorry. I love you, and making love with you is only one way to show it." She managed, after three attempts, to button her blouse. When she looked up, he was at the window, his back to her. "Ty, I came here to tell you some things you must know. When I'm finished, I'll go and give you time to think about them."

"Can't you understand I don't want to think anymore?"

"It's the last thing I'll ask of you."

"All right." In a gesture of fatigue she rarely saw in him, he rubbed both hands over his face. The liquor had burned out of his system—by the anger or the passion, he wasn't sure. But he was cold sober. "Maybe I should tell you first that what Jess said to you three years ago was her own fabrication. I didn't know anything about it until the other day when she told me what she'd done. In her own way, she was trying to protect me."

"I don't understand what you're talking about."

Turning, he gave her a grim smile. "Did you really think I was tired of you? Looking for a way out? Wondering how I could ditch you without raising too much fuss or interfering with my career?"

Asher opened her mouth to speak, then shut it again. How strange that the words still hurt and made her defensive.

"Obviously you did."

"And if I did?" she countered. "Everything she said fit. You'd never made a commitment to me. There'd never been any talk about the future."

"On either side," he reminded her.

Asher pushed away the logic. "If you'd once told me—"

"Or perhaps you were uncertain enough of your own feelings that when Jess dumped that on you, you ran right to Wickerton. Even though you were carrying my baby."

"I didn't know I was pregnant when I married Eric." She saw him shrug her words away. In fury she grabbed both of his arms. "I tell you I didn't know! Perhaps if I had known before I would have simply gone away. I don't know what I would have done. I was already terrified you were growing tired of me before Jess confirmed it."

"And where the hell did you get a stupid idea like that?"

"You'd been so moody, so withdrawn. Everything she said made sense."

"If I was moody and withdrawn, it was because I was trying to work out the best way to ask Asher Wolfe, Miss Society Tennis, to marry Starbuck, from the wrong side of the tracks."

Asher took an uncertain step toward him. "You would have married me?"

"I still have the ring I bought you," he answered.

"A ring?" she repeated stupidly. "You'd bought me a ring?" For some inexplicable reason the thought of it stunned her more than anything else.

"I'd planned to try a very conventional proposal. And if that didn't work, maybe a kidnapping."

She tried to laugh because tears were entirely too close. "It would have worked."

"If you'd told me you were pregnant—"

"Ty, I didn't know! Damn it!" She pounded once against his chest. "Do you think I would have married Eric if I had known? It was weeks afterward that I found out."

"Why the hell didn't you tell me then?"

"Do you think I wanted to get you back that way?" The old pride lifted her chin. "And I was married to another man. I'd made him a promise."

"A promise that meant more than the life of the child we'd made together," he retorted bitterly. "A promise that let you walk into one of those antiseptic clinics and destroy something innocent and beautiful. And mine."

The image was too ugly, the truth too painful. Flying at him,

Asher struck him again and again until he pinned her hands behind her back. *"And mine!"* she shouted at him. "And mine, or doesn't my part matter?"

"You didn't want it." His fingers closed like steel as she tried to pull away. "But you didn't have the decency to ask me if I did. Couldn't you bear the thought of carrying part of me inside you for nine months?"

"Don't ask me what I could bear." She wasn't pale now, but vivid with fury. "I didn't have an abortion," she spat at him. "I miscarried. I miscarried and nearly died in the process. Would you feel better if I had? God knows I tried to."

"Miscarried?" His grip shifted from her wrists to her shoulders. "What are you talking about?"

"Eric hated me too!" she shouted. "When I learned I was pregnant and told him, all he could say was that I'd deceived him. I'd tried to trick him into claiming the baby after you'd refused me. Nothing I said got through to him. We argued and argued. We were near the steps and he was shouting. All I wanted to do was get away." Her hands flew up to cover her face as she remembered again, all too clearly. "I didn't look, I only ran. Then I was falling. I tried to stop, but my head hit the railing, I think. Then I don't remember anything until I woke up and the baby was gone."

Somehow he could see it as vividly as though it were being played on film in front of his eyes. "Oh, God, Asher." When he tried to take her in his arms, she pulled away.

"I wanted you, but I knew you'd never forgive me. It didn't seem to matter anymore, so I did what Eric wanted." To force back the tears, she pressed her fingers to her eyes. "I didn't want you to know, I couldn't have stood it if you had known when you didn't want me." Lowering her hands, she looked at him, dry-eyed. "I paid for losing your baby, Ty. For three years I did without everything that mattered to me, and I grieved alone. I can't mourn any longer."

"No." Going to the window, he flung it up as if he needed air. There was no breeze, nothing to relieve the burning that he felt.

"You've had years to deal with it. I've had days." And she'd had no one, he thought. Years with no one. Ty took several long breaths. "How badly were you hurt?"

Puzzled by the question, she shook her head. "What?"

"Were you badly hurt?" The question was rough and turbulent. When she remained silent he turned. "When you fell, how bad was it?"

"I—I lost the baby."

"I asked about you."

She stared without comprehension. No one had asked her that, not even her father. Looking into Ty's ravaged face, she could only shake her head again.

"Damn it, Asher, did you have a concussion, did you break any bones? You said you almost died."

"The baby died," she repeated numbly.

Crossing to her, he grabbed her shoulders. *"You!"* he shouted. "Don't you know that you're the most important thing to me? We can have a dozen babies if you want. I need to know what happened to you."

"I don't remember very much. I was sedated. There were transfusions..." The full impact of his words penetrated slowly. The anguish in his eyes was for her. "Ty." Burying her face against his chest, she clung. "All that's over."

"I should have been with you." He drew her closer. "We should have gone through that together."

"Just tell me you love me. Say the words."

"You know that I do." He cupped her chin to force her head back. "I love you." He saw the first tear fall and kissed it away. "Don't," he pleaded. "No more tears, Face. No more grieving."

She held him close again until the fullness left her chest. "No more grieving," she repeated, and lifted her face.

He touched it gently, fingertips only. "I hurt you."

"We let other people hurt us," she contradicted. "Never again."

"How could we be stupid enough to almost lose it all twice?" he wondered aloud. "No more secrets, Asher."

She shook her head. "No more secrets. A third chance, Ty?"

"I work best under pressure." He brushed his lips over her temple. "Double break point, Face, I'm on a winning streak."

"You should be celebrating."

"I did my share."

"Not with me." She gave him a light kiss full of promise. "We could go to my place. Pick up a bottle of champagne on the way."

"We could stay here," he countered. "And worry about the champagne tomorrow."

"It is tomorrow," she reminded him.

"Then we've got all day." He began to pull her toward the bedroom.

"Wait a minute." Snatching her hand away, she stepped back. "I'd like to hear that conventional proposal now."

"Come on, Asher." He made another grab for her hand, but she eluded him.

"I mean it."

Flustered, he stuck his hands into his pockets. "You know I want you to marry me."

"That's not a conventional proposal." She folded her arms and waited. "Well," she began when he remained silent, "should I write you a cheat sheet? You say something like, Asher—"

"I know what I'm supposed to say," he muttered. "I'd rather try the kidnapping."

Laughing, she walked over and twined her arms around his neck. "Ask me," she whispered, letting her lips hover an inch from his.

"Will you marry me, Asher?" The lips held tantalizingly near his curved, but she remained silent. His eyes dropped to them, lingered, then rose to hers. "Well?"

"I'm thinking it over," she told him. "I was hoping for something a bit more flowery, maybe some poetry or—" The wind was knocked out of her as he hefted her over his shoulder. "Yes, that's good too," she decided. "I should be able to let you know in a few days."

From the height he dropped her, she bounced twice before she settled on the bed.

"Or sooner," she decided as he began unbuttoning her blouse.

"Shut up."

She cocked a brow. "Don't you want to hear my answer?"

"We'll get the license tomorrow."

"I haven't said—"

"And the blood tests."

"I haven't agreed—"

His mouth silenced her in a long, lingering kiss as his body fit unerringly to hers.

"Of course," Asher sighed, "I could probably be persuaded."

* * * * *

UNTAMED

Chapter 1

At the crack of the whip, twelve lions stood on their haunches and pawed the air. On command, they began to leap from pedestal to pedestal in a quick, close-formation, figure-eight pattern. This required split-second timing. With voice and hand commands the trainer kept the tawny, springing bodies moving.

"Well done, Pandora."

At her name and the signal, the muscular lioness leaped to the ground and lay down on her side. One by one the others followed suit, until, snarling and baring their teeth, they stretched across the tanbark. A male was positioned beside each female; at a sharp reproof from the trainer, Merlin ceased nibbling on Ophelia's ear.

"Heads up!" They obeyed as the trainer walked briskly in front of them. The whip was tossed aside with a flourish, then, with apparent nonchalance, the trainer reclined lengthwise across the warm bodies. The center cat, a full-maned African, let out a great, echoing bellow. As a reward for his response to the cue, his ear was given a good scratching. The trainer rose from the feline couch, clapped hands and brought the lions to their feet. Then, with a hand signal, each was called by name and sent through the chute and into their cages. One stayed behind, a huge, black-maned cat who, like an ordinary tabby, circled and rubbed up against his trainer's legs.

Deftly, a rope was attached to a chain that was hidden under his mane. Then, with swift agility, the trainer mounted the lion's back. As the door of the big cage opened, lion and rider passed through for a tour of the practice ring. When they reached the back door of the ring barn, Merlin, the obliging lion, was transferred to a wheel cage.

"Well, Duffy." Jo turned after the cage was secured. "Are we ready for the road?"

Duffy was a small, round man with a monk's fringe of chestnut hair and a face that exploded with ginger freckles. His open smile and Irish blue eyes gave him the look of an aging choirboy. His mind was sharp, shrewd and scrappy. He was the best manager Prescott's Circus Colossus could have had.

"Since we open in Ocala tomorrow," he replied in a raspy voice, "you'd better be ready." He shifted his fat cigar stump from the right side of his mouth to the left.

Jo merely smiled, then stretched to loosen muscles grown taut during the thirty minutes in the cage. "My cats are ready, Duffy. It's been a long winter. They need to get back on the road as much as the rest of us."

Duffy frowned. As circumstances had it, he stood only inches higher than his animal trainer. Widely spaced, almond-shaped eyes stared back at him. They were as sharp and green as emeralds, surrounded by thick, inky lashes. At the moment they were fearless and amused, but Duffy had seen them frightened, vulnerable and lost. He shifted his cigar again and took two quick puffs as Jo gave a cage hand instructions.

He remembered Steve Wilder, Jo's father. He had been one of the best cat men in the business. Jo was as good with the cats as Wilder had been. In some ways, Duffy acknowledged, even better. But she had the traits of her mother: delicate build; dark, passionate looks. Jolivette Wilder was as slender as her aerialist mother had been, with bold green eyes and straight, raven black hair that fell to just below her waist. Her brows were delicately arched, her nose small and straight, her cheekbones high and elegant, while her mouth was full and soft. Her skin was tawny from the Florida sun; it added to her gypsy-like appearance. Confidence added spark to the beauty.

Finishing her instructions, Jo tucked her arm through Duffy's. She had seen that frown before. "Somebody quit?" she asked as they began to walk toward Duffy's office.

"Nope."

His monosyllabic reply caused Jo to lift a brow. It was not often Duffy answered any question briefly. Years of experience told her to hold her tongue as they moved across the compound.

Rehearsals were going on everywhere. Vito the wire walker informally sharpened his act on a cable stretched between two trees. The Mendalsons called out to each other as they tossed their juggling pins high in the air, while the equestrian act led their horses into the ring barn. She saw one of the Stevenson girls walking on stilts. She'd be six now, Jo mused, tossing the hair from her eyes as she watched the young girl's wavering progress. Jo remembered the year she had been born. It had been that same year that she had been allowed to work the big cage alone. She had been sixteen, and it had been another full year before she had been permitted to work an audience.

For Jo, there had never been any home but the circus. She had been born during the winter break, had been tucked into her parents' trailer the following spring to spend her first year and each subsequent one of her life thereafter on the road. She had inherited both her fascination and her flair with animals from her father, her style and grace of movement from her mother. Though she had lost both parents fifteen years before, they continued to influence her. Their legacy to her had been a world of restlessness, a world of fantasies. She had grown up playing with lion cubs, riding elephants, wearing spangles and traveling like a gypsy.

Jo glanced down at a cluster of daffodils growing by the side of Prescott's winter office and smiled. She remembered planting them when she had been thirteen and in love with a tumbler. She remembered, too, the man who had stooped beside her, offering advice on bulb planting and broken hearts. As Jo thought of Frank Prescott, her smile grew sad.

"I still can't believe he's gone," she murmured as she and Duffy moved inside.

Duffy's office was sparsely furnished with a wooden desk, metal filing cabinets and two spindly chairs. A collage of posters adorned the walls. They promised the amazing, the astounding, the incredible: elephants that danced, men who flew through the air, beautiful girls who spun by their teeth, raging tigers that rode horseback. Tumblers, clowns, lions, strong men, fat ladies, boys who could balance on their forefingers; they brought the magic of the circus into the drab little room.

As Jo glanced over at a narrow pine door, Duffy followed her gaze. "I keep expecting him to come busting through there with some crazy new idea," he mumbled as he began to fiddle with his prize possession, an automatic coffeemaker.

"Do you?" With a sigh Jo straddled a chair, then rested her chin on its back. "We all miss him. It's not going to seem the same without him this year." She looked up suddenly, and her eyes were angry. "He wasn't an old man, Duffy. Heart attacks should be for old men." She brooded into space, touched again with the injustice of Frank Prescott's death.

He had been barely into his fifties and full of laughter and simple kindness. Jo had loved him and trusted him without reservation. At his death she had grieved for him more acutely than she had for her own parents. In her longest memory he had been the core of her life.

"It's been nearly six months," Duffy said gruffly as he studied her face. When Jo glanced up, he stuck out a mug of coffee.

"I know." She took the mug, letting it warm her hands in the chilly March morning. Resolutely, she shook off the mood. Frank would not have wanted to leave sadness behind. Jo studied the coffee, then sipped. It was predictably dreadful. "Rumor has it we're following last year's route to the letter. Thirteen states." Jo smiled, watching Duffy wince over his coffee before he downed it. "Not superstitious, are you?" She grinned, knowing he kept a four-leaf clover in his billfold.

"Pah!" he said indignantly, coloring under his freckles. He set down his empty cup, then moved around his desk and sat behind it. When he folded his hands on the yellow blotter, Jo knew he was getting down to business. Through the open window she could hear the band rehearsing. "We should be in Ocala by six tomorrow," he began. Dutifully, Jo nodded. "Should have the tents up before nine."

"The parade should be over by ten, and the matinee will start at two," Jo finished with a smile. "Duffy, you're not going to ask me to work the menagerie in the sideshow again, are you?"

"Should be a good crowd," he replied, adroitly skirting her question. "Bonzo predicts clear skies."

"Bonzo should stick with pratfalls and unicycles." She watched as Duffy chewed on the stub of a now dead cigar. "Okay," she said firmly, "let's have it."

"Someone's going to be joining us in Ocala, at least temporarily." He pursed his lips as his eyes met Jo's. His were blue, faded with age. "I don't know if he'll finish out the season with us."

"Oh, Duffy, not some first of mayer we have to break in this late?" Jo demanded, using the circus term for novice. "What is he, some energetic writer who wants an epic on the vanishing tent circus? He'll spend a few weeks as a roustabout and swear he knows all there is to know about it."

"I don't think he'll be working as a roustabout," Duffy muttered. Striking a match, he coaxed the cigar back to life. Jo frowned, watching the smoke struggle toward the ceiling.

"It's a bit late to work in a new act now, isn't it?"

"He's not a performer." Duffy swore lightly under his breath, then met Jo's eyes again. "He owns us."

For a moment Jo said nothing. She sat unmoving, as Duffy had seen her from time to time when she trained a young cat. "No!" She rose suddenly, shaking her head. "Not him. Not now. Why does he have to come? What does he want here?"

"It's his circus," Duffy reminded her. His voice was both rough and sympathetic.

"It'll never be his circus," Jo retorted passionately. Her eyes lit and glowed with a temper she rarely let have sway. "It's Frank's circus."

"Frank's dead," Duffy stated in a quiet, final tone. "Now the circus belongs to his son."

"Son?" Jo countered. She lifted her fingers to press them against her temple. Slowly, she moved to the window. Outside, the sun was pouring over the heads of troupers. She watched the members of the trapeze act, in thick robes worn over their tights, head toward the ring barn. The chatter of mixed languages was so familiar she failed to notice it. She placed her palms on the window sill and with a little sigh, steadied her temper. "What sort of son is it who never bothers to visit his father? In thirty years he never came to see Frank. He never wrote. He didn't even come to the funeral." Jo swallowed the tears of anger that rose to her throat and thickened her voice. "Why should he come now?"

"You've got to learn that life's a two-sided coin, kiddo," Duffy said briskly. "You weren't even alive thirty years ago. You don't know why Frank's wife up and left him or why the boy never visited."

"He's not a boy, Duffy, he's a man." Jo turned back, and he saw that she again had herself under control. "He's thirty-one, thirty-two years old now, a very successful attorney with a fancy Chicago office. He's very wealthy, did you know?" A small smile played on her lips but failed to reach her eyes. "And not just from court cases and legal fees; there's quite a lot of money on his mother's side. Nice, quiet, old money. I can't understand what a rich city lawyer would want with a tent circus."

Duffy shrugged his broad, round shoulders. "Could be he wants a tax shelter. Could be he wants to ride an elephant. Could be anything. He might want to take inventory and sell us off, piece by piece."

"Oh, Duffy, no!" Emotion flew back into Jo's face. "He couldn't do that."

"The heck he couldn't," Duffy muttered as he stubbed out his cigar. "He can do as he pleases. If he wants to liquidate, he liquidates."

"But we have contracts through October...."

"You're too smart for that, Jo." Duffy frowned, scratching his rim of hair. "He can buy them off or let them play through. He's a lawyer. He can figure the way out of a contract if he wants to. He can wait till August when we start to negotiate again and let them all lapse." Seeing Jo's distress, he backpedaled. "Listen, kiddo, I didn't say he was going to sell, I said he *could*."

Jo ran a hand through her hair. "There must be something we can do."

"We can show a profit by the end of the season," Duffy said wryly. "We can show the new owner what we have to offer. I think it's important that he sees we're not just a mud show but a profitable three-ring circus with class acts. He should see what Frank built, how he lived, what he wanted to do. I think," Duffy added, watching Jo's face, "that you should be in charge of his education."

"Me?" Jo was too incredulous to be angry. "Why? You're better qualified in the public relations department than I am. I train lions, not lawyers." She could not keep the hint of scorn from her voice.

"You were closer to Frank than anyone. And there isn't anyone here who knows this circus better than you." Again he frowned. "And you've got brains. Never thought much use would come of all those fancy books you read, but maybe I was wrong."

"Duffy." Her lips curved into a smile. "Just because I like to read Shakespeare doesn't mean I can deal with Keane Prescott. Even thinking about him makes me furious. How will I act when I meet him face to face?"

"Well." Duffy shrugged before he pursed his lips. "If you don't think you can handle it…"

"I didn't say I *couldn't* handle it," Jo muttered.

"Of course, if you're afraid…"

"I'm not afraid of anything, and I'm certainly not afraid of some Chicago lawyer who doesn't know sawdust from tanbark." Sticking her hands in her pockets, she paced the length of the small room. "If Keane Prescott, attorney-at-law, wants to spend his summer with the circus, I'll do my best to make it a memorable one."

"Nicely," Duffy cautioned as Jo moved to the door.

"Duffy," she paused and gave him an innocent smile. "You know what a gentle touch I have." To prove it, Jo slammed the door behind her.

Dawn was hovering over the horizon as the circus caravan drew up in a large, grassy field. Colors were just a promise in a pale gray sky. In the distance was grove upon grove of orange trees. As Jo stepped from the cab of her truck, the fragrance met her. It's a perfect day, she decided, then took a long, greedy breath. To her, there was no more beautiful sight than dawn struggling to life.

The air was vaguely chilly. She zipped up her gray sweat jacket as she watched the rest of the circus troupe pouring out of their trucks and cars and trailers. The morning quiet was soon shattered by voices. Work began immediately. As the Big Top canvas was being unrolled out of the spool truck, Jo went to see how her lions had fared the fifty-mile journey.

Three handlers unloaded the traveling cages. Buck had been with Jo the longest. He had worked for her father, and during the interim between his death and Jo's professional debut, he had worked up a small act with four male lions. His shyness had made his retirement from performing a relief. To Buck, two people were a crowd. He stood six-feet-four, and his build was powerful enough for him to pad the sideshow from time to time as Hercules the Strong Man. He had an impressive head of wild blond hair and a full, curling beard. His hands were wide, with thick, strong fingers, but Jo remembered their gentleness when the two of them had delivered a lioness of a pair of cubs.

Pete's small frame seemed puny beside Buck's. He was of indeterminable age. Jo guessed between forty and fifty, but she was never certain. He was a quiet man with skin like polished mahogany and a rich, low-pitched voice. He had come to Jo five years before, asking for a job. She had never asked where he had come from, and he had never told her. He wore a fielder's cap and was never seen without a wad of gum moving gently in his teeth. He read Jo's books and was the undisputed king of the poker table.

Gerry was nineteen and eager. He was nearly six feet and still carried the lankiness of his youth. His mother sewed, and his father was a souvenir salesman, or a candy butcher, as circus jargon had it. Working the big cage was Gerry's dream, and because it had been hers, Jo had finally agreed to tutor him.

"How are my babies?" she demanded as she approached. At each cage she paused and soothed a nervous cat, calling each by name until they had settled. "They've traveled well. Hamlet's still edgy, but it's his first year on the road."

"He's a mean one," Buck muttered, watching Jo move from cage to cage.

"Yes, I know," she replied absently. "He's smart, too." She had twisted her hair into one thick braid and now tossed it to her back. "Look, here come some towners." A few cars and a smattering of bikes drew into the field.

These were the people from the outlying towns who wanted to see a Big Top raised, who wanted to see the circus, if only for a moment, from the other side. Some would watch while others would lend a hand with tent poles, stretching canvas and rigging. They would earn a show pass and an unforgettable experience.

"Keep them clear of the cages," Jo ordered, nodding to Pete before she moved toward the still flaccid canvas. Buck lumbered beside her.

The field was alive with ropes and wire and people. Six elephants were harnessed but idle, with their handlers standing by the stake line. As workers pulled on guy ropes, the dusky brown canvas billowed up like a giant mushroom.

The poles were positioned—side, quarter, center—while the canvas muffled the sounds of scrambling workers. In the east the sun was rising fast, streaking the sky with pink. There were shouted instructions from the head canvas man, laughter from adventuresome boys and an occasional oath. As the quarter poles were driven into the sag of canvas, Jo signaled Maggie, the large African elephant. Obligingly, Maggie lowered her trunk. Jo stepped nimbly into the *u,* then scrambled onto the wide, gray back.

The sun grew higher by the second, shooting the first streams of light onto the field. The scent of orange blossoms mingled with the odor of leather harnesses. Jo had watched the canvas rise under a lightening sky countless times. Each time it was special, and the first raising each season was the most special of all. Maggie lifted her head and trumpeted as if pleased to be around for another season. With a laugh Jo reached back and swatted her rough, wrinkled rump. She felt free and fresh and incredibly alive. If there were a moment, she thought suddenly, that I could capture and bottle, it would be this one. Then, when I'm very old, I could take it out and feel young again. Smiling, she glanced down at the people swarming below her.

Her attention was caught by a man who stood by a coil of cable. Typically, she noted his build first. A well-proportioned body was essential to a performer. He was lean and stood straight. She noted he had good shoulders but doubted if there was much muscle in his arms. Though he was dressed casually in jeans, *city* stood out all over him. His hair was a dark, rich blond, and the early breeze had disturbed it so that it teased his forehead. He was clean-shaven, with a narrow, firm-jawed face. It was an attractive face. It was not, Jo mused, smoothly handsome like Vito the wire walker's but more aware, more demanding. Jo liked the face, liked the shape of the long, unsmiling mouth, liked the hint of bone beneath his tawny skin. Most of all she liked the directness of the amber eyes that stared back at her. They're like Ari's, she observed, thinking of her favorite lion. She was certain that he had been watching her long before she had looked down. Knowing this, Jo was impressed with his unselfconsciousness. He continued to stare, making no effort to camouflage his interest. She laughed, unperturbed, and tossed her braid from her shoulder.

"Want a ride?" she called out. Too many strangers had walked in and out of her world for her to be aloof. She watched his brow lift in acknowledgment of her offer. She would see if it was only his eyes that were like Ari's. "Maggie won't hurt you. She's gentle as a lamb, just bigger." Instantly, she saw he had understood the challenge. He walked across the grass until he stood beside her. He moved well, she noted. Jo tapped Maggie's side with the bull hook she carried. Wearily, the elephant knelt down on her trunklike front legs. Jo held out her hand. With an agility that surprised her, the man mounted the elephant and slid into place behind her.

For a moment she said nothing, a bit stunned by the trembling that had coursed up her arm as her palm had met his. The contact had been brief. Jo decided she had imagined it. "Up, Maggie," she said, giving her mount another tap. With an elephantine sigh, Maggie obeyed, rocking her passengers gently from side to side.

"Do you always pick up strange men?" the voice behind her inquired. It was a smooth, well-keyed voice, a good pitchman's voice.

Jo grinned over her shoulder. "Maggie's doing the picking up."

"So she is. Are you aware that she's remarkably uncomfortable?"

Jo laughed with genuine enjoyment. "You should try riding her a few miles in a street parade while keeping a smile on your face."

"I'll pass. Are you in charge of her?"

"Maggie? No, but I know how to handle her. You have eyes like one of my cats," she told him. "I like them. And since you seemed to be interested in Maggie and me, I asked you up."

This time it was he who laughed. Jo twisted her head, wanting to see his face. There was humor in his eyes now, and his teeth were white and straight. Liking his smile, she answered with one of her own. "Fascinating. You asked me to take a ride on an elephant because I have eyes like your cat's. And no offense to the lady beneath me, but I was looking at you."

"Oh?" Jo pursed her lips in thought. "Why?"

For several seconds he studied her in silence. "Strange, I believe you really don't know."

"I wouldn't ask if I did," she returned, shifting her weight slightly. "It would be a waste of time to ask a question if I knew the answer." She shifted again and turned away from him. "Hold on now. Maggie's got to earn her bale of hay."

The poles hung between the canvas and the ground at forty-five degree angles. Quickly the elephant's chains were hooked to the metal rings at the base of the quarter poles. Jo urged Maggie forward in unison with her coworkers. Poles skidded along the ground, then up into place, pushing the canvas with it. The Big Top billowed to life under the early morning sky.

Her job done, Maggie moved through the flaps and into the light. "Beautiful, isn't it?" Jo murmured. "It's born fresh every day."

Vito walked by, calling out to Jo in Italian. Sending him a wave, she called back in his own language, then signaled to Maggie to kneel again. Jo waited until her passenger had dismounted before she slid off. It surprised her, when they stood face to face, that he was so tall. Tilting back her head, she judged him to be only two inches shy of Buck.

"You looked shorter when I was up on Maggie," she told him with her usual candor.

"You looked taller."

Jo chuckled, patting Maggie behind the ear. "Will you see the show?" She knew that she wanted him to, knew as well that she wanted to see him again. She found this both strange and intriguing. Men had always taken a second place to her cats, and towners had never interested her.

"Yes, I'm going to see the show." There was a slight smile on his face, but he was studying her thoughtfully. "Do you perform?"

"I have an act with my cats."

"I see. Somehow I pictured you in an aerial act, flying from the trapeze."

She sent him an easy smile. "My mother was an aerialist." Someone called her name, and looking, Jo saw Maggie was needed for raising the sideshow tent. "I have to go. I hope you like the show."

He took her hand before she could lead Maggie away. Jo stood still, again surprised by a trembling up her arm. "I'd like to see you tonight."

Glancing up, she met his eyes. They were direct and unselfconscious. "Why?" The question was sincere. Jo knew she wanted to see him as well but was unsure why.

This time he did not laugh. Gently, he ran a finger down the length of her braid. "Because you're beautiful, and you intrigue me."

"Oh." Jo considered. She had never thought of herself as beautiful. Striking, perhaps, in her costume, surrounded by her cats, but in jeans, without makeup, she doubted it. Still, it was an interesting thought. "All right, if there's no trouble with the cats. Ari hasn't been well."

A smile played at the corners of his mouth. "I'm sorry to hear that."

There was another loud summons for Jo, and both looked toward it. "I see you're needed," he said with a nod. "Perhaps you could point out Bill Duffy for me before you go."

"Duffy?" Jo repeated, surprised. "You can't be looking for a job?" There was incredulity in her voice, and he grinned.

"Why can't I?"

"Because you don't fit any of the types."

"Are there types?" he asked, both interested and amused. Jo shook her head in annoyance.

"Yes, of course, and you don't fit into any of them."

"Actually, I'm not looking for a job, so to speak," he told her, still smiling. "But I am looking for Bill Duffy."

It was against Jo's nature to probe. Privacy was both guarded and respected in the circus. Shielding her eyes with her hand, Jo looked around until she spotted Duffy supervising the raising of the cookhouse tent. "There," she said, pointing. "Duffy's the one with the red checked jacket. He still dresses like an outside talker."

"A what?"

"You'd call it a barker, I imagine." With easy grace she mounted the patient Maggie. "That's a towner's term, not a circus one." She smiled at him, then urged Maggie into a walk. "Tell Duffy Jo said to give you a pass," she called over her shoulder, then waved and turned away.

Dawn was over, and it was morning.

Chapter 2

Jo stood at the back door of the Big Top waiting for her cue. Beside her was Jamie Carter, alias Topo. He was a third generation clown and wore his bright face and orange wig naturally. He was young and limber and used these traits as well as his makeup to bring enthusiasm to his craft. To Jo, Jamie was more brother than friend. He was tall and thin, and under his greasepaint his face was mobile and pleasant. He and Jo had grown up together.

"Did she say anything?" Jamie demanded for the third time. With a sigh, Jo tossed closed the flap of the tent. Inside, clowns were performing around the hippodrome track while hands set up the big cage.

"Carmen said nothing. I don't know why you waste your time." Her voice was sharp, and Jamie bristled.

"I don't expect you to understand," he said with great dignity. His thin shoulders drew straight under his red polka dot shirt. "After all, Ari's the closest you've come to being involved with the opposite sex."

"That's very cute," Jo replied, unoffended by the jibe. Her annoyance stemmed from seeing Jamie make a fool of himself over Carmen Gribalti, the middle sister of the flying Gribaltis. She was darkly beautiful, graceful, talented, selfish and sublimely indifferent to Jamie. Looking into his happy, painted face and moody eyes, Jo's irritation dissipated.

"She probably hasn't had a chance to answer the note you sent her," she soothed. "The first day of a new season's always wild."

"I suppose," Jamie muttered with a grudging shrug. "I don't know what she sees in Vito."

Jo thought of the wire walker's dark, cocky looks and rippling muscles. Wisely, she refrained from mentioning them. "Who can account for taste?" She gave him a smacking kiss on his round, red nose. "Personally, I get all wobbly when I see a man with thick, orange hair."

Jamie grinned. "Proves you know what to look for in a man."

Turning, Jo lifted the flap again, noting Jamie's cue was nearly upon them. "Did you happen to notice a towner hanging around today?"

"Only a couple dozen of them," Jamie answered dryly as he lifted the pail of confetti he used to finish the gag now being performed inside.

Jo shot him a half-hearted glare. "Not the usual type. About thirty, I think," she continued. "Wearing jeans and a T-shirt. He was tall, six-one, six-two," she went on as laughter poured out of the open flap to drown out her words. "He had dark blond straight hair."

"Yeah, I saw him." Jamie nudged her out of his way and prepared to make his entrance. "He was going into the red wagon with Duffy." With a wild, high-pitched scream, Topo the clown bounded into the Big Top in size fifteen tennis shoes, brandishing his bucket of confetti.

Thoughtfully, Jo watched Jamie chase three other clowns around the track. It was odd, she thought, for Duffy to take a towner into the administration trailer. He had said he wasn't looking for a job. He wasn't a drifter; there was an unmistakable air of stability about him. He wasn't a circus hand from another show, either. His palm had been too smooth. And, her mind added as she vaulted onto Babette, a pure white mare, there had been an undeniable aura of urbanity about him. Success, as well, she thought. And authority. No, he had not been looking for a job.

Jo shrugged, annoyed that a stranger was crowding into her thoughts. It irritated her further that she had scanned the crowds for him during the parade and that even now she wondered if he sat somewhere in the circular arena. He hadn't been at the matinee. Jo patted the mare's neck absently, then straightened as she heard the ringmaster's whistle.

"Ladies and gentlemen," he called in deep, musical tones. "Presenting the most spectacular exhibition of animal subjugation under the Big Top. Jovilette, Queen of the Jungle Cats!"

Jo nudged Babette with her heels and raced into the arena. The applause rose to meet her as the audience appreciated the dashing figure she cut. Swathed in a black cape, raven hair flying free under a glittering tiara, she galloped bareback on the snow white mare. In each hand she held a long, thin whip, which she cracked alternately overhead. At the entrance to the big cage she leaped from the still racing horse. While Babette galloped out of the back door and into the care of a handler, Jo shifted both whips into one hand, then removed the cape with a flourish. Her costume was a close-fitting, one-piece jumpsuit, dazzling in white and spangled with gold sequins. In dramatic contrast, her hair hung straight and severe down her back.

Make an entrance, Frank had always said. And Jovilette made an entrance.

The twelve cats were already in the cage, banding its inside edge as they perched on blue and white pedestals. Entering the main cage appeared routine to the audience, but Jo knew it was one of the most dangerous moments of the act. To enter, she had to pass directly between two cats as she moved from the safety cage to the main arena. She always stationed her best behaved cats there, but if one was irritated, or even playful, he could easily strike out with a powerful paw. Even with sharp claws retracted, the damage could be deadly.

She entered swiftly and was surrounded by cats on all sides. Her spangles and tiara caught the lights and played with them as she began to move around the cage, cracking the whip for showmanship while using her voice to command the cats to rise on their haunches. She moved them through their routine, adjusting the timing to compensate for any feline reluctance, letting one trick begin where the last ended.

Jo disliked overdone propping, preferring action and movement. The contrast of the big, tawny cats and the small white and gold woman were the best props available to her. She used them well. Hers was a *picture act,* relying on style and flash, rather than a *fighting act,* which emphasized the ferocity of the big cats by employing blank-bulleted guns and rehearsed charges, or *bounces.* Her confidence transmitted itself to the audience, making her handling of the cats appear effortless. In truth, her body was coiled for any danger, and her mind was focused so intently on her cats, there might have been no audience at all.

She stood between two high pedestals as the cats leaped over her head from both directions. They set up a light breeze, which stirred her hair. They roared when she cued them, setting up an echoing din. Now and then one reached out to paw at the stock of her whip, and she stopped him with a quick command. She sent her best leaper through a hoop of flame and coaxed her best balancer to walk on a glistening silver ball. She ended to waves of applause by trotting Merlin around the hippodrome track.

At the back door Merlin jumped into a wheel cage and was turned over to Pete. "Nice show," he said as he handed her a long chenille robe. "Smooth as silk."

"Thanks." Cold, she bundled into the robe. The spring night was frigid in contrast to the hot lights and heat in the big cage. "Listen, Pete, tell Gerry he can feed the cats tonight. They're behaving themselves."

Pete snapped his gum and chuckled. "Won't he be riding high tonight." As he moved to the truck that would pull the cage to the cat area, Jo called after him.

"Pete." She bit her lip, then shrugged when he twisted his head. "You'll keep an eye on him, won't you?"

Pete grinned and climbed into the cab of the truck. "Who you worried about, Jo? Those big cats or that skinny boy?"

"Both," she answered. The rhinestones in her tiara sparkled as she tossed her head and laughed. Knowing she had nearly an hour before the finale parade, Jo walked away from the Big Top. She thought of wandering to the cookhouse for some coffee. Mentally, she began replaying every segment of her act. It had gone well, she thought, pleased with the timing and the flow. If Pete had said it had been smooth, Jo knew it had. She had heard his criticisms more than once over the past five years. True, Hamlet had tested her once or twice, but no one knew that but Jo and the cat. She doubted if anyone but Buck would have seen that he had given her trouble. Closing her eyes a moment, Jo rolled her shoulders, loosening tight, tensed muscles.

"That's quite an act you have."

Jo whirled around at the sound of the voice. She could feel her heart rate accelerate. Though she wondered at her interest in a man she barely knew, Jo was aware that she had been waiting for him. There was a quick surge of pleasure as she watched him approach, and she allowed it to show on her face.

"Hello." She saw that he smoked a cigar, but unlike Duffy's, his was long and slim. Again she admired the elegance of his hands. "Did you like the show?"

He stopped in front of her, then studied her face with a thoroughness that made her wonder if her makeup had smeared. Then he gave a small, surprised laugh and shook his head. "Do you know," he began, "when you told me this morning that you did an act with cats, I had Siamese in mind rather than African."

"Siamese?" Jo repeated blankly, then laughed. "House cats?" He brushed her hair behind her back while Jo giggled at the thought of coaxing a Siamese to jump through a flaming hoop.

"From my point of view," he told her as he let a strand of her hair linger between his fingers, "it made more sense than a little thing like you walking into a cage with a dozen lions."

"I'm not little," Jo corrected good-naturedly. "Besides, size hardly matters to twelve lions."

"No, I suppose it doesn't." He lifted his eyes from her hair and met hers. Jo continued to smile, enjoying looking at him. "Why do you do it?" he asked suddenly.

Jo gave him a curious look. "Why? Because it's my job."

By the way he studied her, Jo could see that he was not satisfied with the simplicity of her answer. "Perhaps I should ask *how* you became a lion tamer."

"Trainer," Jo corrected automatically. To her left, she could hear the audience's muffled applause. "The Beirots are starting," she said with a glance toward the sound. "You shouldn't miss their act. They're first-rate acrobats."

"Don't you want to tell me?" His voice was soft.

She lifted a brow, seeing that he truly wanted to know. "Why, it's not a secret. My father was a trainer, and I have a knack for working with cats. It just followed." Jo had never thought about her career past this point, and she shrugged it aside. "You shouldn't waste your ticket standing out here. You can stand by the back door and watch the rest of the act." Jo turned to lead the way to the performer's entrance but stopped when his hand took hers.

He stepped forward until their bodies were nearly touching. Jo could feel the heat from his as she watched his face. Her heart was thudding in a quick, steady rhythm. She could hear it vibrate through her the same way it did when she approached a new cat for the first time. Here was something new, something untested. She tingled with the excitement of the unknown when he lifted his hand to touch her cheek. She did not move but let the warmth spread while she watched him carefully, gauging him. Her eyes were wide, curious and unafraid.

"Are you going to kiss me?" she asked in a tone that expressed more interest than desire.

His eyes lit with humor and glittered in the dim light. "I had given it some thought," he answered. "Do you have any objections?"

Jo considered a moment, dropping her eyes to his mouth. She liked its shape and wondered how it would feel against hers. He brought her no closer. One hand still held hers while the other slid around to cradle her neck. Jo shifted her gaze until their eyes met again. "No," she decided. "I haven't any objections."

The corners of his mouth twitched as he tightened his hold slightly on the base of her neck. Slowly, he lowered his head toward hers. Curious and a bit wary, Jo kept her eyes open, watching his. She knew from experience that you could tell more about people and about cats from the eyes. To her surprise, his remained open as well, even as their lips met.

It was a gentle kiss, without pressure, only a whisper of a touch. Amazed, Jo thought she felt the ground tremble under her feet. Dimly, she wondered if the elephants were being led by. But it can't be time, she thought in confusion. His lips moved lightly over hers, and his eyes remained steady. Jo's pulse drummed under her skin. They stood, barely touching, as the Big Top throbbed with noise behind them. Lazily, he traced her lips with the tip of his tongue, teasing them open. Still there was no demand in the kiss, only testing. Unhurried, confident, he explored her mouth while Jo felt her breath accelerating. A soft moan escaped her as her lids fluttered down.

For an instant she surrendered utterly to him, to the new sensations swimming through her. She leaned against him, straining toward pleasure, sighing with it as the kiss lingered.

He drew her away, but their faces remained close. Dizzily, Jo realized that she had risen to her toes to compensate for their difference in height. His hand was still light on the back of her neck. His eyes were gold in the darkening night.

"What an incredible female you are, Jovilette," he murmured. "One surprise after another."

Jo felt stunningly alive. Her skin seemed to tingle with new feelings. She smiled. "I don't know your name."

He laughed, releasing her neck to take her other hand in his. Before he could speak, Duffy called out from the direction of the Big Top. Jo turned to watch as he moved toward them in his quick, rolling walk.

"Well, well, well," he said in his jolly, rough voice. "I didn't know you two had met. Has Jo been showing you around already?" Reaching them, he squeezed Jo's shoulder. "Knew I could count on you, kiddo." Jo glanced at him in puzzlement, but he continued before she could form a question. "Yes, sir, this little girl puts on quite a show, doesn't she? Always a grabber. And she knows this circus like the back of her hand. Born and raised to it," he continued. Jo relaxed. She recognized that Duffy was into one of his spiels, and there was no stopping him. "Yessiree, any questions you got, you just ask our Jo, and she'll tell you. 'Course, I'm always at your disposal, too. Anything I can tell you about the books or accounts or contracts and the like, you just let me know." Duffy puffed twice on his cigar as Jo felt her first hint of unease.

Why was Duffy rambling about books and contracts? Jo glanced at the man who still held her hands in his. He was watching Duffy with an easy, amused smile.

"Are you a bookkeeper?" Jo asked, perplexed. Duffy laughed and patted her head.

"You know Mr. Prescott's a lawyer, Jo. Don't miss your cue." He gave them both a friendly nod and toddled off.

Jo had stiffened almost imperceptibly at Duffy's offhand information, but Keane had felt it. His brows lowered as he studied her. "Now you know my name."

"Yes." All warmth fled from Jo. Her voice was as cool as her blood. "Would you let go of my hands, Mr. Prescott?"

After a brief hesitation Keane inclined his head and obliged. Jo stuffed her hands quickly into the pockets of her robe. "Don't you think we've progressed to the first name stage of our relationship, Jo?"

"I assure you, Mr. Prescott, if I had known who you were, we wouldn't have progressed at all." Jo's words were stiff with dignity. Inside, though she tried to ignore it, she felt betrayal, anger, humiliation. All pleasure had died from the evening. Now the kiss that had left her feeling clean and alive seemed cheap and shabby. No, she would not use his first name, she vowed. She would never use it. “If you’ll excuse me, I have some things to do before my cue.”

“Why the turnaround?” he asked, halting her with a hand on her arm. “Don’t you like lawyers?”

Coldly, Jo studied him. She wondered how it was possible that she had completely misjudged the man she had met that morning. “I don’t categorize people, Mr. Prescott.”

“I see.” Keane’s tone became detached, his eyes assessing. “Then it would appear that you have an aversion to my name. Should I assume you hold a grudge against my father?”

Jo’s eyes glittered with quick fury. She jerked her arm from his hold. “Frank Prescott was the most generous, the kindest, most unselfish man I’ve ever known. I don’t even associate you with Frank, Mr. Prescott. You have no right to him.” Though it was nearly impossible, Jo forced herself to speak in a normal tone of voice. She would not shout and draw anyone’s attention. This would be kept strictly between Keane Prescott and herself. “It would have been much better if you had told me who you were right away, then there would have been no mix-up.”

“Is that what we’ve had?” he countered mildly. “A mix-up?”

His cool tone was nearly Jo’s undoing. He watched her with a dispassionate curiosity that tempted her to slap him. She fought to keep her fury from spilling over into her voice. “You have no right to Frank’s circus, Mr. Prescott,” she managed quietly. “Leaving it to you is the only thing I’ve ever faulted him for.” Knowing her control was slipping, Jo whirled, running across the grass until she merged with the darkness.

Chapter 3

The morning was surprisingly warm. There were no trees to block the sun, and the smell of the earth was strong. The circus had moved north in the early hours. All the usual scents merged into the aroma of circus: canvas, leather, sweating horses, greasepaint and powder, coffee and oilcloth. The trailers and trucks sat in the accustomed spots, forming the "back yard" that would always take the same formation each time the circus made a stop along the thousands of miles it traveled. The flag over the cookhouse tent signaled that lunch was being served. The Big Top stood waiting for the matinee.

Rose hurried along the midway toward the animal cages. Her dark hair was pinned neatly in a bun at the back of her neck. Her big brown eyes darted about searchingly, while her mouth sat softly in a pout. She was wrapped in a terry cloth robe and wore tennis shoes over her tights. When she saw Jo standing in front of Ari's cage, she waved and broke into a half-run. Watching her, Jo shifted her attention from Ari. Rose was always a diversion, and Jo felt in need of one.

"Jo!" She waved again as if Jo had not seen her the first time, then came to a breathless halt. "Jo, I only have a few minutes. Hello, Ari," she added out of politeness. "I was looking for Jamie."

"Yes, I gathered." Jo smiled, knowing Rose had set her heart on capturing Topo's alter ego. And if he had any sense, she thought, he'd let himself be caught instead of pining over Carmen. Silly, she decided, dismissing all affairs of the heart. Lions were easier to understand. "I haven't seen him all morning, Rose. Maybe he's rehearsing."

"Drooling over Carmen, more likely," Rose muttered, sending a sulky glare in the direction of the Gribalti trailer. "He makes a fool of himself."

"That's what he's paid for," Jo reminded her, but Rose did not respond to the humor. Jo sighed. She had a true affection for Rose. She was bright and fun and without pretentions. "Rose," she said, keeping her voice both light and kind. "Don't give up on him. He's a little slow, you know," she explained. "He's just a bit dazzled by Carmen right now. It'll pass."

"I don't know why I bother," she grumbled, but Jo saw the dark mood was already passing. Rose was a creature of quick passions that flared and soon died. "He's not so very handsome, you know."

"No," Jo agreed. "But he has a cute nose."

"Lucky for him I like red," Rose returned and grinned. "Ah, now we're speaking of handsome," she murmured as her eyes drifted from Jo. "Who is this?"

At the question, Jo glanced over her shoulder. The humor fled from her eyes. "That's the owner," she said colorlessly.

"Keane Prescott? No one told me he was so handsome. Or so tall," she added, admiring him openly as he crossed the back yard. Jo noted that Rose always became more Mexican around men. "Such shoulders. Lucky for Jamie I'm a one-man woman."

"Lucky for you your mama can't hear you," Jo muttered, earning an elbow in the ribs.

"But he comes here, *amiga,* and he looks at you. La, la, my papa would have Jamie to the altar *pronto* if he looked at me that way."

"You're an idiot," Jo snapped, annoyed.

"Ah, Jo," Rose said with mock despair. "I am a romantic."

Jo was helpless against the smile that tugged at her lips. Her eyes were laughing when she glanced up and met Keane's. Hastily, she struggled to dampen their brilliance, turning her mouth into a sober line.

"Good morning, Jovilette." He spoke her name too easily, she thought, as if he had been saying it for years.

"Good morning, Mr. Prescott," she returned. Rose gave a loud, none-too-subtle cough. "This is Rose Sanches."

"It's a pleasure, Mr. Prescott." Rose extended a hand, trying out a smile she had been saving for Jamie. "I heard you were traveling with us."

Keane accepted the hand and smiled in return. Jo noticed with annoyance that it was the same easy, disarming smile of the stranger she had met the morning before. "Hello, Rose, it's nice to meet you."

Seeing her friend's Mexican blood heat her cheeks, Jo intervened. She would not permit Keane Prescott to make a conquest here. "Rose, you only have ten minutes to get back and into makeup."

"Holy cow!" she said, forgetting her attempt at sophistication. "I've got to run." She began to do so, then called over her shoulder, "Don't tell Jamie I was looking for him, the pig!" She ran a little further, then turned and ran backwards. "I'll look for him later," she said with a laugh, then turned back and streaked toward the midway.

Keane watched her dart across the compound while holding up the long skirts of her robe in one hand. "Charming."

"She's only eighteen," Jo offered before she could stop herself.

When Keane turned to her, his look was one of amusement. "I see," he said. "I'll take that information under advisement. And what does the eighteen-year-old Rose do?" he asked, slipping his thumbs into the front pockets of his jeans. "Wrestle alligators?"

"No," Jo returned without batting an eye. "Rose is Serpentina, your premier sideshow attraction. The snake charmer." She was pleased with the incredulous look that passed over his face. It was replaced quickly, however, with one of genuine humor.

"Perfect." He brushed Jo's hair from her cheek before she could protest by word or action. "Cobras?" he asked, ignoring the flash in her eyes.

"And boa constrictors," she returned sweetly. Jo brushed the dust from the knees of her faded jeans. "Now, if you'll excuse me…"

"No, I don't think so." Keane's voice was cool, but she recognized the underlying authority. She did her best not to struggle against it. He *was* the owner, she reminded herself.

"Mr. Prescott," she began, banking down hard on the urge to mutiny. "I'm very busy. I have to get ready for the afternoon show."

"You've got an hour and a half until you're on," he countered smoothly. "I think you might spare me a portion of that time. You've been assigned to show me around. Why don't we start now?" The tone of the question left room for only one answer. Jo's mind fidgeted in search of a way out.

Tilting her head back, she met his eyes. He won't be easy to beat, she concluded, studying his steady, measuring gaze. I'd better study his moves more carefully before I start a battle. "Where would you like to begin?" she asked aloud.

"With you."

Keane's easy answer brought a deep frown to Jo's brows. "I don't understand what you mean."

For a moment Keane watched her. There was no coyness or guile in her eyes as they looked into his. "No, I can see you don't," he agreed with a nod. "Let's start with your cats."

"Oh." Jo's frown cleared instantly. "All right." She watched as he pulled out a thin cigar, waiting until the flame of his lighter licked the tip before speaking. "I have thirteen—seven males, six females. They're all African lions between four-and-a-half and twenty-two years."

"I thought you worked with twelve," Keane commented as he dropped his lighter into his pocket.

"That's right, but Ari's retired." Turning, Jo indicated the large male lion dozing in a cage. "He travels with me because he always has, but I don't work him anymore. He's twenty-two, the oldest. My father kept him, even though he was born in captivity, because he was born the same day I was." Jo sighed, and her voice became softer. "He's the last of my father's stock. I couldn't sell him to a zoo. It seemed like shoving an old relative into a home and abandoning him. He's been with this circus every day of his life, just as I have. His name is Hebrew for *lion*." Jo laughed, forgetting the man beside her as she sifted through memories. "My father always gave his cats names that meant lion somehow or other. Leo, Leonard, Leonara. Ari was a first-class leaper in his prime. He could climb, too; some cats won't. I could teach Ari anything. Smart cat, aren't you, Ari?" The altered tone of her voice caused the big cat to stir. Opening his eyes, he stared back at Jo. The sound he made was more grumble than roar before he dozed again. "He's tired," Jo murmured, fighting a shaft of gloom. "Twenty-two's old for a lion."

"What is it?" Keane demanded, touching her shoulder before she could turn away. Her eyes were drenched with sadness.

"He's dying," she said unsteadily. "And I can't stop it." Stuffing her hands in her pockets, Jo moved away to the main group of cages. To steady herself, she took two deep breaths while waiting for Keane to join her.

Regaining her composure, she began again. "I work with these twelve," she told him, making a sweeping gesture. "They're fed once a day, raw meat six days a week and eggs and milk on the seventh. They were all imported directly from Africa and were cage broken when I got them."

The faint sound of a calliope reached them, signaling the opening of the midway. "This is Merlin, the one I ride out on at the finish. He's ten, and the most even-tempered cat I've ever worked with. Heathcliff," she continued as she moved down the line of cages, "he's six, my best leaper. And this is Faust, the baby at four and a half." The lions paced their cages as Jo walked Keane down the line. Unable to prevent herself, Jo gave Faust a signal by raising her hand. Obediently, he sent out a huge, deafening roar. To Jo's disappointment, Keane did not scramble for cover.

"Very impressive," he said mildly. "You put him in the center when you lie down on them, don't you?"

"Yes." She frowned, then spoke her thoughts candidly. "You're very observant—and you've got steady nerves."

"My profession requires them, too, to an extent," he returned.

Jo considered this a moment, then turned back to the lions. "Lazareth, he's twelve and a natural ham. Bolingbroke, he's ten, from the same lioness as Merlin. Hamlet," she said stopping again, "he's five. I bought him to replace Ari in the act." Jo stared into the tawny eyes. "He has potential, but he's arrogant. Patient, too. He's just waiting for me to make a mistake."

"Why?" Keane glanced over at Jo. Her eyes were cool and steady on Hamlet's.

"So he can get a good clean swipe at me," she told him without altering her expression. "It's his first season in the big cage. Pandora," Jo continued, pointing out the females. "A very classy lady. She's six. Hester, at seven, my best all-around. And Portia; it's her first year, too. She's mostly a seat-warmer."

"Seat-warmer?"

"Just what it sounds like," Jo explained. "She hasn't mastered any complicated tricks yet. She evens out the act, does a few basics and warms the seat." Jo moved on. "Dulcinea, the prettiest of the ladies. Ophelia, who had a litter last year; and Abra, eight, a bit bad-tempered but a good balancer."

Hearing her name, the cat rose, stretched her long, golden body, then began to rub it against the bars of the cage. A deep sound rumbled in her throat. Jo scowled and jammed her hands into her pockets. "She likes you," she muttered.

"Oh?" Lifting a brow, Keane studied the three-hundred-pound Abra more carefully. "How do you know?"

"When a lion likes you, it does exactly what a house cat does. It rubs against you. Abra's rubbing against the bars because she can't get any closer."

"I see." Humor touched his mouth. "I must admit, I'm at a loss on how to return the compliment." He drew on his cigar, then regarded Jo through a haze of smoke. "Your choice of names is fascinating."

"I like to read," she stated, leaving it at that. "Is there anything else you'd like to know about the cats?" Jo was determined to keep their conversation on a professional level. His smile had reminded her all too clearly of their encounter the night before.

"Do you drug them before a performance?"

Fury sparked Jo's eyes. "Certainly not."

"Was that an unreasonable question?" Keane countered. He dropped his cigar to the ground, then crushed it out with his heel.

"Not for a first of mayer," Jo decided with a sigh. She tossed her hair carelessly behind her back. "Drugging is not only cruel, it's stupid. A drugged animal won't perform."

"You don't touch the lions with that whip," Keane commented. He watched the light breeze tease a few strands of her hair. "Why do you use it?"

"To get their attention and to keep the audience awake." She smiled reluctantly.

Keane took her arm. Instantly, Jo stiffened. "Let's walk," he suggested. He began to lead her away from the cages. Spotting several people roaming the back yard, Jo refrained from pulling away. The last thing she wanted was the story spreading that she was having a tiff with the owner. "How do you tame them?" he asked her.

"I don't. They're not tame, they're trained." A tall blond woman walked by carrying a tiny white poodle. "Merlin's hungry today," Jo called out with a grin.

The woman bundled the dog closer to her breast in mock alarm and began a rapid scolding in French. Jo laughed, telling her in the same language that Fifi was too tough a mouthful for Merlin.

"Fifi can do a double somersault on the back of a moving horse," Jo explained as they began to walk again. "She's trained just as my cats are trained, but she's also domesticated. The cats are wild." Jo turned her face up to Keane's. The sun cast a sheen over her hair and threw gold flecks into her eyes. "A wild thing can never be tamed, and anyone who tries is foolish. If you take something wild and turn it into a pet, you've stolen its character, blanked out its spark. And still, there's always an essence of the wild that can come back to life. When a dog turns on his master, it's ugly. When a lion turns, it's lethal." She was beginning to become accustomed to his hand on her arm, finding it easy to talk to him because he listened. "A full-grown male stands three feet at the shoulder and weighs over five hundred pounds. One well-directed swipe can break a man's neck, not to mention what teeth and claws can do." Jo gave a smile and a shrug. "Those aren't the virtues of a pet."

"Yet you go into a cage with twelve of them, armed with a whip?"

"The whip's window dressing." Jo discounted it with a gesture of her hand. "It would hardly be a defense against even one cat at full charge. A lion is a very tenacious enemy. A tiger is more bloodthirsty, but it normally strikes only once. If it misses, it takes it philosophically. A lion charges again and again. Do you know the line Byron wrote about a tiger's spring? 'Deadly, quick and crushing.'" Jo had completely forgotten her animosity and began to enjoy her walk and conversation with this handsome stranger. "It's a true description, but a lion is totally fearless when he charges, and stubborn. He's not the razzle-dazzle fighter the tiger is, just accurate. I'd bet on a lion against a tiger any day. And a man simply hasn't a prayer against one."

"Then how do you manage to stay in one piece?"

The calliope music was just a hint in the air now. Jo turned, noting with surprise that they had walked a good distance from camp. She could see the trailers and tents, hear occasional shouts and laughter, but she felt oddly separated from it all. She sat down cross-legged on the grass and plucked a blade. "I'm smarter than they are. At least I make them think so. And I dominate them, partly by a force of will. In training, you have to develop a rapport, a mutual respect, and if you're lucky, a certain affection. But you can't trust them to the point where you grow careless.

And above all," she added, glancing over as he sat down beside her, "you have to remember the basic rule of poker. Bluff." Jo grinned, leaning back on her elbows. "Do you play poker?"

"I've been known to." Her hair trailed out along the grass, and he lifted a strand. "Do you?"

"Sometimes. My assistant handler, Pete..." Jo scanned the back yard, then smiled and pointed. "There he is, by the second trailer, sitting with Mac Stevenson, the one with the fielder's cap. Pete organizes a game now and then."

"Who's the little girl on stilts?"

"That's Mac's youngest, Katie. She wants to walk on them in the street parade. She's getting pretty good. There's Jamie," she said, then laughed as he did a pratfall and landed at Katie's wooden stilts.

"Rose's Jamie?" Keane asked, watching the impromptu show in the back yard.

"If she has her way. He's currently dazzled by Carmen Gribalti. Carmen won't give Jamie the time of day. She bats her lashes at Vito, the wire walker. He bats his at everyone."

"A complicated state of affairs," Keane commented. He twisted Jo's hair around his fingers. "Romance seems to be very popular in circus life."

"From what I read," she countered, "it's popular everywhere."

"Who dazzles you, Jovilette?" He gave her hair a tug to bring her face around to his.

Jo hadn't realized he was so close. She need do no more than sway for her mouth to touch his. Her eyes measured his while she waited for her pulse to calm. It was odd, she thought, that he had such an effect on her. With sudden clarity, she could smell the grass, a clean, sweet scent, and feel the sun. The sounds of the circus were muted in the background. She could hear birds call out with an occasional high-pitched trill. She remembered the taste of his mouth and wondered if it would be the same.

"I've been too busy to be dazzled," she replied. Her voice was steady, but her eyes were curious.

For the first time, Jo truly *wanted* to be kissed by a man. She wanted to feel again what she had felt the night before. She wanted to be held, not lightly as he had held her before, but close, with his arms tight around her. She wanted to renew the feeling of weightlessness. She had never experienced a strong physical desire, and for a moment she explored the sensation. There was a quiver in her stomach which was both pleasant and disturbing. Throughout her silent contemplations Keane watched her, intrigued by the intensity of her eyes.

"What are you thinking of?"

"I'm wondering why you make me feel so odd," she told him with simple frankness. He smiled, and she noticed that it grew in his eyes seconds before it grew on his mouth.

"Do I?" He appeared to enjoy the information. "Did you know your hair catches the sunlight?" Keane took a handful, letting it spill from between his fingers. "I've never seen another woman with hair like this. It's a temptation all in itself. In what way do I make you feel odd, Jovilette?" he asked as his eyes trailed back up to hers.

"I'm not sure yet." Jo found her voice husky. Abruptly, she decided it would not do to go on feeling odd or to go on wanting to be kissed by Keane Prescott. She scrambled up and brushed off the seat of her pants.

"Running away?" As Keane rose, Jo's head snapped up.

"I never run away from anything, Mr. Prescott." Ice sharpened her voice. She was annoyed that she had allowed herself to fall under his charm again. "I certainly won't run from a city-bred lawyer." Her words were laced with scorn. "Why don't you go back to Chicago and get someone thrown in jail?"

"I'm a defense attorney," Keane countered easily. "I get people out of jail."

"Fine. Go put a criminal back on the streets, then."

Keane laughed, bringing Jo's temper even closer to the surface. "That covers both sides of the issue, doesn't it? You dazzle me, Jovilette."

"Well, it's strictly unintentional." She took a step back from the amusement in his eyes. She would not tolerate him making fun of her. "You don't belong here," she blurted out. "You have no business here."

"On the contrary," he disagreed in a cool, untroubled voice. "I have every business here. I own this circus."

"Why?" she demanded, throwing out her hands as if to push his words aside. "Because it says so on a piece of paper? That's all lawyers understand, I imagine—pieces of paper with strange little words. Why did you come? To look us over and calculate the profit and loss? What's the liquidation value of a dream, Mr. Prescott? What price do you put on the human spirit? Look at it!" she demanded, swinging her arm to encompass the lot behind them. "You only see tents and a huddle of trailers. You can't possibly understand what it all means. But Frank understood. He loved it."

"I'm aware of that." Keane's voice was still calm but had taken on a thin edge of steel. Jo saw that his eyes had grown dark and guarded. "He also left it to me."

"I don't understand why." In frustration, Jo stuffed her hands in her pockets and turned away.

"Neither do I, I assure you, but the fact remains that he did."

"Not once in thirty years did you visit him." Jo whirled back around. Her hair followed in a passionate arch. "Not once."

"Quite true," Keane agreed. He stood with his weight even on both legs and watched her. "Of course, some might look at it differently. Not once in thirty years did he visit me."

"Your mother left him and took you to Chicago—"

"I won't discuss my mother," Keane interrupted in a tone of clipped finality.

Jo bit off a retort, spinning away from him again. Still she could not find the reins to her control. "What are you going to do with it?" she demanded.

"That's my business."

"Oh!" Jo spun back, then shut her eyes and muttered in a language he failed to understand. "Can you be so arrogant? Can you be so dispassionate?" Her lashes fluttered up, revealing eyes dark with anger. "Do the lives of all those people mean nothing to you? Does Frank's dream mean nothing? Haven't you enough money already without hurting people to get more? Greed isn't something you inherited from Frank."

"I'll only be pushed so far," Keane warned.

"I'd push you all the way back to Chicago if I could manage it," she snapped.

"I wondered how much of a temper there was behind those sharp green eyes," Keane commented, watching her passion pour color into her cheeks. "It appears it's a full-grown one." Jo started to retort, but Keane cut her off. "Just hold on a minute," he ordered. "With or without your approval, I own this circus. It might be easier for you if you adjusted to that. Be quiet," he added when her mouth opened again. "Legally, I can do with my—" he hesitated a moment, then continued in a mordant tone

"—inheritance as I choose. I have no obligation or intention of justifying my decision to you."

Jo dug her nails into her palms to help keep her voice from shaking. "I never knew I could grow to dislike someone so quickly."

"Jovilette." Keane dipped his hands into his pockets, then rocked back on his heels. "You disliked me before you ever saw me."

"That's true," she replied evenly. "But I've learned to dislike you in person in less than twenty-four hours. I have a show to do," she said, turning back toward the lot. Though he did not follow, she felt his eyes on her until she reached her trailer and closed the door behind her.

Thirty minutes later Jamie sprang through the back door of the Big Top. He was breathless after a lengthy routine and hooked one hand through his purple suspenders as he took in gulps of air. He spotted Jo standing beside the white mare. Her eyes were dark and stormy, her shoulders set and rigid. Jamie recognized the signs. Something or someone had put Jo in a temper, and she had barely ten minutes to work her way out of it before her cue.

He crossed to her and gave a tug on her hair. "Hey."

"Hello, Jamie." Jo struggled to keep her voice pleasant, but he heard the traces of emotion.

"Hello, Jo," he replied in precisely the same tone.

"Cut it out," she ordered before taking a few steps away. The mare followed docilely. Jo had been trying for some time to put her emotions back into some semblance of order. She was not succeeding.

"What happened?" Jamie asked from directly behind her.

"Nothing," Jo snapped, then hated herself for the short nastiness of the word.

Jamie persisted, knowing her too well to be offended. "Nothing is one of my favorite topics of conversation." He put his hands on her shoulders, ignoring her quick, bad-tempered jerk. "Let's talk about it."

"There's nothing to talk about."

"Exactly." He began massaging the tension in her shoulders with his white gloved hands.

"Oh, Jamie." His good-heartedness was irresistible. Sighing, she allowed herself to be soothed. "You're an idiot."

"I'm not here to be flattered."

"I had an argument with the owner." Jo let out a long breath and shut her eyes.

"What're you doing having arguments with the owner?"

"He infuriates me." Jo whirled around. Her cape whipped and snapped with the movement. "He shouldn't be here. If he were back in Chicago..."

"Hold it." With a slight shake of her shoulders, Jamie halted Jo's outburst. "You know better than to get yourself worked up like this right before a show. You can't afford to have your mind on anything but what you're doing when you're in that cage."

"I'll be all right," she mumbled.

"Jo." There was censure in his voice mixed with affection and exasperation.

Reluctantly, Jo brought her gaze up to his. It was impossible to resist the grave eyes in the brightly painted face. With something between a sigh and a moan, she dropped her forehead to his chest. "Jamie, he makes me so mad! He could ruin everything."

"Let's worry about it when the time comes," Jamie suggested, patting her hair.

"But he doesn't understand us. He doesn't understand anything."

"Well, then it's up to us to make him understand, isn't it?"

Jo looked up and wrinkled her nose. "You're so logical."

"Of course I am," he agreed and struck a pose. As he wiggled his orange eyebrows, Jo laughed. "Okay?" he asked, then picked up his prop bucket.

"Okay," she agreed and smiled.

"Good, 'cause there's my cue."

When he disappeared behind the flap, Jo leaned her cheek against the mare and nuzzled a moment. "I don't think I'm the one to make him understand, though."

I wish he'd never come, she added silently as she vaulted onto the mare's back. I wish I'd never noticed how his eyes are like Ari's and how nice his mouth is when he smiles, she thought. Jo ran the tip of her tongue gingerly over her lips. I wish he'd never kissed me. *Liar.* Her conscience spoke softly in her ear: *Admit it, you're glad he kissed you. You've never felt anything like that before, and no matter what, you're glad he kissed you last night. You even wanted him to kiss you again today.*

She forced her mind clear, taking deep, even breaths until she heard the ringmaster announce her. With a flick of her heels, she sent the mare sprinting into the tent.

It did not go well. The audience cheered her, oblivious to any problem, but Jo was aware that the routine was far from smooth. And the cats sensed her preoccupation. Again and again they tested her, and again and again Jo was forced to alter her timing to compensate. When the act was over, her head throbbed from the strain of concentration. Her hands were clammy as she turned Merlin over to Buck.

The big man came back to her after securing the cage. "What's the matter with you?" he demanded without preamble. By the underlying and very rare anger in his voice, Jo knew he had observed at least a portion of her act. Unlike the audience, Buck would note any deviation. "You go in the cage like that again, one of those cats is going to find out what you taste like."

"My timing was a little off, that's all." Jo fought against the trembling in her stomach and tried to sound casual.

"A little?" Buck glowered, looking formidable behind the mass of blond beard. "Who do you think you're fooling? I've been around these ugly cats since before you were born. When you go in the cage, you've got to take your brain in with you."

Only too aware that he was right, Jo conceded. "I know, Buck. You're right." With a weary hand she pushed back her hair. "It won't happen again. I guess I was tired and a little off-balance." She sent him an apologetic smile.

Buck frowned and shuffled. Never in his forty-five years had he managed to resist feminine smiles. "All right," he muttered, then sniffed and made his voice firm. "But you go take a nap right after the finale. No coffee. I don't want to see you around again until dinner time."

"Okay, Buck." Jo kept her voice humble, though she was tempted to grin. The weakness was going out of her legs, and the dull buzz of fear was fading from between her temples. Still she felt exhausted and agreeable to Buck's uncharacteristic tone of command. A nap, she decided as Buck drove Merlin away, was just what she needed, not to mention that it was as good a way as any to avoid Keane Prescott for the rest of the day. Shooing this thought aside, Jo decided to while away the time until the finale in casual conversation with Vito the wire walker.

Chapter 4

It rained for three days. It was a solid downpour, not heavy but insistent. As the circus wound its way north, the rain followed. Nevertheless, canvas men pitched the tents in soggy fields and muddy lots while straw was laid on the hippodrome track and performers scurried from trailers to tents under dripping umbrellas.

The lot near Waycross, Georgia, was scattered with puddles under a thick, gray sky. Jo could only be grateful that no evening show had been scheduled. By six, it was nearly dark, with a chill teasing the damp air. She hustled from the cookhouse after an early supper. She would check on the cats, she decided, then closet herself in her trailer, draw the curtains against the rain and curl up with a book. Shivering, she concluded that the idea was inspired.

She carried no umbrella but sought questionable shelter under a gray rolled-brimmed hat and thin windbreaker. Keeping her head lowered, she jogged across the mud, skimming around or hopping over puddles. She hummed lightly, anticipating the simple pleasures of an idle evening. Her humming ended in a muffled gasp as she ran into a solid object. Fingers wrapped around her upper arms. Even before she lifted her head, Jo knew it was Keane who held her. She recognized his touch. Through some clever maneuvering, she had managed to avoid being alone with him since they had walked together and looked back on the circus.

"Excuse me, Mr. Prescott. I'm afraid I wasn't looking where I was going."

"Perhaps the weather's dampened your radar, Jovilette." He made no move to release her. Annoyed, Jo was forced to hold her hat steady with one hand as she tilted her head to meet his eyes. Rain fell cool on her face.

"I don't know what you mean."

"Oh, I think you do," Keane countered. "There's not another soul around. You've been careful to keep yourself in a crowd for days."

Jo blinked rain from her lashes. She admitted ruefully that it had been foolish to suppose he wouldn't notice her ploy. She saw he carried no umbrella either, nor did he bother with a hat. His hair was darkened with rain, much the same color that one of her cats would be if caught in an unexpected shower. It was difficult, in the murky light, to clearly make out his features, but the rain could not disguise his mockery.

"That's an interesting observation, Mr. Prescott," Jo said coolly. "Now, if you don't mind, I'm getting wet." She was surprised when she remained in his hold after a strong attempt on her part to pull away. Frowning, she put both hands against his chest and pushed. She discovered that she had been wrong; under the lean frame was an amazing amount of strength. Infuriated that she had misjudged him and that she was outmatched, Jo raised her eyes again. "Let me go," she demanded between clenched teeth.

"No," Keane returned mildly. "I don't believe I will."

Jo glared at him. "Mr. Prescott, I'm cold and wet and I'd like to go to my trailer. Now, what do you want?"

"First, I want you to stop calling me Mr. Prescott." Jo pouted but she kept silent. "Second, I'd like an hour of your time for going over a list of personnel." He paused. Through her windbreaker Jo could feel his fingers unyielding on her arms.

"Is there anything else?" she demanded, trying to sound bored.

For a moment there was only the sound of rain drumming on the ground and splashing into puddles. "Yes," Keane said quietly. "I think I'll just get this out of my system."

Jo's instincts were swift but they were standing too close for her to evade him. And he was quick. Her protest was muffled against his mouth. Her arms were pinioned to her sides as his locked around her. Jo had felt a man's body against her own before—working out with the tumblers, practicing with the equestrians—but never with such clarity as this. She was aware of Keane in every fiber of her being. His body was whipcord lean and hard, his arms holding the strength she had discounted the first time she had seen him. But more, it was his mouth that mystified her. Now it was not gentle or testing; it took and plundered and demanded more before she could withhold a response.

Jo forgot the rain, though it continued to fall against her face. She forgot the cold. The warmth spread from inside, where her blood flowed fast, as her body was molded to Keane's. She forgot herself, or the woman she had thought herself to be, and discovered another. When he lifted his mouth, Jo kept her eyes closed, savoring the lingering pleasures, inviting fresh ones.

"More?" he murmured as his hand trailed up, then down her spine. Heat raced after it. "Kissing can be a dangerous pastime, Jo." He lowered his mouth again, then nipped at her soft bottom lip. "But you know all about danger, don't you?" He kissed her hard, leaving her breathless. "How courageous are you without your cats?"

Suddenly her heart raced to her throat. Her legs became rubbery, and a tingle sprinted up her spine. Jo recognized the feeling. It was the way she felt when she experienced a close call with the cats. Reaction would set in after the door of the safety cage locked behind her and the crisis had passed. It was then that fear found her. She studied Keane's bold, amber eyes, and her mouth went dry. She shuddered.

"You're cold." His voice was abruptly brisk. "Small wonder. We'll go to my trailer and get you some coffee."

"No!" Jo's protest was sharp and instantaneous. She knew she was vulnerable and she knew as well that she did not yet possess the experience to fight him. To be alone with him now was too great a risk.

Keane drew her away, but his grip remained firm. She could not read his expression as he searched her face. "What happened just now was personal," he told her. "Strictly man to woman. I'm of the opinion that lovemaking should be personal. You're an appealing armful, Jovilette, and I'm accustomed to taking what I want, one way or another."

His words were like a shot of adrenaline. Jo's chin thrust forward, and her eyes flamed. "No one *takes* me, one way or another." She spoke with the deadly calm of fury. "If I make love with anyone, it's only because I want to."

"Of course," Keane agreed with an easy nod. "We're both aware you'll be willing when the time comes. We could make love quite successfully tonight, but I think it best if we know each other better first."

Jo's mouth trembled open and closed twice before she could speak. "Of all the arrogant, outrageous…"

"Truthful," Keane supplied, tossing her into incoherency again. "But for now, we have business, and while I don't mind kissing in the rain, I prefer to conduct business in a drier climate." He held up a hand as Jo started to protest. "I told you, the kiss was between a man and a woman. The business we have now is between the owner of this circus and a performer under contract. Understood?"

Jo took a long, deep breath to bring her voice to a normal level. "Understood," she agreed. Without another word she let him lead her across the slippery lot.

When they reached Keane's trailer, he hustled Jo inside without preliminaries. She blinked against the change in light when he hit the wall switch. "Take off your coat," he said briskly, pulling down her zipper before she could perform the task for herself. Instinctively, her hand reached for it as she took a step backward. Keane merely lifted a brow, then stripped off his own jacket. "I'll get the coffee." He moved down the length of the narrow trailer and disappeared around the corner where the tiny kitchen was set.

Slowly, Jo pulled off her dripping hat, letting her hair tumble free from where it had been piled under its confinement. With automatic movements she hung both her hat and coat on the hooks by the trailer door. It had been almost six months since she had stood in Frank's trailer, and like a woman visiting an old friend, she searched for changes.

The same faded lampshade adorned the maple table lamp that Frank had used for reading. The shade sat straight now, however, not at its usual slightly askew angle. The pillow that Lillie from wardrobe had sewn for him on some long-ago Christmas still sat over the small burn hole in the seat cushion of the couch. Jo doubted that Keane knew of the hole's existence. Frank's pipe stand sat, as always, on the counter by the side window. Unable to resist, Jo crossed over to run her finger over the worn bowl of his favorite pipe.

"Never could pack it right," she murmured to his well-loved ghost. Abruptly, her senses quivered. She twisted her head to see Keane watching her. Jo dropped her hand. A rare blush mantled her cheeks as she found herself caught unguarded.

"How do you take your coffee, Jo?"

She swallowed. "Black," she told him, aware that he was granting her the privacy of her thoughts. "Just black. Thank you."

Keane nodded, then turned to pick up two steaming mugs. "Come, sit down." He moved toward the Formica table that sat directly across from the kitchen. "You'd better take off your shoes. They're wet."

After squeaking her way down the length of the trailer, Jo sat down and pulled at the damp laces. Keane set both mugs on the table before disappearing into the back of the trailer. When he returned, Jo was already sipping at the coffee.

"Here." He offered her a pair of socks.

Surprised, Jo shook her head. "No, that's all right. I don't need..."

Her polite refusal trailed off as he knelt at her feet. "Your feet are like ice," he commented after cupping them in his palms. Briskly, he rubbed them while Jo sat mute, oddly disarmed by the gesture. The warmth was spreading dangerously past her ankles. "Since I'm responsible for keeping you out in the rain," he went on as he slipped a sock over her foot, "I'd best see to it you don't cough and sneeze your way through tomorrow's show. Such small feet," he murmured, running his thumb over the curve of her ankle as she stared wordlessly at the top of his head.

Raindrops still clung to and glistened in his hair. Jo found herself longing to brush them away and feel the texture of his hair beneath her fingers. She was sharply aware of him and wondered if it would always be this way when she was near him. Keane pulled on the second sock. His fingers lingered on her calf as he lifted his eyes. Hers were darkened with confusion as they met his. The body over which she had always held supreme control was journeying into frontiers her mind had not yet explored.

"Still cold?" Keane asked softly.

Jo moistened her lips and shook her head. "No. No, I'm fine."

He smiled a lazy, masculine smile that said as clearly as words that he was aware of his effect on her. His eyes told her he enjoyed it. Unsmiling, Jo watched him rise to his feet.

"It doesn't mean you'll win," she said aloud in response to their silent communication.

"No, it doesn't." Keane's smile remained as his gaze roamed possessively over her face. "That only makes it more interesting. Open and shut cases are invariably boring, hardly worth the trouble of going on if you've won before you've finished your opening statement."

Jo lifted her coffee and sipped, taking a moment to settle her nerves. "Are we here to discuss the law or circus business, counselor?" she asked, letting her eyes drift to his again as she set the mug back on the table. "If it's law, I'm afraid I'm going to disappoint you. I don't know much about it."

"What do you know about, Jovilette?" Keane slid into the chair beside hers.

"Cats," she said. "And Prescott's Circus Colossus. I'll be glad to let you know whatever I can about either."

"Tell me about you," he countered, and leaning back, pulled a cigar from his pocket.

"Mr. Prescott—" Jo began.

"Keane," he interrupted, flicking on his lighter. He glanced at the tip of his cigar, then back up at her through the thin haze of smoke.

"I was under the impression you wanted to be briefed on the personnel."

"You are a member of this circus, are you not?" Casually, Keane blew smoke at the ceiling. "I have every intention of being briefed on the entire troupe and see no reason why you shouldn't start with yourself." His eyes traveled back to hers. "Humor me."

Jo decided to take the line of least resistance. "It's a short enough story," she said with a shrug. "I've been with the circus all my life. When I was old enough, I started work as a generally useful."

"A what?" Keane paused in the action of reaching for the coffeepot.

"Generally useful," Jo repeated, letting him freshen her cup. "It's a circus term that means exactly what it says. Rose's parents, for instance, are generally usefuls. We get a lot of drifters who work that way, too. It's also written into every performer's contract, after the specific terms, that they make themselves generally useful. There isn't room in most circuses, and certainly not in a tent circus, for performers with star complexes. You do what's necessary, what's needed. Buck, my handler, fills in during a slump at the sideshow, and he's one of the best canvas men around. Pete is the best mechanic in the troupe. Jamie knows as much about lighting as most shandies—electricians," she supplied as Keane lifted a brow. "He's also a better-than-average tumbler."

"What about you?" Keane interrupted the flow of Jo's words. For a moment she faltered, and the hands that had been gesturing became still. "Besides riding a galloping horse without reins or saddle, giving orders to elephants and facing lions?" He lifted his cup, watching her as he sipped. A smile lurked in his eyes. Jo frowned, studying him.

"Are you making fun of me?"

His smile sobered instantly. "No, Jo, I'm not making fun of you."

She continued. "In a pinch, I run the menagerie in the sideshow or I fill in the aerial act. Not the trap," she explained, relaxing again. "They have to practice together constantly to keep the timing. But sometimes I fill in on the Spanish Web, the big costume number where the girls hang from ropes and do identical moves. They're using butterfly costumes this year."

"Yes, I know the one." Keane continued to watch her as he drew on his cigar.

"But mostly Duffy likes to use girls who are more curvy. They double as showgirls in the finale."

"I see." A smile tugged at the corners of Keane's mouth. "Tell me, were your parents European?"

"No." Diverted, Jo shook her head. "Why do you ask?"

"Your name. And the ease with which I've heard you speak both French and Italian."

"It's easy to pick up languages in the circus," Jo said.

"Your accent was perfect in both cases."

"What? Oh." She shrugged and absently shifted in her chair, bringing her feet up to sit cross-legged. "We have a wide variety of nationalities here. Frank used to say that the world could take a lesson from the circus. We have French, Italian, Spanish, German, Russian, Mexican, Americans from all parts of the country and more."

"I know. It's like a traveling United Nations." He tipped his cigar ash in a glass tray. "So you picked up some French and Italian along the way. But if you've traveled with the circus all your life, what about the rest of your schooling?"

The hint of censure in his voice brought up her chin. "I went to school during the winter break and had a tutor on the road. I learned my ABC's, counselor, and a bit more, besides. I probably know more about geography and world history than you, and from more interesting sources than textbooks. I imagine I know more about animals than a third-year veterinary student and have more practical experience healing them. I can speak seven languages and—"

"Seven?" Keane interrupted. "Seven languages?"

"Well, five fluently," she corrected grudgingly. "I still have a bit of trouble with Greek and German, unless I can really take my time, and I can't read Greek yet at all."

"What else besides French, Italian and English?"

"Spanish and Russian." Jo scowled into her coffee. "The Russian's handy. I use it for swearing at the cats during the act. Not too many people understand Russian cursing, so it's safe."

Keane's laughter brought Jo's attention from her coffee. He was leaning back in his chair, his eyes gold with their mirth. Jo's scowl deepened. "What's so funny?"

"You are, Jovilette." Stung, she started to scramble up, but his hands on her shoulders stopped her. "No, don't be offended. I can't help but find it amusing that you toss out so offhandedly an accomplishment that any language major would brag about." Carelessly, he ran a finger over her sulky mouth. "You continually amaze me." He brushed a hand through her hair. "You mumbled something at me the other day. Were you swearing at me in Russian?"

"Probably."

Grinning, Keane dropped his hand and settled into his chair again. "When did you start working with the cats?"

"In front of an audience? When I was seventeen. Frank wouldn't let me start any earlier. He was my legal guardian as well as the owner, so he had me both ways. I was ready when I was fifteen."

"How did you lose your parents?"

The question caught her off guard. "In a fire," she said levelly. "When I was seven."

"Here?"

She knew Keane was not referring to their locale but to the circus. Jo sipped her cooling coffee. "Yes."

"Didn't you have any other family?"

"The circus is a family," she countered. "I was never given the chance to be an orphan. And I always had Frank."

"Did you?" Keane's smile was faintly sarcastic. "How was he as a father figure?"

Jo studied him for a moment. Was he bitter? she wondered. Or amused? Or simply curious? "He never took my father's place," she replied quietly. "He never tried to, because neither of us wanted it. We were friends, as close as I think it's possible for friends to be, but I'd already had a father, and he'd already had a child. We weren't looking for substitutes. You look nothing like him, you know."

"No," Keane replied with a shrug. "I know."

"He had a comfortable face, all creases and folds." Jo smiled, thinking of it while she ran a finger absently around the rim of her mug. "He was dark, too, just beginning to gray when…" She trailed off, then brought herself back with a quick shake of her head. "Your voice is rather like his, though; he had a truly beautiful voice. I'll ask you a question now."

Keane's expression became attentive, then he gestured with the back of his hand. "Go ahead."

"Why are you here? I lost my temper when I asked you before, but I do want to know." It was against her nature to probe, and some of her discomfort found its way into her voice. "It must have caused you some difficulty to leave your practice, even for a few weeks."

Keane frowned at the end of his cigar before he slowly crushed it out. "Let's say I wanted to see firsthand what had fascinated my father all these years."

"You never came when he was alive." Jo gripped her hands together under the table. "You didn't even bother to come to his funeral."

"I would've been the worst kind of hypocrite to attend his funeral, don't you think?"

"He was your father." Jo's eyes grew dark and her tone sharp in reproof.

"You're smarter than that, Jo," Keane countered calmly. "It takes more than an accident of birth to make a father. Frank Prescott was a complete stranger to me."

"You resent him." Jo felt suddenly torn between loyalty for Frank and understanding for the man who sat beside her.

"No." Keane shook his head thoughtfully. "No, I believe I actively resented him when I was growing up, but…" He shrugged the thought aside. "I grew rather ambivalent over the years."

"He was a good man," Jo stated, leaning forward as she willed him to understand. "He only wanted to give people pleasure, to show them a little magic. Maybe he wasn't made to be a father—some men aren't—but he was kind and gentle. And he was proud of you."

"Of me?" Keane seemed amused. "How?"

"Oh, you're hateful," Jo whispered, hurt by his careless attitude. She slipped from her chair, but before she could step away, Keane took her arm.

"No, tell me. I'm interested." His hold on her arm was light, but she knew it would tighten if she resisted.

"All right." Jo tossed her head to send her hair behind her back. "He had the Chicago paper delivered to his Florida office. He always looked for any mention of you, any article on a court case you were involved in or a dinner party you attended. Anything. You have to understand that to us a write-up is very important. Frank wasn't a performer, but he was one of us. Sometimes he'd read me an article before he put it away. He kept a scrapbook."

Jo pulled her arm away and strode past Keane into the bedroom. The oversize wooden chest was where it had always been, at the foot of Frank's bed. Kneeling down, Jo tossed up the lid. "This is where he kept all the things that mattered to him." Jo began to shift through papers and mementos quickly; she had not been able to bring herself to sort through the chest before. Keane stood in the doorway and watched her. "He called it his memory box." She pushed at her hair with an annoyed hand, then continued to search. "He said memories were the rewards for growing old. Here it is." Jo pulled out a dark green scrapbook, then sat back on her heels. Silently, she held it out to Keane. After a moment he crossed the room and took it from her. Jo could hear the rain hissing on the ground outside as their eyes held. His expression was unfathomable as he opened the book. The pages rustled to join the quiet sound of the rain.

"What an odd man he must have been," Keane murmured, "to keep a scrapbook on a son he never knew." There was no rancor in his voice. "What was he?" he asked suddenly, shifting his eyes back to Jo.

"A dreamer," she answered. "His watch was always five minutes slow. If he hung a picture on the wall, it was always crooked. He'd never straighten it because he'd never notice. He was always thinking about tomorrow. I guess that's why he kept yesterday in this box." Glancing down, she began to straighten the chaos she had caused while looking for the book. A snatch of red caught her eye. Reaching for it, her fingers found a familiar shape. Jo hesitated, then drew the old doll out of the chest.

It was a sad piece of plastic and faded silk with its face nearly washed away. One arm was broken off, leaving an empty sleeve. The golden hair was straggled but brave under its red cap. Ballet shoes were painted on the dainty feet. Tears backed up behind Jo's eyes as she made a soft sound of joy and despair.

"What is it?" Keane demanded, glancing down to see her clutching the battered ballerina.

"Nothing." Her voice was unsteady as she scrambled quickly to her feet. "I have to go." Though she tried, Jo could not bring herself to drop the doll back into the box. She swallowed. She did not wish to reveal her emotions before his intelligent, gold eyes. Perhaps he would be cynical, or worse, amused. "May I have this, please?" She was careful with the tone of the request.

Slowly, Keane crossed the distance between them, then cradled her chin in his hand. "It appears to be yours already."

"It was." Her fingers tightened on the doll's waist. "I didn't know Frank had kept it. Please," she whispered. Her emotions were already dangerously heightened. She could feel a need to rest her head against his shoulder. The evening had been a roller coaster for her feelings, climaxing now with the discovery of her most prized childhood possession. She knew that if she did not escape, she would seek comfort in his arms. Her own weakness frightened her. "Let me by."

For a moment, Jo read refusal in his eyes. Then he stepped aside. Jo let out a quiet, shaky breath. "I'll walk you back to your trailer."

"No," she said quickly, too quickly. "It isn't necessary," she amended, moving by him and into the kitchen. Sitting down, she pulled on her shoes, too distraught to remember she still wore his socks. "There's no reason for us both to get wet again." She rambled on, knowing he was watching her hurried movement, but unable to stop. "And I'm going to check on my cats before I go in, and..."

She stopped short when he took her shoulders and pulled her to her feet. "And you don't want to take the chance of being alone in your trailer with me in case I change my mind."

A sharp denial trembled on her lips, but the knowledge in his eyes crushed it. "All right," she admitted. "That, too."

Keane brushed her hair from her neck and shook his head. He kissed her nose and moved down to pluck her hat and coat from their hooks. Cautiously, Jo followed him. When he held out her coat, she turned and slipped her arms into the sleeves. Before she could murmur her thanks, he turned her back and pulled up the zipper. For a moment his fingers lingered at her neck, his eyes on hers. Taking her hair into his hand, he piled it atop her head, then dropped on her hat. The gestures were innocent, but Jo was rocked by a feeling of intimacy she had never experienced.

"I'll see you tomorrow," he said, pulling the brim of her hat down further over her eyes.

Jo nodded. Holding the doll against her side, she pushed open the door. The sound of rain was amplified through the trailer. "Good night," she murmured, then moved quickly into the night.

Chapter 5

The morning scent was clean. In the new lot rainbows glistened in puddles. At last the sky was blue with only harmless white puffs of clouds floating over its surface. In the cookhouse a loud, crowded breakfast was being served. Finding herself without appetite, Jo skipped going to the cookhouse altogether. She was restless and tense. No matter how she disciplined her mind, her thoughts wandered back to Keane Prescott and to the evening they had spent together. Jo remembered it all, from the quick passion of the kiss in the rain to the calmness of his voice when he had said good-night. It was odd, she mused, that whenever she began to talk to him, she forgot he was the owner, forgot he was Frank's son. Always she was forced to remind herself of their positions.

Deep in thought, Jo slipped into tights and a leotard. It was true, she admitted, that she had failed to keep their relationship from becoming personal. She found it difficult to corral her urge to laugh with him, to share a joke, to open for him the doorway to the magic of the circus. If he could feel it, she thought, he would understand. Though she could admit her interest in him privately, she could not find a clear reason for his apparent interest in her.

Why me? she wondered with a shake of her head. Turning, she opened her wardrobe closet and studied herself in the full-length glass on the back of the door. There she saw a woman of slightly less-than-average height with a body lacking the generous curves of Duffy's showgirls. The legs, she decided, were not bad. They were long and well-shaped with slim thighs. The hips were narrow, more, she thought with a pout, like a boy's than a woman's; and the bustline was sadly inadequate. She knew many women in the troupe with more appeal and a dozen with more experience.

Jo could see nothing in the mirror that would attract a sophisticated Chicago attorney. She did not note the honesty that shone from the exotically shaped green eyes or the strength in her chin or the full promise of her mouth. She saw the touch of gypsy in the tawny complexion and raven hair but remained unaware of the appeal that came from the hint of something wild and untamed just under the surface. The plain black leotard showed her firm, lithe body to perfection, but Jo thought nothing of the smooth satiny sheen of her skin. She was frowning as she pulled her hair back and began to braid it.

He must know dozens of women, she thought as her hands worked to confine her thick mane of hair. He probably takes a different one to dinner every night. They wear beautiful clothes and expensive perfume, she mused, torturing herself with the thought. They have names like Laura and Patricia, and they have low, sophisticated laughs. Jo lifted a brow at the reflection in the mirror and gave a light, low laugh. She wrinkled her brow at the hollowness of the sound. They discuss mutual friends, the Wallaces or the Jamesons, over candlelight and Beaujolais. And when he takes the most beautiful one home, they listen to Chopin and drink brandy in front of the fire. Then they make love. Jo felt an odd tightening in her stomach but pursued the fantasy to the finish. The lovely lady is experienced, passionate and worldly. Her skin is soft and white. When he leaves, she is not devastated but mature. She doesn't even care if he loves her or not.

Jo stared at the woman in the glass and saw her cheeks were wet. On a cry of frustration, she slammed the door shut. *What's wrong with me?* she demanded, brushing all traces of tears from her face. I haven't been myself for days! I need to shake myself out of this—this…whatever it is that I'm in. Slipping on gymnastic shoes and tossing a robe over her arm, Jo hustled from the trailer.

She moved carefully, avoiding puddles and any further speculation on Keane Prescott's romantic life. Before she was halfway across the lot, she saw Rose. From the expression on her face, Jo could see she was in a temper.

"Hello, Rose," she said, strategically stepping aside as the snake charmer splashed through a puddle.

"He's hopeless," Rose tossed back. "I tell you," she continued, stopping and wagging a finger at Jo, "I'm through this time. Why should I waste my time?"

"You've certainly been patient," Jo agreed, deciding that sympathy was the wisest course. "It's more than he deserves."

"Patient?" Rose raised a dramatic hand to her breast. "I have the patience of a saint. Yet even a saint has her limits!" Rose tossed her hair behind her shoulders. She sighed heavily. "*Adios.* I think I hear Mama calling me."

Jo continued her walk toward the Big Top. Jamie walked by, his hands in his pockets. "She's crazy," he muttered. He stopped and spread his arms wide. His look was that of a man ill-used and innocent. Jo shrugged. Shaking his head, Jamie moved away. "She's crazy," he said again.

Jo watched him until he was out of sight, then darted to the Big Top.

Inside, Carmen watched adoringly while Vito practiced a new routine on the incline wire. The tent echoed with the sounds of rehearsals: voices and thumps, the rattle of rigging, the yapping of clown dogs. In the first ring Jo spotted the Six Beirots, an acrobatic act that was just beginning its warm-ups. Pleased with her timing, Jo walked the length of the arena. A raucous whistle sounded over her head, and she glanced up to shake a friendly fist at Vito. He called from fifteen feet above her as he balanced on a slender wire set at a forty-five-degree angle.

"Hey, chickie, you have a nice rear view. You're almost as cute as me."

"No one's as cute as you, Vito," she called back.

"Ah, I know." With a weighty sigh, he executed a neat pivot. "But I have learned to live with it." He sent down a lewd wink. "When you going into town with me, chickie?" he asked as he always did.

"When you teach my cats to walk the wire," Jo answered as she always did. Vito laughed and began a light-footed cha-cha. Carmen fired Jo a glare. She must have it bad, Jo decided, if she takes Vito's harmless flirting seriously. Stopping beside her, Jo leaned close and spoke in a conspirator's whisper. "He'd fall off his wire if I said I'd go."

"I'd go," Carmen said with a lovely pout, "if he'd just ask me."

Jo shook her head, wondering why romances were invariably complicated. She was lucky not to have the problem. Giving Carmen an encouraging pat on the shoulder, Jo set off toward the first ring.

The Six Beirots were brothers. They were all small-statured, dark men who had immigrated from Belgium. Jo worked out with them often to keep herself limber and to keep her reflexes sharp. She liked them all, knew their wives and children, and understood their unique blending of French and English. Raoul was the oldest, and the stockiest of the six brothers. Because of his build and strength, he was the under-stander in their human pyramid. It was he who spotted Jo and first lifted a hand in greeting.

"Halo." He grinned and ran his palm over his receding hairline. "You gonna tumble?"

Jo laughed and did a quick handspring into the ring. She stuck out her tongue when the unanimous critique was "sloppy." "I just need to warm up," she said, assuming an air of injured dignity. "My muscles need tuning."

For the next thirty minutes Jo worked with them, doing muscle stretches and limbering exercises, rib stretches and lung expanders. Her muscles warmed and loosened, her heart pumped steadily. She was filled with energy. Her mind was clear. Because of her lightened mood, Jo was easily cajoled into a few impromptu acrobatics. Leaving the more complicated feats to the experts, she did simple back flips, handsprings or twists at Raoul's command. She did a brief, semi-successful thirty seconds atop the rolling globe and earned catcalls from her comrades at her dismount.

She stood back as they began the leaps. One after another they lined up to take turns running along a ramp, bounding upon a springboard and flying up to do flips or twists before landing on the mat. There was a constant stream of French as they called out to each other.

"Hokay, Jo." Raoul gestured with his hand. "Your turn."

"Oh, no." She shook her head and reached for her robe. "Uh-uh." There was a chorus of coaxing, teasing French. "I've got to give my cats their vitamins," she told them, still shaking her head.

"Come on, Jo. It's fun." Raoul grinned and wiggled his eyebrows. "Don't you like to fly?" As she glanced at the ramp, Raoul knew she was tempted. "You take a good spring," he told her. "Do one forward somersault, then land on my shoulders." He patted them to show their ability to handle the job.

Jo smiled and nibbled pensively on her lower lip. It had been a long while since she had taken the time to go up on the trapeze and really fly. It did look like fun. She gave Raoul a stern look. "You'll catch me?"

"Raoul never misses," he said proudly, then turned to his brothers. *"N'est-ce pas?"* His brothers shrugged and rolled their eyes to the ceiling with indistinguishable mutters. "Ah." He waved them away with the back of his hand.

Knowing Raoul was indeed a top flight under-stander, Jo approached the ramp. Still she gave him one last narrow-eyed look. "You catch me," she ordered, shaking her finger at him.

"Cherie." He took his position with a stylish movement of his hand. "It's a piece of pie."

"Cake," Jo corrected, took a deep breath, held it and ran. When she came off the springboard, she tucked into the somersault and watched the Big Top turn upside down. She felt good. As the tent began to right itself, she straightened for her landing, keeping herself loose. Her feet connected with Raoul's powerful shoulders, and she tilted only briefly before he took her ankles in a firm grip. Straightening her poor posture, Jo styled elaborately with both arms while she received exaggerated applause and whistles. She leaped down nimbly as Raoul took her waist to give her landing bounce.

"When do you want to join the act?" he asked her, giving her a friendly pat on the bottom. "We'll put you up on the sway pole."

"That's okay." Grinning, Jo again reached for her robe. "I'll stick with the cats." After a cheerful wave, she slipped one arm into a sleeve and started back down the hippodrome track. She pulled up short when she spotted Keane leaning up against the front seat rail.

"Amazing," he said, then straightened to move to her. "But then, the circus is supposed to be amazing, isn't it?" He lifted the forgotten sleeve to her robe, then slipped her other arm into it. "Is there anything here you can't do?"

"Hundreds of things," Jo answered, taking him seriously. "I'm only really proficient with animals. The rest is just show and play."

"You looked amazingly proficient to me for the last half hour or so," he countered as he pulled out her braid from where it was trapped by her robe.

"Have you been here that long?"

"I walked in as Vito was commenting on your rear view."

"Oh." Jo laughed, glancing back to where Vito now stood flirting with Carmen. "He's crazy."

"Perhaps," Keane agreed, taking her arm. "But his eyesight's good enough. Would you like some coffee?"

Jo was reminded instantly of the evening before. Leery of being drawn to his charms again, she shook her head. "I've got to change," she told him, belting her robe. "We've got a show at two. I want to rehearse the cats."

"It's incredible how much time you people devote to your art. Rehearsals seem to run into the beginning of a show, and a show seems to run into more rehearsals."

Jo softened when he referred to circus skills as art. "Performers always look for just a bit more in themselves. It's a constant struggle for perfection. Even when a performance goes beautifully and you know it, you start thinking about the next time. How can I do it better or bigger or higher or faster?"

"Never satisfied?" Keane asked as they stepped out into the sunlight.

"If we were, we wouldn't have much of a reason to come back and do it all over again."

He nodded, but there was something absent in the gesture, as if his mind was elsewhere. "I have to leave this afternoon," he said almost to himself.

"Leave?" Jo's heart skidded to a stop. Her distress was overwhelming and so unexpected that she was forced to take an extra moment to steady herself. "Back to Chicago?"

"Hmm?" Keane stopped, turning to face her. "Oh, yes."

"And the circus?" Jo asked, thoroughly ashamed that it had not been her first concern. She didn't want him to leave, she suddenly realized.

Keane frowned a moment, then continued to walk. "I see no purpose in disrupting this year's schedule." His voice was brisk now and businesslike.

"This year's?" Jo repeated cautiously.

Keane turned and looked at her. "I haven't decided its ultimate fate, but I won't do anything until the end of the summer."

"I see." She let out a long breath. "So we have a reprieve."

"In a manner of speaking," Keane agreed.

Jo was silent for a moment but could not prevent herself from asking, "Then you won't—I mean, you'll be staying in Chicago now; you won't be traveling with us?"

They negotiated their way around a puddle before Keane answered. "I don't feel I can make a judicious decision about the circus after so brief an exposure. There's a complication in one of my cases that needs my personal attention, but I should be back in a week or two."

Relief flooded through her. He would be back, a voice shouted in her ear. It shouldn't matter to you, another whispered. "We'll be in South Carolina in a couple of weeks," Jo said casually. They had reached her trailer, and she took the handle of her door before she turned to face him. *It's just that I want him to understand what this circus means,* she told herself as she looked up into his eyes. *That's the only reason I want him to come back.* Knowing she was lying to herself made it difficult to keep her gaze steady.

Keane smiled, letting his eyes travel over her face. "Yes, Duffy's given me a route list. I'll find you. Aren't you going to ask me in?"

"In?" Jo repeated. "Oh, no, I told you, I have to change, and..." He stepped forward as she talked. Something in his eyes told her a firm stand was necessary. She had seen a similar look in a lion's eyes while he contemplated taking a dangerous liberty. "I simply don't have time right now. If I don't see you before you go, have a good trip." She turned and opened the door. Aware of a movement, she turned back, but not before he had nudged her through the door and followed. As it closed at his back, Jo bristled with fury. She did not enjoy being outmaneuvered. "Tell me, counselor, do you know anything about a law concerning breaking and entering?"

"Doesn't apply," he returned smoothly. "There was no lock involved." He glanced around at the attractive simplicity of Jo's trailer. The colors were restful earth tones without frills. The beige-and brown-flecked linoleum floor was spotlessly clean. It was the same basic floorplan as Frank's trailer, but here there were softer touches. There were curtains rather than shades at the windows; large, comfortable pillows tossed onto a forest green sofa; a spray of fresh wildflowers tucked into a thin, glass vase. Without comment Keane wandered to a black lacquer trunk that sat directly opposite the door. On it was a book that he picked up while

Jo fumed. *"The Count of Monte Cristo,"* he read aloud and flipped it open. "In French," he stated, lifting a brow.

"It was written in French," Jo muttered, pulling it from his hand. "So I read it in French." Annoyed, she lifted the lid on the trunk, preparing to drop the book inside and out of his reach.

"Good heavens, are those all yours?" Keane stopped the lid on its downswing, then pushed books around with his other hand. "Tolstoy, Cervantes, Voltaire, Steinbeck. When do you have time in this crazy, twenty-four-hour world you live in to read this stuff?"

"I make time," Jo snapped as her eyes sparked. "My *own* time. Just because you're the owner doesn't mean you can barge in here and poke through my things and demand an account of my time. This is my trailer. I own everything in it."

"Hold on." Keane halted her rushing stream of words. "I wasn't demanding an account of your time, I was simply astonished that you could find enough of it to do this type of reading. Since I can't claim to be an expert on your work, it would be remarkably foolish of me to criticize the amount of time you spend on it. Secondly," he said, taking a step toward her—and though Jo stiffened in anticipation, he did not touch her, "I apologize for 'poking through your things,' as you put it. I was interested for several reasons. One being I have quite an extensive library myself. It seems we have a common interest, whether we like it or not. As for barging into your trailer, I can only plead guilty. If you choose to prosecute, I can recommend a couple of lousy attorneys who overcharge."

His last comment forced a smile onto Jo's reluctant lips. "I'll give it some thought." With more care than she had originally intended, Jo lowered the lid of the trunk. She was reminded that she had not been gracious. "I'm sorry," she said as she turned back to him.

His eyes reflected curiosity. "What for?"

"For snapping at you." She lifted her shoulders, then let them fall. "I thought you were criticizing me. I suppose I'm too sensitive."

Several seconds passed before he spoke. "Unnecessary apology accepted if you answer one question."

Mystified, Jo frowned at him. "What question?"

"Is the Tolstoy in Russian?"

Jo laughed, pushing loose strands of hair from her face. "Yes, it is."

Keane smiled, enjoying the two tiny dimples that flickered in her cheeks when she laughed. "Did you know that though you're lovely in any case, you grow even more so when you smile?"

Jo's laughter stilled. She was unaccustomed to this sort of compliment and studied him without any idea of how to respond. It occurred to her that any of the sophisticated women she had imagined that morning would have known precisely what to say. She would have been able to smile or laugh as she tossed back the appropriate comment. That woman, Jo admitted, was not Jovilette Wilder. Gravely, she kept her eyes on his. "I don't know how to flirt," she said simply.

Keane tilted his head, and an expression came and went in his eyes before she could analyze it. He stepped toward her. "I wasn't flirting with you, Jo, I was making an observation. Hasn't anyone ever told you that you're beautiful?"

He was much too close now, but in the narrow confines of the trailer, Jo had little room to maneuver. She was forced to tilt back her head to keep her eyes level with his. "Not precisely the way you did." Quickly, she put her hand to his chest to keep the slight but important distance between them. She knew she was trapped, but that did not mean she was defeated.

Gently, Keane lifted her protesting hand, turning it palm up as he brought it to his lips. An involuntary breath rushed in and out of Jo's lungs. "Your hands are exquisite," he murmured, tracing the fine line of blue up the back. "Narrow-boned, long-fingered. And the palms show hard work. That makes them more interesting." He lifted his eyes from her hand to her face. "Like you."

Jo's voice had grown husky, but she could do nothing to alter it. "I don't know what I'm supposed to say when you tell me things like that." Beneath her robe her breasts rose and fell with her quickening heart. "I'd rather you didn't."

"Do you really?" Keane ran the back of his hand along her jawline. "That's a pity, because the more I look at you, the more I find to say. You're a bewitching creature, Jovilette."

"I have to change," she said in the firmest voice she could muster. "You'll have to go."

"That's unfortunately true," he murmured, then cupped her chin. "Come, then, kiss me goodbye."

Jo stiffened. "I hardly think that's necessary...."

"You couldn't be more wrong," he told her as he lowered his mouth. "It's extremely necessary." In a light, teasing whisper, his lips met hers. His arms encircled her, bringing her closer with only the slightest pressure. "Kiss me back, Jo," he ordered softly. "Put your arms around me and kiss me back."

For a moment longer she resisted, but the lure of his mouth nibbling at hers was too strong. Letting instinct rule her will, Jo lifted her arms and circled his neck. Her mouth grew mobile under his, parting and offering. Her surrender seemed to lick the flames of his passion. The kiss grew urgent. His arms locked, crushing her against him. Her quiet moan was not of protest but of wonder. Her fingers found their way into his hair, tangling in its thickness as they urged him closer. She felt her robe loosen, then his hands trail up her rib cage. At his touch, she shivered, feeling her skin grow hot, then cold, then hot again in rapid succession.

When his hand took her breast, she shied, drawing in her breath quickly. "Steady," he murmured against her mouth. His hands stroked gently, coaxing her to relax again. He kissed the corners of her mouth, waiting until she quieted before he took her deep again. The thin leotard molded her body. It created no barrier against the warmth of his searching fingers. They moved slowly, lingering over the peak of her breast, exploring its softness, wandering to her waist, then tracing her hip and thigh.

No man had ever touched her so freely. Jo was helpless to stop him, helpless against her own growing need for him to touch her again. Was this the passion she had read of so often? The passion that drove men to war, to struggle against all reason, to risk everything? She felt she could understand it now. She clung to him as he taught her—as she learned—the demands of her own body. Her mouth grew hungrier for the taste of him. She was certain she remained in his arms while seasons flew by, while decades passed, while worlds were destroyed and built again.

But when he drew away, Jo saw the same sun spilling through her windows. Eternity had only been moments.

Unable to speak, she merely stared up at him. Her eyes were dark and aware, her cheeks flushed with desire. But somehow, though it still tingled from his, her mouth maintained a youthful innocence. Keane's eyes dropped to it as his hands loitered at the small of her back.

"It's difficult to believe I'm the first man to touch you," he murmured. His eyes roamed to hers. "And quite desperately arousing. Particularly when I find you've passion to match your looks. I think I'd like to make love with you in the daylight first so that I can watch that marvelous control of yours slip away layer by layer. We'll have to discuss it when I get back."

Jo forced strength back into her limbs, knowing she was on the brink of losing her will to him. "Just because I let you kiss me and touch me doesn't mean I'll let you make love to me." She lifted her chin, feeling her confidence surging back. "If I do, it'll be because it's what I want, not because you tell me to."

The expression in Keane's eyes altered. "Fair enough," he agreed and nodded. "It'll simply be my job to make it what you want." He took her chin in his hand and lowered his mouth to hers for a brief kiss. As she had the first time, Jo kept her eyes open and watched him. She felt him grin against her mouth before he raised his head. "You are the most fascinating woman I've ever met." Turning, he crossed to the door. "I'll be back," he said with a careless wave before it closed behind him. Dumbly, Jo stared into empty space.

Fascinating? she repeated, tracing her still warm lips with her fingertips. Quickly, she ran to the window, and kneeling on the sofa below it, watched Keane stride away.

She realized with a sudden jolt that she missed him already.

Chapter 6

Jo learned that weeks could drag like years. During the second week of Keane's absence she had searched each new lot for a sign of him. She had scanned the crowds of towners who came to watch the raising of the Big Top, and as the days stretched on and on, she balanced between anger and despair at his continued absence. Only in the cage did she manage to isolate her concentration, knowing she could not afford to do otherwise. But after each performance Jo found it more and more difficult to relax. Each morning she felt certain he would be back. Each night she lay restless, waiting for the sun to rise.

Spring was in full bloom. The high grass lots smelled of it. Often there were wildflowers crushed underfoot, leaving their heavy fragrances in the air. Even as the circus caravan traveled north, the days grew warm, sunlight lingering further into evening. While other troupers enjoyed the balmy air and providentially sunny skies, Jo lived on nerves.

It occurred to her that after returning to his life in Chicago, Keane had decided against coming back. In Chicago he had comfort and wealth and elegant women. Why should he come back? Jo closed her mind against the ultimate fate of the circus, unwilling to face the possibility that Keane might close the show at the end of the season. She told herself the only reason she wanted him to come back was to convince him to keep the circus open. But the memory of being in his arms intruded too often into her thoughts. Gradually, she grew resigned, filling the strange void she felt with her work.

Several times each week she found time to give the eager Gerry more training. At first she had only permitted him to work with the two menagerie cubs, allowing him, with the protection of leather gloves, to play with them and to feed them. She encouraged him to teach them simple tricks with the aid of small pieces of raw meat. Jo was as pleased as he when the cats responded to his patience and obeyed.

Jo saw potential in Gerry, in his genuine affection for animals and in his determination. Her primary concern was that he had not yet developed a healthy fear. He was still too casual, and with casualness, Jo knew, came carelessness. When she thought he had progressed far enough, Jo decided to take him to the next step of his training.

There was no matinee that day, and the Big Top was scattered with rehearsing troupers. Jo was dressed in boots and khakis with a long-sleeved blouse tucked into the waist. She studied Gerry as she ran the stock of her whip through her hand. They stood together in the safety cage while she issued instructions.

"All right, Buck's going to let Merlin through the chute. He's the most tractable of the cats, except for Ari." She paused a moment while her eyes grew sad. "Ari isn't up to even a short practice session." She pushed away the depression that threatened and continued. "Merlin knows you, he's familiar with your voice and your scent." Gerry nodded and swallowed. "When we go in, you're to be my shadow. You move when I move, and don't speak until I tell you. If you get frightened, don't run." Jo took his arm for emphasis. "That's *important,* understand? Don't run. Tell me if you want out, and I'll get you to the safety cage."

"I won't run, Jo," he promised and wiped hands, damp with excitement, on his jeans.

"Are you ready?"

Gerry grinned and nodded. "Yeah."

Jo opened the door leading to the big cage and let Gerry through behind her before securing it. She walked to the center of the arena in easy, confident strides. "Let him in, Buck," she called and heard the immediate rattle of bars. Merlin entered without hurry, then leaped onto his pedestal. He yawned hugely before looking at Jo. "A solo today, Merlin," she said as she advanced toward him. "And you're the star. Stay with me," she ordered as Gerry merely stood still and stared at the big cat. Merlin gave Gerry a disinterested glance and waited.

With an upward move of her arm, she sent Merlin into a sit-up. "You know," she told the boy behind her, "that teaching a cat to take his seat is the first trick. The audience won't even consider it one. The sit-up," she continued while signaling Merlin to bring his front paws back down, "is usually next and takes quite a bit of time. It's necessary to strengthen the cat's back muscles first." Again she signaled Merlin to sit up, then, with a quick command, she had him pawing the air and roaring. "Marvelous old ham," she said with a grin and brought him back down. "The primary move of each cue is always given from the same position with the same tone of voice. It takes patience and repetition. I'm going to bring him down off the pedestal now."

Jo flicked the whip against the tanbark, and Merlin leaped down. "Now I maneuver him to the spot in the arena where I want him to lie down." As she moved, Jo made certain her student moved with her. "The cage is a circle, forty feet in diameter. You have to know every inch of it inside your head. You have to know precisely how far you are from the bars at all times. If you back up into the bars, you've got no room to maneuver if there's trouble. It's one of the biggest mistakes a trainer can make." At her signal Merlin laid down, then shifted to his side. "Over, Merlin," she said briskly, sending him into a series of rolls. "Use their names often; it keeps them in tune with you. You have to know each cat and their individual tendencies."

Jo moved with Merlin, then signaled him to stop. When he roared, she rubbed the top of his head with the stock of her whip. "They like to be petted just like house cats, but they are not tabbies. It's essential that you never give them your complete trust and that you remember always to maintain your dominance. You subjugate not by poking them or beating or shouting, which is not only cruel but makes for a mean, undependable cat, but with patience, respect and will. Never humiliate them; they have a right to their pride. You bluff them, Gerry," she said as she raised both arms and brought Merlin up on his hind legs. "Man is the unknown factor. That's why we use jungle-bred rather than captivity-bred cats. Ari is the exception. A cat born and raised in captivity is too familiar with man, so you lose your edge." She moved forward, keeping her arms raised. Merlin followed, walking on his hind legs. He spread seven feet into the air and towered over his trainer. "They might have a sense of affection for you, but there's no fear and little respect. Unfortunately, this often happens if a cat's been with a trainer a long time. They don't become more docile the longer they're in an act, but they become more dangerous. They test you constantly. The trick is to make them believe you're indestructible."

She brought Merlin down, and he gave another yawn before she sent him back to his seat. "If one swipes at you, you have to stop it then and there, because they try again and again, getting closer each time. Usually, if a trainer's hurt in the cage, it's because he's made a mistake. The cats are quick to spot them; sometimes they let them pass, sometimes they don't. This one's given me a good smack on the shoulder now and again. He's kept his claws retracted, but there's always the possibility that one time he'll forget he's just playing. Any questions?"

"Hundreds," Gerry answered, wiping his mouth with the back of his hand. "I just can't focus on one right now."

Jo chuckled and again scratched Merlin's head when he roared. "They'll come to you later. It's hard to absorb anything the first time, but it'll come back to you when you're relaxed again. All right, you know the cue. Make him sit up."

"Me?"

Jo stepped to the side, giving Merlin a clear view of her student. "You can be as scared as you like," she said easily. "Just don't let it show in your voice. Watch his eyes."

Gerry rubbed his palm on the thighs of his jeans, then lifted it as he had seen Jo do hundreds of times. "Up," he told the cat in a passably firm voice.

Merlin studied him a moment, then looked at Jo. This, his eyes told her clearly, was an amateur and beneath his notice. Carefully, Jo kept her face expressionless. "He's testing you," she told Gerry. "He's an old hand and a bit harder to bluff. Be firm and use his name this time."

Gerry took a deep breath and repeated the hand signal. "Up, Merlin."

Merlin glanced back at him, then stared with measuring, amber eyes. "Again," Jo instructed and heard Gerry swallow audibly. "Put some authority into your voice. He thinks you're a pushover."

"Up, Merlin!" Gerry repeated, annoyed enough by Jo's description to put some dominance into his voice. Though his reluctance was obvious, Merlin obeyed. "He did it," Gerry whispered on a long, shaky breath. "He really did it."

"Very good," Jo said, pleased with both the lion and her student. "Now bring him down." When this was accomplished, Jo had him bring Merlin from the seat. "Here." She handed Gerry the whip. "Use the stock to scratch his head. He likes it best just behind the ear." She felt the faint tremble in his hand as he took the whip, but he held it steady, even as Merlin closed his eyes and roared.

Because he had performed well, Jo afforded Merlin the liberty of rubbing against her legs before she called for Buck to let him out. The rattle of the bars was the cat's cue to exit, and like a trouper, he took it with his head held high. "You did very well," she told Gerry when they were alone in the cage.

"It was great." He handed her back the whip, the stock damp from his sweaty palms. "It was just great. When can I do it again?"

Jo smiled and patted his shoulder. "Soon," she promised. "Just remember the things I've told you and come to me when you remember all those questions."

"Okay, thanks, Jo." He stepped through the safety cage. "Thanks a lot. I want to go tell the guys."

"Go ahead." Jo watched him scramble away, leaping over the ring and darting through the back door. With a grin, she leaned against the bars. "Was I like that?" she asked Buck, who stood at the opposite end of the cage.

"The first time you got a cat to sit up on your own, we heard about it for a week. Twelve years old and you thought you were ready for the big show."

Jo laughed, and wiping the damp stock of her whip against her pants, turned. It was then she saw him standing behind her. "Keane!" She used the name she had sworn not to use as pleasure flooded through her. It shone on her face. Just as she had given up hope of seeing him again, he was there. She took two steps toward him before she could check herself. "I didn't know you were back." Jo gripped the stock of the whip with both hands to prevent herself from reaching out to touch him.

"I believe you missed me." His voice was as she remembered, low and smooth.

Jo cursed herself for being so naïve and transparent. "Perhaps I did, a little," she admitted cautiously. "I suppose I'd gotten used to you, and you were gone longer than you said you'd be." He looks the same, she thought rapidly, exactly the same. She reminded herself that it had only been a month. It had seemed like years.

"*Mmm,* yes. I had more to see to than I had expected. You look a bit pale," he observed and touched her cheek with his fingertip.

"I suppose I haven't been getting much sun," she said with quick prevarication. "How was Chicago?" Jo needed to turn the conversation away from personal lines until she had an opportunity to gauge her emotions; seeing him suddenly had tossed them into confusion.

"Cool," he told her, making a long, thorough survey of her face. "Have you ever been there?"

"No. We play near there toward the end of the season, but I've never had time to go all the way into the city."

Nodding absently, Keane glanced into the empty cage behind her. "I see you're training Gerry."

"Yes." Relieved that they had lapsed into a professional discussion, Jo let the muscles of her shoulders ease. "This was the first time with an adult cat and no bars between. He did very well."

Keane looked back at her. His eyes were serious and probing. "He was trembling. I could see it from where I stood watching you."

"It was his first time—" she began in Gerry's defense.

"I wasn't criticizing him," Keane interrupted with a tinge of impatience. "It's just that he stood beside you, shaking from head to foot, and you were totally cool and in complete control."

"It's my job to be in control," Jo reminded him.

"That lion must have stood seven feet tall when he went up on his hind legs, and you walked under him without any protection, not even the traditional chair."

"I do a picture act," she explained, "not a fighting act."

"Jo," he said so sharply she blinked. "Aren't you ever frightened in there?"

"Frightened?" she repeated, lifting a brow. "Of course I'm frightened. More frightened than Gerry was—or than you would be."

"What are you talking about?" Keane demanded. Jo noted with some curiosity that he was angry. "I could see that boy sweat in there."

"That was mostly excitement," Jo told him patiently. "He hasn't the experience to be truly frightened yet." She tossed back her hair and let out a long breath. Jo did not like to talk of her fears with anyone and found it especially difficult with Keane. Only because she felt it necessary that he understand this to understand the circus did she continue. "Real fear comes from knowing them, working with them, understanding them. You can only speculate on what they can do to a man. I *know.* I know exactly what they're capable of. They have an incredible courage, but more, they have an incredible guile. I've seen what they can do." Her eyes were calm and clear as they looked into his. "My father almost lost a leg once. I was about five, but I remember it perfectly. He made a mistake, and a five-hundred-pound Nubian sunk into his thigh and dragged him around the arena. Luckily, the cat was diverted by a female in season. Cats are unpredictable when they have sex on their minds, which is probably one of the reasons he attacked my father in the first place. They're fiercely jealous once they've set their minds on a mate. My father was able to get into the safety cage before any of the other cats took an interest in him. I can't remember how many stitches he had or how long it was before he could walk properly again, but I do remember the look in that cat's eyes. You learn quickly about fear when you're in the cage, but you control it, you channel it or you find another line of work."

"Then why?" Keane demanded. He took her shoulders before she could turn away. "Why do you do it? And don't tell me because it's your job. That's not good enough."

It puzzled Jo why he seemed angry. His eyes were darkened with temper, and his fingers dug into her shoulders. As if wanting to draw out her answer, he gave her one quick shake. "All right," Jo said slowly, ignoring the ache in her flesh. "That is part of it, but not all. It's all I've ever known, that's part of it, too. It's what I'm good at." While she spoke, she searched his face for a clue to his mood. She wondered if perhaps he had felt it wrong of her to take Gerry into the cage. "Gerry's going to be good at it, too," she told him. "I imagine everyone needs to be good—really good—at something. And I enjoy giving the people who come to see me the best show I can. But over all, I suppose it's because I love them. It's difficult for a layman to understand a trainer's feeling for his animals. I love their intelligence, their really awesome beauty, their strength, the unquenchable streak of wildness that separates them from well-trained horses. They're exciting, challenging and terrifying."

Keane was silent for a moment. She saw that his eyes were still angry, but his fingers relaxed on her shoulders. Jo felt a light throbbing where bruises would certainly show in the morning. "I suppose excitement becomes addicting—difficult to live without once it's become a habit."

"I don't know," Jo replied, grateful that his temper was apparently cooling. "I've never thought about it."

"No, I suppose you'd have little reason to." With a nod, he turned to walk away.

Jo took a step after him. "Keane." His name raced through her lips before she could prevent it. When he turned back to her, she realized she could not ask any of the dozens of questions that flew through her mind. There was only one she felt she had any right to ask. "Have you thought any more about what you're going to do with us...with the circus?"

For an instant she saw temper flare again into his eyes. "No." The word was curt and final. As he turned his back on her again, she felt a spurt of anger and reached for his arm.

"How can you be so callous, so unfeeling?" she demanded. "How is it possible to be so casual when you hold the lives of over a hundred people in your hands?"

Carefully, he removed her hand from his arm. "Don't push me, Jo." There was warning in his eyes and in his voice.

"I'm not trying to," she returned, then ran a frustrated hand through her hair. "I'm only asking you to be fair, to be...kind," she finished lamely.

"Don't ask me anything," he ordered in a brisk, authoritative tone. Jo's chin rose in response. "I'm here," he reminded her. "You'll have to be satisfied with that for now."

Jo battled with her temper. She could not deny that in coming back he had proved himself true to his word. She had the rest of the season if nothing else. "I don't suppose I have any choice," she said quietly.

"No," he agreed with a faint nod. "You don't."

Frowning, Jo watched him stride away in a smooth, fluid gait she was forced to admire. She noticed for the first time that her palms were as damp as Gerry's had been. Annoyed, she rubbed them over her hips.

"Want to talk about it?"

Jo turned quickly to find Jamie behind her in full clown gear. She knew her preoccupation had been deep for her to be caught so completely unaware. “Oh, Jamie, I didn’t see you.”

“You haven’t seen anything but Prescott since you stepped out of the cage,” Jamie pointed out.

“What are you doing in makeup?” she asked, skirting his comment.

He gestured toward the dog at her feet. “This mutt won’t respond to me unless I’m in my face. Do you want to talk about it?”

“Talk about what?”

“About Prescott, about the way you feel about him.”

The dog sat patiently at Jamie’s heels and thumped his tail. Casually, Jo stopped and ruffled his gray fur.

“I don’t know what you’re talking about.”

“Look, I’m not saying it can’t work out, but I don’t want to see you get hurt. I know how it is to be nuts about somebody.”

“What in the world makes you think I’m nuts about Keane Prescott?” Jo gave the dog her full attention.

“Hey, it’s me, remember?” Jamie took her arm and pulled her to her feet. “Not everybody would’ve noticed, maybe, but not everybody knows you the way I do. You’ve been miserable since he went back to Chicago, looking for him in every car that drove on the lot. And just now, when you saw him, you lit up like the midway on Saturday night. I’m not saying there’s anything wrong with you being in love with him, but—”

“In love with him?” Jo repeated, incredulous.

“Yeah.” Jamie spoke patiently. “In love with him.”

Jo stared at Jamie as the realization slid over her. “In love with him,” she murmured, trying out the words. “Oh, no.” She sighed, closing her eyes. “Oh, no.”

“Didn’t you have enough sense to figure it out for yourself?” Jamie said gently. Seeing Jo’s distress, he ran a hand gently up her arm.

“No, I guess I’m pretty stupid about this sort of thing.” Jo opened her eyes and looked around, wondering if the world should look any different. “What am I going to do?”

“Heck, I don’t know.” Jamie kicked sawdust with an oversized shoe. “I’m not exactly getting rave notices myself in that department.” He gave Jo a reassuring pat. “I just wanted you to know that you always have a sympathetic ear here.” He grinned engagingly before he turned to walk away, leaving Jo distracted and confused.

* * *

Jo spent the rest of the afternoon absorbed with the idea of being in love with Keane Prescott. For a short time she allowed herself to enjoy the sensation, the novel experience of loving someone not as a friend but as a lover. She could feel the light and the power spread through her, as if she had caught the sun in her hand. She daydreamed.

Keane was in love with her. He'd told her hundreds of times as he'd held her under a moonlit sky. He wanted to marry her, he couldn't bear to live without her. She was suddenly sophisticated and worldly enough to deal with the country club set on their own ground. She could exchange droll stories with the wives of other attorneys. There would be children and a house in the country. How would it feel to wake up in the same town every morning? She would learn to cook and give dinner parties. There would be long, quiet evenings when they would be alone together. There would be candlelight and music. When they slept together, his arms would stay around her until morning.

Idiot. Jo dragged herself back sternly. As she and Pete fed the cats, she tried to remember that fairy tales were for children. None of those things are ever going to happen, she reminded herself. I have to figure out how to handle this before I get in any deeper.

"Pete," she began, keeping her voice conversational as she put Abra's quota of raw meat on a long stick. "Have you ever been in love?"

Pete chewed his gum gently, watching Jo hoist the meat through the bars. "Well, now, let's see." Thrusting out his lower lip, he considered. "Only 'bout eight or ten times, I guess. Maybe twelve."

Jo laughed, moving down to the next cage. "I'm serious," she told him. "I mean *really* in love."

"I fall in love easy," Pete confessed gravely. "I'm a pushover for a pretty face. Matter of fact, I'm a pushover for an ugly face." He grinned. "Yes sir, the only thing like being in love is drawing an ace-high flush when the pot's ripe."

Jo shook her head and continued down the line. "Okay, since you're such an expert, tell me what you do when you're in love with a person and the person doesn't love you back and you don't want that person to know that you're in love because you don't want to make a fool of yourself."

"Just a minute." Pete squeezed his eyes tight. "I got to think this one through first." For a moment he was silent as his lips moved with his thoughts. "Okay, let's see if I've got this straight." Opening his eyes, he frowned in concentration. "You're in love—"

"I didn't say *I* was in love," Jo interrupted hastily.

Pete lifted his brows and pursed his lips. "Let's just use *you* in the general sense to avoid confusion," he suggested. Jo nodded, pretending to absorb herself with the feeding of the cats. "So, you're in love, but the guy doesn't love you. First off, you've got to be sure he doesn't."

"He doesn't," Jo murmured, then added quickly, "Let's say he doesn't."

Pete shot her a look out of the corner of his eye, then shifted his gum to the other side of his mouth. "Okay, then the first thing you should do is change his mind."

"Change his mind?" Jo repeated, frowning at him.

"Sure." Pete gestured with his hand to show the simplicity of the procedure. "You fall in love with him, then he falls in love with you. You play hard to get, or you play easy to get. Or you play flutter and smile." He demonstrated by coyly batting his lashes and giving a winsome smile. Jo giggled and leaned on the feeding pole. Pete in fielder's cap, white T-shirt and faded jeans was the best show she'd seen all day. "You make him jealous," he continued. "Or you flatter his ego. Girl, there're so many ways to get a man, I can't count them, and I've been gotten by them all. Yes, sir, I'm a real pushover." He looked so pleased with his weakness, Jo smiled. How easy it would be, she thought, if I could take love so lightly.

"Suppose I don't want to do any of those things. Suppose I don't really know how and I don't want to humiliate myself by making a mess of it. Suppose the person isn't—well, suppose nothing could ever work between us, anyway. What then?"

"You got too many supposes," Pete concluded, then shook his finger at her. "And I got one for you. Suppose you ain't too smart because you figure you can't win even before you play."

"Sometimes people get hurt when they play," Jo countered quietly. "Especially if they aren't familiar with the game."

"Hurting's nothing," Pete stated with a sweep of his hand. "Winning's the best, but playing's just fine. This whole big life, it's a game, Jo. You know that. And the rules keep changing all the time. You've got nerve," he continued, then laid his rough, brown hand on her shoulder. "More raw nerve than most anybody I've ever known. You've got brains, too, hungry brains. You going to tell me that with all that, you're afraid to take a chance?"

Meeting his eyes, Jo knew hypothetical evasions would not do. "I suppose I only take calculated risks, Pete. I know my turf; I know my moves. And I know exactly what'll happen if I make a mistake. I take a chance that my body might be clawed, not my emotions. I've never rehearsed for anything like this, and I think playing it cold would be suicide."

"I think you've got to believe in Jo Wilder a little more," Pete countered, then gave her cheek a quick pat.

"Hey, Jo." Looking over, Jo saw Rose approaching. She wore straight-leg jeans, a white peasant blouse and a six-foot boa constrictor over her shoulders.

"Hello, Rose." Jo handed Pete the feeding pole. "Taking Baby out for a walk?"

"He needed some air." Rose gave her charge a pat. "I think he got a little carsick this morning. Does he look peaked to you?"

Jo looked down at the shiny, multicolored skin, then studied the tiny black eyes as Rose held Baby's head up for inspection. "I don't think so," she decided.

"Well, it's a warm day," Rose observed, releasing Baby's head. "I'll give him a bath. That might perk him up."

Jo noticed Rose's eyes darting around the compound. "Looking for Jamie?"

"Hmph." Rose tossed her black curls. "I'm not wasting my time on that one." She stroked the latter half of Baby's anatomy. "I'm indifferent."

"That's another way to do it," Pete put in, giving Jo a nudge. "I forgot about that one. It's a zinger."

Rose frowned at Pete, then at Jo. "What's he talking about?"

With a laugh, Jo sat down on a water barrel. "Catching a man," she told her, letting the warm sun play on her face. "Pete's done a study on it from the male point of view."

"Oh." Rose threw Pete her most disdainful look. "You think I'm indifferent so he'll get interested?"

"It's a zinger," Pete repeated, adjusting his cap. "You get him confused so he starts thinking about you. You make him crazy wondering why you don't notice him."

Rose considered the idea. "Does it usually work?"

"It's got an eighty-seven percent success average," Pete assured her, then gave Baby a friendly pat. "It even works with cats." He jerked his thumb behind him and winked at Jo. "The pretty lady cat, she sits there and stares off into space like she's got important things occupying her mind. The boy in the next cage is doing everything but standing on his head to get her attention. She just gives herself a wash, pretending she doesn't even know he's there. Then, maybe after she's got him banging his head against the bars, she looks over, blinks her big yellow eyes and says, 'Oh, were you talking to me?'" Pete laughed and stretched his back muscles. "He's hooked then, brother, just like a fish on a line."

Rose smiled at the image of Jamie dangling from her own personal line. "Maybe I won't put Baby in Carmen's trailer after all," she murmured. "Oh, look, here comes Duffy and the owner." An inherent flirt, Rose instinctively fluffed her hair. "Really, he is the most handsome man. Don't you think so, Jo?"

Jo's eyes had already locked on Keane's. She seemed helpless to release herself from the gaze. Gripping the edge of the water barrel tightly, she reminded herself not to be a fool. "Yes," she agreed with studied casualness. "He's very attractive."

"Your knuckles are turning white, Jo," Pete muttered next to her ear.

Letting out a frustrated breath, Jo relaxed her hands. Straightening her spine, she determined to show more restraint. Control, she reminded herself, was the basic tool of her trade. If she could train her emotions and outbluff a dozen lions, she could certainly outbluff one man.

"Hello, Duffy." Rose gave the portly man a quick smile, then turned her attention to Keane. "Hello, Mr. Prescott. It's nice to have you back."

"Hello, Rose." He smiled into her upturned face, then lifted a brow as his eyes slid over the reptile around her neck and shoulders. "Who's your friend?"

"Oh, this is Baby." She patted one of the tan-colored saddle marks on Baby's back.

"Of course." Jo noticed how humor enhanced the gold of his eyes. "Hello, Pete." He gave the handler an easy nod before his gaze shifted and then lingered on Jo.

As on the first day they had met, Keane did not bother to camouflage his stare. His look was cool and assessing. He was reaffirming ownership. It shot through Jo that yes, she was in love with him, but she was also afraid of him. She feared his power over her, feared his capacity to hurt her. Still, her face registered none of her thoughts. Fear, she reminded herself as her eyes remained equally cool on his, was something she understood. Love might cause impossible problems, but fear could be dealt with. She would not cower from him, and she would honor the foremost rule of the arena. She would not turn and run.

Silently, they watched each other while the others looked on with varying degrees of curiosity. There was the barest touch of a smile on Keane's lips. The battle of wills continued until Duffy cleared his throat.

"Ah, Jo."

Calmly, without hurry, she shifted her attention. "Yes, Duffy?"

"I just sent one of the web girls into town to see the local dentist. Seems she's got an abscess. I need you to fill in tonight."

"Sure."

"Just for the web and the opening spectacular," he continued. Unable to prevent himself, he cast a quick look at Keane to see if he was still staring at her. He was. Duffy shifted uncomfortably and wondered what the devil was going on. "Take your usual place in the finale. We'll just be one girl shy in the chorus. Wardrobe'll fix you up."

"Okay." Jo smiled at him, though she was very much aware of Keane's eyes on her. "I guess I'd better go practice walking in those three-inch heels. What position do I take?"

"Number four rope."

"Duffy," Rose chimed in and tugged on his sleeve. "When are you going to let me do the web?"

"Rose, how's a pint-sizer like you going to stand up with that heavy costume on?" Duffy shook his head at her, keeping a respectable distance from Baby. After thirty-five years of working carnies, sideshows and circuses, he still was uneasy around snakes.

"I'm pretty strong," Rose claimed, stretching her spine in the hope of looking taller. "And I've been practicing." Anxious to demonstrate her accomplishments, Rose deftly unwound Baby. "Hold him a minute," she requested and dumped several feet of snake into Keane's arms.

"Ah..." Keane shifted the weight in his arms and looked dubiously into Baby's bored eyes. "I hope he's eaten recently."

"He had a nice breakfast," Rose assured him, going into a fluid backbend to show Duffy her flexibility.

"Baby won't eat owners," Jo told Keane. She did not bother to suppress her grin. It was the first time she had seen him disconcerted. "Just a stray towner, occasionally. Rose keeps him on a strict diet."

"I assume," Keane began as Baby slithered into a more comfortable position, "that he's aware I'm the owner."

Grinning at Keane's uncomfortable expression, Jo turned to Pete. "Gee, I don't know. Did anybody tell Baby about the new owner?"

"Haven't had a chance, myself," Pete drawled, taking out a fresh stick of gum. "Looks a lot like a towner, too. Baby might get confused."

"They're just teasing you, Mr. Prescott," Rose told him as she finished her impromptu audition with a full split. "Baby doesn't eat people at all. He's docile as a lamb. Little kids come up and pet him during a demonstration." She rose and brushed off her jeans. "Now, you take a cobra..."

"No, thank you," Keane declined, unloading the six-foot Baby back into Rose's arms.

Rose slipped the boa back around her neck. "Well, Duffy, I'm off. What do you say?"

"Get one of the girls to teach you the routine," he said with a nod. "Then we'll see." Smiling, he watched Rose saunter away.

"Hey, Duffy!" It was Jamie. "There's a couple of towners looking for you. I sent them over to the red wagon."

"Fine. I'll just go right on along with you." Duffy winked at Jo before turning to catch up with Jamie's long stride.

Keane was standing very close to the barrels. Jo knew getting down from her perch was risky. She knew, too, however, that her pulse was beginning to behave erratically despite her efforts to control it. "I've got to see about my costume." Nimbly, she came down, intending to skirt around him. Even as her boots touched the ground, his hands took her waist. Exercising every atom of willpower, she neither jerked nor struggled but lifted her eyes calmly to his.

His thumbs moved in a lazy arch. She could feel the warmth through the fabric of her blouse. With her entire being she wished he would not hold her. Then, perversely, she wished he would hold her closer. She struggled not to weaken as her lips grew warm under the kiss of his eyes. Her heart began to hammer in her ears.

Keane ran a hand down the length of her long, thick braid. Slowly, his eyes drifted back to hers. Abruptly, he released her and backed up to let her pass. "You'd best go have wardrobe take a few tucks in that costume."

Deciding she was not meant to decipher his changing moods, Jo stepped by him and crossed the compound. If she spent enough time working, she could keep her thoughts from dwelling on Keane Prescott. Maybe.

Chapter 7

The Big Top was packed for the evening show. Jo watched the anticipation in the range of faces as she took her temporary position in the opening spectacular. The band played jumpy, upbeat music, leaning heavily on brass as the theme parade marched around the hippodrome track. As the substitute Bo Peep, Jo wore a demure mobcap and a wide crinoline skirt and led a baby lamb on a leash. Because her act came so swiftly on the tail of the opening, she rarely participated in the spectacular. Now she enjoyed a close-up look at the audience. In the cage, she blocked them out almost completely.

They were, she decided, a well-mixed group: young babies, older children, parents, grandparents, teenagers. They gave the pageant enthusiastic applause. Jo smiled and waved as she performed the basic choreography with hardly a thought.

After a quick costume change, she took her cue as Queen of the Jungle Cats. After that followed another costume change that transformed her into one of the Twelve Spinning Butterflies.

"Just heard," Jamie whispered in her ear as she took the customary pose by the rope. "You got the job for the next week. Barbara won't be able to handle the teeth grip."

Jo shifted her shoulders to compensate for the weight of her enormous blue wings. "Rose is going to learn the routine," she mumbled back, smiling in the flood of the sunlight. "Duffy's giving her the job if she can stand up under this blasted costume." She made a quick, annoyed sound and smiled brightly. "It weighs a ton."

Slowly, to the beat of the waltz the band played, Jo climbed hand over hand up the rope. "Ah, show biz," she heard Jamie sigh. She vowed to poke him in the ribs when she took her bow. Then, hooking her foot in the hoop, she began the routine, imitating the other eleven Spinning Butterflies.

She was able to share a cup of coffee with Rose's mother when she returned the butterfly costume to wardrobe and changed into her own white and gold jumpsuit. Her muscles complained a bit due to the unfamiliar weight of the wings, and she gave a passing thought to a long, luxurious bath. That was a dream for September, she reminded herself. Showers were the order of the day on the road.

Jo's last duty in the show was to stand on the head of Maggie, the key elephant in the finale's long mount. Sturdy and dependable, Maggie stood firm while four elephants on each side of her rose on their hind legs, resting their front legs on the back of the one in front. Atop Maggie's broad head, Jo stood glittering under the lights with both arms lifted in the air. It was here, more than any other part of the show, that the applause washed over her. It merged with the music, the ringmaster's whistle, the laughter of children. Where she had been weary, she was now filled with energy. She knew the fatigue would return, so she relished the power of the moment all the more. For those few seconds there was no work, no long hours, no predawn drives. There was only magic. Even when it was over and she slid from Maggie's back, she could still feel it.

Outside the tent, troupers and roustabouts and shandies mingled. There were anecdotes to exchange, performances to dissect, observations to be made. Gradually, they drifted away alone, in pairs or in groups. Some would change and help strike the tents, some would sleep, some would worry over their performances. Too energized to sleep, Jo planned to assist in the striking of the Big Top.

She switched on a low light as she entered her trailer, then absently braided her hair as she moved to the tiny bath. With quick moves she creamed off her stage makeup. The exotic exaggeration of her eyes was whisked away, leaving the thick fringe of her lashes and the dark green of her irises unenhanced. The soft bloom of natural rose tinted her cheeks again, and her mouth, unpainted, appeared oddly vulnerable. Accustomed to the change, Jo did not see the sharp contrast between Jovilette the performer and the small, somewhat fragile woman in the glittering jumpsuit. With her face naked and the simple braid hanging down her back, the look of the wild, of the gypsy, was less apparent. It remained in her movements, but her face rinsed of all artifice and unframed, was both delicate and young, part ingenue, part flare. But Jo saw none of this as she reached for her front zipper. Before she could pull it down, a knock sounded on her door.

"Come in," she called out and flicked her braid behind her back as she started down the aisle. She stopped in her tracks as Keane stepped through the door.

"Didn't anyone ever tell you to ask who it is first?" He shut the door behind him and locked it with a careless flick of his wrist. "You might not have to lock your door against the circus people," he continued blandly as she remained still, "but there are several dozen curious towners still hanging around."

"I can handle a curious towner," Jo replied. The offhand quality of his dominance was infuriating. "I never lock my door."

There was stiffness and annoyance in her voice. Keane ignored them both. "I brought you something from Chicago."

The casual statement succeeded in throwing Jo's temper off the mark. For the first time, she noticed the small package he carried. "What is it?" she asked.

Keane smiled and crossed to her. "It's nothing that bites," he assured her, then held it out.

Still cautious, Jo lifted her eyes to his, then dropped her gaze back to the package. "It's not my birthday," she murmured.

"It's not Christmas, either," Keane pointed out.

The easy patience in the tone caused Jo to lift her eyes again. She wondered how it was he understood her hesitation to accept presents. She kept her gazed locked on his. "Thank you," she said solemnly as she took the gift.

"You're welcome," Keane returned in the same tone.

The amenities done, Jo recklessly ripped the paper. "Oh! It's Dante," she exclaimed, tearing off the remaining paper and tossing it on the table. With reverence she ran her palm over the dark leather binding. The rich scent drifted to her. She knew her quota of books would have been limited to one a year had she bought a volume so handsomely bound. She opened it slowly, as if to prolong the pleasure. The pages were heavy and rich cream in color. The text was Italian, and even as she glanced over the first page, the words ran fluidly through her mind.

"It's beautiful," she murmured, overcome. Lifting her eyes to thank him again, Jo found Keane smiling down at her. Shyness enveloped her suddenly, all the more intense because she had so rarely experienced it. A lifetime in front of crowds had given her a natural confidence in almost any situation. Now color began to surge into her cheeks, and her mind was a jumble of words that would not come to order.

"I'm glad you like it." He ran a finger down her cheek. "Do you always blush when someone gives you a present?"

Because she was at a loss as to how to answer his question, Jo maneuvered around it. "It was nice of you to think of me."

"It seems to come naturally," Keane replied, then watched Jo's lashes flutter down.

"I don't know what to say." She was able to meet his eyes again with her usual directness, but he had again touched her emotions. She felt inadequate to deal with her feelings or with his effect on her.

"You've already said it." He took the book from Jo's hand and paged through it. "Of course, I can't read a word of it. I envy you that." Before Jo could ponder the idea of a man like Keane Prescott envying her anything, he looked back up and smiled. Her thoughts scattered like nervous ants. "Got any coffee?" he asked and set the book back down on the table.

"Coffee?"

"Yes, you know, coffee. They grow it in quantity in Brazil."

Jo gave him a despairing look. "I don't have any made. I'd fix you a cup, but I've got to change before I help strike the tents. The cookhouse will still be serving."

Keane lifted a brow as he let his eyes wander over her face. "Don't you think that between Bo Peep, lions and butterflies, you've done enough work tonight? By the way, you make a very appealing butterfly."

"Thank you, but—"

"Let's put it this way," Keane countered smoothly. He took the tip of her braid in his fingers. "You've got the night off. I'll make the coffee myself if you show me where you keep it."

Though she let out a windy sigh, Jo was more amused than annoyed. Coffee, she decided, was the least she could do after he had brought her such a lovely present. "I'll make it," she told him, "but you'll probably wish you'd gone to the cookhouse." With this dubious invitation, Jo turned and headed toward the kitchen. He made no sound, but she knew he followed her. For the first time, she felt the smallness of her kitchen.

Setting an undersized copper kettle on one of the two burners, Jo flicked on the power. It was a simple matter to keep her back to him while she plucked cups from the cupboard. She was well aware that if she turned around in the compact kitchen, she would all but be in his arms.

"Did you watch the whole show?" she asked conversationally as she pulled out a jar of instant coffee.

"Duffy had me working props," Keane answered. "He seems to be making me generally useful."

Amused, Jo twisted her head to grin at him. Instantly, she discovered her misstep in strategy. Keane's face was only inches from hers, and in his eyes she read his thoughts. He wanted her, and he intended to have her. Before she could shift her position, Keane took her shoulders and turned her completely around. Jo knew she had backed up against the bars.

Leisurely, he began to loosen her hair, working his fingers through it until it pooled over her shoulders. "I've wanted to do that since the first time I saw you. It's hair to get lost in." His voice was soft as he took a generous handful. The gesture itself seemed to stake his claim. "In the sun it shimmers with red lights, but in the dark it's like night itself." It came to her that each time she was close to him, she was less able to resist him. She became more lost in his eyes, more beguiled by his power. Already her mouth tingled with the memory of his kiss, with the longing for a new one. Behind them the kettle began a feverish whistle.

"The water," she managed and tried to move around him. With one hand in her hair, Keane kept her still as he turned off the burner. The whistle sputtered peevishly, then died. The sound echoed in Jo's head.

"Do you want coffee?" he murmured as his fingers trailed to her throat.

Jo's eyes clung to his. Hers were enormous and direct, his quiet and searching. "No," she whispered, knowing she wanted nothing more at that moment than to belong to him. He circled her throat with his hand and pressed his fingers against her pulse. It fluttered wildly.

"You're trembling." He could feel the light tremor of her body as he brought her closer. “Is it fear?” he demanded as his thumbs brushed over her lips. “Or excitement?”

“Both,” she answered in a voice thickened with emotion. She made a tiny, confused sound as his palm covered her heart. Its desperate thudding increased. “Are you…” She stopped a moment because her voice was breathless and unsteady. “Are you going to make love to me?” Did his eyes really darken? she wondered dizzily. Or is it my imagination?

“Beautiful Jovilette,” he murmured as his mouth lowered to hers. “No pretentions, no evasions…irresistible.” The quality of the kiss altered swiftly. His mouth was hungry on hers, and her response leaped past all caution. If loving him was madness, her heart reasoned, could making love take her further beyond sanity? Past wisdom and steeped in sensation, she let her heart rule her will. When her lips parted under his, it was not in surrender but in equal demand.

Keane gentled the kiss. He kept her shimmering on the razor’s edge of passion. His mouth teased, promised, then fed her growing need. He found the zipper at the base of her throat and pulled it downward slowly. Her skin was warm, and he sought it, giving a low sound of pleasure as her breast swelled under his hand. He explored without hurry, as if memorizing each curve and plane. Jo no longer trembled but became pliant as her body moved to the rhythm he set. Her sigh was spontaneous, filled with wonder and delight.

With a suddenness that took her breath away, Keane crushed her mouth beneath his in fiery urgency. Jo’s instincts responded, thrusting her into a world she had only imagined. His hands grew rougher, more insistent. Jo realized he had relinquished control. They were both riding on the tossing waves of passion. This sea had no horizon and no depth. It was a drowning sea that pulled the unsuspecting under while promising limitless pleasure. Jo did not resist but dove deeper.

At first she thought the knocking was only the sound of her heart against her ribs. When Keane drew away, she murmured in protest and pulled him back. Instantly, his mouth was avid, but as the knocking continued, he swore and pulled back again.

“Someone’s persistent,” he muttered. Bewildered, Jo stared up at him. “The door,” he explained on a long breath.

“Oh.” Flustered, Jo ran a hand through her hair and tried to collect her wits.

"You'd better answer it," Keane suggested as he pulled the zipper to her throat in one quick move. Jo broke the surface into reality abruptly. For a moment Keane watched her, taking in her flushed cheeks and tousled hair before he moved aside. Willing her legs to carry her, Jo walked to the front of the trailer. The door handle resisted, then she remembered that Keane had locked it, and she turned the latch.

"Yes, Buck?" she said calmly enough when she opened the door to her handler.

"Jo." His face was in shadows, but she heard the distress in the single syllable. Her chest tightened. "It's Ari."

He had barely finished the name before Jo was out of the trailer and running across the compound. She found both Pete and Gerry standing near Ari's cage.

"How bad?" she demanded as Pete came to meet her.

He took her shoulders. "Really bad this time, Jo."

For a moment she wanted to shake her head, to deny what she read in Pete's eyes. Instead, she nudged him aside and walked to Ari's cage. The old cat lay on his side as his chest lifted and fell with the effort of breathing. "Open it," she ordered Pete in a voice that revealed nothing. There was the jingle of keys, but she did not turn.

"You're not going in there." Jo heard Keane's voice and felt a restraining grip on her shoulders. Her eyes were opaque as she looked up at him.

"Yes, I am. Ari isn't going to hurt me or anyone else. He's just going to die. Now leave me alone." Her voice was low and toneless. "Open it," she ordered again, then pulled out of Keane's loosened hold. The bars rattled as he slid the door open. Hearing it, Jo turned, then hoisted herself into the cage.

Ari barely stirred. Jo saw, as she knelt beside him, that his eyes were open. They were glazed with weariness and pain. "Ari," she sighed, seeing there would be no tomorrow for him. His only answer was a hollow wheezing. Putting a hand to his side, she felt the ragged pace of his breathing. He made an effort to respond to her touch, to his name, but managed only to shift his great head on the floor. The gesture tore at Jo's heart. She lowered her face to his mane, remembering him as he had once been: full of strength and a terrifying beauty. She lifted her face again and took one long, steadying breath. "Buck." She heard him approach but kept her eyes on Ari. "Get the medical kit. I want a hypo of pentobarbital." She could feel Buck's brief hesitation before he spoke.

"Okay, Jo."

She sat quietly, stroking Ari's head. In the distance were the sounds of the Big Top going down, the call of men, the rattle of rigging, the clang of wood against metal. An elephant trumpeted, and three cages down, Faust roared half-heartedly in response.

"Jo." She turned her head as Buck called her and pushed her hair from her eyes. "Let me do it."

Jo merely shook her head and held out her hand.

"Jo." Keane stepped up to the bars. His voice was gentle, but his eyes were so like the cat's at her knees, Jo nearly sobbed aloud. "You don't have to do this yourself."

"He's my cat," she responded dully. "I said I'd do it when it was time. It's time." Her eyes shifted to Buck. "Give me the hypo, Buck. Let's get it done." When the syringe was in her hand, Jo stared at it, then closed her fingers around it. Swallowing hard, she turned back to Ari. His eyes were on her face. After more than twenty years in captivity there was still something not quite tamed in the dying cat. But she saw trust in his eyes and wanted to weep. "You were the best," she told him as she passed a hand through his mane. "You were always the best." Jo felt a numbing cold settling over her and prayed it would last until she had finished. "You're tired now. I'm going to help you sleep." She pulled the safety from the point of the hypodermic and waited until she was certain her hands were steady. "This won't hurt, nothing is going to hurt you anymore."

Involuntarily, Jo rubbed the back of her hand over her mouth, then, moving quickly, she plunged the needle into Ari's shoulder. A quiet whimper escaped her as she emptied the syringe. Ari made no sound but continued to watch her face. Jo offered no words of comfort but sat with him, methodically stroking his fur as his eyes grew cloudy. Gradually, the effort of his breathing lessened, becoming quieter and quieter until it wasn't there at all. Jo felt him grow still, and her hand balled into a fist inside the mass of his mane. One quick, convulsive shudder escaped her. Steeling herself, she moved from the cage, closing the door behind her. Because her bones felt fragile, she kept them stiff, as though they might shatter. Even as she stepped back to the ground, Keane took her arm and began to lead her away.

"Take care of things," he said to Buck as they moved past.

"No." Jo protested, trying and failing to free her arm. "I'll do it."

"No, you won't." Keane's tone held a quiet finality. "Enough's enough."

"Don't tell me what to do," she said sharply, letting her grief take refuge in anger.

"I *am* telling you," he pointed out. His hand was firm on her arm.

"You *can't* tell me what to do," she insisted as tears rose treacherously in her throat. "I want you to leave me alone."

Keane stopped, then took her by the shoulders. His eyes caught the light of a waning moon. "There's no way I'm going to leave you alone when you're so upset."

"My emotions have nothing to do with you." Even as she spoke, he took her arm again and pulled her toward her trailer. Jo wanted desperately to be alone to weep out her grief in private. The mourning belonged to her, and the tears were personal. As if her protests were nonexistent, he pulled her into the trailer and closed the door behind them. "Will you get out of here?" she demanded, frantically swallowing tears.

"Not until I know you're all right." Keane's answer was calm as he walked back to the kitchen.

"I'm perfectly all right." Her breath shuddered in and out quickly. "Or I will be when you leave me alone. You have no right to poke your nose in my business."

"So you've told me before," Keane answered mildly from the back of the trailer.

"I just did what had to be done." She held her body rigid and fought against her own quick, uneven breathing. "I put a sick animal out of his misery; it's as simple as that." Her voice broke, and she turned away, hugging her arms. "For heaven's sake, Keane, go away!"

Quietly, he walked back to her carrying a glass of water. "Drink this."

"No." She whirled back to him. Tears spilled out of her eyes and trickled down her cheeks despite her efforts to banish them. Hating herself, she pressed the heel of her hand between her brows and closed her eyes. "I don't want you here." Keane set down the glass, then gathered her into his arms. "No, don't. I don't want you to hold me."

"Too bad." He ran a hand gently up and down her back. "You did a very brave thing, Jo. I know you loved Ari. I know how hard it was to let him go. You're hurting, and I'm not leaving you."

"I don't want to cry in front of you." Her fists were tight balls at his shoulders.

"Why not?" The stroking continued up and down her back as he cradled her head in the curve of his shoulder.

"Why won't you let me be?" she sobbed as her control slipped. Her fingers gripped his shirt convulsively. "Why am I always losing what I love?" She let the grief come. She let his arms soothe her. As desperately as she had protested against it, she clung to his offer of comfort.

She made no objection as he carried her to the couch and cradled her in his arms. He stroked her hair, as she had stroked Ari, to ease the pain of what couldn't be changed. Slowly, her sobbing quieted. Still she lay with her cheek against his chest, with her hair curtaining her face.

"Better?" he asked as the silence grew calmer. Jo nodded, not yet trusting her voice. Keane shifted her as he reached for the glass of water. "Drink this now."

Gratefully, Jo relieved her dry throat, then went without resistance back against his chest. She closed her eyes, thinking it had been a very long time since she had been held in anyone's lap and soothed. "Keane," she murmured. She felt his lips brush over the top of her head.

"Hmm?"

"Nothing." Her voice thickened as she drifted toward sleep. "Just Keane."

Chapter 8

Jo felt the sun on her closed lids. There was the summer morning sound of excited birds. Her mind, levitating slowly toward the surface, told her it must be Monday. Only on Monday would she sleep past sunrise. That was the enroute day, the only day in seven the circus held no show. She thought lazily of getting up. She would set aside two hours for reading. Maybe I'll drive into town and see a movie. What town are we in? With a sleepy sigh she rolled onto her stomach.

I'll give the cats a good going-over, maybe hose them down if it gets hot enough. Memory flooded back and snapped her awake. *Ari.* Opening her eyes, Jo rolled onto her back and stared at the ceiling. Now she recalled vividly how the old cat had died with his eyes trusting on her face. She sighed again. The sadness was still there, but not the sharp, desperate grief of the night before. Acceptance was settling in. She realized that Keane's insistence on staying with her during the peak of her mourning had helped her. He had given her someone to rail at, then someone to hold on to. She remembered the incredible comfort of being cradled in his lap, the solid dependability of his chest against her cheek. She had fallen asleep with the sound of his heart in her ear.

Turning her head, Jo looked out the window, then at the patch of white light the sun tossed on the floor. But it isn't Monday, she remembered suddenly. It's Thursday. Jo sat up, pushing at her hair, which seemed to tumble everywhere at once. What was she doing in bed on a Thursday when the sun was up? Without giving herself time to work out the answer, she scrambled out of bed and hurried from the room. She gave a soft gasp as she ran headlong into Keane.

His hand ran down the length of her hair before he took her shoulder. "I heard you stirring," he said easily, looking down into her stunned face.

"What are you doing here?"

"Making coffee," he answered as he gave her a critical study. "Or I was a moment ago. How are you?"

"I'm all right." Jo lifted her hand to her temple as if to gain her bearings. "I'm a bit disoriented, I suppose. I overslept. It's never happened before."

"I gave you a sleeping pill," Keane told her matter-of-factly. He slipped an arm around her shoulder as he turned back to the kitchen.

"A pill?" Jo's eyes flew to his. "I don't remember taking a pill."

"It was in the water you drank." On the stove the kettle began its piercing whistle. Moving to it, Keane finished making the coffee. "I had my doubts as to whether you'd take it voluntarily."

"No, I wouldn't have," Jo agreed with some annoyance. "I've never taken a sleeping pill in my life."

"Well, you did last night." He held out a mug of coffee. "I sent Gerry for it while you were in the cage with Ari." Again he gave her a quick, intense study. "It didn't seem to do you any harm. You went out like a light. I carried you to bed, changed your clothes—"

"Changed my…" All at once Jo became aware that she wore only a thin white nightshirt. Her hand reached instinctively for the top button that nestled just above her bosom. Thinking hard, she found she could recall nothing beyond falling asleep in his arms.

"I don't think you'd have spent a very comfortable night in your costume," Keane pointed out. Enjoying his coffee, he smiled at the nervous hand she held between her breasts. "I've had a certain amount of experience undressing women in the dark." Jo dropped her hand. It was an unmistakable movement of pride. Keane's eyes softened. "You needed a good night's sleep, Jo. You were worn out."

Without speaking, Jo lifted her coffee to her lips and turned away. Walking to the window, she could see that the back yard was deserted.

Her sleep must indeed have been deep to have kept her unaware of camp breaking.

"Everyone's gone but a couple of roustabouts and a generator truck. They'll take off when you don't need power anymore."

The vulnerability Jo felt was overwhelming. Several times in the course of the evening before, she had lost control, which had always been an essential part of her. Each time, it had been Keane who had been there. She wanted to be angry with him for intruding on her privacy but found it impossible. She had needed him, and he had known it.

"You didn't have to stay behind," she said, watching a crow swoop low over the ground outside.

"I wasn't certain you'd be in any shape to drive fifty miles this morning. Pete's driving my trailer."

Her shoulders lifted and fell before she turned around. Sunlight streamed through the window at her back and poured through the thin folds of her nightshirt. Her body was a slender shadow. When she spoke, her voice was low with regret. "I was horribly rude to you last night."

Keane shrugged and lifted his coffee. "You were upset."

"Yes." Her eyes were an open reflection of her sorrow. "Ari was very important to me. I suppose he was an ongoing link with my father, with my childhood. I'd known for some time he wouldn't make it through the season, but I didn't want to face it." She looked down at the mug she held gripped in both hands. A faint wisp of steam rose from it and vanished. "Last night was a relief for him. It was selfish of me to wish it otherwise. And I was wrong to strike out at you the way I did. I'm sorry."

"I don't want your apology, Jo." Because he sounded annoyed, she looked up quickly.

"I'd feel better if you'd take it, Keane. You've been very kind."

To her astonishment, he swore under his breath and turned back to the stove. "I don't care for your gratitude any more than your apology." He set down his mug and poured in more coffee. "Neither of them is necessary."

"They are to me," Jo replied, then took a step toward him. "Keane..." She set down her coffee and touched his arm. When he turned, she let impulse guide her. She rested her head on his shoulder and slipped her arms around his waist. He stiffened, putting his hands to her shoulders as if to draw her away. Then she heard his breath come out in a long sigh as he relaxed. For an instant he brought her closer.

"I never know precisely what to expect from you," he murmured. He lifted her chin with his finger. In automatic response, Jo closed her eyes and offered her mouth. She felt his fingers tighten on her skin before his lips brushed hers lightly. "You'd better go change." His manner was friendly but cool as he stepped away. "We'll stop off in town, and I'll buy you some breakfast."

Puzzled by his attitude but satisfied he was no longer annoyed, Jo nodded. "All right."

Spring became summer as the circus wound its way north. The sun stayed longer, peeking into the Big Top until well after the evening show began. Heavy rain came infrequently, but there were quick summer storms with thunder and lightning. Through June, Prescott's Circus Colossus snaked through North Carolina and into western Tennessee.

During the long weeks while spring tripped over into summer, Jo found Keane's attitude a paradox. His friendliness toward her was offhand. He laughed if she said something amusing, listened if she had a complaint and to her confusion, slipped a thin barrier between them. At times she wondered if the passion that had flared between them the night he had returned from Chicago had truly existed. Had the desire she had tasted on his lips been a fantasy? The closeness she had felt blooming between them had withered and blown away. They were only owner and trouper now.

Keane flew back to Chicago twice more during this period, but he brought no surprise presents back with him. Not once during those long weeks did he come by her trailer. Initially, his altered manner confused her. He was not angry. His mood was neither heated nor icy with temper but fell into an odd middle ground she could not understand. Jo ached with love. As days passed into weeks, she was forced to admit that Keane did not seem to be interested in a close relationship.

On the eve of the July Fourth show, Jo sat sleepless in her bed. In her hand she held the volume of Dante, but the book was only a reminder of the emptiness she felt. She closed it, then stared at the ceiling. It's time to snap out of it, she lectured herself. It's time to stop pretending he was ever really part of my life. Loving someone only makes him a part of your wishes. He never talked about love, he never promised anything, never offered anything but what he gave to me. He's done nothing to hurt me. Jo squeezed her eyes shut and pressed the book between her fingers. How I wish I could hate him for showing me what life could be like and then turning away, she thought.

But I can't. Jo let out a shaky breath and relaxed her grip on the book. Gently, she ran a finger down its smooth, leather binding. I can't hate him, but I can't love him openly, either. How do I stop? I should be grateful he stopped wanting me. I would have made love with him. Then I'd hurt a hundred times more. Could I hurt a hundred times more? For several moments she lay still, trying to quiet her thoughts.

It's best not to know, she told herself sternly. It's best to remember he was kind to me when I needed him and that I haven't a right to make demands. Summer doesn't last forever. I may never see him again when it's over. At least I can keep the time we have pleasant.

The words sounded hollow in her heart.

Chapter 9

The Fourth of July was a full day with a run to a new lot, the tent raising, a street parade and two shows. But it was a holiday. Elephants wore red, white and blue plumes atop their massive heads. The evening performance would be held an hour earlier to allow for the addition of a fireworks display. Traditionally, Prescott's circus arranged to spend the holiday in the same small town in Tennessee. The license and paperwork for the display were seen to in advance, and the fireworks were shipped ahead to be stored in a warehouse. The procedure had been precisely the same for years. It was one of the circus's most profitable nights. Concessions thrived.

Jo moved through the day with determined cheerfulness. She refused to permit the distance between her and Keane to spoil one of the highlights of the summer. Brooding, she decided, would not change things. The mood of the crowd helped to keep her spirits light.

Between shows came the inevitable lull. Some troupers sat outside their trailers exchanging small talk and enjoying the sun. Others got in a bit more practice or worked out a few kinks. Bull hands washed down the elephants, causing a minor flood in the pen area.

Jo watched the bathing process with amusement. She never ceased to enjoy this particular aspect of circus life, especially if there were one or two inexperienced bull hands involved. Invariably, Maggie or one of the other veteran bulls would spray a trunkful of water over the new hands to initiate them. Though Jo knew the other hands encouraged it, they always displayed remarkable innocence.

Spotting Duffy, Jo moved away from the elephant area and wandered toward him. She could see he was deep in discussion with a towner. He was as short as Duffy but wider, with what she had once heard Frank call a successful frame. His stomach started high and barreled out to below his waist. He had a ruddy complexion and pale eyes that squinted hard against the sun. Jo had seen his type before. She wondered what he was selling and how much he wanted for it. Since Duffy was puffing with annoyance, Jo assumed it was quite a lot.

"I'm telling you, Carlson, we've already paid for storage. I've got a signed receipt. And we pay fifteen bucks delivery, not twenty."

Carlson was smoking a small, unfiltered cigarette and dropped it to the ground. "You paid Myers for storage, not me. I bought the place six weeks ago." He shrugged his wide shoulders. "Not my problem you paid in advance."

Looking over, Jo saw Keane approaching with Pete. Pete was talking rapidly, Keane nodding. As Jo watched, Keane glanced up and gave Carlson a quick study. She had seen that look before and knew the older man had been assessed. Keane caught her eye, smiled and began to move past her. "Hello, Jo."

Unashamedly curious, Jo fell into step beside him. "What's going on?"

"Why don't we find out?" he suggested as they stopped in front of Duffy and Carlson. "Gentlemen," Keane said in an easy tone. "Is there a problem?"

"This character," Duffy spouted, jerking a scornful thumb at Carlson's face, "wants us to pay twice for storage on the fireworks. Then he wants twenty for delivery when we agreed on fifteen."

"Myers agreed on fifteen," Carlson pointed out. He smiled without humor. "I didn't agree on anything. You want your fireworks, you gotta pay for them first—cash," he added, then spared Keane a glance. "Who's this guy?"

Duffy began to wheeze with indignation, but Keane laid a restraining hand on his shoulder. "I'm Prescott," he told him in untroubled tones. "Perhaps you'd like to fill me in."

"Prescott, huh?" Carlson stroked both his chins as he studied Keane.

Seeing youth and amiable eyes, he felt closer to success. "Well, now we're getting somewhere," he said jovially and stuck out his hand. Keane accepted it without hesitation. "Jim Carlson," he continued as he gave Keane's hand a brisk pump. "Nice circus you got here, Prescott. Me and the missus see it every year. Well, now," he said again and hitched up his belt. "Seeing as you're a businessman, too, I'm sure we can straighten all this out. Problem is, your fireworks've been stored in my warehouse. Now, I gotta make a living, they can't just sit there for free. I bought the place off Myers six weeks ago. I can't be held responsible for a deal you made with him, can I?" Carlson gave a stretched-lip smile, pleased that Keane listened so politely. "And as for delivery, well…" He made a helpless gesture and patted Keane's shoulder. "You know about gas prices these days, son. But we can work that out after we settle this other little problem."

Keane nodded agreeably. "That sounds reasonable." He ignored Duffy's huffing and puffing. "You do seem to have a problem, Mr. Carlson."

"I don't have a problem," Carlson countered. His smile suffered a fractional slip. "You've got the problem, unless you don't want the fireworks."

"Oh, we'll have the fireworks, Mr. Carlson," Keane corrected with a smile Jo thought more wolfish than friendly. "According to paragraph three, section five, of the small business code, the lessor is legally bound by all contracts, agreements, liens and mortgages of the previous lessor until such time as all aforesaid contracts, agreements, liens and mortgages are expired or transferred."

"What the…" Carlson began with no smile at all, but Keane continued blandly.

"Of course, we won't pursue the matter in court as long as we get our merchandise. But that doesn't solve your problem."

"My problem?" Carlson sputtered while Jo looked on in frank admiration. "I haven't got a problem. If you think…"

"Oh, but you do, Mr. Carlson, though I'm sure there was no intent to break the law on your part."

"Break the law?" Carlson wiped damp hands on his slacks.

"Storing explosives without a license," Keane pointed out. "Unless, of course, you obtained one after your purchase of the warehouse."

"Well, no, I…"

"I was afraid of that." Keane lifted his brow in pity. "You see, in paragraph six of section five of the small business code it states that all licenses, permits and warrants shall be nontransferable. Authorization for new licenses, permits or warrants must be requested in writing by the current owner. Notarized, naturally." Keane waited a bit to allow Carlson to wrestle with the idea. "If I'm not mistaken," he continued conversationally, "the fine's pretty hefty in this state. Of course, sentencing depends on—"

"Sentencing?" Carlson paled and mopped the back of his neck with a handkerchief.

"Look, tell you what." Keane gave Carlson a sympathetic smile. "You get the fireworks over here and off your property. We don't have to bring the law in on something like this. Just an oversight, after all. We're both businessmen, aren't we?"

Too overwrought to detect sarcasm, Carlson nodded.

"That was fifteen on delivery, right?"

Carlson didn't hesitate but stuck the damp handkerchief back in his pocket and nodded again.

"Good enough. I'll have the cash for you on delivery. Glad to help you out."

Relieved, Carlson turned and headed for his pickup. Jo managed to keep her features grave until he pulled off the lot. Simultaneously, Pete and Duffy began to hoot with laughter.

"Was it true?" Jo demanded and took Keane's arm.

"Was what true?" Keane countered, merely lifting a brow over the hysterics that surrounded him.

"'Paragraph three, section five, of the small business code,'" Jo quoted.

"Never heard of it," Keane answered mildly, nearly sending Pete into orbit.

"You made it up," Jo said in wonder. "You made it all up!"

"Probably," Keane agreed.

"Smoothest con job I've seen in years," Duffy stated and gave Keane a parental slap on the back. "Son, you could go into business."

"I did," Keane told him and grinned.

"I ever need a lawyer," Pete put in, pushing his cap further back on his head, "I know where to go. You come on by the cookhouse tonight, Captain. We're having ourselves a poker game. Come on, Duffy, Buck's gotta hear about this."

As they moved off, Jo realized that Keane had been officially accepted. Before, he had been the legal owner but an outsider, a towner. Now he was one of them. Turning, she lifted her face to his. "Welcome aboard."

"Thank you." She saw he understood precisely what had been left unsaid.

"I'll see you at the game," she said before her smile became a grin. "Don't forget your money."

She turned away, but Keane touched her arm, bringing her back to him. "Jo," he began, puzzling her by the sudden seriousness of his eyes.

"Yes?"

There was a brief hesitation, then he shook his head. "Nothing, never mind. I'll see you later." He rubbed his knuckles over her cheek, then walked away.

Jo studied her hand impassively. On the deal, she had missed a heart flush by one card and now waited for someone to open. Casually, she moved her glance around the table. Duffy was puffing on a cigar, apparently unconcerned with the dwindling chips in front of him. Pete chewed his gum with equal nonchalance. Amy, the wife of the sword swallower, sat beside him, then Jamie, then Raoul. Directly beside Jo was Keane, who, like Pete, was winning consistently.

The pot grew. Chips clinked on the table. Jo discarded and was pleased to exchange a club for the fifth heart. She slipped it into her hand without blinking. Frank had taught her the game. Before the second round of betting, Jamie folded in disgust. "Should never have taken Buck's seat," he muttered and frowned when Pete raised the bet.

"You got out cheap, kiddo," Duffy told him dolefully as he tossed in chips. "I'm only staying in so I don't change my standard of living. Money'll do that to you," he mumbled obscurely.

"Three kings," Pete announced when called, then spread his cards. Amid a flutter of complaints cards were tossed down.

"Heart flush," Jo said mildly before Pete could rake in the pot. Duffy leaned back and gave a hoot of laughter.

"Attagirl, Jo. I hate to see him win all my money."

During the next two hours the cookhouse tent grew hot and ripe with the scents of coffee and tobacco and beer. Jamie's luck proved so consistently poor that he called for Buck to relieve him.

Jo found herself with an indifferent pair of fives. Almost immediately the betting grew heavy as Keane raised Raoul's opening. Curiosity kept Jo in one round, but practicality had her folding after the draw. Divorced from the game, she watched it with interest. Leaning on her elbows, she studied each participant. Keane played a good game, she mused. His eyes gave nothing away. They never did. Casually, he nursed the beer beside him while Duffy, Buck and Amy folded. Studying him closely, Pete chewed his gum. Keane returned the look, keeping the stub of his cigar clamped between his teeth. Raoul muttered in French and scowled at his cards.

"Could be bluffing," Pete considered, seeing Keane's raise. "Let's raise it five more and see what's cooking." Raoul swore in French, then again in English, before he tossed in his hand. Taking his time, Keane counted out the necessary chips and tossed them into the pot. It was a plastic mountain of red, white and blue. Then, he counted out more.

"I'll see your five," he said evenly, "and raise it ten."

There was mumbling around the table. Pete looked into his hand and considered. Shifting his eyes, he took in the generous pile of chips in front of him. He could afford to risk another ten. Glancing up, he studied Keane's face while he fondled his chips. Abruptly, he broke into a grin.

"Nope," he said simply, turning his cards face down. "This one's all yours."

Setting down his cards, Keane raked in a very sweet pot. "Gonna show 'em?" Pete asked. His grin was affable.

Keane pushed a stray chip into the pile and shrugged. With his free hand he turned over the cards. The reaction ranged from oaths to laughter.

"Trash," Pete mumbled with a shake of his head. "Nothing but trash. You've got nerve, Captain." His grin grew wide as he turned over his own cards. "Even I had a pair of sevens."

Raoul gnashed his teeth and swore elegantly in two languages. Jo grinned at his imaginative choice of words. She rose on a laugh and snatched off the soft felt hat Jamie wore. Deftly, she scooped her chips into it. "Cash me in later," she requested, then gave him a smacking kiss on the mouth. "But don't play with them."

Duffy scowled over at her. "Aren't you cashing in early?"

"You've always told me to leave 'em wanting more," she reminded him. With a grin and a wave, she swung through the door.

"That Jo," said Raoul, chuckling as he shuffled the cards. "She's one smart cracker."

"Cookie," Pete corrected, opening a fresh stick of gum. He noticed that Keane's gaze had drifted to the door she had closed behind her. "Some looker, too," he commented and watched Keane's eyes wander back to his. "Don't you think, Captain?"

Keane slipped his cards into a pile as they were dealt to him. "Jo's lovely."

"Like her mother," Buck put in, frowning at his cards. "She was a beaut, huh, Duffy?" Duffy grunted in agreement and wondered why Lady Luck refused to smile on him. "Always thought it was a crime for her to die that way. Wilder, too," he added with a shake of his head.

"A fire, wasn't it?" Keane asked as he picked up his cards and spread them.

"Electrical fire." Buck nodded and lifted his beer. "A short in their trailer's wiring. What a waste. If they hadn't been in bed asleep, they'd probably still be alive. The trailer was halfway gone before anybody set up an alarm. Just plain couldn't get to the Wilders. Their side of the trailer was like a furnace. Jo's bedroom was on the other side, and we nearly lost her. Frank busted in the window and pulled her out. Poor little tyke. She was holding onto this old doll like it was the last thing she had left. Kept it with her for I don't know how long. Remember, Duffy?" He glanced into his hand and opened for two. "It only had one arm." Duffy grunted again and folded. "Frank sure knew how to handle that little girl."

"She knew how to handle him, more likely," Duffy mumbled. Raoul bumped the pot five, and Keane folded.

"Deal me out the next hand," he said as he rose and moved to the door. One of the Gribalti brothers took the chair Jo had vacated, and Jamie slipped into Keane's. Curious, he lifted the tip of the cards. He saw a jack-high straight. With a thoughtful frown, he watched the door swing shut.

Outside, Jo moved through the warm night. With a glance at the sky, she thought of the fireworks. They had been wonderful, she mused, stirring up the stars with exploding color. Though it was over and a new day hovered, she felt some magic remained in the night. Far from sleepy, she wandered toward the Big Top.

"Hello, pretty lady."

Jo looked into the shadows and narrowed her eyes. She could just barely make out a form. "Oh, you're Bob, aren't you?" She stopped and gave him a friendly smile. "You're new."

He stepped toward her. "I've been on for nearly three weeks." He was young, Jo guessed about her own age, with a solid build and sharp-featured face. Just that afternoon she had watched Maggie give him a shower.

Jo pushed her hands into the pockets of her cut-offs and continued to smile. It appeared he thought his tenure made him a veteran. "How do you like working with the elephants?"

"It's okay. I like putting up the tent."

Jo understood his feeling. "So do I. There's a game in the cookhouse," she told him with a gesture of her arm. "You might like to sit in."

"I'd rather be with you." As he moved closer, Jo caught the faint whiff of beer. He's been celebrating, she thought and shook her head.

"It's a good thing tomorrow's Monday," she commented. "No one's going to be in any shape to pitch a tent. You should go to bed," she suggested. "Or get some coffee."

"Let's go to your trailer." Bob weaved a little, then took her arm.

"No." Firmly, Jo turned in the opposite direction. "Let's go to the cookhouse." His advances did not trouble her. She was close enough to the cookhouse tent that if she called out, a dozen able-bodied men would come charging. But that was precisely what Jo wanted to avoid.

"I want to go with you," he said, stumbling over the words as he veered away from the cookhouse again. "You look so pretty in that cage with those lions." He put both arms around her, but Jo felt it was as much for balance as romance. "A fella needs a pretty lady once in a while."

"I'm going to feed you to my lions if you don't let me go," Jo warned.

"Bet you can be a real wildcat," he mumbled and made a fumbling dive for her mouth.

Though her patience was wearing thin, Jo endured the kiss that landed slightly to the left of bull's-eye. His hands, however, had better aim and grabbed the firm roundness of her bottom. Losing her temper, Jo pushed away but found his hold had taken root. In a quick move, she brought up her fist and caught him square on the jaw. With only a faint sound of surprise, Bob sat down hard on the ground.

"Well, so much for rescuing you," Keane commented from behind her.

Turning quickly, Jo pushed at her hair and gave an annoyed sigh. She would have preferred no witnesses. Even in the dim light, she could see he was furious. Instinctively, she stepped between him and the man who sat on the ground fingering his jaw and shaking the buzzing from his ears.

"He—Bob just got a bit overenthusiastic," she said hastily and put a restraining hand on Keane's arm. "He's been celebrating."

"I'm feeling a bit enthusiastic myself," Keane stated. As he made to brush her aside, Jo clung with more fervor.

"No, Keane, please."

Looking down, he fired a glare. "Jo, would you let go so that I can deal with this?"

"Not until you listen." The faint hint of laughter in her eyes only enraged him further, and Jo fought to suppress it. "Keane, please, don't be hard on him. He didn't hurt me."

"He was attacking you," Keane interrupted. He barely resisted the urge to shake her off and drag the still seated Bob by the scruff of the neck.

"No, he was really more just leaning on me. His balance is a trifle impaired. He only tried to kiss me," she pointed out, wisely deleting the wandering hands. "And I hit him much harder than I should have. He's new, Keane, don't fire him."

Exasperated, he stared at her. "Firing was the least of what I had in mind for him."

Jo smiled, unable to keep the gleam from her eyes. "If you were going to avenge my honor, he really didn't do much more than breathe on it. I don't think you should run him through for that. Maybe you could just put him in the stocks for a couple of days."

Keane swore under his breath, but a reluctant smile tugged at his mouth. Seeing it, Jo loosened her hold. "Miss Wilder wants to give you a break," he told the dazed Bob in a tough, no-nonsense voice that Jo decided he used for intimidating witnesses. "She has a softer heart than I do. Therefore, I won't knock you down several more times or kick you off the lot, as I had entertained doing." He paused, allowing Bob time to consider this possibility. "Instead, I'll let you sleep off your—enthusiasm." In one quick jerk, he pulled Bob to his feet. "But if I ever hear of you breathing uninvited on Miss Wilder or any other of my female employees, we'll go back to the first choice. And before I kick you out," he added with low menace, "I'll let it be known that you were decked by one punch from a hundred-pound woman."

"Yes, sir, Mr. Prescott," said Bob as clearly as possible.

"Go to bed," Jo said kindly, seeing him pale. "You'll feel better in the morning."

"Obviously," Keane commented as Bob lurched away, "you haven't done much drinking." He turned to Jo and grinned. "The one thing he's not going to feel in the morning is better." Jo smiled, pleased to have Keane talk to her without the thin shield of politeness. "And where," he asked and took her hand for examination, "did you learn that right jab?"

Jo laughed, allowing Keane's fingers to interlock with hers. "It would hardly have knocked him down if he hadn't already been tilting in that direction." Her face turned up to his and sparkled with starlight. In his eyes an expression she couldn't comprehend came and went. "Is something wrong?"

For a moment he said nothing. In her breast her heart began to hammer as she waited to be kissed. "No, nothing," he said. The moment was shattered. "Come on, I'll walk you back to your trailer."

"I wasn't going there." Wanting to put him back into an easy mood, she linked her arm with his. "If you come with me, I'll show you some magic." Her smile slanted invitingly. "You like magic, don't you, Keane? Even a sober, dedicated lawyer must like magic."

"Is that how I strike you?" Jo almost laughed at the trace of annoyance in his voice. "As a sober, dedicated lawyer?"

"Oh, not entirely, though that's part of you." She enjoyed feeling that for the moment she had him to herself. "You've also got a streak of adventure and a rather nice sense of humor. And," she added with generous emphasis, "there's your temper."

"You seem to have me all figured out."

"Oh, no." Jo stopped and turned to him. "Not at all. I only know how you are here. I can only speculate on how you are in Chicago."

His brow lifted as she caught his attention. "Would I be different there?"

"I don't know." Jo's forehead wrinkled in thought. "Wouldn't you be? Circumstances would. You probably have a house or a big apartment, and there's a housekeeper who comes in once—no, twice—a week." Caught up in the picture, she gazed off into the distance and built it further. "You have an office with a view of the city, a very efficient secretary and a brilliant law clerk. You go to business lunches at the club. In court you're deadly and very successful. You have your own tailor and work out at the gym three times a week. There's the theater on the weekends, along with something physical. Tennis maybe, not golf. No, handball."

Keane shook his head. "Is this the magic?"

"No." Jo shrugged and began to walk again. "Just guesswork. You don't have to have a great deal of money to know how people who do behave. And I know you take the law seriously. You wouldn't choose a career that wasn't very important to you."

Keane walked in silence. When he spoke, his voice was quiet. "I'm not certain I'm comfortable with your little outline of my life."

"It's very sketchy," Jo told him. "I'd have to understand you better to fill in the gaps."

"Don't you?"

"What?" Jo asked, pausing. "Understand you?" She laughed, tickled at the absurdity of his question. "No, I don't understand you. How could I? You live in a different world." With this, she tossed aside the flap of the Big Top and stepped into its darkness. When she hit the switch, two rows of overhead lights flashed on. Shadows haunted the corners and fell over the arena seats.

"It's wonderful, isn't it?" Her clear voice ran the length of the tent and echoed back. "It's not empty, you know. They're always here—the troupers, the audience, the animals." She walked forward until she stood beside the third ring. "Do you know what this is?" she asked Keane, tossing out her arms and turning a full circle. "It's an ageless wonder in a changing world. No matter what happens on the outside, this is here. We're the most fragile of circuses, at the mercy of the elephants, of emotions, of mechanics, of public whims. But six days a week for twenty-nine weeks we perform miracles. We build a world at dawn, then disappear into the dark. That's part of it—the mystery." She waited until Keane moved forward to join her.

"Tents pop up on an empty lot, elephants and lions walk down Main Street. And we never grow old, because each new generation discovers us all over again." She stood slender and exquisite in a circle of light. "Life here's crazy. And it's hard. Muddy lots, insane hours, sore muscles, but when you've finished your act and you get that feeling that tells you it was special, there's nothing else like it in the world."

"Is that why you do it?" Keane asked.

Jo shook her head and moved out of the circle of light into the dark and into another ring. "It's all part of the same thing. We all have our own reasons, I suppose. You've asked me that before; I'm not certain I can explain. Maybe it's that we all believe in miracles." She turned under the light, and it shimmered around her. "I've been here all my life. I know every trick, every illusion. I know how Jamie's dad gets twenty clowns into a two-seater car. But each time I see it, I laugh and I believe it. It's not just the excitement, Keane, it's the anticipation of the excitement. It's knowing you're going to see the biggest or the smallest or the fastest or the highest." Jo ran to the center ring and threw up her arms.

"Ladies and gentlemen," she announced with a toss of her head. "For your amazement and astonishment, for the first time in America, a superabundance of mountainous, mighty pachyderms led in a stupendous exhibition of choreography by the Great Serena." Jo laughed and shifted her hair to her back with a quick movement of her hand. "Dancing elephants!" she said to Keane, pleased that he was smiling. "Or you listen to the talker in the sideshow when he starts his spiel. Step right up. Come a little closer." She curled her fingers in invitation. "See the Amazing Serpentina and her monstrous, slithering vipers. Watch the beautiful young girl charm a deadly cobra. Watch her accept the reptilian embrace of the gargantuan boa. Don't miss the chance to see the enchantress of the evil serpent!"

"I suppose Baby might sue for slander."

Jo laughed and stepped up on the ring. "But when the crowds see little Rose with a boa constrictor wrapped around her shoulders, they've gotten their money's worth. We give them what they come for: color, fantasy, the unique. Thrills. You've seen the audience when Vito does his high wire act without a net."

"A net seems little enough protection when he's balancing on a wire at two hundred feet." Keane stuck his hands in his pockets and frowned. "He risks his life every day."

"So does a police officer or a fire fighter." Jo spoke quietly and rested her hands on his shoulders. It seemed more necessary than ever that she make him understand his father's dream. "I know what you're saying, Keane, but you have to understand us. The element of danger is essential to many of the acts. You can hear the whole audience suck in their breath when Vito does his back somersault on the wire. They'd be impressed if he used a net, but they wouldn't be terrified."

"Do they need to be?"

Jo's sober expression lightened. "Oh, yes! They need to be terrified and fascinated and mesmerized. It's all included in the price of a ticket. This is a world of superlatives. We test the limit of human daring, and every day it changes. Do you know how long it took before the first man accomplished the triple on the trapeze? Now it's nearly a standard." A light of anticipation flared in her eyes. "One day someone will do a quadruple. If a man stands in this ring and juggles three torches today, tomorrow someone will juggle them on horseback and after that there'll be a team tossing them back and forth while swinging on a trap. It's our job to do the incredible, then, when it's done, to do the impossible. It's that simple."

"Simple," Keane murmured, then lifted a hand to caress her hair. "I wonder if you'd think so if you could see it from the outside."

"I don't know." Her fingers tightened on his shoulders as he buried his other hand in her hair. "I never have."

As if his thoughts centered on it, Keane combed his fingers through her hair. Gradually, he pushed it back until only his hands framed her face. They stood in a pool of light that threw their shadows long behind them. "You are so lovely," he murmured.

Jo neither spoke nor moved. There was something different this time in the way he touched her. There was a gentleness and a hesitation she had not felt before. Though they looked directly into hers, she could not read his eyes. Their faces were close, and his breath fluttered against her mouth. Jo slid her arms around his neck and pressed her mouth to his.

Not until that moment had she realized how empty she had felt, how desperately she had needed to hold him. Her lips were hungry for his. She clung while all gentleness fled from his touch. His hands were greedy. The weeks that he had not touched her were forgotten as her skin warmed and hummed with quickening blood. Passion stripped her of inhibitions, and her tongue sought his, taking the kiss into wilder and darker depths.

Their lips parted, only to meet again with sharp new demands. She understood that all needs and all desires were ultimately only one—Keane.

His mouth left hers, and for an instant he rested his cheek against her hair. For that moment Jo felt a contentment more complete than she had ever known. Abruptly, he drew away.

Puzzled, she watched as he drew out a cigar. She lifted a hand to run it through the hair he had just disturbed. He flicked on his lighter. "Keane?" She looked at him, knowing her eyes offered everything.

"You've had a long day," he began in an oddly polite tone. Jo winced as if he had struck her. "I'll walk you back to your trailer."

She stepped off the ring and away from him. Pain seared along her skin. "Why are you doing this?" To her humiliation, tears welled in her eyes and lodged in her throat. The tears acted as a prism, refracting the light and clouding her vision. She blinked them back. Keane's brows drew together at the gesture.

"I'll take you back," he said again. The detached tone of his voice accelerated all Jo's fury and grief.

"How dare you!" she demanded. "How dare you make me…" The word *love* nearly slipped through her lips, and she swallowed it. "How dare you make me want you, then turn away! I was right about you from the beginning. I thought I'd been wrong. You're cold and unfeeling." Her breath came quickly and unevenly, but she refused to retreat until she had said it all. Her face was pale with the passion of her emotions. "I don't know why I thought you'd ever understand what Frank had given you. You need a heart to see the intangible. I'll be glad when the season's over and you do whatever it is you're going to do. I'll be glad when I never have to see you again. I won't let you do this to me anymore!" Her voice wavered, but she made no attempt to steady it. "I don't want you to ever touch me again."

Keane studied her for a long moment, then took a careful drag on his cigar. "All right, Jo."

The very calmness of his answer tore a sob from her before she turned and ran from the Big Top.

Chapter 10

In July the troupe circled through Virginia, touched the tip of West Virginia on their way into Kentucky, then moved into Ohio. Audiences fanned themselves as the temperatures in the Big Top rose, but they still came.

Since the evening of the Fourth, Jo had avoided Keane. It was not as difficult as it might have been, as he spent half the month in Chicago dealing with his business. Jo functioned. She ate because eating was necessary in order to maintain her strength. She slept because rest was essential to remaining alert in the cage. She did not find any enjoyment in food nor was her sleep restful. Because so many in the troupe knew her well, Jo struggled to keep on a mask of normalcy. Above all, she needed to avoid any questions, any advice, any sympathy. It was necessary, because of her profession, to put her emotions on hold a great deal of the time. After some struggle and some failure, Jo achieved a reasonable success.

Her training of Gerry continued, as did his progress. The additional duty of working with him helped fill her small snatches of spare time. On afternoons when no matinee was scheduled, Jo took him into the big cage. As he grew more proficient, she brought other cats in to join Merlin. By the first week in August they were working together with her full complement of lions.

The only others who were rehearsing in the Big Top were the equestrian act. They ran through the Thread the Needle routine in the first ring. Hooves echoed dully on tanbark. Jo supervised while Gerry sent the cats into a pyramid. At his urging, Lazarus climbed up the wide, arched ladder that topped the grouping. Twice he balked, and twice Gerry was forced to reissue the command.

"Good," Jo commented when the pyramid was complete.

"He wouldn't go." Gerry began to complain, but she cut him off.

"Don't be in too much of a hurry. Bring them down." Her tone was brisk and professional. "Make certain they dismount and take their seats in the right order. It's important to stick to routine."

Hands resting on hips, Jo watched. In her opinion, Gerry had true potential. His nerves were good, he had a feeling for the animals, and he was slowly developing patience. Still she balked at the next step in his training: leaving him alone in the arena. Even with only Merlin, she felt it too risky. He was still too casual. Not yet did he possess enough respect for the lion's guile.

Jo moved around the arena, and the lions, used to her, were not disturbed. As the cats settled onto their pedestals, she once more moved to stand beside Gerry. "Now we'll walk down the line. You make each do a sit-up before we send them out."

One by one the cats rose on their haunches and pawed the air. Jo and Gerry moved down their ranks. The heat was becoming oppressive, and Jo shifted her shoulders, longing for a cool shower and a change of clothes. When they came to Hamlet, he ignored the command with a rebellious snarl.

Bad-tempered brute, thought Jo absently as she waited for Gerry to reissue the command. He did so but moved forward as if to emphasize the words.

"No, not so close!" Jo warned quickly. Even as she spoke, she saw the change in Hamlet's eyes.

Instinctively, she stepped over, nudging Gerry back and shielding his body with hers. Hamlet struck out, claws extended. There was a moment of blind heat in her shoulder as the skin ripped. Swiftly, she was facing the cat, holding tightly onto Gerry's arm as they stood just out of range.

"Don't run," she ordered, feeling his jerk of panic. Her arm was on fire as the blood began to flow freely. Keeping her movements quick but smooth, she took the whip from Gerry's nerveless hand and cracked it hard, using her left arm. She knew that if Hamlet continued his defiance and attacked, it was hopeless. The other cats were certain to join in a melee. It would be over before anything could be done. Already, Abra shifted restlessly and bared her teeth.

"Open the chute," Jo called out. Her voice was cool as ice. "Back toward the safety cage," she instructed Gerry as she gave the cats their signal to leave the arena. "I've got to get them out one at a time. Move slow, and if I tell you to stop, you stop dead. Understand?"

She heard him swallow as she watched the cats begin to leap off their pedestals and file into the chute. "He got you. Is it bad?" The words were barely a whisper and drenched in terror.

"I said go." Half the cats were gone, and still Hamlet's eyes were locked on hers. There was no time to waste. One part of her brain heard shouting outside the cage, but she blocked it out and focused all her concentration on the cat. "Go now," she repeated to Gerry. "Do as you're told."

He swallowed again and began to back away. Long seconds dragged until she heard the rattle of the safety cage door. When his turn came, Hamlet made no move to leave his seat. Jo was alone with him. She could smell the heat, the scent of the wild and the fragrance of her own blood. Her arm was alive with pain. Slowly, she tested him by backing up. The safety cage seemed hundreds of miles away. The cat tensed immediately, and she stopped. She knew he would not let her cross the arena. Outrunning him was impossible, as the distance between them could be covered in one spring. She had to outbluff him instead.

"Out," she ordered firmly. "Out, Hamlet." As he continued to watch her, Jo felt a trickle of sweat slide down between her shoulder blades. Her skin was clammy with it in contrast to the warmth of the blood that ran down her arm. There was a sudden, vivid picture inside her head of her father being dragged around the cage. Fear tripped inside her throat. There was a lightness fluttering in the top of her head, and she knew that a moment's terror would cause her to faint. She stiffened her spine and pushed it away.

Speed was important. The longer she allowed the cat to remain in the arena after his cue, the more defiant he would become. And the more dangerous. As yet he was unaware that he held her at such a sharp disadvantage. "Out, Hamlet." Jo repeated the command with a crack of the whip. He leaped from the pedestal. Jo's stomach trembled. She locked every muscle, and as the cat hesitated, she repeated the command. He was confused, and she knew this could work as an advantage or a curse. Confused, he might spring or retreat. Her fingers tightened on the stock of the whip and trembled. The cat paced nervously and watched her.

"Hamlet!" She raised her voice and bit off each syllable. "Go out." To the words she added the hand signal she had used before he was fully trained to voice command.

As if rebuffed, Hamlet relaxed his tail and padded into the chute. Before the door slid completely closed, Jo sank to her knees. Her body began to quake fiercely with the aftershock. No more than five minutes had passed since Hamlet had defied Gerry's command, but her muscles bore the strain of hours. For an instant her vision blurred. Even as she shook her head to clear it, Keane was on the ground beside her.

She heard him swear, ripping the tattered sleeve of her blouse from her arm. He fired questions at her, but she could do no more than shake her head and gulp in air. Focusing on him, she noticed his eyes were unusually dark against his face.

"What?" She followed his voice but not the words. He swore again, sharply enough to penetrate the first layer of her shock. He pulled her to her feet, then continuing the motion smoothly, lifted her into his arms. "Don't." Her mind struggled to break through the fog and function. "I'm all right."

"Shut up," he said harshly as he carried her from the cage. "Just shut up."

Because speaking cost her some effort, Jo obeyed. Closing her eyes, she let the mixture of excited voices whirl around her. Her arm screamed with pain, but the throbbing reassured her. Numbness would have terrified her. Still she kept her eyes shut, not yet having the courage to look at the damage. Being alive was enough.

When she opened her eyes again, Keane was carrying her into the administration wagon. At the sound of the chaos that followed them, Duffy strode through from his office. "What the..." he began, then stopped and paled beneath his freckles. He moved quickly forward as Keane set Jo in a chair. "How bad?"

"I don't know yet," Keane muttered. "Get a towel and the first-aid kit."

Buck had come in behind them and, already having secured the items, handed them to Keane. Then he moved to a cabinet and located a bottle of brandy.

"It's not too bad," Jo managed. Because her voice was tolerably steady, she screwed up her courage and looked down. Keane had fastened a rough bandage from the remains of her sleeve. Though the flow of blood had slowed, there were streaks of it down her arm, and too much spreading from the wound to be certain how extensive the cuts were. Nausea rocked in her stomach.

"How do you know?" Keane demanded between his teeth as he began to clean the wound. He wrung out the towel in the basin Buck set beside him.

"It's not bleeding that badly." Jo swallowed the queasiness. As her mind began to clear, she frowned at the tone of Keane's voice. Feeling her stare, he glanced up. In his eyes was such fury, she pulled away.

"Be still," he ordered roughly and gave his attention back to her arm.

The cat had delivered only a glancing blow, but even so, there were four long slices in her upper arm. Jo set her jaw as pain ripped through her. Keane's brusqueness brought more hurt, and she fought to show no reaction to either. The aftermath of fear was bubbling through her. She longed to be held, to be soothed by the hands that tended to her wound.

"She's going to need stitches," Keane said without looking at her.

"And an antitoxin shot," Buck added, handing Jo a generous glass of brandy. "Drink this, honey. It'll help settle you."

The gentleness in his voice nearly undid her. He laid his big hand against her cheek, and for a moment she pressed against it.

"Drink now," Buck ordered again. Obediently, Jo lifted the glass and swallowed. The room whirled, then snapped into focus. She made a small sound and pressed the glass to her forehead. "Tell me what happened in there." Buck crouched down beside her as Keane began to apply a temporary bandage.

Jo took a moment to draw air in and out of her lungs. She lowered the glass and spoke steadily. "Hamlet didn't respond, and Gerry repeated a command, but he stepped forward. Too close. I saw Hamlet's eyes, and I knew. I should have moved faster. I should have been watching him more carefully. It was a stupid mistake." She stared into the brandy as she berated herself.

"She stepped between the boy and the cat." Keane bit off the words as he completed the bandaging. Rising, he moved to the brandy and poured. Not once did he turn to look at Jo. Hurt, she stared at his back before looking back at Buck.

"How's Gerry?"

Buck urged the glass back to her lips. A faint tint of pink was creeping into her cheeks. "Pete's with him. Got his head between his knees. He'll be fine."

Jo nodded. "I guess I'll have to go to town and have this seen to." She handed the glass to Buck and wondered if she dare attempt to rise yet. With another deep breath, she glanced at Duffy. "Make sure he's ready to go in when I get back."

Keane turned from the window. "Go in where?" His face was set in hard lines.

In response, Jo's voice was chilled. "In the cage." She turned her eyes to Buck. "We should be able to have a short run-through before the evening show."

"No." Jo's head snapped up as Keane spoke. For a long moment they stared at each other with odd, unreasonable antagonism. "You're not going back in there today." His voice held curt authority.

"Of course I am," Jo countered, managing to keep the combination of pain and anger from her words. "And if Gerry wants to be a cat man, he's going in, too."

"Jo's right," Buck put in, trying to soothe what he sensed was an explosive situation. "It's like falling off a horse. You can't wait too long before you get back up, or you won't ride again."

Keane never took his eyes from Jo. He continued as if Buck hadn't spoken. "I won't permit it."

"You can't stop me." Indignation forced her to her feet. The brisk movement caused her arm to protest, and her struggle against it showed momentarily in her eyes.

"Yes, I can." Keane took a long swallow of brandy. "I own this circus."

Jo's fists tightened at his tone, at his careless use of his authority. Not once since he had knelt beside her in the cage had he given her any sign of comfort or reassurance. She had needed it from him. To masquerade its trembling, she kept her voice low. "But you don't own me, Mr. Prescott. And if you'll check your papers and the legalities, you'll see you don't own the lions or my equipment. I bought them, and I maintain them out of my salary. My contract doesn't give you the right to tell me when I can or can't rehearse my cats."

Keane's face was granite hard. "Neither does it give you the right to set up in the Big Top without my permission."

"Then I'll set up someplace else," she tossed back. "But I *will* set up. That cat will be worked again today. I won't take the risk of losing months of training."

"But you will risk being killed," Keane shot back and slammed down his glass.

"What do you care?" Jo shouted. All control deserted her. The cuts were deep on her emotions as well as her flesh. She had passed through a terror more acute than she had known since the night of her parents' death. More than anything else, she wanted to feel Keane's arms around her. She wanted to know the security she had felt when he had let her weep out her grief for Ari in his arms. "I'm nothing to you!" Her head shook quickly, tossing her hair. There was a bubble of hysteria in her voice, and Buck reached out to lay a hand on her shoulder.

"Jo," he warned in his soft, rumbling voice.

"No!" She shook her head and spoke rapidly. "He hasn't the right. You haven't the right to interfere with my life." She flared at Keane again with eyes vivid with emotion. "I know what I have to do. I know what I *will* do. Why should it matter to you? You aren't legally responsible if I get mauled. No one's going to sue you."

"Hold on, Jo." This time Buck spoke firmly. As he took her uninjured arm, he felt the tremors shooting through her. "She's too upset to know what she's saying," he told Keane.

There was a mask over Keane's face which concealed all emotion. "Oh, I think she knows what she's saying," he disagreed quietly. For a moment there was only the sound of Jo shuddering and the splash of brandy being poured into a glass. "You do what you have to do, Jo," he said after drinking again. "You're perfectly correct that I haven't any rights where you're concerned. Take her into town," he told Buck, then turned back to the window.

"Come on, Jo." Buck urged her to the door, slipping a supportive arm around her waist. Even as they stepped outside, Rose came running from the direction of the midway.

"Jo!" Her face was white with concern. "Jo, I just heard." She glanced at the bandage with wide, terrified eyes. "How bad is it?"

"Just scratches, really," Jo assured her. She added the best smile she could muster. "Buck's going to take me into town for a couple of stitches."

"Are you sure?" She looked up at the tall man for reassurance. "Buck?"

"Several stitches," he corrected but patted Rose's hand. "But it's not too bad."

"Do you want me to come with you?" She fell into step beside them as Buck began to lead Jo again.

"No. Thank you, Rose." Jo smiled with more feeling. "I'll be fine."

Because of the smile, Rose was able to relax. "I thought when I heard… well, I imagined all sorts of terrible things. I'm glad you're not badly hurt." They had reached Buck's truck, and Rose leaned over to kiss Jo's cheek. "We all love you so."

"I know." Squeezing her hand, Jo let Buck help her into the cab of his truck. As he maneuvered from the lot, Jo rested her head against the back of the seat and shut her eyes. Never could she remember feeling more spent, more battered.

"Hurt bad?" Buck asked as they switched to an asphalt road.

"Yes," she answered simply, thinking of her heart as much as her arm.

"You'll feel better when you're patched up."

Jo kept her eyes shut, knowing some wounds never heal. Or if they did, they left scars that ached at unexpected times.

"You shouldn't have gone off on him that way, Jo." There was light censure in Buck's voice.

"He shouldn't have interfered," Jo retorted. "It's none of his business. *I'm* none of his business."

"Jo, it's not like you to be so hard."

"Hard?" She opened her eyes and turned to Buck. "What about him? Couldn't he have been kinder, shown even the barest trace of compassion? Did he have to speak to me as if I were a criminal?"

"Jo, the man was terrified. You're only looking at this from one side." He scratched his beard and gave a gusty sigh. "You can't know what it's like to be outside that cage, helpless when someone you care about is facing down death. I had to all but knock him unconscious to keep him out of there until we got it through his head that he'd just get you killed for sure. He was scared, Jo. We were all scared."

Jo shook her head, certain Buck exaggerated because of his affection for her. Keane's voice had been hard, his eyes angry. "He doesn't care," she corrected quietly. "Not like the rest of you. You didn't swear at me. You weren't cold."

"Jo, people have different ways—" Buck began, but she interrupted.

"I know he wouldn't want to see me hurt, Buck. He's not heartless or cruel." She sighed as all the force of anger and fear washed out of her body and left her empty. "Please, I don't want to talk about him."

Buck heard the weariness in her voice and patted her hand. "Okay, honey, just relax. We'll have you all fixed up in no time."

Not all fixed up, Jo thought. Far from all fixed up.

Chapter 11

As the weeks passed, Jo's arm lost its stiffness. She healed cleanly. The only traces were thin scars that promised to fade but not disappear. She found, however, that some spark had gone out of her life. Constantly, she fought against a vague dissatisfaction. Nothing—not her work, not her friends, not her books—brought about the contentment she had grown up with. She had become a woman, and her needs had shifted. Jo knew the root of her problem was Keane, but the knowledge was not a solution. He had left the circus again on the very night of her accident. Nearly four weeks later he had not returned.

Three times Jo had sat down to write him, needing to assuage her guilt for the harsh things she had said to him. Three times she had torn up the paper in frustration. No matter how she rearranged the words, they were wrong. Instead, she clung to the hope that he would come back one last time. If, she felt, they could part as friends, without bitterness or hard words, she could accept the separation. Willing this to happen, she was able to return to her routine with some tranquility. She rehearsed, performed, joined in the daily duties of circus life. She waited. The caravan moved closer to Chicago.

Jo stood in the steaming Big Top on a late August afternoon. Dressed in a leotard, she worked on ground exercises with the Beirot Brothers.

It was this daily regimentation that had aided in keeping her arm limber. She could now move into a back walk-over without feeling any protest in her injured arm.

"I feel good," Jo told Raoul as they worked out. "I feel really good." She did a quick series of pirouettes.

"You don't keep your shoulder in shape by dancing on your feet," Raoul challenged.

"My shoulder's fine," she tossed back, then proved her point by bending into a handstand. Slowly, she lowered her legs to a forty-five degree angle, bringing one foot to rest on the knee of the opposite leg. "It's perfect." She executed a forward roll and sprang to her feet. "I'm strong as an ox," she claimed and did a quick back handspring followed by a back flip.

She landed at Keane's feet.

The cascade of emotions that raced through her reflected briefly in her eyes before she regained her balance. "I didn't—I didn't know you were back." Instantly, she regretted the inanity of the words but could find no others. The longing was raw in her to hurl herself into his arms. She wondered that he could not feel her need through the pores of her skin.

"I just got in." His eyes continued to search her face after his hands dropped to his sides. "This is my mother," he added. "Rachael Loring, Jovilette Wilder."

At his words, Jo's gaze moved from his face. She saw the woman beside him. If she had seen Rachael Loring in a crowd of two thousand, she would have known her for Keane's mother. The bone structure was the same, though hers was more elegant. Her brows were golden wings, flaring out at the end, as Keane's did. Her hair was smooth, brushed up and away from her face with no gray to mar its tawny perfection. But it was the eyes that sent a jolt through Jo. She had not thought to see them in anyone's face but Keane's. The woman was dressed simply in an unpretentiously tailored suit that bespoke taste and wealth. There was, however, none of the cool, distant polish that Jo had always attributed to the woman who had taken her son and left Frank. There was a charm to the smile that curved in greeting.

"Jovilette, such a lovely name. Keane's told me of you." She extended her hand, and Jo accepted, intending a quick, impersonal shake. Rachael Loring, however, laid her other hand atop their joined ones and added warmth. "Keane tells me you were very close to Frank. Perhaps we could talk."

The affection in her voice confused Jo into a stumbling reply. "I—Yes. I—if you'd like."

"I should like very much." She squeezed Jo's hand again before releasing it. "Perhaps you have time to show me around?" She smiled with the question, and Jo found it increasingly difficult to remain aloof. "I'm sure there've been some changes since I was here last. You must have some business to attend to," she said, looking up at Keane. "I'm sure Jovilette will take good care of me. Won't you, dear?" Without waiting for either to respond, Rachael tucked her arm through Jo's and began to walk. "I knew your parents," she said as Keane watched them move away. "Not terribly well, I'm afraid. They came here the same year I left. But I recall they were both thrilling performers. Keane tells me you've followed your father's profession."

"Yes, I..." She hesitated, feeling oddly at a disadvantage. "I did," she finished lamely.

"You're so young." Rachael gave her a gentle smile. "How terribly brave you must be."

"No...no, not really. It's my job."

"Yes, of course." Rachael laughed at some private memory. "I've heard that before."

They were outside now, and she paused to look thoughtfully around her. "I think perhaps I was wrong. It hasn't really changed, not in thirty years. It's a wonderful place, isn't it?"

"Why did you leave?" As soon as the words were spoken, Jo regretted them. "I'm sorry," she said quickly. "I shouldn't have asked."

"Of course you should." Rachael sighed and patted Jo's hand. "It's only natural. Duffy's still here, Keane tells me." At the change in subject, Jo imagined her question had been evaded.

"Yes, I suppose he always will be."

"Could we have some coffee, or some tea, perhaps?" Rachael smiled again. "It's such a long drive from town. Is your trailer nearby?"

"It's just over in the back yard."

"Oh, yes." Rachael laughed and began to walk again. "The neighborhood that never changes over thousands of miles. Do you know the story of the dog and the bones?" she asked. Though Jo knew it well, she said nothing. "One version is that a roustabout gave his dog a bone every night after dinner. The dog would bury the bone under the trailer, then the next day try to dig it back up. Of course, it was fifty miles behind in an empty lot. He never figured it out." Quietly, she laughed to herself.

Feeling awkward, Jo opened the door to her trailer. How could this woman be the one she had resented all of her life? How could this be the cold, heartless woman who had left Frank? Oddly, Rachael seemed totally at ease in the narrow confines of the trailer.

"How efficient these are." She looked around with interest and approval. "You must barely realize you're on wheels." Casually, she picked up the volume of Thoreau which lay on Jo's counter. "Keane told me you have an avid interest in literature. In language, too," she added, glancing up from the book. Her eyes were golden and direct like her son's. Jo was tossed back suddenly to the first morning of the season when she had looked down and found Keane's eyes on her.

It made her uncomfortable to learn Keane had discussed her with his mother. "I have some tea," Jo told her as she moved toward the kitchen. "It's a better gamble than my coffee."

"That's fine," Rachael said agreeably and followed her. "I'll just sit here while you fix it." She settled herself with apparent ease at the tiny table across from the kitchen.

"I'm afraid I haven't anything else to offer you." Jo kept her back turned as she routed through her cupboard.

"Tea and conversation," Rachael answered in mild tones, "will be fine."

Jo sighed and turned. "I'm sorry." She shook her head. "I'm being rude. I just don't know what to say to you, Mrs. Loring. I've resented you for as long as I can remember. Now you're here and not at all as I imagined." She managed to smile, albeit ruefully. "You're not cold and hateful, and you look so much like…" She stopped, horrified that she had nearly blurted out Keane's name. For a moment her eyes were utterly naked.

Rachael smoothed over the awkwardness. "I don't wonder you resented me if you were as close to Frank as Keane tells me. Jovilette," she said softly, "did Frank resent me, too?"

Helpless, Jo responded to the hint of sadness. "No. Not while I knew him. I don't think Frank was capable of resentments."

"You understood him well, didn't you?" Rachael watched as Jo poured boiling water into mugs. "I understood him, too," she continued as Jo brought the mugs to the table. "He was a dreamer, a marvelous free spirit." Absently, she stirred her tea.

Consumed with curiosity, Jo sat across from her and waited for the story she sensed was coming.

"I was eighteen when I met him. I had come to the circus with a cousin. The Colossus was a bit smaller in those days," she added with a reminiscent smile, "but it was all the same. Oh, the magic!" She shook her head and sighed. "We tumbled into love so fast, married against all my family's objections and went on the road. It was exciting. I learned the web routine and helped out in wardrobe."

Jo's eyes widened. "You performed?"

"Oh, yes." Rachael's cheeks tinted a bit with pride. "I was quite good. Then I became pregnant. We were both like children waiting for Christmas. I wasn't quite nineteen when I had Keane, and I'd been with the circus for nearly a year. Things became difficult over the next season. I was young and a bit frightened of Keane. I panicked if he sneezed and was constantly dragging Frank into town to see doctors. How patient he was."

Rachael leaned forward and took Jo's hand. "Can you understand how hard this life is for one not meant for it? Can you see that through the magic of it, the excitement and wonder, there are hardships and fears and impossible demands? I was little more than a child myself, with an infant to care for, without the endurance or vocation of a trouper, without the experience or confidence of a mother. I lived on nerves for an entire season." She let out a little rush of breath. "When it was over, I went home to Chicago."

For the first time, Jo imagined the flight from Rachael's point of view. She could see a girl, younger than herself, in a strange, demanding world with a baby to care for. Over the years Jo had seen scores of people try the life she'd led and last only weeks. Still she shook her head in confusion.

"I think I understand how difficult it must have been for you. But if you and Frank loved each other, couldn't you have worked it out somehow?"

"How?" Rachael countered. "Should I have taken a house somewhere and lived with him half a year? I would have hated him. Should he have given up his life here and settled down with me and Keane? It would have destroyed everything I loved about him." Rachael shook her head, giving Jo a soft smile. "We did love each other, Jovilette, but not enough. Compromise isn't always possible, and neither of us were capable of adjusting to the needs of the other. I tried, and Frank would have tried had I asked him. But it was lost before it had really begun. We did the wisest thing under the circumstances." Looking into Jo's eyes, she saw youth and confidence. "It seems cold and hard to you, but it was no use dragging out a painful situation. He gave me Keane and two years I've always treasured. I gave him his freedom without bitterness. Ten years after Frank, I found happiness again." She smiled softly with the memory. "I loved Frank, and that love remains as young and sweet as the day I met him."

Jo swallowed. She searched for some way to apologize for a grudge held for a lifetime. "He—Frank kept a scrapbook on Keane. He followed the Chicago papers."

"Did he?" Rachael beamed, then leaned back in her chair and lifted her mug. "How like him. Was he happy, Jovilette? Did he have what he wanted?"

"Yes," Jo answered without hesitation. "Did you?"

Rachael's eyes came back to Jo's. For a moment the look was speculative, then it grew warm. "What a good heart you have, generous and understanding. Yes, I had what I wanted. And you, Jovilette, what do you want?"

At ease now, Jo shook her head and smiled. "More than I can have."

"You're too smart for that," Rachael observed, studying her. "I think you're a fighter, not a dreamer. When the time comes to make your choice, you won't settle for anything less than all." She smiled at Jo's intent look, then rose. "Will you show me your lions? I can't tell you how I'm looking forward to seeing you perform."

"Yes, of course." Jo stood, then hesitated. She held out her hand. "I'm glad you came."

Rachael accepted the gesture. "So am I."

Throughout the rest of the day Jo looked for Keane without success. After meeting and talking with his mother, it had become even more imperative that she speak with him. Her conscience would have no rest until she made amends. By showtime she had not yet found him.

Each act seemed to run on and on as she fretted for the finish. He would be with his mother in the audience, and undoubtedly she would find him after the show. She strained with impatience as the acts dragged.

After the finale she stood at the back door, unsure whether to wait or to go to his trailer. She was struck with both relief and alarm when she saw him approaching.

"Jovilette." Rachael spoke first, taking Jo's hands in hers. "How marvelous you were, and how stunning. I see why Keane said you had an untamed beauty."

Surprised, Jo glanced up at Keane but met impassive amber eyes. "I'm glad you enjoyed it."

"Oh, I can't tell you how much. The day has brought me some very precious memories. Our talk this afternoon meant a great deal to me." To Jo's surprise, Rachael leaned over and kissed her. "I hope to see you again. I'm going to say goodbye to Duffy before you drive me back, Keane," she continued. "I'll meet you in the car. Goodbye, Jovilette."

"Goodbye, Mrs. Loring." Jo watched her go before she turned to Keane. "She's a wonderful person. She makes me ashamed."

"There's no need for that." He tucked his hands into his pockets and watched her. "We both had our reasons for resentments, and we were both wrong. How's your arm?"

"Oh." Jo's fingers traveled to the wound automatically. "It's fine. There's barely any scarring."

"Good." The word was short and followed by silence. For a moment Jo felt her courage fail her.

"Keane," she began, then forced herself to meet his eyes directly. "I want to apologize for the horrible way I behaved after the accident."

"I told you once before," he said coolly, "I don't care for apologies."

"Please." Jo swallowed her pride and touched his arm. "I've been saving this one for a very long time. I didn't mean those things I said," she added quickly. "I hope you'll forgive me." It wasn't the eloquent apology she had planned, but it was all she could manage. His expression never altered.

"There's nothing to forgive."

"Keane, please." Jo grabbed his arm again as he turned to go. "Don't leave me feeling as if you don't forgive me. I know I said dreadful things. You have every right to be furious, but couldn't you—can't we be friends again?"

Something flickered over his face. Lifting his hand, he touched the back of it to her cheek. "You have a habit of disconcerting me, Jovilette." He dropped his hand, then thrust it into his pocket. "I've left something for you with Duffy. Be happy." He walked away from her while she dealt with the finality of his tone. He was walking out of her life. She watched him until he disappeared.

Jo had thought she would feel something, but there was nothing; no pain, no tears, no desperation. She had not known a human being could be so empty and still live.

"Jo." Duffy lumbered up to her, then held out a thick envelope. "Keane left this for you." Then he moved past her, anxious to see that all straggling towners were nudged on their way.

Jo felt all emotions had been stripped away. Absently, she glanced at the envelope as she walked to her trailer. Without enthusiasm, she stepped inside, then tore it open. She remained standing as she pulled out the contents. It took her several moments to decipher the legal jargon. She read the group of papers through twice before sitting down.

He's given it to me, she thought. Still she could not comprehend the magnitude of it. *He's given me the circus.*

Chapter 12

O'Hare Airport was an army of people and a cacophony of sound. Nearly losing herself in the chaos of it, Jo struggled through the masses and competed for a cab. At first she had merely gawked at the snow like a towner seeing his first sword swallower. Then, though she shivered inside the corduroy coat she had bought for the trip, she began to enjoy it. It was beautiful as it lay over the city, and it helped to turn her mind from the purpose of her journey. Never had she been north so late in the year. Chicago in November was a sensational sight.

She had learned, after the initial shock had worn off, that Keane had not only given her the circus but a responsibility as well. Almost immediately there had been contracts to negotiate. She had been tossed into a sea of paperwork, forced to rely heavily on Duffy's experience as she tried to regain her balance. As the season had come to a close, Jo had attempted a dozen times to call Chicago. Each time, she had hung up before Keane's number could be dialed. It would be, she had decided, more appropriate to see him in person. Her trip had been postponed a few weeks due to Jamie and Rose's wedding.

It was there, as she had stood as maid of honor, that Jo had realized what she must do. There was only one thing she truly wanted, and that was to be with Keane. Watching Rose's face as their vows had been exchanged, Jo had recalled her unflagging determination to win the man she loved.

And will I stay here? Jo had demanded of herself thousands of miles away from him. No. Her heart had begun to thud as she had mapped out a plan. She would go to Chicago to see him. She would not be turned away. He had wanted her once; she would make him want her again. She would not live out her life without at least some small portion of it being part of his. He didn't have to love her. It was enough that she loved him.

And so, shivering against the unfamiliar cold, Jo scrambled into a cab and headed across town. She brushed her hair free of snow with chilled fingers, thinking how idiotic she had been to forget to buy a hat and gloves. What if he isn't home? she thought suddenly. What if he's gone to Europe or Japan or California? Panic made her giddy, and she pushed it down. He has to be home. It's Sunday, and he's sitting at home reading or going over a brief—or entertaining a woman, she thought, appalled. I should stop and call. I should tell the driver to take me back to the airport. Closing her eyes, Jo fought to regain her calm. She took long, deep breaths and stared at the buildings and sidewalks. Gradually, she felt the tiny gurgle of hysteria dissipate.

I won't be afraid, she told herself and tried to believe it. I won't be afraid. But Jovilette, the woman who reclined on a living rug of lions, was very much afraid. What if he rejected her? I won't let him reject me, she told herself with a confident lift of her chin. *I'll seduce him.* She pressed her fingers to her temples. *I wouldn't know how to begin.* I've got to tell the driver to turn around.

But before she could form the words, the cab pulled up to a curb. With the precision of a robot, Jo paid the fare, overtipping in her agitation, and climbed out.

Long after the cab had pulled away, she stood staring up at the massive glass-girdled building. Snow waltzed around her, sprinkling her hair and shoulders. A jostle from a rushing pedestrian broke the spell. She picked up her suitcases and hurried through the front door of the apartment buildings.

The lobby was enormous, with smoked glass walls and a deep shag carpet. Not knowing she should give her name at the desk, Jo wandered toward the elevators, innocently avoiding detection by merging with a group of tenants. Once inside the car, Jo pushed the button for the penthouse with a nerveless forefinger. The chatter of those in the elevator with her registered only as a distant humming. She never noticed when the car stopped for their departure.

When it stopped a second time and the doors slid open, she stared at the empty space for ten full seconds. Only as the automatic doors began to close did she snap out of her daze. Pushing them open again, she stepped through and into the hall. Her legs were wobbly, but she forced them to move forward in the direction of the penthouse. Panic sped up and down her spine until she set down her bags and leaned her brow against Keane's door. She urged air in and out of her lungs. She remembered that Rachael Loring had called her a fighter. Jo swallowed, lifted her chin and knocked. The wait was mercifully brief before Keane opened the door. She saw surprise light his eyes as he stared at her.

Her hair was dusted with snow as it lay over the shoulders of her coat. Her face glowed with the cold, and her eyes were bright, nearly feverish with her struggle for calm. Only once did her mouth tremble before she spoke.

"Hello, Keane."

He only stared, his eyes running over her in disbelief. He was leaner, she thought as she studied his face. As she filled herself with the sight of him, she saw he wore a sweatshirt and jeans. His feet were bare. He hadn't shaved, and her hand itched to test the roughness of his beard.

"What are you doing here?" Jo felt a resurgence of panic. His tone was harsh, and he had not answered her smile. She strained for poise.

"May I come in?" she asked, her smile cracking.

"What?" He seemed distracted by the question. His brows lowered into a frown.

"May I come in?" she repeated, barely defeating the urge to turn tail and run.

"Oh, yes, of course. I'm sorry." Running a hand through his hair, Keane stepped back and gestured her inside.

Instantly, Jo's shoes sank into the luxurious pile of the buff-colored carpet. For a moment she allowed herself to gaze around the room, using the time for the additional purpose of regaining her composure. It was an open, sweeping room with sharp, contrasting colors. There was a deep brown sectional sofa with a chrome and glass coffee table. There were high-backed chairs in soft creams and vivid slashes of blue in chunky floor pillows. There were paintings, one she thought she recognized as a Picasso, and a sculpture she was certain was a Rodin.

On the far right of the room there was an elevation of two steps. Just beyond was a huge expanse of glass that featured a spreading view of Chicago. Jo moved toward it with undisguised curiosity. Now, inexplicably, fear had lessened. She found that once she had stepped over the threshold she had committed herself. She was no longer afraid.

"It's wonderful," she said, turning back to him. "How marvelous to have a whole city at your feet every day. You must feel like a king."

"I've never thought of it that way." With half the room between them, he studied her. She looked small and fragile with the bustling city at her back.

"I would," she said, and now her smile came easily. "I'd stand at the window and feel regal and pompous."

At last she saw his lips soften and curve. "Jovilette," he said quietly. "What are you doing in my world?"

"I needed to talk to you," she answered simply. "I had to come here to do it."

He moved to her then, but slowly, with his eyes on hers. "It must be important."

"I thought so."

His brow lifted, then he shrugged. "Well, then, we'll talk. But first, let's have your coat."

Jo's cold fingers fumbled with the buttons and caused Keane to frown again. "Good heavens, you're frozen." He captured her hands between his and swore. "Where are your gloves?" he demanded like an irate parent. "It must be all of twelve degrees outside."

"I forgot to buy any," Jo told him as she dealt with the heavenly feeling of his hands restoring warmth to hers.

"Idiot. Don't you know better than to come to Chicago in November without gloves?"

"No." Jo responded to his anger with a cheerful smile. "I've never been to Chicago in November before. It's wonderful."

His eyes lifted from her hands to her face. He watched her for a long moment, then she heard him sigh. "I'd nearly convinced myself I could be cured."

Jo's eyes clouded with concern. "Have you been ill?"

Keane laughed with a shake of his head, then he pushed away the question and became brisk again. "Here, let's have your coat. I'll get you some coffee."

"You needn't bother," she began as he undid the buttons on the coat himself and drew it from her shoulders.

"I'd feel better if I was certain your circulation was restored." He paused and looked down at her as he laid her coat over his arm. She wore a green angora sweater with pearl buttons and a gray skirt in thin wool. The soft fabric draped softly at her breasts and over her hips and thighs. Her shoes were dainty and impractical sling-back heels.

"Is something wrong?"

"I've never seen you wear anything but a costume or jeans."

"Oh." Jo laughed and combed her fingers through her damp hair. "I expect I look different."

"Yes, you do." His voice was low, and there was a frown in his eyes. "Right now you look as if you've come from college for the holidays." He touched the ends of her hair, then turned away. "Sit down. I'll get the coffee."

A bit puzzled by his mercurial moods, Jo wandered about the room, finally ignoring a chair to kneel beside one of the pillows near the picture window. Though the carpet swallowed Keane's footsteps, she sensed his return.

"How wonderful to have a real winter, if just for the snow." She turned a radiant face his way. "I've always wondered what Christmas is like with snow and icicles." Images of snowflakes danced in her eyes. Seeing he carried two mugs of coffee, she rose and took one. "Thank you."

"Are you warm enough?" he asked after a moment.

Jo nodded and sat in one of the two chairs opposite the sofa. The novelty of the city made her mission seem like a grand adventure. Keane sat beside her, and for a moment they drank in companionable silence.

"What did you want to talk to me about, Jo?"

Jo swallowed, ignoring the faint trembling in her chest. "A couple of things. The circus, for one." She shifted in her chair until she faced him. "I didn't write because I felt it too important. I didn't phone for the same reason. Keane…" All her carefully thought-out speeches deserted her. "You can't just give something like that away. I can't take it from you."

"Why not?" He shrugged and sipped his coffee. "We both know it's always been yours. A piece of paper doesn't change that one way or the other."

"Keane, Frank left it to you."

"And I gave it to you."

Jo made a small sound of frustration. "Perhaps if I could pay you for it..."

"Someone asked me once what was the value of a dream or the price of a human spirit." Jo shifted her eyes to his helplessly. "I didn't have an answer then. Do you have one now?"

She sighed and shook her head. "I don't know what to say to you. 'Thank you' is far from adequate."

"It's not necessary, either," Keane told her. "I simply gave back what was yours in any case. What else was there, Jo? You said there were a couple of things."

This was it, Jo's brain told her. Carefully, she set down the coffee and rose. Waiting for her stomach to settle, she walked a few feet out into the room, then turned. She allowed herself a deep breath before she met Keane's eyes.

"I want to be your mistress," she said with absolute calm.

"*What?*" Both Keane's face and voice registered utter shock.

Jo swallowed and repeated. "I want to be your mistress. That's still the right term, isn't it, or is it antiquated? Is *lover* right? I've never done this before."

Slowly, Keane set his mug beside hers and rose. He did not move toward her but watched her with probing eyes. "Jo, you don't know what you're saying."

"Oh, yes, I do," she cut him off and nodded. "I might not have the terminology exactly right, but I do know what I mean, and I'm sure you do, too. I want to be with you," she continued and took a step toward him. "I want you to make love to me. I want to live with you if you'll let me, or at least close by."

"Jo, you're not talking sensibly." Sharply, Keane broke into her speech. Turning away, he thrust his hands into his pockets and balled them into fists. "You don't know what you're asking."

"Don't I appeal to you anymore?"

Keane whirled, infuriated with the trace of curiosity in her voice.

"How can you ask me that?" he demanded. "Of course you appeal to me! I'm not dead or in the throes of senility!"

She moved closer to him. "Then if I want you, and you want me, why can't we be lovers?"

Keane swore violently and grabbed her shoulders. "Do you think I could have you for a winter and then blithely let you go? Do you think I could untangle myself at the start of the season and watch you stroll out of my life? Haven't you the sense to see what you do to me?" He shook her hard with the question, stealing any breath she might have used to answer him.

"You make me crazy!" Abruptly, he dragged her against him. His mouth bruised hers, his fingers dug into her flesh. Jo's head spun with confusion and pain and ecstasy. It seemed centuries since she had tasted his mouth on hers. She heard him groan as he tore himself away. He turned, leaving her to find her own balance as the room swayed. "What do I have to do to be rid of you?" His words came in furious undertones.

Jo blew out a breath. "I don't think kissing me like that is a very good start."

"I'm aware of that," he murmured. She watched the rise and fall of his shoulders. "I've been trying to avoid doing it since I opened the door."

Quietly, Jo walked to him and put a hand on his arm. "You're tense," she discovered and automatically sought to soothe the muscles. "I'm sorry if I'm going about this the wrong way. I thought telling you outright would be better than trying to seduce you. I don't think I'd be very good at that."

Keane made a sound somewhere between a laugh and a moan. "Jovilette," he murmured before he turned and gathered her into his arms. "How do I resist you? How many times must I pull away before I'm free of you? Even the thought of you drives me mad."

"Keane." She sighed and shut her eyes. "I've wanted you to hold me for so long. I want to belong to you, even for just a little while."

"No." He pulled away, then forced her chin up with his thumb and forefinger. "Don't you see that once would be too much and a lifetime wouldn't be enough? I love you too much to let you go and enough to know I have to." Shock robbed her of speech. She only stared as he continued. "It was different when I didn't know, when I thought I was—how did you put it? 'Dazzled.'" He smiled briefly at the word. "I was certain if I could make love to you, I could get you out of my system. Then, the night Ari died, I held you while you slept. I realized I was in love with you, had been in love with you right from the beginning."

"But you..." Jo shook her head as if to clear it. "You never told me, and you seemed so cold, so distant."

"I couldn't touch you without wanting more." He pulled her close again and for a moment buried his face in her hair. "But I couldn't stay away. I knew if I wanted to have you, to really have you, one of us had to give up what we did, what we were. I wondered if I could give up the law; it was really all I ever wanted to do. I discovered I wanted you more."

"Oh, Keane." She shook her head, but he put her from him suddenly.

"Then I found out that wouldn't work, either." Keane turned, paced to the window and stared out. The snow was falling heavily. "Every time you walked into that cage, I walked into hell. I thought perhaps I'd get used to it, but it only got worse. I tried leaving, coming back here, but I could never shake you loose. I kept coming back. The day you were hurt..." Keane paused. Jo heard him draw in his breath, and when he continued, his voice was deeper. "I watched you step in front of that boy and take the blow. I can't tell you what I felt at that moment; there aren't words for it. All I could think of was getting to you. I wonder if Pete ever told you that I decked him before Buck got to me. He took it very well, considering. Then I had to—to just stand there and watch while that cat stalked you. I've never known that kind of fear before. The kind that empties you out, body and soul."

He lapsed into silence. "Then it was over," he continued, "and I got to you. You were so white, and you were bleeding in my arms." He muttered an oath, then was silent again. He shook his head. "I wanted to burn the place down, get you away, strangle the cats with my bare hands. Anything. I wanted to hold you, but I couldn't get past the fear and the unreasonable anger at having been helpless. Before my hands stopped shaking, you were making plans to go back into that damnable cage. I wanted to kill you myself then and be done with it."

Slowly, Keane turned and walked back to her. "I saw it happen again every time I closed my eyes for weeks afterward. I can show you exactly where the scars are." He lifted a finger and traced four lines on her upper arm precisely where the claws had ripped her skin. He dropped his hand and shook his head. "I can't watch you go in the cage, Jo." He lifted his hand again and let it linger over her hair. "If I let you stay with me now, I wouldn't be able to let you go back to your own life. And I can't ask you to give it up."

"I wish you would." Solemn-eyed, Jo watched him. "I very much wish you would."

"Jo." Shaking his head, he turned away. "I know what it means to you."

"No more than the law means to you, I imagine," she said briskly. "But you said you were willing to give that up."

"Yes, but..."

"Oh, very well." She pushed back her hair. "If you won't ask me, I'll have to ask you. Will you marry me?"

Keane turned back, giving her his lowered brow frown. "Jo, you can't..."

"Of course I can. This is the twentieth century. If I want to ask you to marry me, then I will. I did," she pointed out.

"Jo, I don't..."

"Yes or no, please, counselor. This isn't an easy question." She stepped forward until they stood toe to toe. "I'm in love with you, and I want to marry you and have several babies. Is that agreeable?"

Keane's mouth opened and closed. He gave her an odd smile and lifted his hands to her shoulders. "This is rather sudden."

Jo felt a wild surge of joy. "Perhaps it is," she admitted. "I'll give you a minute to think about it. But I might as well tell you, I won't take no for an answer."

Keane's fingers traced the curve of her neck. "It seems I have little choice."

"None at all," she corrected. Boldly, she locked her arms around him and pulled his mouth down to hers. The kiss was instantly urgent, instantly searching. Joined, they lowered to the rug and clung. For a long, long moment, their lips were united in a language too complex for words. Then, as if to reassure himself she was real, Keane searched the familiar curves of her body, tasted the longed-for flavor of her skin.

"Why did I think I could live without you?" he whispered. His mouth came desperately back to hers. "Be sure, Jo, be sure." Roughened with emotion, his voice was low while the words were spoken against her lips. "I'll never be able to let you go. I'm asking you for everything."

"No. No, it's not like that. Hold me tighter. Kiss me again," she demanded as his lips roamed her face. "Kiss me." She wondered if the sound of pleasure she heard was his or her own. She had not known a kiss could be so intimate, so terrifyingly exciting. No, she thought as she soared with the knowledge that he loved her. He wasn't asking everything, he was giving it.

"I'm leaving something behind," she told him when their lips parted, "and replacing it with something infinitely more important." She buried her face in the curve of his neck. "When you realize how much I love you, you'll understand."

Keane drew away and stared down at her. At last he spoke, but it was only her name. It was a soft sigh of a sound. She smiled at it and lifted a hand to his cheek. "If there's a way to compromise…"

"No." She shook her head, remembering his mother's words. "Sometimes there can't be a compromise. We love each other enough not to need one. Please, don't think I'm making a sacrifice; I'm not." She smiled a little and rubbed her palm experimentally over the stubble of his neglected beard. "I don't regret one minute of my life in the circus, and I don't regret changing it. You've given me the circus, so I'll always be a part of it." Her smile faded, and her eyes grew serious. "Will you belong to me, Keane?"

He took her hand from his cheek and pressed it to his lips. "I already do. I love you, Jovilette. I'll spend a lifetime loving you."

"That's not long enough," she said as their lips met again. "I want more. I want forever."

With slow, building passion, his hands moved over her. Taking his time, he loosened the buttons on her sweater. "So beautiful," he murmured as his lips trailed down her throat and found the gentle swell. Jo's breath caught at the new intimacy. "You're trembling. I love knowing I can make your skin tremble under my hands." His lips roamed back to hers before he cradled her in his arms. "I've wanted to be with you, to hold you, just hold you, for so long. I can't remember not wanting it."

With a sigh washed with contentment, Jo snuggled against him. "Keane," she murmured.

"Hmm?"

"You never answered me."

"About what?" He kissed her closed lids, then tangled his fingers in her hair.

Jo opened her eyes. Her brows arched over them. "Are you going to marry me or not?"

Keane laughed, rolled her onto her back and planted a long, lingering kiss on her mouth. "Is tomorrow soon enough?"

* * * * *

HER MOTHER'S KEEPER

Chapter 1

The taxi zipped through the airport traffic. Gwen let out a long sigh as the Louisiana heat throbbed around her. She shifted as the thin material of her ivory lawn blouse dampened against her back. The relief was brief. Squinting out of the window, she decided the July sun hadn't changed in the two years she had been away. The cab veered away from downtown New Orleans and cruised south. Gwen reflected that very little else here had changed in the past two years but herself. Spanish moss still draped the roadside trees, giving even the sun-drenched afternoon a dreamlike effect. The warm, thick scent of flowers still wafted through the air. The atmosphere was touched with an easygoing indolence she nearly had forgotten during the two years she'd spent in Manhattan. Yes, she mused, craning her neck to catch a glimpse of a sheltered bayou, I'm the one who's changed. I've grown up.

When she had left Louisiana, she'd been twenty-one and a starry-eyed innocent. Now, at twenty-three, she felt mature and experienced. As an assistant to the fashion editor of *Style* magazine, Gwen had learned how to cope with deadlines, soothe ruffled models, and squeeze in a personal life around her professional one. More, she had learned how to cope alone, without the comfort of familiar people and places. The gnawing ache of homesickness she had experienced during her first months in New York was forgotten, the torture of insecurity and outright fear of being alone were banished from her memory. Gwen Lacrosse had not merely survived the transplant from magnolias to concrete, she felt she had triumphed. This is one small-town southern girl who can take care of herself, she reflected with a flash of defiance. Gwen had come home not merely for a visit, a summer sabbatical. She had come on a mission. She folded her arms across her chest in an unconscious gesture of determination.

In the rearview mirror, the taxi driver caught a glimpse of a long, oval face surrounded by a shoulder-length mass of caramel curls. The bone structure of his passenger's face was elegant, but the rather sharp features were set in grim lines. Her huge brown eyes were focused on some middle distance, and her full, wide mouth was unsmiling. In spite of her severe expression, the cabbie decided, the face was a winner. Unaware of the scrutiny, Gwen continued to frown, absorbed by her thoughts. The landscape blurred, then disappeared from her vision.

How, she wondered, could a forty-seven-year-old woman be so utterly naive? What a fool she must be making of herself. Mama's always been dreamy and impractical, but this! It's all *his* fault, she thought resentfully. Her eyes narrowed as she felt a fresh surge of temper, and color rose to warm the ivory tone of her skin. *Luke Powers*—Gwen gritted her teeth on the name—successful novelist and screenwriter, sought-after bachelor and globe-trotter. *And rat,* Gwen added, unconsciously twisting her leather clutch bag in a movement suspiciously akin to that of wringing a neck. A thirty-five-year-old rat. Well, Mr. Powers, Gwen's thoughts continued, your little romance with my mother is through. I've come all these miles to send you packing. And by hook or crook, fair means or foul, that's what I'm going to do.

Gwen sat back, blew the fringe of curls from her eyes and contemplated the pleasure of ousting Luke Powers from her mother's life. Researching a new book, she sniffed. He'll have to research his book without researching my mother. She frowned, remembering the correspondence from her mother over the past three months. Luke Powers had been mentioned on almost every page of the violet-scented paper; helping her mother garden, taking her to the theater, hammering nails, making himself generally indispensable.

At first Gwen had paid little attention to the constant references to Luke. She was accustomed to her mother's enthusiasm for people, her flowery, sentimental outlook. And, to be honest, Gwen reflected with a sigh, I've been preoccupied with my own life, my own problems. Her thoughts flitted back to Michael Palmer—practical, brilliant, selfish, dependable Michael. A small cloud of depression threatened to descend on her as she remembered how miserably she had failed in their relationship. He deserved more than I could give him, she reflected sadly. Her eyes became troubled as she thought of her inability to share herself as Michael had wanted. Body and mind, she had held back both, unwilling or unable to make the commitment. Quickly shaking off the encroaching mood, Gwen reminded herself that while she had failed with Michael, she was succeeding in her career.

In the eyes of most people, the fashion world was glamorous, elegant, full of beautiful people moving gaily from one party to the next. Gwen almost laughed out loud at the absurdity of the illusion. What it really was, as she had since learned, was crazy, frantic, grueling work filled with temperamental artists, high-strung models and impossible deadlines. And I'm good at handling all of them, she mused, automatically straightening her shoulders. Gwen Lacrosse was not afraid of hard work any more than she was afraid of a challenge.

Her thoughts made a quick U-turn back to Luke Powers. There was too much affection in her mother's words when she wrote of him, and his name cropped up too often for comfort. Over the past three months, Gwen's concern had deepened to worry, until she felt she had to do something about the situation and had arranged for a leave of absence. It was, she had decided, up to her to protect her mother from a womanizer like Luke Powers.

She was not intimidated by his reputation with words or his reputation with women. He might be said to be an expert with both, she mused, but I know how to take care of myself and my mother. Mama's trouble is that she's too trusting. She sees only what she wants to see. She doesn't like to see faults. Gwen's mouth softened into a smile, and her face was suddenly, unexpectedly breathtaking. I'll take care of her, she thought confidently, I always have.

The lane leading to Gwen's childhood home was lined with fragile magnolia trees. As the taxi turned in and drove through patches of fragrant shade, Gwen felt the first stirrings of genuine pleasure. The scent of wisteria reached her before her first glimpse of the house. It had three graceful stories and was made of white-washed brick with high French windows and iron balconies like lacework. A veranda flowed across the entire front of the house, where the wisteria was free to climb on trellises at each end. It was not as old or as elaborate as many other antebellum houses in Louisiana, but it had the charm and grace so typical of that period. Gwen felt that the house suited her mother to perfection. They were both fragile, impractical and appealing.

She glanced up at the third story as the taxi neared the end of the drive. The top floor contained four small suites that had been remodeled for "visitors," as her mother called them, or as Gwen more accurately termed them, boarders. The visitors, with their monetary contributions, made it possible to keep the house in the family and in repair. Gwen had grown up with these visitors, accepting them as one accepts a small itch. Now, however, she scowled up at the third-floor windows. One of the suites housed Luke Powers. Not for long, she vowed, as she slipped out of the cab with her chin thrust forward.

As she paid her fare, Gwen glanced absently toward the sound of a low, monotonous thudding. In the side yard, just past a flourishing camellia, a man was in the process of chopping down a long-dead oak. He was stripped to the waist, and his jeans were snug over narrow hips and worn low enough to show a hint of tan line. His back and arms were bronzed and muscled and gleaming with sweat. His hair was a rich brown, touched with lighter streaks that showed a preference for sun. It curled damply at his neck and over his brow.

There was something confident and efficient in his stance. His legs were planted firmly, his swing effortless. Though she could not see his face, she knew he was enjoying his task: the heat, the sweat, the challenge. She stood in the drive as the cab drove off and admired his raw, basic masculinity, the arrogant efficiency of his movements. The ax swung into the heart of the tree with a violent grace. It occurred to her suddenly that for months she had not seen a man do anything more physical than jog in Central Park. Her lips curved in approval and admiration as she watched the rise and fall of the ax, the tensing and flow of muscle. The ax, tree and man were a perfect whole, elemental and beautiful. Gwen had forgotten how beautiful simplicity could be.

The tree shuddered and moaned, then hesitated briefly before it swayed and toppled to the ground. There was a quick whoosh and thump. Gwen felt a ridiculous urge to applaud.

"You didn't say timber," she called out.

He had lifted a forearm to wipe the sweat from his brow, and at her call, he turned. The sun streamed behind his back. Squinting against it, Gwen could not see his face clearly. There was an aura of light around him, etching the tall, lean body and thickly curling hair. He looks like a god, she thought, like some primitive god of virility. As she watched, he leaned the ax against the stump of the tree and walked toward her. He moved like a man more used to walking on sand or grass than on concrete. Ridiculously, Gwen felt as though she were being stalked. She attributed the strange thrill she felt to the fact that she could not yet make out his features. He was a faceless man, therefore somehow the embodiment of man, exciting and strong. In defense against the glare of the sun, she shaded her eyes with her hand.

"You did that very well." Gwen smiled, attracted by his uncomplicated masculinity. She had not realized how bored she had become with three-piece suits and smooth hands. "I hope you don't mind an audience."

"No. Not everyone appreciates a well-cut tree." His voice was not indolent with vowels. There was nothing of Louisiana in his tone. As his face at last came into focus, Gwen was struck with its power. It was narrow and chiseled, long-boned and with the faintest of clefts in the chin. He had not shaved, but the shadow of beard intensified the masculinity of the face. His eyes were a clear blue-gray. They were calm, almost startlingly intelligent under rough brows. It was a calm that suggested power, a calm that captivated the onlooker. Immediately, Gwen knew he was a man who understood himself. Though intrigued, she felt discomfort under the directness of his gaze. She was almost sure he could see beyond her words and into her thoughts.

"I'd say you have definite talent," she told him. There was an aloofness about him, she decided, but it was not the cold aloofness of disinterest. He has warmth, she thought, but he's careful about who receives it. "I'm sure I've never seen a tree toppled with such finesse." She gave him a generous smile. "It's a hot day for ax swinging."

"You've got too many clothes on," he returned simply. His eyes swept down her blouse and skirt and trim, stockinged legs, then up again to her face. It was neither an insolent assessment nor an admiring one; it was simply a statement. Gwen kept her eyes level with his and prayed she would not do anything as foolish as blushing.

"More suitable for plane travelling than tree chopping I suppose," she replied. The annoyance in her voice brought a smile to the corners of his mouth. Gwen reached for her bags, but her hand met his on the handle. She jerked away and stepped back as a new source of heat shot through her. It seemed to dart up her fingers, then explode. Stunned by her own reaction, she stared into his calm eyes. Confusion flitted across her face and creased her brow before she smoothed it away. Silly, she told herself as she struggled to steady her pulse. Absolutely silly. He watched the shock, confusion and annoyance move across her face. Like a mirror, her eyes reflected each emotion.

"Thank you," Gwen said, regaining her poise. "I don't want to take you away from your work."

"No hurry." He hoisted her heavy bags easily. As he moved up the flagstone walk, she fell into step beside him. Even in heels, she barely reached his shoulder. Gwen glanced up to see the sun play on the blond highlights in his hair.

"Have you been here long?" she asked as they mounted the steps to the veranda.

"Few months." He set down her bags and placed his hand on the knob. Pausing, he studied her face with exacting care. Gwen felt her lips curve for no reason at all. "You're much lovelier than your picture, Gwenivere," he said unexpectedly. "Much warmer, much more vulnerable." With a quick twist, he opened the door, then again picked up her bags.

Breaking out of her trance, Gwen followed him inside, reaching for his arm. "How do you know my name?" she demanded. His words left her puzzled and defenseless. He saw too much too quickly.

"Your mother talks of you constantly," he explained as he set her bags down in the cool, white-walled hallway. "She's very proud of you." When he lifted her chin with his fingers, Gwen was too surprised to protest. "Your beauty is very different from hers. Hers is softer, less demanding, more comfortable. I doubt very much that you inspire comfort in a man." His eyes were on her face again, and fascinated, Gwen stood still. She could nearly feel the heat flowing from his body into hers. "She worries about you being alone in New York."

"One can't be alone in New York, it's a contradiction in terms." A frown shadowed her eyes and touched her mouth with a pout. "She's never told me she worried."

"Of course not, then you'd worry about her worrying." He grinned.

Resolutely Gwen ignored the tingle of pleasure his touch gave her. "You seem to know my mother quite well." Her frown deepened and spread. The grin reminded her of someone. It was charming and almost irresistible. Recognition struck like a thunderbolt. *"You're Luke Powers,"* she accused.

"Yes." His brows lifted at the tone of her voice, and his head tilted slightly, as if to gain a new perspective. "Didn't you like my last book?"

"It's your current one I object to," Gwen snapped. She jerked her chin from his hold.

"Oh?" There was both amusement and curiosity in the word.

"To the fact that you're writing it here, in this house," Gwen elaborated.

"Have you a moral objection to my book, Gwenivere?"

"I doubt you know anything about morals," Gwen tossed back as her eyes grew stormy. "And don't call me that, no one but my mother calls me that."

"Pity, such a romantic name," he said casually. "Or do you object to romance, as well?"

"When it's between my mother and a Hollywood Casanova a dozen years younger than she, I have a different name for it." Gwen's face flushed with the passion of her words. She stood rigid. The humor faded from Luke's face. Slowly, he tucked his hands in his pockets.

"I see. Would you care to tell me what you'd call it?"

"I won't glorify your conduct with a title," Gwen retorted. "It should be sufficient that you understand I won't tolerate it any longer." She turned, intending to walk away from him.

"Won't you?" There was something dangerously cold in his tone. "And your mother has no voice in the matter?"

"My mother," Gwen countered furiously, "is too gentle, too trusting and too naive." Whirling, she faced him again. "I won't let you make a fool of her."

"My dear Gwenivere," he said smoothly. "You do so well making one of yourself."

Before Gwen could retort, there was the sharp click of heels on wood. Struggling to steady her breathing, Gwen moved down the hall to greet her mother.

"Mama." She embraced a soft bundle of curves smelling of lilac.

"Gwenivere!" Her mother's voice was low and as sweet as the scent she habitually wore. "Why, darling, what are you doing here?"

"Mama," Gwen repeated and pulled away far enough to study the rosy loveliness of her mother's face. Her mother's skin was creamy and almost perfectly smooth, her eyes round and china blue, her nose tilted, her mouth pink and soft. There were two tiny dimples in her cheeks. Looking at her sweet prettiness, Gwen felt their roles should have been reversed. "Didn't you get my letter?" She tucked a stray wisp of pale blond hair behind her mother's ear.

"Of course, you said you'd be here Friday."

Gwen smiled and kissed a dimpled cheek. "This is Friday, Mama."

"Well, yes, it's *this* Friday, but I assumed you meant *next* Friday, and… Oh, dear, what does it matter?" Anabelle brushed away confusion with the back of her hand. "Let me look at you," she requested and, stepping back, subjected Gwen to a critical study. She saw a tall, striking beauty who brought misty memories of her young husband. Widowed for more than two decades, Anabelle rarely thought of her late husband unless reminded by her daughter. "So thin," she clucked, and sighed. "Don't you eat up there?"

"Now and again." Pausing, Gwen made her own survey of her mother's soft, round curves. How could this woman be approaching fifty? she wondered with a surge of pride and awe. "You look wonderful," Gwen murmured, "but then, you always look wonderful."

Anabelle laughed her young, gay laugh. "It's the climate," she claimed as she patted Gwen's cheek. "None of that dreadful smog or awful snow you have up there." New York, Gwen noted, would always be "up there." "Oh, Luke!" Anabelle caught sight of him as he stood watching the reunion. A smile lit up her face. "Have you met my Gwenivere?"

Luke shifted his gaze until his eyes met Gwen's. His brow tilted slightly in acknowledgement. "Yes." Gwen thought his smile was as much a challenge as a glove slapped across her cheek. "Gwen and I are practically old friends."

"That's right." Gwen let her smile answer his. "Already we know each other quite well."

"Marvelous." Anabelle beamed. "I do want you two to get along." She gave Gwen's hand a happy squeeze. "Would you like to freshen up, darling, or would you like a cup of coffee first?"

Gwen struggled to keep her voice from trembling with rage as Luke continued to smile at her. "Coffee sounds perfect," she answered.

"I'll take your bags up," Luke offered as he lifted them again.

"Thank you, dear." Anabelle spoke before Gwen could refuse. "Try to avoid Miss Wilkins until you have a shirt on. The sight of all those muscles will certainly give her the vapors. Miss Wilkins is one of my visitors," Anabelle explained as she led Gwen down the hall. "A sweet, timid little soul who paints in watercolors."

"Hmm," Gwen answered noncommittally as she glanced back over her shoulder. Luke stood watching them with sunlight tumbling over his hair and bronzed skin. "Hmm," Gwen said again, and turned away.

The kitchen was exactly as Gwen remembered: big, sunny and spotlessly clean. Tillie, the tall, waspishly thin cook stood by the stove. "Hello, Miss Gwen," she said without turning around. "Coffee's on."

"Hello, Tillie." Gwen walked over to the stove and sniffed at the fragrant steam. "Smells good."

"Cajun jambalaya."

"My favorite," Gwen murmured, glancing up at the appealingly ugly face. "I thought I wasn't expected until next Friday."

"You weren't," Tillie agreed, with a sniff. Lowering her thick brows, she continued to stir the roux.

Gwen smiled and leaned over to peck Tillie's tough cheek. "How are things, Tillie?"

"Comme ci, comme ça," she muttered, but pleasure touched her cheeks with color. Turning, she gave Gwen a quick study. "Skinny" was her quick, uncomplimentary conclusion.

"So I'm told." Gwen shrugged. Tillie never flattered anyone. "You have a month to fatten me up."

"Isn't that marvellous, Tillie?" Anabelle carefully put a blue delft sugar and creamer set on the kitchen table. "Gwen is staying for an entire month. Perhaps we should have a party! We have three visitors at the moment. Luke, of course, and Miss Wilkins and Mr. Stapleton. He's an artist, too, but he works in oils. Quite a talented young man."

Gwen seized the small opening. "Luke Powers is considered a gifted young man, too." She sat across from her mother as Anabelle poured the coffee.

"Luke *is* frightfully talented," Anabelle agreed with a proud sigh. "Surely you've read some of his books, seen some of his movies? Overwhelming. His characters are so real, so vital. His romantic scenes have a beauty and intensity that just leave me weak."

"He had a naked woman in one of his movies," Tillie stated in an indignant mutter. "Stark naked."

Anabelle laughed. Her eyes smiled at Gwen's over the rim of her cup. "Tillie feels Luke is singlehandedly responsible for the moral decline in the theater," Anabelle continued.

"Not a stitch on," Tillie added, setting her chin.

Though Gwen was certain Luke Powers had no morals whatsoever, she made no reference to them. Her voice remained casual as instead she commented, "He certainly has accomplished quite a bit for a man of his age. A string of best-sellers, a clutch of popular movies...and he's only thirty-five."

"I suppose that shows how unimportant age really is," Anabelle said serenely. Gwen barely suppressed a wince. "And success hasn't spoiled him one little bit," she went on. "He's the kindest, sweetest man I've ever known. He's so generous with his time, with himself." Her eyes shone with emotion. "I can't tell you how good he's been for me. I feel like a new woman." Gwen choked on her coffee. Anabelle clucked in sympathy as Tillie gave Gwen a sturdy thump on the back. "Are you all right, honey?"

"Yes, yes, I'm fine." Gwen took three deep breaths to steady her voice. Looking into her mother's guileless blue eyes, she opted for a temporary retreat. "I think I'll go upstairs and unpack."

"I'll help you," Anabelle volunteered, and started to rise.

"No, no, don't bother." Gwen placed a gentle hand on her shoulder. "It won't take long. I'll shower and change and be down in an hour." In an hour, Gwen hoped to have her thoughts more in order. She looked down at her mother's smooth, lovely face and felt a hundred years old. "I love you, Mama," she sighed, and kissed Anabelle's brow before she left her.

As Gwen moved down the hall, she realigned her strategy. Obviously, there was little she could say to her mother that would discourage her relationship with Luke Powers. It was going to be necessary, she decided, to go straight to the source. While climbing the stairs, she searched her imagination for an appropriate name for him. She could find nothing vile enough.

Chapter 2

A shaft of sunlight poured over the floor in Gwen's room. The walls were covered in delicate floral paper. Eggshell-tinted sheer curtains were draped at the windows, matching the coverlet on the four-poster bed. As she always did when she entered the room, Gwen crossed to the French windows and threw them open. Scents from Anabelle's flower garden swam up to meet her. Across the lawn was a spreading cypress, older than the house it guarded, festooned with gray-green moss. The sun filtered through it, making spiderweb patterns on the ground. Birdsong melded with the drone of bees. She could barely glimpse the mystery of the bayou through a thick curtain of oaks. New York's busy streets seemed nonexistent. Gwen had chosen that world for its challenges, but she discovered that coming home was like a sweet dessert after a full meal. She had missed its taste. Feeling unaccountably more lighthearted, she turned back into her room. She plucked up her white terry-cloth robe and headed for the shower.

Mama's romanticizing again, Gwen mused as the water washed away her travel weariness. She simply doesn't understand men at all. *And you do?* her conscience asked as she thought uncomfortably of Michael. Yes, I do understand them, she answered defiantly as she held her face up to the spray. I understand them perfectly. I won't let Luke hurt my mother, she vowed. I won't let him make a fool of her. I suppose he's used to getting his own way because he's successful and attractive. Well, I deal with successful, attractive people every day, and I know precisely how to handle them. Refreshed and ready for battle, Gwen stepped from the shower. With her confidence restored, she hummed lightly as she towel-dried her hair. Curls sprang to life on her forehead. Slipping on her robe, she tied the belt at her waist and strolled back into the bedroom.

"You!" Gwen jerked the knot tight as she spied Luke Powers standing beside her dresser. "What are you doing in my room?"

Calmly, his eyes traveled over her. The frayed robe was short, revealing slender legs well above the knee. Its simplicity outlined her nearly boyish slenderness. Without makeup, her eyes were huge and dark and curiously sweet. Luke watched her damp curls bounce with the outraged toss of her head.

"Anabelle thought you'd like these," he said as he indicated a vase of fresh yellow roses on the dresser. His hand made the gesture, but his eyes remained on Gwen. Gwen frowned.

"You should have knocked," she said ungraciously.

"I did," he said easily. "You didn't answer." To her amazement, he crossed the distance between them and lifted a hand to her cheek. "You have incredibly beautiful skin. Like rose petals washed in rainwater."

"Don't!" Knocking his hand away, Gwen stepped back. "Don't touch me." She pushed her hair away from her face.

Luke's eyes narrowed fractionally at her tone, but his voice was calm. "I always touch what I admire."

"I don't want you to admire me."

Humor lit his face and added to its appeal. "I didn't say I admired you, Gwen, I said I admired your skin."

"Just keep your hands off my skin," she snapped, wishing the warmth of his fingers would evaporate and leave her cheek as it had been before his touch. "And keep your hands off my mother."

"What gives you the notion I've had my hands on your mother?" Luke inquired, lifting a bottle of Gwen's scent and examining it.

"Her letters were clear enough." Gwen snatched the bottle from him and slammed it back on the dresser. "They've been full of nothing but you for months. How you went to the theater or shopping, how you fixed her car or sprayed the peach trees. Especially how you've given her life fresh meaning." Agitated, Gwen picked up her comb, then put it down again. His direct, unruffled stare tripped her nerves.

"And from that," Luke said into the silence, "you've concluded that Anabelle and I are having an affair."

"Well, of course." His tone confused her for a moment. Was he amused? she wondered. His mouth was beautiful, a smile lurking on it. Furious with herself, Gwen tilted her chin. "Do you deny it?"

Luke slipped his hands into his pockets and wandered about the room. Pausing, he studied the view from the open French windows. "No, I don't believe I will. I believe I'll simply tell you it's none of your business."

"None of my..." Gwen sputtered, then swallowed in a torrent of fury. "None of my business? She's my mother!"

"She's also a person," Luke cut in. When he turned back to face her, there was curiosity on his face. "Or don't you ever see her that way?"

"I don't feel it's—"

"No, you probably don't," he interrupted. "It's certainly time you did, though. I doubt you feel Anabelle should approve of every man you have a relationship with."

Color flared in Gwen's cheeks. "That's entirely different," she fumed, then stalked over to stand in front of him. "I don't need you to tell me about my mother. You can flaunt your affairs with actresses and socialites all you want, but—"

"Thank you," Luke replied evenly. "It's nice to have your approval."

"I won't have you flaunting your affair with my mother," Gwen finished between her teeth. "You should be ashamed," she added with a toss of her head, "seducing a woman a dozen years older than you."

"Of course, it would be perfectly acceptable if I were a dozen years older than she," he countered smoothly.

"I didn't *say* that," Gwen began. Her brow creased with annoyance.

"You look too intelligent to hold such views, Gwen. You surprise me." His mild voice was infuriating.

"I don't!" she denied hotly. Because the thought made her uncomfortable, her mouth moved into a pout. Luke's eyes dropped to her lips and lingered.

"A very provocative expression," he said softly. "I thought so the first time I saw it, and it continues to intrigue me." In one swift motion, he gathered her into his arms. At her gasp of surprised protest, he merely smiled. "I told you I always touch what I admire." Gwen squirmed, but she was pinned tight against him, helpless as his face lowered toward her.

His lips feathered lightly along her jawline. Gwen was caught off guard by the gentleness. Though his chest was solid and strong against her yielding breasts, his mouth was soft and sweet. Disarmed, she stood still in the circle of his arms as his mouth roamed her face. Through the slight barrier of the robe, she could feel every line of his body. They merged together as if destined to do so. Heat began to rise in her, a sudden, unexpected heat as irresistible as his mouth. Her lips throbbed for the touch of his. She moaned softly as he continued to trace light, teasing kisses over her skin. Her hands slipped up from his chest to find their way into his hair, urging him to fulfill a silent promise. At last his lips brushed hers. They touched, then clung, then devoured.

Lost in pleasure, riding on sensations delirious and new, Gwen answered his demands with fervor. She rose on her toes to meet them. The kiss grew deeper. The roughness of his beard scratched her skin and tripled her heartbeat. A tenuous breeze fanned the curtains at the open windows, but Gwen felt no lessening of heat. Luke moved his hands down her spine, firmly caressing her curves before he took her hips and drew her away.

Gwen stared up at him with dark, cloudy eyes. Never had a kiss moved her more, never had she been so filled with fire and need. Her soft mouth trembled with desire for his. The knowledge of what could be hers lay just beyond her comprehension. Luke lifted his hand to her damp curls, tilting back her head for one last, brief kiss. "You taste every bit as good as you look."

Abruptly Gwen remembered who and where she was. The fires of passion were extinguished by fury. "Oh!" She gave Luke's chest a fierce push and succeeded in putting an entire inch between them. "How could you?"

"It wasn't hard," he assured her.

Gwen shook her head. Tiny droplets of water danced in the sunlight. "You're despicable!"

"Why?" Luke's smile broadened. "Because I made you forget yourself for a moment? You made me forget myself for a moment too." He seemed to enjoy the confession. "Does that make you despicable?"

"I didn't… It was you…I just…" Her words stumbled to a halt, and she made ineffectual noises in her throat.

"At least try to be coherent," Luke said.

"Just let me go," Gwen demanded. She began a violent and fruitless struggle. "Just let me go!"

"Certainly," Luke said obligingly. He brushed back her disheveled hair with a friendly hand. "You know, one day you might just be the woman your mother is."

"Oh!" Gwen paled in fury. "You're disgusting."

Luke laughed with pure masculine enjoyment. "Gwenivere, I wasn't speaking of your rather exceptional physical virtues." He sobered, then shook his head. "Anabelle is the only person I know who looks for the good in everyone and finds it. It's her most attractive asset." His eyes were calm again and thoughtful. "Perhaps you should take time to get to know your mother while you're here. You might be surprised."

Gwen retreated behind a film of ice. "I told you, I don't need you to tell me about my mother."

"No?" Luke smiled, shrugged, and moved to the door. "Perhaps I'll spend my time teaching you about yourself, then. See you at dinner." He closed the door on her furious retort.

The front parlor had both the color and the scent of roses. It was furnished in Anabelle's delicate and feminine style. The chairs were small and elegant, with dusky pink cushions; the lamps, china and terrifyingly fragile; the rugs, faded and French. Even when she was not there, Anabelle's presence could be felt.

Gwen pushed aside a pale pink curtain and watched the sun go down while Anabelle chattered happily. The sky gradually took on the hues of sunset, until it glowed with defiant gold and fiery reds. Its passion suited Gwen much more than the soft comfort of the room at her back. She lifted her palm to the glass of the window, as if to touch that explosion of nature. She still felt the aftershocks of the explosion that had burst inside her only a few hours before in the arms of a stranger.

It meant nothing, she assured herself for the hundredth time. I was off guard, tired, confused. I'm sure most of what I felt was pure imagination. I'm on edge, that's all, everything's exaggerated. She ran the tip of her tongue experimentally along her lips, but found no remnants of the heady flavor she remembered. Exaggerated, she told herself again.

"A month's quite a long time for you to be away from your job,"

Anabelle said conversationally as she sorted through a basket of embroidery thread.

Gwen shrugged and made a small sound of agreement. "I haven't taken more than a long weekend in nearly two years."

"Yes, darling, I know. You work too hard."

The cerulean blue dress suited Gwen well, but as Anabelle glanced up at her, she again thought how thin her daughter looked. She was slim and straight as a wand. Gwen's hair caught some of the last flames of the sun, and the mass of curls became a flood of rose-gold light. *How did she get to be twenty-three?* Anabelle wondered. She went back to sorting her thread. "You always were an overachiever. You must get that from your father's side. His mother had two sets of twins, you know. That's overachievement."

With a laugh, Gwen rested her forehead against the glass of the window. It was as refreshing as her mother. "Oh, Mama, I do love you."

"I love you, too, dear," she answered absently as she scrutinized two tones of green. "You haven't mentioned that young man you were seeing, the attorney. Michael, wasn't it?"

"It was," Gwen returned dryly. Dusk began to fall as she watched. With the mellowing of light came an odd, almost reverent hush. She sighed. Dusk, she thought, was the most precious time, and the most fleeting. The sound of the first cricket brought her out of her reverie. "I'm not seeing Michael anymore."

"Oh, dear." Anabelle looked up, distressed. "Did you have a disagreement?"

"A series of them. I'm afraid I don't make the ideal companion for a corporate attorney." Gwen made a face in the glass and watched it reflect. "I have too many deep-rooted plebeian values. Mostly, I like to see the little guy get a break."

"Well, I hope you parted friends."

Gwen closed her eyes and stifled a sardonic laugh as she recalled the volatile parting scene. "I'm sure we'll exchange Christmas cards for years to come."

"That's nice," Anabelle murmured comfortably as she threaded her needle. "Old friends are the most precious."

With a brilliant smile, Gwen turned toward her mother. The smile faded instantly as she spotted Luke in the doorway. As her eyes locked with his, she felt herself trembling. He had changed into tan slacks and a rust-colored shirt. The effect was casual and expensive. But somehow there seemed little difference between the clean-shaven, conventionally clad man Gwen now saw and the rugged woodsman she had met that morning. Clothes and a razor could not alter the essence of his virility.

"It's a fortunate man who has two exquisite women to himself."

"Luke!" Anabelle's head lifted. Instantly, her face was touched with pleasure. "How lovely it is to be flattered! Don't you agree, Gwen?"

"Lovely," Gwen assented, as she sent him her most frigid smile.

With easy assurance, Luke crossed the room. From Gwen's grandmother's Hepplewhite server, he lifted a crystal decanter. "Sherry?"

"Thank you, darling." Anabelle turned her smile from him to Gwen. "Luke bought the most delightful sherry. I'm afraid he's been spoiling me."

I'll just bet he has, Gwen muttered silently. Temper flared in her eyes. Had she seen it, Anabelle would have recognized the look. Luke both saw it and recognized it. To Gwen's further fury, he grinned.

"We shouldn't dawdle long," Anabelle said, unconscious of the war being waged over her head. "Tillie has a special supper planned for Gwen. She dotes on her, you know, though she wouldn't admit it for the world. I believe she's missed Gwen every bit as much as I have these past two years."

"She's missed having someone to scold," Gwen smiled ruefully. "I still carry the stigma of being skinny and unladylike that I acquired when I was ten."

"You'll always be ten to Tillie, darling." Anabelle sighed and shook her head. "I have a difficult time realizing you're more than twice that myself."

Gwen turned toward Luke as he offered her a glass of sherry. "Thank you," she said in her most graciously insulting voice. She sipped, faintly disappointed to find that it was excellent. "And will you be spoiling me, as well, Mr. Powers?"

"Oh, I doubt that, Gwenivere." He took her hand, although she stiffened and tried to pull it away. His eyes laughed over their joined fingers. "I doubt that very much."

Chapter 3

Over dinner Gwen met Anabelle's two other visitors. Though both were artists, they could not have been more different from each other. Monica Wilkins was a small, pale woman with indifferent brown hair. She spoke in a quiet, breathy voice and avoided eye contact at all costs. She had a supply of large, shapeless smocks, which she wore invariably and without flair. Her art was, for the most part, confined to illustrating textbooks on botany. With a touch of pity, Gwen noticed that her tiny, birdlike eyes often darted glances at Luke, then shifted away quickly and self-consciously.

Bradley Stapleton was tall and lanky, casually dressed in an ill-fitting sweater, baggy slacks and battered sneakers. He had a cheerful, easily forgettable face and a surprisingly beautiful voice. He studied his fellow humans with unquenchable curiosity and painted for the love of it. He yearned to be famous but had settled for regular meals.

Gwen thoroughly enjoyed dinner, not only because of Tillie's excellent jambalaya but for the oddly interesting company of the two artists. Separately, she thought each might be a bore, but somehow together, the faults of one enhanced the virtues of the other.

"So, you work for *Style,*" Bradley stated as he scooped up a second, generous helping of Tillie's jambalaya. "Why don't you model?"

Gwen thought of the frantic, nervous models, with their fabulous faces. She shook her head. "No, I'm not at all suitable. I'm much better at stroking."

"Stroking?" Bradley repeated, intrigued.

"That's what I do, basically." Gwen smiled at him. It was better, she decided, that her mother had seated her next to Luke rather than across from him. She would have found it uncomfortable to face him throughout an entire meal. "Soothe, stroke, bully. Someone has to keep the models from using their elegant nails on each other and remind them of the practical side of life."

"Gwen's so good at being practical," Anabelle interjected. "I'm sure I don't understand why. I've never been. Strange," she said, and smiled at her daughter. "She grew up long before I did."

"Practicality wouldn't suit you, Anabelle," Luke told her with an affectionate smile.

Anabelle dimpled with pleasure. "I told you he was spoiling me," she said to Gwen.

"So you did." Gwen lifted her water glass and sipped carefully.

"You must sit for me, Gwen," Bradley said, as he buttered a biscuit.

"Must I?" Knowing the only way she could get through a civilized meal was to ignore Luke, Gwen gave Bradley all her attention.

"Absolutely." Bradley held both the biscuit and knife suspended while he narrowed his eyes and stared at her. "Fabulous, don't you agree, Monica? A marvelous subject," he went on without waiting for her answer. "In some lights the hair would be the color Titian immortalized, in others, it would be quieter, more subtle. But it's the eyes, isn't it, Monica? It's definitely the eyes. So large, so meltingly brown. Of course, the bone structure's perfect, and the skin's wonderful, but I'm taken with the eyes. The lashes are real, too, aren't they, Monica?"

"Yes, quite real," she answered as her gaze flew swiftly to Gwen's face and then back to her plate. "Quite real."

"She gets them from her father," Anabelle explained as she added a sprinkle of salt to her jambalaya. "Such a handsome boy. Gwen favors him remarkably. His eyes were exactly the same. I believe they're why I first fell in love with him."

"They're very alluring," Bradley commented with a nod to Anabelle. "The size, the color, the shape. Very alluring." He faced Gwen again. "You will sit for me, won't you, Gwen?"

Gwen gave Bradley a guileless smile. "Perhaps."

The meal drifted to a close, and the evening waned. The artists retreated to their rooms, and Luke wandered off to his. At Gwen's casual question, Anabelle told her that Luke "worked all the time." It was odd, Gwen mused to herself, that a woman as romantic as her mother wasn't concerned that the man in her life was not spending his evening with her.

Anabelle chattered absently while working tiny decorative stitches into a pillowcase. Watching her, Gwen was struck with a sudden thought. Did Anabelle seem happier? Did she seem more vital? If Luke Powers was responsible, should she, Gwen, curse him or thank him? She watched Anabelle delicately stifle a yawn and was swept by a fierce protective surge. She needs me to look out for her, she decided, and that's what I plan to do.

Once in her bedroom, however, Gwen could not get to sleep. The book she had brought with her to pass the time did not hold her attention. It grew late, but her mind would not allow her body to rest. A breeze blew softly in through the windows, lifting the curtains. It beckoned. Rising, Gwen threw on a thin robe and went outside to meet it.

The night was warm and lit by a large summer moon. The air was filled with the scent of wisteria and roses. She could hear the continual hum of the crickets. Now and then, there was the lonely, eerie call of an owl. Leaves rustled with the movements of night birds and small animals. Fireflies blinked and soared.

As Gwen breathed in the moist, fragrant air, an unexpected peace settled over her. Tranquility was something just remembered, like a childhood friend. Tentatively Gwen reached out for it. For two years, her career had been her highest priority. Independence and success were the goals she had sought. She had worked hard for them. And I've got them, she thought as she plucked a baby coral rose from its bush. Why aren't I happy? I am happy, she corrected as she lifted the bloom and inhaled its fragile scent, but I'm not as happy as I should be. Frowning, she twisted the stem between her fingers. *Complete.* The word came from nowhere. I don't feel complete. With a sigh, she tilted her head and studied the star-studded sky. Laughter bubbled up in her throat suddenly and sounded sweet in the silence.

"Catch!" she cried as she tossed the bloom in the air. She gasped in surprise as a hand plucked the rose on its downward journey. Luke had appeared as if from nowhere and was standing a few feet away from her twirling the flower under his nose. "Thanks," he said softly. "No one has ever tossed me a rose."

"I wasn't tossing it to you." Automatically, Gwen clutched her robe together where it crossed her breasts.

"No?" Luke smiled at her and at the gesture. "Who then?"

Feeling foolish, Gwen shrugged and turned away. "I thought you were working."

"I was. The muse took a break so I called it a night. Gardens are at their best in the moonlight." He paused, and there was an intimacy in his voice. Stepping closer, he added, "I've always thought the same held true for women."

Gwen felt her skin grow warm. She struggled to keep her tone casual as she turned to face him.

Luke tucked the small flower into her curls and lifted her chin. "They are fabulous eyes, you know. Bradley's quite right."

Her skin began to tingle where his fingers touched it. Defensively, she stepped back. "I wish you wouldn't keep doing that." Her voice trembled, and she despised herself for it.

Luke gave her an odd, amused smile. "You're a strange one, Gwenivere. I haven't got you labeled quite yet. I'm intrigued by the innocence."

Gwen stiffened and tossed back her hair. "I don't know what you're talking about."

Luke's smile broadened. The moonlight seemed trapped in his eyes. "Your New York veneer doesn't cover it. It's in the eyes. Bradley doesn't know why they're appealing, and I won't tell him. It's the innocence and the promise." Gwen frowned, but her shoulders relaxed. Luke went on, "There's an unspoiled innocence in that marvelous face, and a warmth that promises passion. It's a tenuous balance."

His words made Gwen uncomfortable. A warmth was spreading through her that she seemed powerless to control. Tranquility had vanished. An excitement, volatile and hot, throbbed through the air. Suddenly she was afraid. "I don't want you to say these things to me," she whispered, and took another step in retreat.

"No?" The amusement in his voice told her that a full retreat would be impossible. "Didn't Michael ever use words to seduce you? Perhaps that's why he failed."

"Michael? What do you know about…?" Abruptly she recalled the conversation with her mother before dinner. "You were listening!" she began, outraged. "You had no right to listen to a private conversation! No gentleman listens to a private conversation!"

"Nonsense," Luke said calmly. "Everyone does, if he has the chance."

"Do you enjoy intruding on other people's privacy?"

"People interest me, emotions interest me. I don't apologize for my interests."

Gwen was torn between fury at his arrogance and admiration for his confidence. "What *do* you apologize for, Luke Powers?"

"Very little."

Unable to do otherwise, Gwen smiled. Really, she thought, he's outrageous.

"Now that was worth waiting for," Luke murmured, as his eyes roamed her face. "I wonder if Bradley can do it justice? Be careful," he warned, "you'll have him falling in love with you."

"Is that how you won Monica?"

"She's terrified of me," Luke corrected as he reached up to better secure the rose in her hair.

"Some terrific observer of humanity you are." Gwen sniffed, fiddling with the rose herself and managing to dislodge it. As it tumbled to the ground, both she and Luke stooped to retrieve it. Her hair brushed his cheek before she lifted her eyes to his. As if singed, she jolted back, but before she could escape, he took her arm. Slowly, he rose, bringing her with him. Involuntarily, she shivered as he brought her closer until their bodies touched. Just a look from him, just the touch of him, incited her to a passion that she had not known she possessed. His hands slid up her arms and under the full sleeves of her robe to caress her shoulders. She felt her mantle of control slip away as she swayed forward and touched her lips to his.

His mouth was avid so quickly, her breath caught in her throat. Then all was lost in pleasure. Lights fractured and exploded behind her closed lids as her lips sought to give and to take with an instinct as old as time. Beneath her palms she felt the hard, taut muscles of his back. She shuddered with the knowledge of his strength and the sudden realization of her own frailty. But even her weakness had a power she had never tapped, never experienced.

His hands roamed over her, lighting fires, learning secrets, teaching and taking. Gwen was pliant and willing. He was like a drug flowing into her system, clouding her brain. Only the smallest grain of denial struggled for survival, fighting against the growing need to surrender. Reason surfaced slowly, almost reluctantly. Suddenly, appalled by her own behavior, she began to struggle. But when she broke away, she felt a quick stab of loneliness.

"No." Gwen lifted her hands to her burning cheeks. "No," she faltered.

Luke watched in silence as she turned and fled to the house.

Chapter 4

The morning was hazy and heavy. So were Gwen's thoughts. As dawn broke with a gray, uncertain light, she stood by her window.

How could I? she demanded of herself yet again. Closing her eyes and groaning, Gwen sank down onto the window seat. I kissed him. *I* kissed *him.* Inherent honesty kept her from shifting what she considered blame. I can't say I was caught off guard this time. I knew what was going to happen, and worse yet, I *enjoyed* it. She brought her knees up to her chin. I enjoyed the first time he kissed me too. The silent admission caused her to shut her eyes again. *How could I?* As she wrestled with this question, she rose and paced the room. I came thousands of miles to get Luke Powers out of Mama's life, and I end up kissing him in the garden in the middle of the night. And liking it, she added wretchedly. What kind of a person am I? What kind of a daughter am I? I never thought of Mama once in that garden last night. Well, I'll think of her today, she asserted, and pulled a pair of olive-drab shorts from her drawer. I've got a month to move Luke Powers out, and that's just what I'm going to do.

As she buttoned up a short-sleeved khaki blouse, Gwen nodded confidently at herself in the mirror. No more moonlit gardens. I won't take the chance of having midsummer madness creep over me again. That's what it was, wasn't it? she asked the slender woman in the glass. She ran a nervous hand through her hair. Another answer seemed just beyond her reach. Refusing any attempt to pursue it, Gwen finished dressing and left the room.

Not even Tillie was in the kitchen at such an early hour. There was a certain enjoyment in being up alone in the softly lit room. She made the first pot of coffee in the gray dawn. She sipped at a cupful while watching dark clouds gather. Rain, she thought, not displeased. The sky promised it, the air smelled of it. It gave an excitement to the quiet, yawning morning. There would be thunder and lightning and cooling wind. The thought inexplicably lifted Gwen's spirits. Humming a cheerful tune, she began searching the cupboards. The restless night was forgotten.

"What are you up to?" Tillie demanded, sweeping into the room. Hands on her bony hips, she watched Gwen.

"Good morning, Tillie." Used to the cook's abrasiveness, Gwen answered good-naturedly.

"What do you want in my kitchen?" she asked suspiciously. "You made coffee."

"Yes, it's not too bad." Gwen's tone was apologetic, but her eyes danced with mischief.

"I make the coffee," Tillie reminded her. "I always make the coffee."

"I've certainly missed it over the past couple of years. No matter how I try, mine never tastes quite like yours." Gwen poured a fresh cup. "Have some," she offered. "Maybe you can tell me what I do wrong."

Tillie accepted the cup and scowled. "You let it brew too long," she complained. Lifting her hand, she brushed curls back from Gwen's forehead. "Will you never keep your hair out of your eyes? Do you want to wear glasses?"

"No, Tillie," Gwen answered humbly. It was an old gesture and an old question. She recognized the tenderness behind the brisk words and quick fingers. Her lips curved into a smile. "I made Mama's breakfast." Turning, Gwen began to arrange cups and plates on a tray. "I'm going to take it up to her, she always liked it when I surprised her that way."

"You shouldn't bother your *maman* so early in the morning," Tillie began.

"Oh, it's not so early," Gwen said airily as she lifted the tray. "I didn't leave much of a mess," she added with the carelessness of youth. "I'll clean it up when I come back." She whisked through the door before Tillie could comment.

Gwen moved quickly up the stairs and down the corridor. Balancing the tray in one hand, she twisted the knob on her mother's door with the other. She was totally stunned to find it locked. Automatically, she jiggled the knob in disbelief. Never, as far back as her childhood memories stretched, did Gwen remember the door of Anabelle's room being locked.

"Mama?" There was a question in her voice as she knocked. "Mama, are you up?"

"What?" Anabelle's voice was clear but distracted. "Oh, Gwen, just a minute, darling."

Gwen stood outside the door listening to small, shuffling sounds she could not identify. "Mama," she said again, "are you all right?"

"Yes, yes, dear, one moment." The creaks and shuffles stopped just before the door opened. "Good morning, Gwen." Anabelle smiled. Though she wore a gown and robe and her hair was mussed by sleep, her eyes were awake and alert. "What have you got there?"

Blankly, Gwen looked down at the tray she carried. "Oh, chocolate and *beignets*. I know how you like them. Mama, what were you…?"

"Darling, how sweet!" Anabelle interrupted, and drew Gwen into the room. "Did you really make them yourself? What a treat. Come, let's sit on the balcony. I hope you slept well."

Gwen evaded a lie. "I woke early and decided to test my memory with the *beignet* recipe. Mama, I don't remember you ever locking your door."

"No?" Anabelle smiled as she settled herself in a white, wrought-iron chair. "It must be a new habit, then. Oh, dear, it looks like rain. Well, my roses will be thankful."

The locked door left Gwen feeling slighted. It reminded her forcibly that Anabelle Lacrosse was a person, as well as her mother. Perhaps she would do well to remember it, Gwen silently resolved. She set the tray on a round, glass-topped table and bent to kiss Anabelle's cheek. "I've really missed you. I don't think I've told you that yet."

"Gwenivere." Anabelle smiled and patted her daughter's fine-boned hand. "It's so good to have you home. You've always been such a pleasure to me."

"Even when I'd track mud on the carpet or lose frogs in the parlor?" Grinning, Gwen sat and poured the chocolate.

"Darling." Anabelle sighed and shook her head. "Some things are best forgotten. I never understood how I could have raised such a hooligan.

But even as I despaired of you ever being a lady, I couldn't help admiring your freedom of spirit. Hot-tempered you might have been," Anabelle added as she tasted her chocolate, "but never malicious and never dishonest. No matter what dreadful thing you did, you never did it out of spite, and you always confessed."

Gwen laughed. Her curls danced as she tossed back her head. "Poor Mama, I must have done so many dreadful things."

"Well, perhaps a bit more than your share," Anabelle suggested kindly. "But now you're all grown up, so difficult for a mother to accept. Your job, Gwen, you do enjoy it?"

Gwen's automatic agreement faltered on her lips. Enjoy, she thought. I wonder if I do. "Strange," she said aloud, "I'm not at all certain." She gave her mother a puzzled smile. "But I need it, not just for the money, I need the responsibility it imposes, I need to be involved."

"Yes, you always did… My, the *beignets* look marvelous."

"They are," Gwen assured her mother as she rested her elbows on the table and her chin on her open palms. "I felt obligated to try one before I offered them to you."

"See, I've always told you you were sensible," Anabelle said with a smile before she tasted one of the oddly shaped doughnuts. "Delicious," she proclaimed. "Tillie doesn't make them any better, though that had best be our secret."

Gwen allowed time to pass with easy conversation until she poured the second cup of chocolate. "Mama," she began cautiously, "how long does Luke Powers plan to stay here?"

The lifting of Anabelle's delicate brows indicated her surprise. "Stay?" she repeated as she dusted powdered sugar from her fingers. "Why, I don't know precisely, Gwen. It depends, I should say, on the stage of his book. I know he plans to finish the first draft before he goes back to California."

"I suppose," Gwen said casually as she stirred her chocolate, "he'll have no reason to come back here after that."

"Oh, I imagine he'll be back." Anabelle smiled into her daughter's eyes. "Luke is very fond of this part of the country. I wish I could tell you what his coming here has meant to me." Dreamily, she stared out into the hazy sky. Gwen felt a stab of alarm. "He's given me so much. I'd like you to spend some time with him, dear, and get to know him."

Gwen's teeth dug into the tender inside of her lip. For the moment, she felt completely at a loss. She raged in silence while Anabelle smiled secretly at rain clouds. Despicable man. How can he do this to her? Gwen glanced down into the dregs of her cup and felt a weight descend on her heart. And what is he doing to me? No matter how she tried to ignore it, Gwen could still feel the warmth of his lips on hers. The feeling clung, taunting and enticing. She was teased by a feeling totally foreign to her, a longing she could neither identify nor understand. Briskly, she shook her head to clear her thoughts. Luke Powers was only a problem while he was in Louisiana. The aim was to get him back to the West Coast and to discourage him from coming back.

"Gwen?"

"Hmm? Oh, yes, Mama." Blinking away the confused images and thoughts of Luke, Gwen met Anabelle's curious look.

"I said blueberry pie would be nice with supper. Luke's very fond of it. I thought perhaps you'd like to pick some berries for Tillie."

Gwen pondered briefly on the attractive prospect of sprinkling arsenic over Luke's portion, then rejected the idea. "I'd love to," she murmured.

The air was thick with moisture when, armed with a large bucket, Gwen went in search of blueberries. With a quick glance and shrug at the cloudy sky, she opted to risk the chance of rain. She would use her berry picking time to devise a plan to send Luke Powers westward. Swinging the bucket, she moved across the trim lawn and into the dim, sheltering trees that formed a border between her home and the bayou. Here was a different world from her mother's gentle, tidy, well-kept home. This was a primitive world with ageless secrets and endless demands. It had been Gwen's refuge as a child, her personal island. Although she remembered each detail perfectly, she stood and drank in its beauty anew.

There was a mist over the sluggish stream. Dull and brown, cattails peeked through the surface in search of the hidden sun. Here and there, cypress stumps rose above the surface. The stream itself moved in a narrow path, then curved out of sight. Gwen remembered how it twisted and snaked and widened. Over the straight, slender path, trees arched tunnellike, garnished with moss. The water was silent, but Gwen could hear the birds and an occasional plop of a frog. She knew the serenity was a surface thing. Beneath the calm was a passion and violence and wild, surging life. It called to her as it always had.

With confidence, she moved along the riverbank and searched out the plump wild berries. Silence and the simplicity of her task were soothing. Years slipped away, and she was a teenager again, a girl whose most precious fantasy was to be a part of a big city. She had dreamed in the sheltered bayou of the excitement, the mysteries of city life, the challenges of carving out her own path. Hard work, determination and a quick mind had hurried her along that path. She had earned a responsible job, established an interesting circle of friends and acquired just lately a nagging sense of dissatisfaction.

Overwork, Gwen self-diagnosed, and popped a berry into her mouth. Its juice was sweet and full of memories. And, of course, there's Michael. With a frown, Gwen dropped a handful of berries into the bucket. Even though it was my idea to end things between us, I could be suffering from the backlash of a terminated romance. And those things he said... Her frown deepened, and unconsciously she began to nibble on berries. That I was cold and unresponsive and immature...I must not have loved him. Sighing, Gwen picked more berries and ate them, one by one. If I had loved him, I'd have wanted him to make love to me.

I'm not cold, she thought. I'm not unresponsive. Look at the way I responded to Luke! She froze with a berry halfway to her mouth. Her cheeks filled with color. That was different, she assured herself quickly. Entirely different. She popped the berry into her mouth. That was simply physical, it had nothing to do with emotion. Chemistry, that's all. Why, it's practically scientific.

She speculated on the possibility of seducing Luke. She could flirt and tease and drive him to the point of distraction, make him fall in love with her and then cast him off when all danger to Anabelle was past. It can't be too difficult, she decided. I've seen lots of the models twist men around their fingers. She looked down at her own and noted they were stained with berry juice.

"Looks as though you've just been booked by the FBI."

Whirling, Gwen stared at Luke as he leaned back comfortably against a thick cypress. Again he wore jeans and a T-shirt, both faded and well worn. His eyes seemed to take their color from the sky and were more gray now than blue. Gwen's heart hammered at the base of her throat.

"Must you continually sneak up on me?" she snapped. Annoyed with the immediate response of her body to his presence, she spoke heatedly. "You have the most annoying habit of being where you're not wanted."

"Did you know you become more the Southern belle when you're in a temper?" Luke asked with an easy, unperturbed smile. "Your vowels flow quite beautifully."

Gwen's breath came out in a frustrated huff. "What do you want?" she demanded.

"To help you pick berries. Though it seems you're doing more eating than picking."

It trembled on her tongue to tell him that she didn't need or want his help. Abruptly, she remembered her resolve to wind him around her berry-stained finger. Carefully she smoothed the frown from between her brows and coaxed her mouth into a charming smile. "How sweet of you."

Luke raised a quizzical eyebrow at her change of tone. "I'm notoriously sweet," he said dryly. "Didn't you know?"

"We don't know each other well, do we?" Gwen smiled and held out the bucket. "At least, not yet."

Slowly, Luke straightened from his stance and moved to join her. He accepted the bucket while keeping his eyes fastened on hers. Determinedly, Gwen kept her own level and unconcerned. She found it difficult to breathe with him so close. "How is your book going?" she asked, hoping to divert him while she regained control of her respiratory system.

"Well enough." He watched as she began to tug berries off the bush again.

"I'm sure it must be fascinating." Gwen slid her eyes up to his in a manner she hoped was provocative and exciting. "I hope you won't think me a bore if I confess I'm quite a fan of yours. I have all your books." This part was easier because it was true.

"It's never a bore to know one's work is appreciated."

Emboldened, Gwen laid her hand on his on the handle of the bucket. Something flashed in his eyes, and her courage fled. Quickly slipping the bucket from his hold, she began to pick berries with renewed interest while cursing her lack of bravery.

"How do you like living in New York?" Luke asked as he began to add to the gradually filling bucket.

"New York?" Gwen cleared her head with a quick mental shake. Resolutely, she picked up the strings of her plan again. "It's very exciting—

such a sensual city, don't you think?" Gwen lifted a berry to Luke's lips. She hoped her smile was invitingly alluring, and wished she had thought to practice in a mirror.

Luke opened his mouth to accept her offering. His tongue whispered along the tips of her fingers. Gwen felt them tremble. It took every ounce of willpower not to snatch her hand away. "Do you—do you like New York?" Her voice was curiously husky as she began to pull berries again. The tone was uncontrived and by far the most enticing of her tactics.

"Sometimes," Luke answered, then brushed the hair away from her neck.

Moistening her lips, Gwen inched away. "I suppose you live in Louisiana."

"No, I have a place near Carmel, at the beach. What marvellously soft hair you have," he murmured, running his hand through it.

"The beach," Gwen repeated, swallowing. "It must be wonderful. I've—I've never seen the Pacific."

"It can be very wild, very dangerous," Luke said softly before his lips brushed the curve of Gwen's neck.

There was a small, strangled sound from Gwen's throat. She moved farther away and fought to keep up a casual front. "I've seen pictures, of course, and movies, but I expect it's quite different to actually see it. I'm sure it's a wonderful place to write."

"Among other things." From behind, Luke dropped his hands to her hips as he caught the lobe of her ear between his teeth. For a moment, Gwen could only lean back against him. Abruptly she stiffened, straightened, and put a few precious inches between them.

"You know," she began, completely abandoning her plans to seduce him, "I believe we have enough." As she turned around, her breasts brushed against his chest. She began to back up, stammering. "Tillie won't want to make more than two—two pies, and there's plenty here for that." Her eyes were wide and terrified.

Luke moved forward. "Then we won't have to waste any more time picking berries, will we?" The insinuation was clear.

"No, well..." Her eyes clung helplessly to his as she continued to back up. "Well, I'll just take these in to Tillie. She'll be waiting."

He was still advancing, slowly. Just as Gwen decided to abandon her dignity and run, she stepped backward into empty space. With a sharp cry, she made a desperate grab for Luke's hand. He plucked the bucket from her as she tumbled into the stream.

"Wouldn't want to lose the berries," he explained as Gwen surfaced, coughing and sputtering. "How's the water?"

"Oh!" After beating the surface of the water violently with her fists, Gwen struggled to her feet. "You did that on purpose!" Her hair was plastered to her face, and impatiently she pushed it out of her eyes.

"Did what?" Luke grinned, appreciating the way her clothes clung to her curves.

"Pushed me in." She took two sloshing steps toward the bank.

"My dear Gwenivere," Luke said in a reasonable tone. "I never laid a hand on you."

"Exactly." She kicked at the water in fury. "It's precisely the same thing."

"I suppose it might be from your point of view," he agreed. "But then, you were getting in over your head in any case. Consider the dunking the lesser of two evils. By the way, you have a lily pad on your..." His pause for the sake of delicacy was belied by the gleam in his eyes.

Flushing with embarrassment and fury, Gwen swiped a hand across her bottom. "As I said before, you are no gentleman."

Luke roared with laughter. "Why, Miss Gwenivere, ma'am, your opinion devastates me." His drawl was mocking, his bow low.

"At least," she began with a regal sniff, "you could help me out of this mess."

"Of course." With a show of gallantry, Luke set down the bucket and reached for Gwen's hand. Her wet shoes slid on the slippery bank. To help balance her, he offered his other hand. Just as she reached the top edge, Gwen threw all her weight backward, tumbling them both into the water. This time, Gwen surfaced convulsed with laughter.

As she stood, she watched him rise from the water and free his eyes of wet hair with a jerk of his head. Laughter blocked her speech. In silence, Luke watched as the sounds of her uninhibited mirth filled the air.

"How's the water?" she managed to get out before dissolving into fresh peals of laughter. Though she covered her mouth with both hands, it continued to escape and dance on the air. A quick hoot of laughter emerged as she saw his eyes narrow. He took a step toward her, and she began a strategic retreat. She moved with more speed than grace through the water, kicking it high. Giggles caused her to stumble twice. She scrambled up the slope but before she could rise to her feet, Luke caught her ankle. Pulling himself up onto the grass, he pinned Gwen beneath him.

Breathless, Gwen could still not stop laughing. Water dripped from Luke's hair onto her face, and she shook her head as it tickled her skin. A smile lurked in Luke's eyes as he looked down on her.

"I should have known better, I suppose," he commented. "But you have such an innocent face."

"You don't." Gwen took deep gulps of air in a fruitless effort to control her giggles. "Yours isn't innocent at all."

"Thank you."

Abruptly, the heavens opened and rain fell, warm and wild. "Oh!" Gwen began to push against him. "It's raining."

"So it is," Luke agreed, ignoring her squirms. "We might get wet."

The absurdity of his statement struck her suddenly. After staring up at him a moment, Gwen began to laugh again. It was a young sound, appealing and free. Gradually, Luke's expression sobered. In his eyes appeared a desire so clear, so unmistakable, that Gwen's breath caught in her throat. She opened her mouth to speak, but no words came.

"My God," he murmured. "You are exquisite."

His mouth took hers with a raw, desperate hunger. Her mouth was as avid as his, her blood as urgent. Their wet clothing proved no barrier as their bodies fused together in ageless intimacy. His caress was rough, and she reveled in the exquisite pain. The soft moan might have come from either of them. He savaged the vulnerable curve of her neck, tasting, arousing, demanding. His quick, desperate loving took her beyond the edge of reason and into ecstasy.

She felt no fear, only excitement. Here was a passion that sought and found her hidden fires and set them leaping. Rain poured over them unfelt, thunder bellowed unheard. His hands were possessive as they moved over her. Through the clinging dampness of her blouse, his mouth found the tip of her breast. She trembled, murmuring his name as he explored the slender smoothness of her thigh. She wanted him as she had never wanted anyone before.

"Luke?" His name was half question, half invitation.

Lightning flashed and illuminated the bayou. Just as swiftly they were plunged again into gloom.

"We'd better get back," Luke said abruptly, rising. "Your mother will be worried."

Gwen shut her eyes on a sudden stab of hurt. Hurriedly, she scrambled to her feet, avoiding Luke's outstretched hand. She swayed under a dizzying onslaught of emotions. "Gwen," Luke said, and took a step toward her.

"No." Her voice shook with the remnants of passion and the beginning of tears. Her eyes as they clung to his were young and devastated. "I must be losing my mind. You had no right," she told him shakily, "you had no right."

"To what?" he demanded roughly and grasped her shoulders. "To begin to make love with you or to stop?" Anger crackled in his voice.

"I wish I'd never seen you! I wish you'd never touched me."

"Oh, yes." Temper whipped through Luke's voice as he pulled her close to him again. "I can only say I wish precisely the same, but it's too late now, isn't it?" She had never seen his eyes so lit with fury. "Neither of us seems pleased with what's been started, but perhaps we should finish it." Rain swept around them, slicing through the trees and battering the ground. For a moment, Gwen knew terror. He could take her, she knew, even if she fought him. But worse, she knew he would need no force, no superior strength, after the first touch. Abruptly, he released her and stepped away. "Unless that's what you want," he said softly, "you'd best get out of here."

This time Gwen took his advice. Sobbing convulsively, she darted away among the moss-draped trees. Her one thought…to reach the safety of home.

Chapter 5

The rain had awakened the garden. Twenty-four hours later it was still vibrant. Rose petals dried lazily in the sun while dew clung tenaciously to the undersides of leaves. Without enthusiasm, Gwen moved from bush to bush, selecting firm young blooms. Since the day before, she had avoided Luke Powers. With a determination born of desperation, she had clung to her mother's company, using Anabelle as both a defense and an offense. If, she had decided, *she* was always with Anabelle, Luke could not be. Nor could he take another opportunity to confuse and humiliate Gwen herself.

The basket on her arm was half filled with flowers, but she felt no pleasure in their colors and scents. Something was happening to her—she knew it, felt it, but could not define it. More and more often, she caught her thoughts drifting away from whatever task she was performing. It is, she reflected as she snipped a slender, thorny rose stem with Anabelle's garden shears, as if even my thoughts aren't wholly mine any longer.

When she considered her behavior over the past two days, Gwen was astounded. She had come to warn her mother about her relationship with Luke Powers and instead had found herself responding to him as she had never responded to Michael or any other man. But then, she admitted ruefully, she had never come into contact with a man like Luke Powers. There was a basically sensual aura about him despite his outward calm.

She felt that he, like the bayou, hid much below the surface. Gwen was forced to admit that she had no guidelines for dealing with such a man. Worse, he had kindled in her a hitherto-buried part of her nature.

She had always thought her life and her needs simple. But suddenly, the quiet dreams inside her had risen to the surface. She was no longer the uncomplicated, controlled woman she had thought herself to be. The somewhat volatile temper she possessed had always been manageable, but in just two days the reins of restraint had slipped through her fingers.

His fault, Gwen grumbled to herself as she glared at a pale pink peony. He shouldn't be here—he should be in his beach house in California. If he were in California, perhaps battling an earthquake or hurricane, I'd be having a nice, uncomplicated visit with Mama. Instead he's here, insinuating himself into my life and making me feel… Gwen paused a moment and bit her lip. How does he make me feel? she thought. With a sigh, she let her gaze wander over the variety of colors and hues in the garden. I'm not sure how he makes me feel. He frightens me. The knowledge came to her swiftly, and her eyes reflected her surprise. Yes, he frightens me, though I'm not altogether sure why. It's not as if I thought he'd hurt me physically, he's not that sort of man, but still… Shaking her head, Gwen moved slowly down the walkway, digesting the new thought. He's a man who controls people and situations so naturally you're hardly aware you've been controlled.

Unconsciously, Gwen lifted her finger and ran it along her bottom lip. Vividly she remembered the feel of his mouth on hers. Its touch had ranged from gentle and coaxing to urgent and demanding, but the power over her had been the same. It was true—there was something exhilarating about fencing with him, like standing on the bow of a ship in a storm. But no matter how adventurous she might be, Gwen was forced to concede that there was one level on which she could not win. When she was in his arms, it was not surrender she felt, but passion for passion, need for need. Discovering this new facet of herself was perhaps the most disturbing knowledge of all.

I won't give up. Gwen lifted her chin and straightened her shoulders. I won't let him intimidate me or dominate my thoughts any longer. Her eyes glittered with challenge. Luke Powers won't control me. He'll find out that Gwen Lacrosse is perfectly capable of taking care of herself *and* her mother.

"Just a minute longer." Bradley Stapleton held up a pencil briefly, then continued to scrawl with it on an artist's pad. He sat crosslegged in the middle of the walkway, his feet sandaled, wearing paint-spattered carpenter's pants, a checked sport shirt unbuttoned over his thin chest and a beige fisherman's cap on his head. Surprised and intrigued, Gwen stopped in her tracks.

"Wonderful!" With surprising agility, Bradley unfolded himself and rose. His eyes smiled with genuine pleasure as he strolled over to Gwen. "I knew you'd be a good subject, but I didn't dare hope you'd be spectacular. Just look at this range of emotions!" he commanded as he flipped back several pages in his pad.

Gwen's initial amusement altered to astonishment. That the pencil sketches were exceptionally good was obvious, but it was not his talent as much as the content of the sketches that surprised her. She saw a woman with loose, curling hair and a coltish slenderness. There was a vulnerability she had never perceived in herself. As Gwen turned the pages, she saw herself dreaming, pouting, thinking and glaring. There was something disturbing about seeing her feelings of the past half hour so clearly defined. She lifted her eyes to the artist.

"They're fabulous," she told him. Bradley's face crinkled into a grin. "Bradley," she searched for the right words. "Am I really…so, well… artless as it seems here?" She looked back down at the sketches with a mixture of conflicting emotions. "What I mean is, are my thoughts, my feelings, so blatantly obvious? Am I so transparent?"

"That's precisely what makes you such a good model," Bradley said. "Your face is so expressive."

"But—" With a gesture of frustration, Gwen ran a hand through her hair. "Do they always show? Are they always there for people to examine? I feel defenseless and, well, naked somehow."

Bradley gave her a sympathetic smile and patted her cheek with his long, bony fingers. "You have an honest face, Gwen, but if it worries you, remember that most people don't see past the shape of a nose or the color of eyes. People are usually too busy with their own thoughts to notice someone else's."

"Yet you certainly did," Gwen replied, but she felt more comfortable.

"It's my business."

"Yes." With a smile, Gwen began flipping through the pages again.

"You're very good..." She stopped, speechless as the pad fell open to a sketch of Luke.

It was a simple sketch of him sitting on the rail of the veranda. He was dressed casually, and his hair was tousled, as though he had been working. Bradley had captured the strength and intelligence in his face, as well as the sensual quality she had not expected another man to notice. But it was Luke's eyes, which seemed to lock on to hers, that impressed her. The artist had caught the strange melding of serenity and power that she had felt in them. Gwen was conscious of an odd quickening of her breath. Irresistibly, she was drawn to the picture just as she was drawn to the man.

"I'm rather pleased with it." Gwen heard Bradley's voice and realized with a jolt that he had been speaking for several seconds.

"It's very good," she murmured. "You understand him." She was unaware of the wistfulness and touch of envy in her voice.

After a brief, speculative glance at her lowered head, Bradley nodded. "To an extent, I suppose. I understand he's a complicated man. In some ways, he's much like you."

"Me?" Genuinely shocked, Gwen lifted her eyes.

"You're both capable of a wide range of emotions. Not everyone is, you know. The main difference is, he channels his, while yours are fully expressed. Will you sit for me?"

"What?" Gwen tried to focus on him again. The question was out of context with the rest of his statement. She shook her head to clear it of the disturbing thoughts his words had aroused in her.

"Will you sit for me?" Bradley repeated patiently. "I very much want to do you in oils."

"Yes, of course." She shrugged and conjured up a smile to dispel her own mood. "It sounds like fun."

"You won't think so after a couple of hours of holding a pose," Bradley promised good-naturedly. "Come on, we'll get started now, before you change your mind." Taking her hand, he pulled her up the walkway.

Several hours later, Gwen clearly understood the truth of Bradley's statement. Posing for a temperamental artist, she discovered, was both exhausting and demanding. Her face had been sketched from a dozen angles while she stood or sat or twisted in accordance with his commands. She began to feel more sympathy for the models at *Style*.

She had been amused at first when Bradley rooted through her wardrobe in search of attire suitable to sitting for the portrait. When he selected a thin white silk robe, she had taken what she considered a firm stand against his choice. He ignored her objections and, to her amazement, Gwen found herself doing exactly as he instructed.

Now, tired and alone, Gwen stretched out on her bed and relaxed her muscles. A smile lurked at the corners of her mouth as she recalled how Bradley had gently steamrolled her. Any embarrassment she had felt about wearing only the robe while he studied her or moved her this way and that had been swiftly eradicated. She might as easily have been an interesting tree or a fruit bowl. He had not been interested in the body beneath the robe but in the way the material draped.

I don't have to worry about fending off a passionate attack, Gwen reflected as she shut her eyes, only about stiffening joints. With a deep sigh, she snuggled into the pillow.

Her dreams were confused. She dreamed she was roaming through the bayou picking roses and blueberries. As she passed through a clearing, she saw Luke chopping down a thick, heavy tree. The sound of the ax was like thunder. The tree fell soundlessly at her feet. As Luke watched, she walked to him and melted into his arms. For an instant she felt violent joy, then, just as suddenly, she found herself hurled into the cool stream.

From behind a curtain of water, Gwen saw Anabelle, a gentle smile on her lips as she offered her hand to Luke. Gwen struggled for the surface but found it just beyond her reach. Abruptly she was standing on the bank with Bradley sitting at her feet sketching. Ax in hand, Luke approached her, but Gwen found her arms and legs had turned to stone. As he walked, he began to change, his features dissolving, his clothing altering.

It was Michael who came to her now, a practical briefcase taking the place of the ax. He shook his head at her stone limbs and reminded her in his precise voice that he had told her she was cold. Gwen tried to shake her head in denial, but her neck had turned to stone, as well. When Michael took her by the shoulders and prepared to carry her away, she could only make a small sound of protest. From a distance, she heard Luke call her name. Michael dropped her, and as her stone limbs shattered, she awoke. Dazed, Gwen stared into blue-gray eyes. "Luke," she murmured, "I'm not cold."

"No." He brushed the hair from her cheek, then let his palm linger. "You're certainly not."

"Kiss me again, I don't want to turn to stone." She made the request petulantly. Amusement touched Luke's mouth as he lowered it to hers.

"Of course not, who could blame you?"

Sighing, Gwen locked her arms around his neck and enjoyed the warm gentleness of the kiss. Her limbs grew warm and fluid, her lips parted and begged for more. The kiss deepened until dream and reality mixed. A sharp stab of desire brought Gwen crashing through the barriers of lingering sleep. She managed a muffled protest against his mouth as she struggled for release. Luke did not immediately set her free but allowed his lips to linger on hers until he had had his fill. Even then, his face remained dangerously close. His mouth was only a sigh away.

"That must've been some dream," he murmured. With easy intimacy, he rubbed his nose against hers. "Women are so irresistibly soft and warm when they've been sleeping."

Cheeks flaming, Gwen managed to struggle up to a sitting position. "You have a nerve," she flared. "What do you mean by coming into my bedroom and molesting me?"

"Take a guess," he invited with a wolfish grin. Her color grew yet deeper as she gripped the V of her robe. "Relax," Luke continued. "I didn't come to steal your virtue, I came to wake you for dinner." He ran a fingertip along her jawline. "The rest was your idea."

Indignation stiffened Gwen's spine but muddled her speech. "You—you…I was asleep, and you took advantage…"

"I certainly did," Luke agreed, then pulled her close for a hard, brief kiss. "And we both enjoyed every second of it." He rose gracefully. "White suits you," he commented, his gaze wandering over the soft folds of the robe, "but you might want to change into something a bit less informal for dinner, unless your object is to drive Bradley into a frenzy of desire."

Gwen rose, wrapping the robe more tightly about her. "Don't worry about Bradley," she said icily. "He spent all afternoon sketching me in this robe."

The humor disappeared so swiftly from Luke's face, Gwen wondered if she had imagined its existence. His mouth was grim as he stepped toward her. "What?" The one word vibrated in the room.

"You heard me. I've agreed to let Bradley paint me."

"In that?" Luke's eyes dropped the length of the robe, then returned to her face.

"Yes, what of it?" Gwen tossed her head and turned to walk away from him. The silk of her robe floated around her legs and clung to her hips as she moved. When she reached the window, she turned and leaned back against the sill. Her stance was at once insolent and sensual. "What business is it of yours?"

"Don't play games unless you're prepared to lose," Luke warned softly.

"You're insufferable." The brown of her eyes grew molten.

"And you're a spoiled child."

"I'm not a child," Gwen retorted. "I make my own decisions. If I want to pose for Bradley in this robe or in a suit of armor or in a pair of diamond earrings and nothing else, that's nothing to do with you."

"I'd consider the diamond earrings carefully, Gwen." The soft tone of Luke's voice betrayed his rising temper. "If you try it, I'd have to break all of Bradley's fingers."

His calm promise of violence added fuel to Gwen's fire. "If that isn't typical male stupidity! If something doesn't work, kick it or swear at it! I thought you were more intelligent."

"Did you?" A glimmer of amusement returned to Luke's eyes. Reaching out, he gave her hair a sharp tug. "Too bad you were wrong."

"Men!" she expostulated, lifting her palms and eyes to the ceiling. "You're all the same."

"You speak, of course, from vast personal experience."

The sarcasm in his voice did not escape Gwen. "You're all arrogant, superior, selfish—"

"Beasts?" Luke suggested amiably.

"That'll do," she agreed with a nod.

"Glad to help." Luke sat back on the edge of the bed and watched her. The flickering lights of the setting sun accentuated the hollows and shadows of her face.

"You always think you know best and that women are too muddleheaded to decide things for themselves. All you do is give orders, orders, orders, and when you don't get your own way, you shout or sulk or, worse, patronize. I hate, loathe and despise being patronized!" Balling her hands into fists, Gwen thrust them into the pockets of her robe. "I don't like being told I'm cute in a tone of voice that means I'm stupid. I don't like being patted on the head like a puppy who can't learn to fetch. Then, after you've finished insulting my intelligence, you want to breathe all over me. Of course, I should be grateful for the attention because I'm such a sweet little simpleton." Unable to prevent herself any longer, Gwen gave the bedpost a hard slap. "I am not," she began, and her voice was low with fury, "I am *not* cold and unresponsive and sexually immature."

"Good Lord, child." Gwen, jolted by Luke's voice, blinked as she refocused on him. "What idiot ever told you that you were?"

Gwen stared at Luke in frozen silence.

"Your opinion of men obviously comes from the same source," he continued. "Your Michael must have been really convincing." Embarrassed, Gwen shrugged and turned back to the window. "Were you in love with him?"

The question caught her so off balance that she answered automatically. "No, but I thought I was, so it amounts to the same thing, I imagine."

"Bounced around a bit, were you?" His tone was surprisingly gentle as were the hands that descended to her shoulders.

"Oh, please." Quickly, Gwen moved away as she felt a strange, sweet ache. "Don't be kind to me. I can't fight you if you're kind."

"Is that what you want to do?" Luke took her shoulders firmly now and turned her around to face him. "Do you want to fight?" His eyes dropped to her lips. Gwen began to tremble.

"I think it's better if we do." Her voice was suddenly breathless. "I think fighting with you is safer."

"Safer than what?" he inquired. He smiled, a quick, flashing movement that was both charming and seductive. The room grew dim in the dusk, silhouetting them in the magic light of a dying day. "You are beautiful," he murmured, sliding his hand along the slope of her shoulders until his fingers traced her throat.

Mesmerized, Gwen stared up at him. "No, I—I'm not. My mouth's too wide, and my chin's pointed."

"Of course," Luke agreed as he drew her closer. "I see it now, you're quite an ugly little thing. It's a pity to waste velvet eyes and silken skin on such an unfortunate-looking creature."

"Please." Gwen turned her head, and his mouth brushed her cheek rather than her lips. "Don't kiss me. It confuses me—I don't know what to do."

"On the contrary, you seem to know precisely what to do."

"Luke, please." She caught her breath. "Please, when you kiss me, I forget everything, and I only want you to kiss me again."

"I'll be happy to do so."

"No, don't." Gwen pushed away and looked at him with huge, pleading eyes. "I'm frightened."

He studied her with quiet intensity. He watched her lip tremble, her teeth digging into it to halt the movement. The pulse in her neck throbbed under his palm. Letting out a long breath, he stepped back and slipped his hands into his pockets. His look was thoughtful. "I wonder, if I make love to you, would you lose that appealing air of innocence?"

"I'm not going to let you make love to me." Even to herself, Gwen's voice sounded shaky and unsure.

"Gwen, you're much too honest to make a statement like that, let alone believe it yourself." Luke turned and walked to the door. "I'll tell Anabelle you'll be down in a few minutes."

He closed the door behind him, and Gwen was left alone with her thoughts in the darkening room.

Chapter 6

Gwen endured Bradley's sketching for nearly an hour. His eyes were much sharper in his plain, harmless face than she had originally thought. And, she had discovered, he was a quiet tyrant. Once she had agreed to pose for him, he had taken over with mild but inescapable efficiency. He placed her on a white wrought-iron chair in the heart of the garden.

The morning was heavy and warm, with a hint of rain hovering despite the sunshine. A dragonfly darted past, zooming over a rosebush to her right. Gwen turned her head to watch its flight.

"Don't do that!" Bradley's beautifully modulated voice made Gwen guiltily jerk her head back. "I'm only sketching your face today," he reminded her. She murmured something unintelligible that had him smiling. "Now I understand why you work behind the scenes at *Style* and not in front of the camera." His pencil paused in midair. "You've never learned how to sit still!"

"I always feel as though I should be doing something," Gwen admitted. "How does anyone ever just sit like this? I had no idea how difficult it was."

"Where's your Southern languor?" Bradley asked, sketching in a stray wisp of hair. She would sit more quietly if he kept up a conversation, he decided, even though he did not particularly care for splitting his concentration between sketching and talking.

"Oh, I don't think I ever had it," Gwen told him. She brought up her foot to rest on the chair and laced her hands around her knee. Enjoying the heady perfumes of the garden, she took a deep breath. "And living in New York has made it worse. Although…" She paused, looking around her again, though this time remembering to move only her eyes. "There is something peaceful here, isn't there? I'm discovering how much I've missed that."

"Is your work very demanding?" Bradley asked, perfecting the line of her chin with a dash of his pencil.

"Hmm." Gwen shrugged and longed to take a good stretch. "There's always some deadline that no one could possibly meet that, of course, we meet. Then there are the models and photographers who need their artistic egos soothed—"

"Are you good at soothing artistic egos?" Bradley narrowed his eyes to find the perspective.

"Surprisingly, yes." She smiled at him. "And I like the challenge of meeting deadlines."

"I've never been good with deadlines," he murmured. "Move your chin, so." He gestured with a fingertip, and Gwen obeyed.

"No, some people aren't, but I have to be. When you're a monthly publication, you have no choice."

For a moment, Gwen fell silent, listening to the hum of bees around the azalea bushes in back of her. Somewhere near the house, a bird sent up a sudden, jubilant song. "Where are you from, Bradley?" she asked at length, turning her eyes back to him. He was a strange man, she thought, with his gangly body and wise eyes.

"Boston." His eyes went briefly to her, then back to his sketch pad. "Turn your head to the right a bit… There, good."

"Boston. I should have guessed. Your voice is very…elegant." Bradley chuckled. "How did you decide to become an artist?"

"It's my favorite mode of communication. I've always loved sketching. In school my teachers had to confiscate my sketchbooks. And some people are very impressed when they hear you're an artist."

Gwen laughed. "The last's not a real reason."

"Don't be too sure," Bradley murmured, involved with the curve of her cheek. "I enjoy flattery. Not everyone is as self-sufficient as you."

Forgetting his instructions, Gwen turned to him again. "Is that the way you see me?"

"Sometimes." He lifted a brow and motioned for her to turn away again. For a moment he studied her profile before beginning to draw again. "To be an artist, a good one, without the driving passion to be a great one, suits me perfectly." He smiled at her thoughtful expression. "It wouldn't suit you at all. You haven't the patience for it."

Gwen thought of the brisk, no-nonsense Gwen Lacrosse of *Style* magazine—a practical, efficient woman who knew her job and did it well, a woman who knew how to handle details and people, who was good at facts and figures. And yet…there was another Gwen Lacrosse who loved old, scented gardens and watched weepy movies on television, who hopped into hansom cabs in the rain. Michael had been attracted to the first Gwen but despaired of the second. She sighed. Perhaps she had never understood the mixture herself. She had not even questioned it. At least not until she had met Luke Powers.

Luke Powers. She didn't want to think about him. Things were not working out quite the way she had planned in that department. Worse yet, she wasn't at all sure they ever would.

Gwen tilted her head up to the sky. Bradley opened his mouth to remonstrate, then finding a new angle to his liking, continued sketching. The sun lit reddish sparks in her hair. She noticed that the clouds were rolling in from the west. A storm was probably brewing, she thought. It was still far off, hovering, taking its time. She had a feeling that it would strike when least expected. Though the day appeared to be sunny and pleasant, she felt the passion there, just below the surface. The air throbbed with it. In spite of the heat, Gwen shivered involuntarily. Irresistibly, her eyes were drawn to the house and up.

Luke was watching her from the window of his room. She wondered how long he had been there, looking down with that quiet, direct expression that she had come to expect from him. His eyes never wavered as hers met them.

He stared without apology, without embarrassment. For the moment, Gwen found herself compelled to stare back. Even with the distance between them, she could feel the intrusion of his gaze. She stiffened against it.

As if sensing her response, Luke smiled…slowly, arrogantly, never shifting his eyes from hers. Gwen read the challenge in them. She tossed her head before turning away.

Bradley cocked a brow at Gwen's scowling face. "It appears," he said mildly, "that we're done for the day." He rose from his perch on a stone, unexpectedly graceful. "Tomorrow morning, I want you in the robe. I've a pretty good idea on the pose I want. I'm going in to see if I can charm Tillie out of a piece of that chocolate cake. Want some?"

Gwen smiled and shook her head. "No, it's a bit close to lunch for me. I think I'll give Mama a hand and do some weeding." She glanced down at the petunia bed. "She seems to be neglecting it a bit."

"Busy lady," Bradley said and, sticking the pencil behind his ear, sauntered down the path.

Busy lady? Gwen frowned after him. Her mother did not seem preoccupied…but *what* precisely was she doing? Perhaps it was just her way of intimating to Gwen that she, too, had a life, just as important as Gwen's big-city profession. Moving over to the petunia bed, Gwen knelt down and began to tug at stray weeds.

Anabelle had developed a habit of disappearing from time to time—that was something new. Unable to do otherwise, she glanced up at Luke's window again. He was gone. With a scowl, she went back to her weeding.

If only he would leave, she thought, everything would be fine. Her mother was a soft, gentle creature who trusted everyone. She simply had no defenses against a man like Luke Powers. And you do? she mocked herself. Swearing, Gwen tugged and unearthed a hapless petunia.

"Oh!" She stared down at the colorful blossom, foolishly guilty. A shadow fell across her, and she stiffened.

"Something upsetting you?" Luke asked. He crouched down beside her; taking the blossom from her hand, he tucked it behind her ear. Gwen remembered the rose and blushed before she could turn her face away.

"Go away. I'm busy," she said.

"I'm not." His voice was carelessly friendly. "I'll help."

"Don't you have work to do?" She shot him a scornful glance before ripping savagely at another weed.

"Not at the moment." Luke's tone was mild as he felt his way among the flowers. His fingers were surprisingly deft. "The advantage of being self-employed is that you make your own hours—at least most of the time."

"Most of the time?" Gwen queried, curiously overcoming her dislike for this annoying man.

"When it works, you're chained to the typewriter, and that's that."

"Strange," Gwen mused aloud, forgetting to ignore him. "I can't picture you chained to anything. You seem so free. But it must be difficult putting all those words on paper, making the people inside your head walk and talk and think. Why did you decide to become a writer?"

"Because I have an affection for words," he said. "And because those people in my head are always scrambling to get out. Now I've answered your question frankly." Luke turned to her as he twirled a blade of grass between his fingers. "It's my turn to ask one. What were you thinking of when you were watching the sky?"

Gwen frowned. She wasn't at all sure she wanted to share her private thoughts with Luke Powers. "That we're in for some rain," she compromised. "Must you watch me that way?"

"Yes."

"You're impossible," she told him crossly.

"You're beautiful." His look was suddenly intense, shooting a quiver up her spine. He cupped her chin before she could turn away. "With the sunlight on your hair and your eyes misty, you were all I have ever dreamed of. I wanted you." His mouth drew closer to hers. His breath fluttered over her skin.

"Don't!" Gwen started to back away, but his fingers on her chin held her steady.

"Not so fast," Luke said softly.

His kiss was surprisingly gentle, brushing her mouth like a butterfly's wing. Instinctively, she parted her lips to receive his probing tongue. With a sigh, she succumbed to the mood of the waiting garden. Her passion had lain sleeping, like the threatened storm behind the layer of soft clouds. She trembled with desire as his fingers carefully traced the planes of her face. They caressed her cheekbones, the line of her jaw, the thick tousle of her hair at her temples, before he kissed her again. His tongue teased and tasted with only the slightest pressure. She gripped his shirt front tightly and moaned his name. Her skin was alive with him. Wanting, needing, she twined her arms around his neck and pulled him against her. Her mouth was avid, seeking.

For one blazing moment, the flame rose and consumed them both, as they embraced in the fragrant morning heat. Then he had drawn her away, and Gwen was staring up at him, trying to catch her breath.

"No." She shook her head, pressing her hands to her temples as she waited for her thoughts to steady. "No." Before she could turn and flee, Luke had sprung up, grabbing her wrist.

"No what?" His voice was deeper, but still calm.

"This isn't right." The words tumbled out of her as she tried to find reason. "Let me go."

"In a minute." Luke kept his hand on her wrist and stepped toward her. A sweeping gaze took in her frantic color and widened eyes. "You want it, and so do I."

"No, no, I don't!" She shot out the fierce denial and jerked her arm. Her wrist stayed in his grip.

"I don't remember your protesting too much!" he said mildly. She was annoyed to recognize amusement in his eyes. "Yes, I distinctly recall it was you who took matters to the boiling point."

"All right, all right. You win." She took a breath. "I did. I forgot, that's all."

He smiled. "Forgot what?"

Gwen narrowed her eyes at his amusement. It fanned her temper more than his anger would have. "Forgot that I don't like you," she tossed out. "Now let me go, my memory's back."

Luke laughed a joyous masculine laugh before he pulled Gwen back into his arms. "You tempt me to make you forget again, Gwenivere." He kissed her again, a hard and possessive kiss. It was over almost before it had begun, but her senses were already reeling from it. "Shall we go back to weeding?" he asked pleasantly, as he released her.

She drew herself straight, indignant, furious. "You can go…"

"Gwen!" Anabelle's soft voice cut off Gwen's suggestion. Her mother had drifted into the garden. "Oh, here you are, both of you. How nice."

"Hello Anabelle." Luke gave her an easy smile. "We thought we'd give you a hand with the garden!"

"Oh?" She looked vaguely at her flowers, then her face brightened with a smile. "That's sweet, I'm sure I haven't been as diligent as I should be, but…" She trailed off, watching a bee swoop down on a rosebud. "Perhaps we can all get back to this later. Tillie's got lunch ready and insists on serving right away. It's her afternoon off, you know." She turned her smile on Gwen. "You'd better wash your hands, dear," she looked anxiously at Gwen, "and perhaps you should stay out of the sun for a while, you're a bit flushed."

Gwen could feel Luke grin without looking at him. "You're probably right," she mumbled. Detestable man! Why did he always succeed in confusing her?

Unaware of the fires raging in her daughter, Anabelle smilingly laid a hand on Gwen's cheek, but whatever she planned to say was distracted by the drone of a furry bee. "My, my," she said, watching it swoop greedily down on an azalea blossom. "He's certainly a big one." Having forgotten Tillie's instructions, she glanced back up at Gwen. "You were sitting for Bradley this morning, weren't you, dear?"

"Yes." Gwen made a face. "For almost two hours."

"Isn't that exciting?" Anabelle glanced up at Luke for his confirmation, then continued before he could comment. "A portrait painted by a real artist! I can hardly wait to see it when it's all finished! Why, I'll have to buy it, I suppose." Her blue eyes brightened. "Perhaps I'll hang it right over the mantel in the parlor. That is..." Another thought intruded, and she stopped her planning and rearranging to look at her daughter. "Unless you want it for you and your Michael."

"He isn't *my* Michael, Mama, I told you." Gwen stuck her hands in her pockets, wishing Luke would say something instead of simply watching her with those cool blue-gray eyes. Why was it never possible to tell what he was thinking? "And in any case, he'd never buy a painting from an unknown. He wouldn't be assured of the investment value," she added. She was sorry that a note of rancor slipped into her voice.

Luke's eyes remained cool, but Gwen saw his brow lift fractionally. He doesn't miss anything, she thought with a stab of resentment. Turning, she began to pull loose petals from an overbloomed rose.

"Oh, but surely, if it were a portrait of you..." Anabelle began. Observing her daughter's expression, she hastily changed her course. "I'm sure it's going to be just beautiful," she said brightly. She turned to Luke. "Don't you think so, Luke?"

"Undoubtedly," he agreed as Gwen gave the rose her fiercest attention. "Bradley has the raw material to work with. That is..." He paused and, unable to resist, Gwen looked over her shoulder to meet his eyes again. "If Gwenivere manages to hold still until it's finished."

Gwen's spine stiffened at the amusement in his voice, but before she could retort, Anabelle laughed gaily. "Oh, yes, Gwen's a ball of fire, I declare," she emoted. "Even as a youngster, flitting here and there, quicker than a minute. Why, I'd have to nearly chain her to a chair to braid her hair." She smiled in maternal memory, absently fluffing her own hair. "Then, at the end of the day, or most times long before, it looked as though I had never touched it! And her clothes!" She clucked her tongue and rolled her eyes. "Oh, what a time I used to have with torn knees and ripped seams."

"Mama." Gwen interrupted before Anabelle could launch into another speech on her girlhood. "I'm sure Luke's not interested in the state of my clothes."

He grinned at that, widely, irreverently. Gwen blushed to the roots of her hair. "On the contrary," he said as she groped around for something scathing and dignified to say. "I'm extremely interested." His eyes softened as he smiled at Anabelle. "It's all grist for my mill—just the sort of background material a writer needs."

"Why, yes, I suppose so." Gwen saw that her mother found this extremely profound. Anabelle lapsed into silence again, dreaming off into the middle distance. Luke grinned at Gwen over her head.

"And I've always had a fondness for little girls," he told her. "Particularly ones whose braids won't stay tied, and who regularly scrape their knees." He glanced down, letting his eyes run over Gwen's French-cut T-shirt and cinnamon-colored shorts. "I imagine over the years Anabelle was pretty busy administering first aid." His eyes traveled up on the same slow, casual journey before meeting hers.

"I didn't make a habit of falling down," Gwen began, feeling ridiculous.

Anabelle came out of her trance for a moment. "Oh, yes." She picked up on Luke's comment. "I don't think a day went by when I wasn't patching up some hurt. A fishhook in your hand one day..." She shuddered at the memory. "And a lump the size of a goose egg on your forehead the next. It was always one thing or another."

"Mama." Gwen crushed what was left of the rose between her fingers. "You make it sound as if I had been a walking disaster."

"You were just spirited, darling." Anabelle frowned a bit at the damaged rose, but made no comment. "Though there were times, I admit, I wasn't certain you'd live to grow up. But, of course, you have, so I probably shouldn't have worried so much."

"Mama." Gwen was suddenly touched. How difficult it must have been, she reflected, for such a young, dreamy woman to raise a lively youngster all on her own! How many sacrifices Anabelle must have made that Gwen had never even considered. Stepping over, Gwen put her hands on Anabelle's soft rounded shoulders. "I love you, and I'm terribly glad you're my mother."

With a sound of surprised pleasure, Anabelle framed Gwen's face and kissed both her cheeks. "What a sweet thing to hear, and from a grown daughter, too." She gave Gwen a quick, fragrant hug.

Over her mother's shoulder, Gwen saw that Luke was still watching them. His direct intensity made her feel self-conscious.

How do I really feel about him? she asked herself. And how can I feel anything, anything at all, when the woman I love most in the world stands between us? She felt trapped, and something of her panic showed in her eyes.

Luke tilted his head. "You're very fortunate, Anabelle." He spoke to the mother, though his eyes remained on the daughter. "Love is very precious."

"Yes." She kissed Gwen's cheek again, then linked her arm through her daughter's. "I'm in a festive mood," she told them both, glowing. "I think we should be daring and have some wine with lunch." Her eyes widened. "*Lunch!* Oh, dear, Tillie will be furious! I completely forgot." She rested a hand against her heart as if to calm it. "I'll go smooth things along. Give me a minute." She assumed a businesslike air. "Then come right in. And see that you make a fuss over whatever she's fixed. We don't want to hurt her feelings any more than we have." She gave the final instructions as she swept back up the path and disappeared.

Gwen started to follow. Luke neatly cut off her retreat by taking her hand. "You'd better let her play diplomat first," he told her.

Gwen swung around to face him. "I don't want to be here with you."

Luke lifted a brow, letting his eyes play over her face. "Why not? I can't imagine more attractive circumstances. This lovely garden… A beautiful day… Tell me something," he continued, interrupting whatever retort she might have made. Casually, he tangled the fingers of his other hand in her hair. "What were you thinking of when you hugged your mother and looked at me?"

"That's none of your business." Gwen jerked her head, trying to free her hair from his curious fingers.

"Really?" He lifted and stroked a straying lock of her hair. Somewhere in the distant west, she heard the first rumbles of thunder. "I had the impression whatever was going through your mind at that moment was very much my business." He brought his eyes back down to hers and held them steady. "Why do you suppose I did?"

"I haven't the faintest idea," Gwen returned coolly. "Probably an author's overheated imagination."

Luke's smile moved slowly, touching his eyes seconds before it touched his lips. "I don't think so, Gwen. I prefer thinking of it as a writer's intuition."

"Or a man's overinflated ego," she shot back, lifting her hand to her hair in an attempt to remove his exploring fingers. "Would you stop that!" she demanded, trying to ignore the dancing of nerves at the back of her neck.

"Or a man's sensitivity to a woman," he countered, bringing her hand to his lips. He kissed her fingers one at a time until she regained the presence of mind to try to jerk free. Instead of releasing her, Luke simply laced fingers with hers. They stood, joined as carelessly as schoolchildren, while she frowned at him. The thunder came again, closer. "Sensitive enough to know when a woman who is attracted to me," he went on lazily, "is not willing to admit it."

Her eyes narrowed. "You're impossibly conceited."

"Hopelessly honest," he corrected. "Shall I prove it to you?"

Gwen lifted her chin. "There's nothing to prove." She knew the hopelessness of attempting to pull her hand from his. Casually, she looked past him to the sky. "The clouds are coming in. I don't want to get caught in the rain."

"We've got a minute," he said, without even glancing at the sky. He smiled. "I believe I make you nervous."

"Don't flatter yourself," she tossed back, and kept her hands calm in his.

"The pulse in your throat is hammering." His eyes dropped and lingered on it, further increasing its pace. "It's strangely attractive—"

"It always does when I'm annoyed," she said, fighting for poise as the sweep of his eyes from her throat to her face threatened to destroy her composure.

"I like you when you're annoyed. I like to watch the different expressions on your face and to see your eyes darken…but…" He trailed off, slipping his hands to her wrists. "At the moment, I believe it's nerves."

"Believe what you like." It was impossible to prevent her pulse from pounding against his fingers. She tried to calm her rebel blood. "You don't make me the least bit nervous."

"No?" His grin turned wolfish. Gwen braced for a struggle. "A difference of opinion," he observed. "And one I'm tempted to resolve." He drew her closer, letting his eyes rest on her mouth. Gwen knew he was baiting her and held her ground. She said nothing, waiting for him to make his move.

"At the moment, however, I'm starved." Luke grinned, then gave her a quick, unexpected kiss on the nose. "And I'm too much of a coward to risk Tillie's bad temper." He dropped one of her hands, but kept the other companionably linked with his. "Let's eat," he suggested, ignoring Gwen's frown.

Chapter 7

Gwen noticed several small changes in Anabelle. There was an air of secrecy about her that Gwen found out of character. She disappears so often, Gwen thought as she seated herself in front of the vintage Steinway in the parlor. She's here one minute and gone the next. And she spends too much time with Luke Powers. There are too many discussions that stop abruptly when I walk in on them. They make me feel like an intruder. With little interest, she began to pick out a melody. The breeze came softly through the window, barely stirring the curtain. The scent of jasmine was elusive, teasing the senses.

I'm jealous, Gwen realized with a jolt of surprise. I expected Mama's undivided attention, and I'm not getting it. With a rueful laugh, Gwen began to play Chopin. Now when have I ever had Mama's undivided attention? She's always had her "visitors," her antiques, her flowers.

Thinking back over childhood memories, Gwen played with absent-minded skill. She had forgotten how soothing the piano was to her. I haven't given myself enough time for this, she reflected. I should take a step back and look at where my life is going. I need to find out what's missing. Her fingers stilled on the last note, which floated quietly through the air and then vanished.

"Lovely," Luke said. "Really lovely."

Gwen suppressed the desire to jump at the sound of his voice. She forced herself to raise her eyes and meet his, struggling to keep the color from tinting her cheeks. It was difficult, after what she had said the evening before, to face him. She felt her defenses were shaky, her privacy invaded. He knew more of her now than she wanted him to.

"Thank you," she said politely. "I am, as Mama always said I would be, grateful for the music lessons she forced me to take."

"Forced?" To Gwen's consternation, Luke sat down on the stool beside her.

"As only she can." Gwen relieved a portion of her tension by giving her attention to another melody. "With quiet, unarguable insistence."

"Ah." Luke nodded in agreement. "And you didn't want to study piano?"

"No, I wanted to study crawfishing." She was stunned when he began to play along with her, picking out the melody on the treble keys. "I didn't know you played." The utter disbelief in her voice brought on his laugh.

"Believe it or not, I, too, had a mother." He gave Gwen his swift, conspiratorial grin. "I wanted to study rock skipping."

Totally disarmed, Gwen smiled back at him. Something passed between them. It was as strong and as real as the passion that had flared with their kiss, as gentle and soothing as the music drifting from the keys.

"Isn't that sweet." Anabelle stood in the doorway and beamed at both of them. "Duets are so charming."

"Mama." Gwen was relieved her voice did not tremble. "I looked for you earlier."

"Did you?" Anabelle smiled. "I'm sorry, dear, I've been busy with... this and that," she finished vaguely. "Aren't you sitting for Bradley today?"

"I've already given him his two hours this morning," Gwen answered. "It's lucky for me he wants the early light, or I'd be sitting all day. I thought perhaps you had something you'd like me to do or someplace you'd like me to take you. It's such a lovely day."

"Yes, it is, isn't it?" Anabelle agreed. Her eyes drifted momentarily to Luke's. Abruptly, her cheeks dimpled and her lips curved. "Why, as a matter of fact, darling, there *is* something you could do for me. Oh—" She paused and shook her head. "But it's so much trouble."

"I don't mind," Gwen interrupted, falling into a childhood trap.

"Well, if it really isn't a bother," Anabelle continued, beaming again. "I especially wanted some embroidery thread, very unusual shades, difficult to find, I'm afraid. There's a little shop in the French Market that carries them."

"In New Orleans?" Gwen's eyes widened.

"Oh, it is a bother, isn't it?" Anabelle sighed. "It's not important, dear. Not important at all," she added.

"It's not a bother, Mama," Gwen corrected, smiling at the old ruse. "Besides, I'd like to get into New Orleans while I'm home. I can be a tourist now."

"What a marvelous idea!" Anabelle enthused. "Wouldn't it be fun? Roaming through the Vieux Carré, wandering through the shops, listening to the music in Bourbon Street. Oh, and dinner at some lovely gallery restaurant. Yes." She clapped her hands together and glowed. "It's just the thing."

"It sounds perfect." Anabelle's childlike enthusiasm caused Gwen to smile. Shopping, she remembered, had always been Anabelle's favorite pastime. "I can't think of a better way to spend the day."

"Good. It's settled, then." She turned to Luke with a pleased smile. "You'll go with Gwen, won't you, dear? It wouldn't do for her to go all alone."

"Alone?" Gwen cut in, confused. "But, Mama, aren't you—?"

"It's such a long drive, too," Anabelle bubbled on. "I'm sure Gwen would love the company."

"No, Mama, I—"

"I'd love to." Luke easily overruled Gwen's objections. He gave Gwen an ironic smile. "I can't think of a better way to spend the day."

"Gwen, dear, I'm so glad you thought of it." The praise was given with a sigh as Anabelle moved over to pat Gwen's cheek.

Looking up into the ingenuous eyes, Gwen felt the familiar sensations of affection and frustration. "I'm very clever," she murmured, moving her lips into a semblance of a smile.

"Yes, of course you are," Anabelle agreed, and gave her a quick, loving hug. "I would change, though, darling. It wouldn't do to go into the city in those faded old jeans. Didn't I throw those out when you were fifteen? Yes, I'm sure I did. Well, run along and have fun," she ordered as she began to drift from the room. "I've just so much to do, I can't think of it all."

"Mama." Gwen called after her. Anabelle turned at the door, lifting her brows in acknowledgement. "The thread?"

"Thread?" Anabelle repeated blankly. "Oh, yes, of course. I'll write down the colors and the name of the shop." She shook her head with a self-deprecating smile. "My, my, I'm quite the scatterbrain. I'll go in right now and tell Tillie you won't be here for dinner. She gets so annoyed with me when I forget things. Do change those pants, Gwen," she added as she started down the hall.

"I'd hide them," Luke suggested confidentially. "She's liable to throw them out again."

Rising with what she hoped was dignity, Gwen answered, "If you'll excuse me?"

"Sure." Before she could move away, Luke took her hand in a light but possessive grip. "I'll meet you out front in twenty minutes. We'll take my car."

A dozen retorts trembled on Gwen's tongue and were dismissed. "Certainly. I'll try not to keep you waiting." She walked regally from the room.

The weather was perfect for a drive—sunny and cloudless, with a light breeze. Gwen had replaced her jeans with a snowy crepe de chine dress. It had a high, lacy neck and pleated bodice, its skirt flowing from a trim, tucked waist. She wore no jewelry. Her hair lay free on her shoulders. Hands primly folded in her lap, she answered Luke's easy conversation with polite, distant monosyllables. I'll get Mama's thread, she determined, have a token tour of the city and drive back as quickly as possible. I will be perfectly polite the entire time.

An hour later, Gwen found that maintaining her aloof sophistication was a difficult task. She had forgotten how much she loved the Vieux Carré. It was not just the exquisite iron grillwork balconies, the profusion of flowering plants, the charm of long wooden shutters and buildings that had stood for centuries. It was the subtle magic of the place. The air was soft and seemed freshly washed, its many scents ranging from flowery to spicy to the rich smell of the river.

"Fabulous, isn't it?" Luke asked as they stood on the curb of a street too narrow for anything but pedestrian traffic. "It's the most stable city I know."

"Stable?" Gwen repeated, intrigued enough to turn and face him directly.

"It doesn't change," he explained with a gesture of his hand. "It just continues on." Before she realized his intent, he laced his fingers with hers and began to walk. She tugged and was ignored.

"There's no reason to hold my hand," Gwen told him primly.

"Sure there is," he corrected, giving her a friendly smile. "I like to."

Gwen subsided into silence. Luke's palm was hard, the palm of a man used to doing manual labor. She remembered suddenly the feel of it caressing her throat. He sighed, turned and pulled her hard against him, covering her mouth in an unexpected and dizzying kiss. Gwen had no time to protest or respond before she was drawn away again. Along the crowded street, several people applauded.

Gwen and Luke walked past the many street artists in Jackson Square. They paused briefly to admire the chalk portraits of tourists, the oils of city scenes and the mysterious studies of the bayous. Gwen was torn between her desire to share her pleasure at returning to the city of her childhood and the feeling that she should ignore the dominating man by her side. She was not here to have a good time, she reminded herself sternly. She was here to do an errand. It was on the tip of her tongue to remind Luke of the purpose of their trip when she saw the magician. He was dressed in black, with spangles and a rakish beret and a flowing moustache.

"Oh, look!" Gwen pointed. "Isn't he wonderful?" She moved closer, unconsciously pulling Luke along by tightening her grip on his hand.

They watched brilliantly colored scarves appear from nowhere, huge bouquets of paper flowers grow from the magician's palm and coins sprout from the ears of onlookers. Two young clowns in whiteface entertained the stragglers by twisting balloons into giraffe and poodle shapes. Some distance away, guitarists sold their songs to passing tourists. Gwen could just hear their close-knit harmony.

Forgetting all her stern resolutions, she turned to grin at Luke. He dropped a bill into the cardboard box that served as the portable cash register for the magician. Reaching out, he pinched her chin between his thumb and forefinger. "I knew it wouldn't last too long."

"What wouldn't?" She brushed the hair from her eyes in a habitual gesture.

"You enjoy things too much to remain cool for long," he told her. "No, now don't do that," he ordered, running a finger down her nose as she frowned. He smiled, then brushed his lips over her fingertips. "Shall we be friends?"

Her hand, already warm from his, grew warmer at the kiss. She knew his charm was practiced, his smile a finely tuned weapon. She forced herself to be cautious.

"I don't know that I'd go as far as that," she replied, studying him with eyes that were warily amused.

"Fellow tourists?" he suggested. His thumb moved gently across her knuckles. "I'll buy you an ice cream cone."

Gwen knew she was losing to the smile and the persuasive voice. "Well..." It would do no harm to enjoy the day. No harm in enjoying the city, the magic...in enjoying him. "Two scoops," she demanded, answering his smile with her own.

They moved at an easy pace through the park, enjoying both shade and sun. All around was the soft, continuous cooing from hundreds of pigeons. They flocked along the ground, scattered when chased by children, sunned atop the statue of Andrew Jackson on a rearing horse. Here and there people sat or slept on curved black benches. A young girl sat in a patch of shade and played softly on a recorder.

They walked along the levee and looked at the brown waters of the Mississippi. Lazy music from calliopes provided a pleasant background as they talked of everything and of nothing. The bells of Saint Louis Cathedral chimed the hour. They laughed at the toddler who escaped from his mother and splashed in the cool waters of a fountain.

They walked along Bourbon Street, listening to the tangled, continuous music that poured from open doors. Jazz and country and rock merged into one jumbled, compelling sound. They applauded the old man who danced in the street to the demanding strains of "Tiger Rag." They listened to the corner saxophone player whose lonely song brought Gwen to tears.

On a gallery overlooking a narrow street surging with people, they ate shrimp gumbo and drank cold, dry wine. They lingered over the leisurely meal, watching the sun slowly disappear. Pleasantly weary, Gwen toyed with the remains of her cheesecake and watched the first stars come out. Laughter rose from the street below. When she turned, she found Luke studying her over the rim of his glass.

"Why do you look at me like that?" Her smile was completely relaxed as she rested her chin on her palm.

"A remarkably foolish question," Luke answered as he set down his glass. "Why do you think?"

"I don't know." She took a deep breath. The scent of the city assailed her senses. "No one's ever looked at me quite the way you do. You can tell too much about people. It's not fair. You study them and steal their thoughts. It's not a very comfortable feeling."

Luke smiled, and his fingers were light on the back of her hand.

Gwen lifted an eyebrow, then strategically moved her hand out of reach. "You also have a way of making people say things. Yesterday I..." Gwen hesitated and twisted the stem of her glass between her fingers. "I said things to you I shouldn't have. It's disturbing to know you've revealed your emotions to someone else." She sipped her wine. "Michael always says I'm too open."

"Your emotions are beautiful." Gwen looked up, surprised at the tenderness in his voice. "Michael is a fool."

Quickly she shook her head. "Oh, no, he's really quite brilliant, and he never does anything foolish. He has an image to maintain. It's just that I was beginning to feel as if I were being molded into his conception of a proper attorney's wife."

"He asked you to marry him?" Luke asked, as he poured wine into both glasses.

"He was sure that I would. He was furious when I didn't jump at the offer." Gwen sighed and made a restless movement with her shoulders. "I kept seeing a long, narrow tunnel, very straight, no curves, no detours, no surprises. I guess I developed claustrophobia." She made a frustrated sound, wrinkling her nose. "There, you've done it again."

"I have?" He smiled as he leaned back in his seat. Moonlight spilled over her hair.

"I'm telling you things...things I've barely told myself. You always manage to find out what's in a person's mind, but you keep your own thoughts all tidy and tucked away."

"I put them in print," he corrected. "For anyone who cares to read them."

"Yes," she said slowly. "But how does one know if they're your real thoughts? Your books are interesting, but how do I know who you really are?"

"Do you want to?" There was a soft challenge in his voice.

Gwen hesitated, but the answer was already moving to her lips. "Yes, I do."

"But you're not quite sure." He rose, then held out his hand to her. "The wine's made you sleepy," he said, looking down into her heavy eyes. "Shall I take you home?"

"No." Gwen shook her head. "No, not yet." She slipped her hand back into his.

Luke drove down the magnolia-lined lane. The scent of the night was delicate, mixing with the fragrance of the woman who slept on his shoulder. After stopping the car, he turned his head and looked down at her. Gwen's mouth was soft and vulnerable in sleep. There was a moment's hesitation before he lifted her chin and drew away from her.

"Gwen." He moved his thumb gently over her lips. She gave a soft, pleased sigh. "Gwen," he said again with more firmness. Her lashes fluttered and opened. "We're home." He massaged her shoulders lightly, and she stretched under his hands.

"Did I fall asleep?" Her eyes were huge and dark as she smiled at him. "I didn't mean to."

"It's late."

"I know." She smiled sleepily. "I had fun. Thank you." On impulse, she bent forward and brushed her lips over his. His fingers tightened on her shoulders as he pulled away from her sharply. Gwen blinked in confusion. "Luke?"

"I have my limits," he said tersely. He made a quick, impatient sound as her face registered consternation. "I told you once, women are very soft and warm when they've been sleeping. I have a weakness for soft, warm women."

"I didn't mean to fall asleep," she murmured as his hand slipped around to cradle the back of her neck. Her head felt light, her limbs heavy.

A cloud drifted over the moon. The light shifted, dimmed and glowed again. He was watching her, studying each feature with absorption. She could feel his fingers on the base of her neck. They were hard and long, their strength obvious even in the gentle touch. She whispered, "What do you want?"

In answer, he bent slowly toward her. His mouth was easy, teasing the corners of hers, drifting to her closed lids, exploring the hollows of her cheeks. Passion lay simmering beneath the surface as he began to caress her body with slow, patient hands. He traced her parted lips with the tip of his tongue. "Beautiful," he murmured, moving his mouth to her ear. She shivered with pleasure as his thumb lingered on the point of her breast. "When I touch you, I feel your body melt under my hands." He met her mouth with a long, tender kiss. "What do I want?" he answered as he tasted the heated skin of her throat. "What I want more than anything at this moment is to make love with you. I want to take you slowly, until I know all of you."

She felt her body growing fluid, and her will flowed with it. "Will you make love with me?" She heard herself ask, heard the tone that was request rather than question. Luke's mouth paused on her skin. Slowly he tightened his grip on her hair, then drew her head back until their eyes met. For a moment, they hung suspended in silence with only the echo of her voice between them.

"No." His answer was cool and quick as a slap. Gwen jerked away from it and him and fumbled with the handle of the door. She stumbled out of the car, but before she could escape into the house, Luke captured her arms in a firm grip. "Wait a minute."

Shaking her head, Gwen pushed against him. "No, I want to go in. I didn't know what I was saying. It was crazy."

"You knew exactly what you were saying," Luke corrected, tightening his grasp.

Gwen wanted to deny it, but found it impossible. She had wanted him, she knew she still wanted him. "All right, I knew what I was saying. Now will you let me go?"

"I won't apologize for touching you," he said.

"I'm not asking for apologies, Luke," she told him evenly. "I'm simply asking for my freedom." She realized uncomfortably that it was not freedom from his arms that she meant, but freedom from the power he held over her. The struggle inside her was reflected briefly in her face. Luke's frown deepened before he released her arms. "Thank you," she said.

She walked quickly inside the house before he could say another word.

Chapter 8

A yellow butterfly fluttered delicately over a pot of white impatiens. From the veranda, Gwen watched its dance until it skimmed away, light as the air. Sitting in the white porch rocker, dressed in a yellow sundress, Anabelle looked as fragile as the butterfly. Gwen studied her mother's soft pink cheeks and gentle blue eyes. Anabelle's small hands were busy with the domestic task of shelling peas, but her eyes were, as always, dreamy. Watching her, Gwen was swamped with waves of love and helplessness.

Who am I? she demanded of herself. Who am I to advise anyone on men? For a moment, Gwen wished desperately that she could seek from Anabelle advice for herself. Her own emotions were chaotic. She was terrified that her own feelings for Luke were approaching a dangerous level. Falling in love with a man like Luke was courting disaster. And yet, Gwen wondered unhappily, is it really possible for the mind to control the heart? In this case it must...there's no choice. I have to forget about last night. The sigh escaped before she could stop it. Priorities, she reminded herself. Gwen watched a bumblebee dive into a cluster of wisteria, then took a deep breath and turned to Anabelle. "Mama." Anabelle went on shelling peas, a misty smile on her lips. "Mama," Gwen repeated more sharply, placing a hand over her mother's.

"Oh, yes, dear?" Anabelle looked up with the open, expectant look of a child. "Did you say something?"

For an instant, Gwen teetered on the brink, then plunged. "Mama, don't you think twelve years is a terribly big gap?"

Gravely, Anabelle considered. "Why, I suppose it could be, Gwenivere, but then, as you grow older, twelve years is hardly any time at all." Her momentary seriousness vanished with a fresh smile. "Why, it seems like yesterday that you were twelve years old. I remember quite clearly when you fell out of that old cypress in the backyard and broke your arm. Such a brave child..." She began shelling peas again. "Never shed a tear. I cried enough for both of us, though."

"But, Mama." Valiantly Gwen tried to keep Anabelle's thoughts from straying. "Twelve years, when you're speaking of a man and a woman...." Anabelle failed to respond to the prompting, only nodding to indicate she was listening. "The age difference, Mama," Gwen blurted out. "Isn't twelve years a terribly wide age gap?"

"Sally Deumont's girls are nearly twelve years apart," Anabelle stated with another series of nods. "I suppose having children that far apart has its drawbacks."

"No, Mama." Gwen ran both hands through her hair.

"And its advantages, certainly," Anabelle said soothingly, not wanting to be critical of an old friend.

"No, Mama, I don't mean that at all. I'm speaking of men and women... of relationships. Romantic relationships."

"Oh!" Anabelle blinked in surprise and smiled. "That's a different matter altogether, isn't it?" Gwen resisted grinding her teeth as her mother continued to shell peas for a moment in silence. "I'm surprised," Anabelle said at length, giving Gwen a look of gentle curiosity. "I'm surprised you would think that age and love had anything to do with each other. I've always thought of the heart as ageless."

The words caused Gwen to falter a moment. Slowly she leaned forward and took both her mother's hands in hers. "Mama, don't you think, sometimes, that love can blind people to what's right for them? Don't people often put themselves into a position where getting hurt is the only possible outcome?"

"Yes, of course." Anabelle shook her head, as if startled by the question. "That's part of life. If you never open yourself for pain, you never open yourself for joy. How empty life would be then. This Michael of yours," Anabelle continued with a light of concern in her eyes, "did he hurt you terribly?"

"No." Gwen released her mother's hands and rose to walk the length of the veranda. "No, basically only my pride."

"That can happen by a fall off a horse," Anabelle stated. Abandoning her peas, she moved to join Gwen. "Darling, how young you are." She turned to face her, studying her with rare total concentration. "I sometimes forget that, because you're so much more practical and organized than I am. I suppose I always let you take care of me, much more than I took care of you."

"Oh, no, Mama," Gwen protested, but Anabelle placed a finger on her lips.

"It's true. I never like to look at the unpleasant side of things. I'm afraid I've always let you do that for me. In some ways you matured so quickly, but in others…" Anabelle sighed and slipped an arm around Gwen's waist. "Perhaps at last we've found something I can help you with."

"But, Mama, it's not me…" Gwen began, only to be ignored.

"Did you know I was only eighteen when I first saw your father? I fell instantly, wildly in love." The soft look in Anabelle's eyes halted Gwen's interruption. "Who would have thought his life would be so short? He never even got to see you. I always thought that the greatest tragedy. He would have been so proud to see himself in you." She sighed, then smiled at Gwen. "Ours was a first love, a desperate love, and often I've wondered if it would have withstood all the tests of time. I'll never know." Gwen remained silent, fascinated by a side of her mother she was seeing for the first time. "I learned so many things from that short, crowded marriage. I learned you must always accept love when it's offered, always give it when it's needed. There might not be a second chance. And I know, too, that until your heart's been broken, you never know the full beauty of love."

Gwen watched a squirrel dart across the lawn and scurry up a tree. It was an odd feeling, hearing her mother speak of being in love. She wondered if their relationship had blinded her from seeing Anabelle as a woman with needs and desires. Looking down, Gwen saw the smooth, untroubled skin of a woman at the peak of her beauty. There was still a youthful sweetness in the shape of the mouth, an impossible air of innocence in the eyes. Impulsively, Gwen asked the question that had lurked in her mind for years.

"Mama, why haven't you ever gotten married again?"

"I haven't wanted to," Anabelle answered instantly. She moved away with a swish of her skirts. "At first, I was too much in love with your father's memory, and later I was having too much fun raising you." She plucked a withered fuchsia bloom from a hanging basket and dropped it over the railing of the veranda. "I'm quite good with babies, you know. Later you became more and more independent, so I moved on to the next stage. I've had some admirers." She smiled, pleased with the thought. "I've simply never had the urge to settle down with any of them." In silence, Gwen watched Anabelle move from flower to flower. It occurred to her for the first time that her mother had probably enjoyed love affairs over the past twenty years. She had not been exclusively Gwen's dreamy, gentle mother but Anabelle Lacrosse, a lovely, desirable woman. For one brief moment, Gwen felt ridiculously like an orphan.

I'm being a fool, Gwen told herself, resting her head against the rail post. She's still the same person—I'm the one who's changing. I grew up, but I've kept her locked in a childhood image. It's time I let her out. But I can't bear to see her hurt, and I'm so afraid Luke will leave her wounded. He can't love her, not when he can kiss me the way he does. No… She closed her eyes. He wants me, but it has nothing to do with his heart. He wants me, but he turned away from me. Why else would he have done that, if not for her? A bright flash of jealousy both stunned and shamed her. With a shuddering sigh, she turned to find Anabelle studying her.

"You're not happy," her mother said simply.

"No." Gwen shook her head with the word.

"Confused?"

"Yes." Quickly she swallowed the tears that threatened to come.

"Men do that to us so easily." Anabelle smiled as if the prospect was not altogether unappealing. "Try a rare piece of advice from your mother, darling. Do nothing." With a little laugh, she tossed back a stray wisp of golden hair. "I know how difficult that is for you, but do try. Just let the pieces fall into place around you for a time. Sometimes doing nothing is doing everything."

"Mama." Gwen was forced to smile. "How can something so silly make so much sense?"

"Luke says I've an intuitive understanding," Anabelle replied with a glow of pride.

"He has a way with words," Gwen muttered.

"Tools of the trade." Luke spoke as the screen door swung shut behind him. His eyes met Gwen's. There was something intimate in the glance, something possessive. Even as the stirring began inside her, she lifted her chin in defense. A smile teased his mouth. "Guns primed, Gwenivere?"

"I'm a dead shot," she returned evenly.

"Oh dear." Anabelle moved lightly across the veranda and began to gather her peas. "You didn't tell me you were going hunting. I hope Tillie packed you a lunch."

Luke grinned over her head with such easy boyish charm, Gwen was helpless to resist. Her eyes warmed and her mouth softened as they shared the intimacy of a joke.

"Actually, I had fishing in mind," Luke countered, keeping his eyes on Gwen's. "I thought I'd walk down to Malon's cabin."

"That's nice." Anabelle straightened and smiled. "Malon still brings up fresh fish," she told Gwen. "You run along, too, darling. You know he would be hurt if you didn't visit."

"Oh, well, I..." Seeing the amusement on Luke's face, Gwen continued smoothly, "I'll visit him, Mama, another time. I told Tillie I'd help her do some canning."

"Nonsense." Anabelle flitted to the screen door, beaming at Luke as he held it open for her. "Thank you, darling," she said before giving Gwen a look over her shoulder. "You're on vacation. That's no time to be standing in a hot kitchen over boiling tomatoes. Run along and have fun. She's always loved to fish," she added to Luke before she stepped inside. "Tell Malon I'd adore some fresh shrimp." The door closed behind her. Gwen had the odd feeling that she had just been pushed gently out of the way. Luke gave her slim blue jeans and plain white T-shirt a cursory glance.

"Looks like you're dressed for fishing," he said with a nod. "Let's go."

"I have no intention of going anywhere with you." Gwen dusted her hands on her hips and started to move by him. She was brought up short by his hand on her arm. They stood side by side. Gwen let her eyes rest on his imprisoning hand and then slid them slowly to meet his. It was her most disdainful stare. "I beg your pardon?" she said icily. To her dismay, Luke burst out laughing. The warm, deep tones of it caused a bird to dart from the lawn to the shelter of a tree. "Let me go, you…you…"

"Wasn't it 'beast' before?" he asked as he began to assist her down the stairs.

"You are the most outrageous man." She continued to struggle as she trotted to keep pace.

"Thanks."

Gwen dug in her heels and managed to persuade Luke to stop. Staring up at him, she took a long, deep breath. "You are the most arrogant, officious, egotistical, thick-skinned man I have ever met."

"You forgot unreasonable, tyrannical and incredibly attractive. Really, Gwen, you surprise me. I thought you had more imagination. Are those your best insults?"

"Off the cuff, yes." She sniffed and tried not to respond to the humor in his eyes. "If you'll give me a little time, I can be more articulate."

"Don't trouble, I got the idea." He released her arm, held up one hand in the air, and the other out to her. "Truce?"

Gwen's guard relaxed before she realized it. Her hand moved to meet his.

"Truce," she agreed, with only a token trace of reluctance.

"Until…?" he asked as he rubbed his thumb lightly across the back of her hand.

"Until I decide to be annoyed with you again." Gwen smiled, tossing back her curls as she enjoyed his laugh. It was, she decided, the most pleasing, infectious laugh she had ever heard.

"Well, will you fish with me?" he asked.

"Perhaps I will." For a moment she pursed her lips in thought. When she smiled again, it was the smile of challenge. "Ten bucks says I catch a bigger fish than you."

"Done." Casually, Luke laced his fingers through hers. This time Gwen made no objection.

Gwen knew every twist of the river and every turn of the paths in the bayou. Automatically, she moved north toward Malon's cabin. They walked under cascading moss and filtered sunlight.

"Do you really know how to can tomatoes, Gwenivere?" Luke asked as he bent under a low-hanging branch.

"Certainly, and anything else that comes out of a garden. When you're poor, a garden can mean the difference between eating or not."

"I've never known poor people who eat with Georgian silver," Luke commented dryly.

"Heirlooms." Gwen gave a sigh and a shrug. "Mama always considered heirlooms a sacred trust. One can't sell a sacred trust. Nor," she added with a wry smile, "can one comfortably wear or eat a sacred trust. Mama loves that house, it's her Camelot. She's a woman who needs a Camelot."

"And Gwenivere doesn't?" A great egret, startled by their intrusion, unfolded himself from the water and rose into the sky. Gwen felt an old, familiar stir of pleasure as she watched.

"I suppose I've always wanted to find my own. Heirlooms belong to someone else first. I'd nearly forgotten the scent of wild jasmine," she murmured as the fragrance drifted to her.

There was a dreamlike stillness around them. Beside them, the stream moved on its lackadaisical journey to the Gulf. Its water mirrored the moss-dripping trees. Gwen tossed a pebble and watched the ripples spread and vanish. "I spent most of my leisure time out here when I was younger," she said. "I felt more at home here than inside my own house. There was never any real privacy there, with strangers always coming and going. I never wanted to share my kingdom with anyone before...."

She could feel Luke's big hand tighten his grasp on hers. He met her eyes with perfect understanding.

Chapter 9

Malon's cabin hung over the water. It was built of split logs with a low, wide A roof and a porch that doubled as a dock for his pirogue. On a small, spare patch of grass beside the cabin, half a dozen chickens clucked and waddled. Somewhere deep in the marsh, a woodpecker drummed. A scratchy recording of music by Saint-Saëns came from the cabin to compete with the drumming and clucking. Stretched lengthwise on a narrow railing above the water, a tabby cat slept.

"It's just the same," Gwen murmured. She was unaware of the relief in her voice or the pleasure that lit her face. She smiled up at Luke and pulled him quickly across the lawn and up the three wooden steps. "Raphael," she said to the snoozing cat. Lazily he opened one eye, made a disinterested noise and shut it again. "Affectionate as ever," Gwen remarked. "I was afraid he'd forget me."

"Raphael is too old to forget anything."

Gwen turned quickly at the sound of the voice. Malon stood in the cabin doorway, a mortar and pestle in his hand. He was a small man, barely taller than Gwen herself, but with powerful arms and shoulders. His middle had not gone to flesh with age, but remained as flat as a boxer's, as he had indeed once been. His hair was white, thick and curly, his face brown and lined, his eyes were a faded blue under dark brows. His age was a mystery. The bayou had been his home for an unspecified number of years. He took from the stream what he needed and was content. He had both a passionate love and a deep respect for the bayou. These he had passed on to the young girl who had found his cabin more than fifteen years before. Gwen checked the impulse to run into his arms.

"Hello, Malon. How are you?"

"Comme ci, comme ça." He gave a tiny shrug, then set down his mortar and pestle. He nodded a greeting to Luke before concentrating on Gwen. For a full minute she stood silent under his scrutiny. At length he said, "Let me see your hands." Obediently, Gwen held them out. "Soft," Malon said with a snort. "Lady's hands now, *hein?* Why didn't you get a lady's figure in New York, too?"

"I could only afford the hands. I'm still saving up for the rest. And Tillie's still pressing your shirts, I see," Gwen ran an experimental finger over the faded but crisp material of his cotton shirt. "When are you going to marry her?"

"I'm too young to get married," he said. "I have not finished sowing wild oats."

Gwen laughed and laid her cheek against his. "Oh, I've missed you, Malon." He answered her laugh and gave her one quick, bruising and unexpected hug. From the outset, they had spoken in Cajun French, a dialect that Gwen used again without the slightest thought. She closed her eyes a moment, enjoying the strength in his burly arms, the feel of his leathery cheek against hers, the scent of woodsmoke and herbs that was his personal cologne. She realized suddenly why she had not come to see him earlier. He had been the one constant male figure in her life. She had been afraid she would find him changed.

"Everything's the same," she murmured.

"But you." There was a smile in his voice, and she heard it.

"I should have come sooner." For the first time since she had known him, Gwen dared kiss his cheek.

"You are forgiven," he said.

Gwen was suddenly conscious of Luke beside her. She flushed. "I'm sorry," she said to him, "I—I didn't realize that we were rambling on in French."

Luke smiled while absently scratching Raphael's ears. "You don't have to apologize—I enjoyed it."

Gwen forced her thoughts into order. She would not fall under the charm of that smile again. "Do you speak French?" she asked with casual interest.

"No. But I still enjoyed it." She had the uncomfortable feeling he knew precisely how deeply his smile affected her. He turned his clear, calm eyes to Malon. "Anabelle says she'd like some shrimp."

"I go shrimping tomorrow," Malon answered with an agreeable nod. "Your book goes well?"

"Well enough."

"So, you take the day off, *hein?* You take this one fishing?" A jerk of his thumb in Gwen's direction accompanied the question.

"Thought I might," Luke replied without glancing at her.

Malon shrugged and sniffed. "Use t'be she knew which end of the pole to hold and which to put in the water, but that was before she went up there." A snap of his head indicated "up there." Even a town twenty miles from Lafitte was regarded with suspicion.

"Perhaps she remembers," Luke suggested. "She seems reasonably intelligent."

"She was raised good," Malon added, softening a bit. "Her papa was a good boy. She has his face. She don't favor her mama."

Gwen straightened her shoulders and raised her brows ever so slightly. "*She* remembers *everything.* My mother can outfish both of you in her sleep."

"Poo-yie!" Malon shook his hand and wrist as if he had touched something hot. "This city girl, she scare me out of my shoe. You take her. Me, I'm too old to fight with mean women."

"A minute ago you were too young to get married," Gwen reminded him.

"Yes, it's a good age I have." He smiled contentedly. "*Allez,* I have medicine to make. Take the poles and the pirogue and bring me a fish for my dinner." Without another word, he walked into the cabin, letting the screen door slam shut behind him.

"He hasn't changed," Gwen stated, trying to sound indignant.

"No," Luke agreed, taking two fishing poles and putting them across his shoulder. "He's still crazy about you." After stepping into the pirogue, he held out a hand to her. With the ease of experience, Gwen settled into the canoe. Soundlessly, Raphael leaped from rail to boat and fell instantly back to sleep.

"He doesn't want to miss the fun," Gwen explained.

Luke poled away from the dock. "Tell me, Gwenivere," he asked, "how do you come to speak the dialect so fluently? Anabelle can barely read a French menu." Sunshine dappled their heads as they passed under a canopy of trees.

"Tillie taught me." Gwen leaned her head back and let the warm sunlight play on her face. She remembered Malon saying long ago that his pirogue could ride on a film of dew. "I've spoken the coastal dialect for as long as I can remember. For the most part, the people here treat outsiders as beneath their notice; it's a very closed society. But I speak Cajun—therefore, I *am* Cajun. I'm curious, though, why Malon accepts you. It's obvious that you're on easy terms."

"I don't speak Cajun." Luke stood in the pirogue and poled down the river as if born to it. "But we speak the same language nonetheless."

They cleared the trees and drifted into a ghost forest shadowed by stumps of cypress. The boat moved through floating mats of hyacinths. Tiny baby crawfish clung to the clumped roots, while a fat cottonmouth disappeared into the lavender blooms. The winding river was teeming with life. Gwen watched a marsh raccoon fishing from the sloping bank.

"How is it," Gwen mused aloud, "that a Pulitzer Prize winner speaks the same language as a Louisiana *traiteur?*"

"Traiteur?" Luke repeated, meeting the frank curiosity in her eyes.

"Folk doctor. Malon fishes and trades and lumbers sometimes, but primarily he's the local *traiteur.* He cures snakebites, illness and spells. Spells are his specialty."

"Hmm. Did you ever wonder why he lives here, alone with his cat, his music and his books?" Gwen did not answer, content to watch Luke pole through the scattered stumps. "He's been to Rome and London and Budapest, but he lives here. He's driven tanks, broken horses, boxed and flown planes. Now he fishes and cures spells. He knows how to fix a carburetor, how to play classical guitar and how to cure snakebites. He does as he pleases and no more. He's the most successful man I know."

"How did you find out so much about him in such a short time?"

"I asked," Luke told her simply.

"No. No, it's not as easy as that." Gwen made a frustrated gesture with her hand. "People tell you things, I don't know why. I've told you things I have no business telling you, and I tell you before I realize it." She examined his face. "And worse, you don't always need to be told, you know. You see people much too clearly."

He smiled down at her. "Does it make you uncomfortable that I know who you are?"

The river widened. Gwen's pout became a frown. "Yes, I think it does. It makes me feel defenseless, the same way I felt when I first saw Bradley's sketches."

"An invasion of privacy?"

"Privacy's important to me," Gwen admitted.

"I understand," Luke leaned on the pole. "You grew up having to share your home with strangers, having to share Anabelle. The result is a desire for privacy and independence. I apologize for invading your privacy, but, after all, it's partly my profession."

"Are we all characters to you?" Gwen asked as she baited her hook and cast her line.

"Some more than others," he returned dryly, casting his line on the opposite side of the boat from hers.

Gwen shook her head. "You know," she began, then settled back, stretching her legs and crossing them, "I'm finding it very hard not to like you."

At the other end of the canoe, Luke mirrored her position. "I'm a very charming person."

"Unfortunately, that's true." With a contented sigh, Gwen closed her eyes. "You're not at all how I pictured you."

"Oh?"

"You look more like a woodchopper than a world-renowned writer."

Luke grinned. "And how should a world-renowned writer look?"

"Several different ways, I suppose. Intellectual, with small glasses and narrow shoulders. Or prominent..."

"Heaven forbid."

"Or prominent," Gwen continued, ignoring him. "Wearing a well-cut suit and with just a hint of a paunch. Dashing, maybe, with a faint scar along the jawline. Or Byronic..."

"Oh, good Lord."

"With a romantic pallor and tragic eyes."

"It's difficult to maintain a pallor in California."

"The trouble is, you're too physical." Gwen was enjoying the gentle drift of the boat and the warm fingers of sun. "What's your new book about?"

"A man and a woman."

"It's been done before," Gwen commented as she opened her eyes.

Luke smiled. His legs made a friendly tangle with hers. "It's *all* been done before, child. It's simply that each person believes his is a fresh experience."

Gwen tilted her head, waiting for his explanation.

Luke obliged. "Endless numbers of symphonies are composed on the same eighty-eight keys." He closed his eyes, and Gwen took the opportunity to study him.

"Will you let me read it?" she asked suddenly. "Or are you temperamental and sensitive?"

"I'm only temperamental when it's to my advantage," Luke told her lazily, opening one eye. "How's your spelling?"

"Comme ci, comme ça," Gwen grinned across at him.

"You can proof my rough draft, my spelling's only half that good."

"That's generous of you." Abruptly she let out a cry. "Oh, I've got one!" Instantly she was sitting up, giving all her attention to the fish on the end of her line. Her face was animated as she tossed her hair back with an impatient jerk of her head. There was competence in her hands and a gleam of challenge in her eyes. "Eight pounds easy," she announced as she plopped the defeated fish on deck. "And that was just for practice." Raphael roused himself to inspect the first catch, then curled up beside Gwen's hip and went back to sleep.

The silence lay comfortably between them. There was no need for conversation or small talk. Dragonflies streaked by now and then with a flash of color and a quick buzz. Occasionally birds called to each other. It seemed natural to Gwen to loll drowsily across from Luke under the hazy sun. Her legs crossed over his with absent camaraderie. The shadows lengthened. Still they lingered, drifting among the stumps of once-towering cypress.

"The sun'll be gone in a couple of hours," Luke commented. Gwen made an unintelligible sound of agreement. "We should be heading back." The boat rocked gently as Luke got to his feet.

Under the cover of gold-tipped lashes, Gwen watched him. He

stretched, and muscles rippled. His eyes were clear and light, an arresting contrast to the burnished tone of his skin. They flicked over her as she lay still, too comfortable to stir herself. She knew that he was aware of her scrutiny.

"You owe me ten dollars," she reminded him smiling.

"A small price to pay for the afternoon." The water sighed as the boat glided over it. "Did you know you have five pale gold freckles on your nose?"

Gwen laughed as she stretched her arms luxuriously over her head. "I believe you're quite mad."

He watched her as the lashes shadowed her cheeks and her mouth sweetened with a smile. "I begin to be sure of it," he murmured.

It wasn't until the pirogue bumped noiselessly against its home dock that Gwen stirred again. The thin wisps of clouds were pink now with the setting sun, and there was a coolness in the air.

"Mmm." Her sigh was filled with the simple pleasure of the moment. "What a lovely ride."

"Next time, you pole," Luke stated. He watched Raphael stand, stretch and leap nimbly onto the dock and then joined him. After securing the boat, he offered a hand to Gwen.

"I suppose that's only fair." Gwen stood in one fluid movement. As nimbly as Raphael, she leaped onto the dock. She tilted back her head to give Luke a flippant grin, but found her lips captured by his.

One hand tangled in her hair while his other pressed into the small of her back, demanding she come closer. His mouth was desperate in its need for possession. There was a tension in him, a whisper of power held tightly in check. Gwen's pulses hammered at the thought of it unleashed. There was no gentleness in the mouth that claimed hers nor in the arms that held her, and she asked for none. There was a wild, restless thing in her that cried for release. She explored the strength of his arms, then the softness of his hair, as she plunged deeper into sensations she could no longer measure. Touching him, she felt there were no limits to the power flooding her. What filled her was more than the quick heat of passion, more than a transient surge of desire. It was an all-consuming need to be his. She wanted to travel where only he could take her and to learn what only he could teach her. Then Luke's hands were on her shoulders, pushing her away.

"Gwen," he began in a voice roughened with desire.

"No, don't talk," she murmured, and pulled his mouth back to hers. It was his taste, and his taste only, that could satisfy her growing hunger. She was famished, only now aware that she had fasted all her life. For a soaring, blinding moment, his mouth bruised hers; then he wrenched away. He held her shoulders in a crushing grip, but Gwen felt no pain as his eyes met hers. She could only stare. Her confusion, her need, her willingness, were plain on her face. Luke's oath was savage and swift as he turned away.

"You should know better than to look at a man like that."

Gwen heard the harsh journey of air in and out of his lungs. Her fingers shook as she ran them nervously through her hair. "I—I don't know how I looked."

"Malleable," Luke muttered. He stared down at the sluggish river before turning back to her. "Pliant, willing and outrageously innocent. Do you know how difficult it is to resist the untouched, the uncorrupted?"

Helplessly, Gwen shook her head. "No, I…."

"Of course you don't," Luke cut in sharply. She winced at his tone, and he let out a long breath. "Good heavens, how easy it is to forget what a child you are."

"I'm not, I…" Gwen shook her head in mute denial. "It happened so fast, I didn't think. I just…"

"I can hardly deny that it's my fault." His tone had cooled, and its marked disinterest had the edge of a knife. "You're an extraordinary creature, part will-o'-the-wisp, part Amazon, and I have a problem keeping my hands off you. Knowing I can have you is not exactly an incentive to restrain myself."

His matter-of-fact tone scraped at Gwen's raw pride, even as it tripped her temper. "You're hateful."

"Agreed," Luke said with a brief nod. "But still, I think, civilized enough not to take advantage of an innocent girl."

"I am not…" Gwen managed before she felt the need to swallow. "I am not an innocent girl, I'm a grown woman!"

"As you wish. Do you still want me to take advantage of you?" Luke's tone was agreeable now.

"No!" Impatiently, she brushed at the hair on her forehead. "I mean, it wouldn't be… Certainly not!"

"In that case…" Taking her arm, Luke firmly guided Gwen inside Malon's cabin.

Chapter 10

Knocking on Luke's door was not the easiest thing Gwen had ever done, but it was necessary. She felt it necessary to prove to herself that she would not succumb to a newly discovered weakness again. She was a grown woman, capable of handling herself. She had asked to read Luke's manuscript, had agreed to proof it. She would not back down because of a kiss or a moment of madness. Still, Gwen braced herself as she lifted her knuckles to the wood. She held her breath.

"Come in."

These simple, ordinary words from inside the room caught at her heart. Letting out her breath slowly, she arranged her features in casual, almost indifferent lines and opened the door. Luke did not even bother to look up.

Reference books were piled on the table and scattered over the floor. Papers—typewritten, handwritten, crumpled and smooth—were strewn everywhere. On the table in the midst of the chaos was a battered portable typewriter. There sat the creator of the havoc, frowning at the keys while he pounded on them. The curtains were still drawn, closing out the late-morning sun, and the bed was a tangle of sheets. Everywhere were books, papers, folders.

"What a mess," Gwen murmured involuntarily. At her voice, Luke glanced up. There was at first a crease of annoyance between his brows, then a look of mild surprise before all was smoothed away.

"Hello," he said easily. He did not rise, but leaned back in his chair to look at her.

Gwen advanced, stepping over books and around papers on the journey. "This is incredible." She lifted her hand to gesture around the room, then dropped it to her side. "How do you live like this?"

Luke looked around, shrugged and met the curiosity in her eyes. "I don't, I work like this. If you've come to tidy up, I'll tell you the same thing I told the girl Anabelle used to send up here. Mess with my papers, and I'll toss you out the window."

Amused, Gwen stuck her hands in her pockets and nudged a book out of her way with her toe. "So, you're temperamental after all." This, she felt, was a trait she could understand and deal with.

"If you like," he agreed. "This way, if I lose something, I can only swear at myself, not at some hapless maid or well-meaning secretary. I have an aversion for well-meaning secretaries. What can I do for you? I'm afraid the coffee's cold."

The formality in his tone made it clear this was his domain. Gwen schooled her voice to sound briskly professional. "You said yesterday you'd like me to proof your manuscript. I'd be glad to do it. If," she added with a glance around the room, "you can find it."

He smiled his charming, irresistible smile. Gwen hardened herself against it. "Are you an organized soul, Gwenivere? I've always admired organization as long as it doesn't infringe on my habits. Sit," he invited with a gesture of his hand.

Gwen stepped over two dictionaries and an encyclopedia. "Would you mind if I opened the drapes first?" she asked.

"If you wish," he answered as he reached for a pile of typewritten pages. "Just don't get domestic."

"Nothing could be further from my mind," she assured him, and had the pleasure of seeing him wince at the brilliance of the sunlight that streamed into the room. "There," she said, adopting the tone of a nursery school teacher, "isn't that better?"

"Sit."

Gwen did so after removing a pile of magazines from the chair across from him.

"You look older with your hair up," Luke commented mildly. "Nearly sixteen."

A fire lit in her eyes, but she managed to keep her voice cool. "Do you mind if I get started?"

"Not at all." Luke handed her a stack of typewritten material. "You'll find a pencil and a dictionary somewhere. Do as much as you like, just be quiet about it."

Gwen's mouth opened to retort, but as he was typing again, she closed it. After locating a pencil under a pile of discarded magazines, she picked up the first page. She refused to admit that the project excited her, that she wanted the job because it meant sharing something with him. Dismissing such thoughts, she resolved to read with objective professionalism. Minutes later, her pencil was forgotten—she was enthralled.

Time passed. Gwen no longer heard the clicking of the typewriter. Dust motes danced in the insistent sunlight, but Gwen was unaware of them. Luke's characters were flesh and blood to her. She felt she knew them, cared about them. She was even unaware that her eyes had filled with tears. She felt as the woman in Luke's story felt; desperately in love, confused, proud, vulnerable. She wept for the beauty of the words and the despair of the heroine. Suddenly, she lifted her eyes.

Luke had stopped typing, but for how long, she did not know. She blinked to clear her vision. He was watching her. His eyes were intent and searching, his mouth unsmiling. Helplessly Gwen stared back, letting the tears fall freely. Her weakness frightened her. He was not touching her, not speaking to her, yet her whole body felt attuned to him. She opened her mouth, but no words came. She shook her head, but he neither moved nor spoke. Knowing her only defense was escape, Gwen stood and darted from the room.

The bayou offered a haven, so she abandoned the house and fled toward it. She had calmed herself considerably by the time she neared Malon's cabin. Taking long, deep breaths, Gwen slowed her steps. It would not do to have Malon see her out of breath and distressed. As she rounded the last bend in the path, she saw Malon stepping from his pirogue onto the dock. Already, she felt reason returning.

"A good catch?" she asked, grateful she could smile at him without effort.

"Not bad," he answered with typical understatement. "Did you come for dinner?"

"Dinner?" Gwen repeated, glancing automatically at the sun. "Is it so late?" Could the afternoon have gone so swiftly? she wondered.

"It is late enough because I'm hungry," Malon replied. "We'll cook up some shrimp and eat, then you can take your mama her share. Can you still make coffee?"

"Of course I can still make coffee—just don't tell Tillie." Gwen followed him inside, letting the screen door slam behind them.

Before long the cabin was filled with the pungent scent of shrimp gumbo cooking and the quiet strains of Chopin. Raphael sunned on the windowsill, leaving the humans to deal with the domestic chores. Gwen felt the tension draining from her system. She ate, surprised at her appetite until she recalled she had eaten nothing since breakfast.

"You still like my cooking, *hein?*" Pleased, Malon spooned more gumbo onto her plate.

"I just didn't want to hurt your feelings," Gwen told him between bites. Malon watched her clean her plate and chuckled. With a contented sigh, Gwen sat back. "I haven't eaten that much in two years."

"That's why you're skinny." Malon leaned back, too, and lit a strong French cigarette. Gwen remembered the scent as well as she remembered the tastes. She had been twelve—curious and ultimately sick—when she persuaded Malon to let her try one. He had offered no sympathy and no lecture. Grinning at the memory, Gwen watched the thin column of smoke rise.

"Now you feel better," Malon commented. At his statement, she shifted her eyes back to his. Instantly, she saw he was not referring to her hunger. Her shoulders lifted and then fell with her sigh.

"Some. I needed to come here—it's helped. I'm having trouble understanding myself, and there's...well, there's this man."

"There is bound to be," Malon agreed, blowing a series of smoke rings. "You are a woman."

"Yes, but not a very smart one. I don't know very much about men. And he's nothing like the men I've known in any case." She turned to Malon. "The trouble is..." She made a small, frustrated sound and walked to the window. "The trouble is, I'm becoming more involved, more emotionally involved with...this man than I can afford to."

"'Afford to,'" he repeated with a snort. "What do you mean, 'afford to'? Emotions cost you nothing."

"Oh, Malon." When she turned back to him, her eyes were unhappy. "Sometimes they cost everything. I'm beginning to need him, beginning to feel an—an attachment that can lead nowhere."

"And why can it lead nowhere?"

"Because I need love." After running a hand through her hair, Gwen paced the width of the cabin.

"So does everyone," Malon told her, carefully crushing out his cigarette.

"But he doesn't love me," she said miserably. Her hands made a futile gesture. "He doesn't love me, yet I can't stop thinking about him. When I'm with him I forget everything else. It's wrong, he's involved with someone else, and… Oh, Malon, it's so complicated." Her voice faltered away.

"Life is not simple, little girl," he said, reverting to her childhood title, "but we live it." Rising, he moved toward her, then patted her cheek. "Complications provide spice."

"Right now," she said with a small smile, "I'd rather be bland."

"Did you come for advice or for sympathy?" His eyes were small and sharp, his palm rough. He smelled of fish and tobacco. Gwen felt the ground was more solid where he stood.

"I came to be with you," she told him softly, "because you are the only father I have." Slipping her arms around his waist, she rested her head on one of his powerful shoulders. She felt his wide hand stroke her hair. "Malon," she murmured. "I don't want to be in love with him."

"So, do you come for an antilove potion? Do you want a snakeskin for his pillow?"

Gwen laughed and tilted back her head. "No."

"Good. I like him. I would feel bad putting a hex on him."

She realized Malon had known all along she had been speaking of Luke. Always she had been as clear as a piece of glass to him. Still, she was more comfortable with him than with anyone else. Gwen studied him, wondering what secrets he held behind the small blue eyes. "Malon, you never told me you'd been to Budapest."

"You never asked."

She smiled and relaxed. "If I asked now, would you tell me?"

"I'll tell you while you do the dishes."

* * *

Bradley frowned at his canvas, then at his model. "You're not giving me the spark," he complained as he pushed the fisherman's cap further back on his head.

Three nights of fitful sleep had dimmed Gwen's spark considerably. She sat, as Bradley had directed her, in the smoothly worn U formed by two branches of an ancient oak. She wore the robe he had chosen, with a magnolia tucked behind her ear. Following his instructions, she had left her hair free and kept her makeup light. Because of their size and color, her eyes dominated the picture. But they did not, as Bradley had anticipated, hold the light he had seen before. There was a listlessness in the set of her shoulders, a moodiness in the set of her mouth.

"Gwen," Bradley said with exaggerated patience, "depression is not the mood we're seeking."

"I'm sorry, Bradley." Gwen shrugged and sent him a weary smile. "I haven't been sleeping well."

"Warm milk," Monica Wilkins stated from her perch on a three-legged stool. She was painting, with quiet diligence, a tidy clump of asters. "Always helps me."

Gwen wanted to wrinkle her nose at the thought, but instead she answered politely. "Maybe I'll try that next time."

"Don't scald it, though," Monica warned as she perfected her image of a petal.

"No, I won't," Gwen assured her with equal gravity.

"Now that we've got that settled…." Bradley began, in such a martyrlike voice that Gwen laughed.

"I'm sorry, Bradley, I'm afraid I'm a terrible model."

"Nonsense," Bradley said. "You've just got to relax."

"Wine," Monica announced, still peering critically at her asters.

"I beg your pardon?" Bradley turned his head and frowned.

"Wine," Monica repeated. "A nice glass of wine would relax her beautifully."

"Yes, I suppose it might, if we had any." Bradley adjusted the brim of his cap and studied the tip of his brush.

"I have," Monica told him in her wispy voice.

"Have what?"

Gwen's eyes went back to Bradley. I'm beginning to feel as though I was at a tennis match, she thought, lifting a hand to the base of her neck.

"Wine," Monica answered, carefully adding a vein to a pale green leaf. "I have a thermos of white wine in my bag. It's nicely chilled."

"How clever of you," Bradley told her admiringly.

"Thank you." Monica blushed. "You're certainly welcome to it, if you think it might help." Carefully she opened a bulky macramé sack and pulled out a red thermos.

"Monica, I'm in your debt." Gallantly, Bradley bowed over the thermos. Monica let out what sounded suspiciously like a giggle before she went back to her asters.

"Bradley, I really don't think this is necessary," Gwen began.

"Just the thing to put you into the mood," he disagreed as he unscrewed the thermos lid. Wine poured, light and golden, into the plastic cup.

"But Bradley, I hardly drink at all."

"Glad to hear it." He held out the cup. "Bad for your health."

"Bradley," Gwen began again, trying to keep her voice firm. "It's barely ten o'clock in the morning."

"Yes, drink up, the light will be wrong soon."

"Oh, good grief." Defeated, Gwen lifted the plastic cup to her lips and sipped. With a sigh, she sipped again. "This is crazy," she muttered into the wine.

"What's that, Gwen?" Monica called out.

"I said this is lovely," Gwen amended. "Thank you, Monica."

"Glad to help." As the women exchanged smiles, Bradley tipped more wine into the cup.

"Drink it up," he ordered, like a parent urging medicine on a child. "We don't want to lose the light."

Obediently, Gwen tilted the cup. When she handed it back to Bradley, she heaved a huge sigh. "Am I relaxed?" she asked. There was a pleasant lightness near the top of her head. "My, it's gotten warm, hasn't it?" She smiled at no one in particular as Bradley replaced the lid on the thermos.

"I hope I haven't overdone it," he muttered to Monica.

"One never knows about people's metabolisms," Monica said. With a noncommittal grunt, Bradley returned to his canvas.

"Now look this way, love," he ordered as Gwen's attention wandered. "Remember, I want contrasts. I see the delicacy of your bone structure, the femininity in the pose, but I want to see character in your face. I want spirit—no, more—I want challenge in your eyes. Dare the onlooker to touch the untouched."

"Untouched," Gwen murmured as her memory stirred. "I'm not a child," she asserted, and straightened her shoulders.

"No," Bradley agreed as he studied her closely. "Yes, yes, that's perfect!" He grabbed his brush. Glancing over his shoulder, he caught sight of Luke approaching, and then he gave his full attention to his work. "Ah, the mouth's perfect," he muttered, "just between sulky and a pout. Don't change it, don't change a thing. Bless you, Monica!"

Bradley worked feverishly, unaware that the wine was a far less potent stimulant to his model than the man who now stood beside him. It was his presence that brought the rush of color to her cheeks, that brightened her eyes with challenge and made her mouth grow soft, sulky and inviting. Luke's own face was inscrutable as he watched. Though he stood in quiet observation, there was an air of alertness about him. Bradley muttered as he worked. A crow cawed monotonously in the distance.

A myriad of thoughts and feelings rushed through Gwen's mind. Longing warred fiercely with pride. Luke had infuriated her, charmed her, laughed at her, rejected her. I will not fall in love with him, she told herself. I will not allow it to happen. *He won't make a fool of me again.*

"Magnificent," Bradley murmured.

"Yes, it is." Luke slipped his hands into his pockets as he studied the portrait. "You've caught her."

"It's rare," Bradley muttered, touching up the shadows of Gwen's cheeks in the portrait. "Her looks are just a bonus. It's that aura of innocence mixed with the hint of banked fires. Incredible combination. Every man who sees this portrait will want her."

A flash of irritation crossed Luke's face as he lifted his eyes to Gwen's. "Yes, I imagine so."

"I'm calling it *The Virgin Temptress.* It suits, don't you think?"

"Hmm."

Taking this as full agreement, Bradley lapsed back into unintelligible mutters. Abruptly, he put down his brush and began packing his equipment. "You did beautifully," he told Gwen. "We're losing the morning light. We should start a bit earlier, I think. Three more good sittings should do it now."

"I'll walk back with you, Bradley." Monica rose. "I've done about all I can do on this one." Gathering up her paints, easel and stool, she started after Bradley.

Gwen slipped down from her seat in the fork of the tree with a quick flutter of white. As her bare feet touched the grass, the wine spun dizzily in her head. Instinctively she rested her hand against the tree for support. Watching her, Luke lifted a brow in speculation. With exaggerated care, she straightened, swallowed the odd dryness in her throat and started to walk. Her legs felt strangely weak. It was her intention to walk past Luke with icy dignity, but he stopped her easily with a hand on her arm.

"Are you all right?"

The sun had the wine bubbling inside her. Clearing her throat, Gwen spoke distinctly. "Of course. I am just fine."

Luke placed two fingers under her chin and lifted it. He studied her upturned face. Humor leaped into his eyes. "Why, Gwenivere, you're sloshed."

Knowing the truth of his statement only stiffened her dignity. "I have no idea what you are talking about. If you would kindly remove your hand from my face, I would greatly appreciate it."

"Sure. But don't blame me if you fall on it once the support's gone." Luke dropped his hand, and Gwen swayed dangerously. She gripped Luke's shirt to right herself.

"If you will excuse me," she said regally, but neither moved nor dropped her hand. Heaving a deep sigh, Gwen raised her face again and frowned. "I'm waiting for you to stand still."

"Oh. Sorry. May one ask how you came to be in this condition?"

"Relaxed," Gwen corrected.

"I beg your pardon?"

"That's what I am. It was either wine or warm milk. Monica's a whiz at these things. I'm not too fond of warm milk, and there wasn't any handy in any case."

"No, I can see it might be difficult to come by," Luke agreed, slipping a supporting arm around her waist as she began to weave her way across the lawn.

"I only had a topful, you know."

"That should do it."

"Oh, dear." Gwen stopped abruptly. "I've stepped on a bee." She sat down in a floating film of white. "I suppose the poor little thing will go off and die." Lifting her foot, she frowned at the small welt on the ball of her foot.

"Happily bombed, I should think." Luke sat down and took her foot in his hand. "Hurt?" he asked as he drew out the stinger.

"No, I don't feel anything."

"Small wonder. I think it might be wise to tell Bradley you don't want to be quite so relaxed at ten in the morning."

"He's very serious about his art," Gwen said confidentially. "He believes I'll become immoral."

"A distinct possibility if you continue to relax before noon," Luke agreed dryly. "But I believe you mean 'immortal.'"

"Do you think so, too?" Gwen lifted her face to the sun. "I really thought he and Monica were macadamias."

"What?"

"Nuts." Gwen lay back in the grass and shut her eyes. "I think it would be rather sweet if they fell in love, don't you?"

"Adorable."

"You're just cynical because you've been in love so many times."

"Have I?" He traced a finger over her ankle as he watched the sun highlight her hair. "Why do you say that?"

"Your books. You know how women think, how they feel. When I was reading yesterday, I hurt because it was too real, too personal." The robe shifted lightly with her sigh. "I imagine you've made love with dozens of women."

"Making love and being in love are entirely separate things."

Gwen opened her eyes. "Sometimes," she agreed. "For some people."

"You're a romantic," Luke told her with a shrug. "Only a romantic can wear floating white or toss flowers to the stars or believe a magician's illusions."

"How odd." Gwen's voice was genuinely puzzled as she closed her eyes again. "I've never thought of myself as a romantic. Is it wrong?"

"No." The word was quick and faintly annoyed. Luke rose and stared down at her. Her hair was spread out under her, glinting with golden lights. The robe crossed lightly over her breasts, making an inviting shadow. Swearing under his breath, he bent and scooped her into his arms.

"Mmm, you're very strong." Her head spun gently, so she rested it against his shoulder. "I noticed that the first day, when I watched you chop down the tree. Michael lifts weights."

"Good for Michael."

"No, actually, he strained his back." With a giggle, Gwen snuggled deeper into the curve of his shoulder. "Michael isn't very physical, you see. He plays bridge." Gwen lifted her face and smiled cheerfully. "I'm quite hopeless at bridge. Michael says my mind needs discipline."

"I simply must meet this Michael."

"He has fifty-seven ties, you know."

"Yes, I imagine he does."

"His shoes are always shined," Gwen added wistfully, and traced Luke's jawline with her fingertip. "I really must try to be more tidy. He tells me continually that the image a person projects is important, but I tend to forget. Feeding pigeons in the park isn't good for a corporate image."

"What is?"

"Opera," she said instantly. "German opera particularly, but I fall asleep. I like to watch murder mysteries on the late-night TV."

"Philistine," Luke concluded as his mouth twitched into a smile.

"Exactly," Gwen agreed, feeling more cheerful than she had in weeks. "Your face is leaner than his, too, and he never forgets to shave."

"Good for Michael," Luke mumbled again as he mounted the porch steps.

"He never made me feel the way you do." At these words Luke stopped and stared down into Gwen's eyes. Cushioned by the wine, Gwen met his look with a gentle smile. "Why do you suppose that is?"

Luke's voice was edged with roughness. "Can you really be so utterly guileless?"

She considered the question, then shrugged. "I don't know. I suppose so. Do you want me to be?"

For a moment, Luke's arms tightened, shifting her closer against him. In immediate response, Gwen closed her eyes and offered her mouth. When his lips brushed over her brow, she sighed and cuddled closer. "Sometimes you're a very nice man," she murmured.

"Am I?" He frowned down at her. "Let's say sometimes I remember there are a few basic rules. At the moment, I'm finding my memory unfortunately clear."

"A very nice man," Gwen repeated, and kissed a spot under his jaw.

With a yawn, she settled comfortably against him. "But I won't fall in love with you."

Luke looked down at her quiet face with its aureole of soft curls. "A wise decision," he said softly, and carried her into the house.

Chapter 11

It was dark when Gwen awoke. Disoriented, she stared at the dim shapes of furniture and the pale silver moonlight. It was a knock at the door that had awakened her, and it came again, soft and insistent. Brushing her hair from her face, she sat up. The room spun once, then settled. Gwen moaned quietly and swallowed before she rose to answer the knock. In the hallway the light was bright. She put her hand over her eyes to shield them.

"Oh, darling, I'm sorry to wake you." Anabelle gave a sympathetic sigh. "I know how these headaches are."

"Headaches?" Gwen repeated, gingerly uncovering her eyes.

"Yes, Luke told me all about it. Did you take some aspirin?"

"Aspirin?" Gwen searched her memory. Abruptly, color rushed to her cheeks. "Oh!"

Taking this as an affirmative response, Anabelle smiled. "Are you feeling better now?"

"I haven't got a headache," Gwen murmured.

"Oh, I'm so glad, because you have a phone call." Anabelle smiled more brightly. "It's from New York, so I really thought it best to wake you. It's that Michael of yours. He has a lovely voice."

"Michael," Gwen echoed softly. She sighed, wishing she could return to the comforting darkness of her room. She felt only weariness at the sound of his name. Glancing down, she saw she still wore the white robe. She could clearly remember her conversation with Luke and, more disturbing, the feel of his arms as he carried her.

"You really shouldn't keep him waiting, darling." Anabelle interrupted Gwen's thoughts with gentle prompting. "It's long-distance."

"No, of course not." Gwen followed her mother to the foot of the stairs.

"I'll just run along and have Tillie warm up some dinner for you." Anabelle retreated tactfully, leaving Gwen staring down at the waiting receiver. She took a deep breath, blew it out and picked up the phone.

"Hello, Michael."

"Gwen—I was beginning to think I'd been left on hold." His voice was even, well pitched and annoyed.

"I'm sorry." The apology was automatic, and immediately, she swore at herself for giving it. Why does he always intimidate me? she demanded silently of herself. "I was busy," she added in a firmer voice. "I wasn't expecting to hear from you."

"I hope it's a pleasant surprise," he replied. From the tone of his voice, Gwen knew he had already concluded it was. "I've been busy myself," he went on without bothering to hear her answer. "Right up to my chin in a lawsuit against Delron Corporation. Tricky business. It's had me chained to my desk."

"I'm sorry to hear that, Michael," Gwen said. Glancing up, she saw Luke coming down the steps. *Oh, perfect,* she thought in despair. She feigned unconcern with a faint nod of greeting, but when he stopped and leaned against the newel post, she frowned. "Do you mind?" she whispered sharply to Luke.

"No, not a bit." He smiled but made no effort to move. "Say hello for me."

Her eyes narrowed into furious slits. "You're horrible, absolutely horrible."

"What?" came Michael's puzzled voice. "What did you say?"

"Oh, nothing," Gwen said sharply.

"For heaven's sake, Gwen, I'm simply trying to tell you about the Delron case. You needn't get testy."

"I am not testy. Why did you call, Michael?"

"To see when you'd be coming home, sweetheart. I miss you." He was using his quiet, persuasive tone, and Gwen sighed. Closing her eyes, she rested the receiver against her forehead a moment.

"Does he always make you feel guilty?" Luke asked conversationally. Gwen jerked up her chin and glared.

"Shut up," she ordered, furious that he could read her so accurately.

"What?" Michael's voice shouted through the receiver. Luke gave a quick laugh at the outraged voice. "We must have a bad connection," he concluded.

"Must have," Gwen muttered. Taking a deep breath, Gwen decided to clear the air once and for all. "Michael, I…"

"I thought I'd given you enough time to cool off," Michael said pleasantly.

"Cool off?"

"It was foolish of us to fight that way, sweetheart. Of course I know you didn't mean the things you said."

"I didn't?"

"You know you have a tendency to say rash things when you're in a temper," Michael reminded her in a patient, forgiving tone. "Of course," he went on, "I suppose I was partially to blame."

"You were?" Gwen struggled to keep her voice quiet and reasonable. "How could you be partially to blame for my temper?" Glancing up, she saw Luke still watching her.

"I'm afraid I rushed you. You simply weren't ready for a sudden proposal."

"Michael, we've been seeing each other for nearly a year," Gwen reminded him, pushing her fingers through her hair in irritation. The gesture caused the V of her bodice to widen enticingly.

"Of course, sweetheart," he said soothingly. "But I should have prepared you."

"*Prepared me?* I don't want to be prepared, Michael, do you understand? I want to be surprised. And if you call me sweetheart again in that patronizing voice, I'm going to scream."

"Now, now, Gwen, don't get upset. I'm more than willing to forgive and forget."

"Oh." Gwen swallowed her rage. "Oh, that's generous of you, Michael. I don't know what to say."

"Just say when you'll be back, sweetheart. We'll have a nice celebration dinner and set the date. Tiffany's has some lovely rings. You can take your pick."

"Michael," Gwen said, "please listen to me. Really listen this time. I'm not what you want... I can't be what you want. If I tried, I'd shrivel up inside. Please, I do care about you, but don't ask me to be someone I'm not."

"I don't know what you're talking about, Gwen," he interrupted. "I'm not asking you—"

"Michael," Gwen said, cutting him off. "I just can't go through all this again. I did mean the things I said, but I don't want to have to say them all again. I'm not good for you, Michael. Find someone who knows how to fix vodka martinis for twenty."

"You're talking nonsense." It was his cool attorney's voice, and Gwen closed her eyes, knowing arguments were futile. "We'll straighten all this out when you get home."

"No, Michael," she said, knowing he wouldn't hear.

"Give me a call and I'll meet your plane. Goodbye, Gwen."

"Goodbye, Michael," she murmured, even while she replaced the receiver. She felt a wave of sorrow and guilt. Lifting her eyes, she met Luke's. There was no amusement in them now, only understanding. She felt that amusement would have been easier to handle. "I'd appreciate it very much," she said quietly, "if you wouldn't say anything just now." She walked past him and up the stairs while he looked after her.

Gwen stood on her balcony under a moonlit sky. Moss-draped cypress trees appeared ghostly and tipped with silver. There was a bird singing in a sweet, clear voice, and she wondered if it was a nightingale. The time seemed right for nightingales. She sighed, remembering that Luke had called her a romantic. Perhaps he was right. But it was not the soft night or the song of a bird that kept her out of bed and on the balcony.

Of course you can't sleep, she berated herself silently. How can you expect to sleep at night when you slept all afternoon? Color rushed to her cheeks as she recalled the reason for her peaceful midday nap. I certainly managed to make a first-class fool of myself. Did he have to be there? Couldn't I have stumbled into the house without an audience? Why can I never be cool and dignified around him?

And then the call from Michael. Gwen lifted her hand to the base of her neck and tried to massage away the tension. Again she played over the telephone conversation in her mind, attempting to find some way she could have made her feelings clearer. It's all been said before, she reminded herself, but he doesn't listen. *He forgives me.* With a quiet laugh, Gwen pressed her fingers to her eyes. He forgives me but thinks nothing of the cruel things he said. He doesn't even love me. He loves the woman he'd like me to be.

As she watched, a star shivered and fell in a speeding arc of light. Gwen caught her breath at the fleeting flash from heaven. Abruptly her thoughts centered on Luke. With him, she had felt a meteoric intensity, a brilliant heat. But she knew she could not hold him any more than the night sky could hold the trailing shimmer of light. Feeling a sudden chill, Gwen slipped back into her room. The middle of the night's a bad time for thinking, she decided. I'd be much better off if I went downstairs and tried some of Monica's detestable warm milk.

Gwen moved quickly down the hall, not bothering to switch on a light. She knew her way, just as she knew which steps creaked and which boards moaned. An unexpected sound made her whirl around as she reached the head of the stairs.

"Mama!" Stunned, Gwen watched her mother creep down the third-floor staircase. Anabelle started at Gwen's voice, and her hand fluttered to her heart.

"Gwenivere, you scared the wits out of me!" Anabelle's soft bosom rose with her breath. Her hair was charmingly disordered around her face. The robe she wore was frilly, pink and feminine. "Whatever are you doing out here in the dark?"

"I couldn't sleep." Gwen moved closer and caught the familiar scent of lilac. "Mama...."

"Of course, you're probably starving." Anabelle gave a sympathetic cluck. "It doesn't do to miss meals, you know."

"Mama, what were you doing upstairs?"

"Upstairs?" Anabelle repeated, then glanced back over her shoulder. "Oh, why, I was just up with Luke." She smiled, not noticing Gwen's draining color.

"W-with Luke?"

"Yes." She made a token gesture of tidying her hair. "He's such a marvelous, generous man."

Gwen gently took her mother's hand. "Mama." She bit her lip to steady her voice and took a deep breath. "Are you certain this is what you want?"

"Is what what I want, darling?"

"This—this relationship with Luke," Gwen managed to get out, although the words hurt her throat.

"Oh, Gwen, I simply couldn't get along without Luke." She gave Gwen's icy hand a squeeze. "Goodness, you're cold. You'd best get back to bed, dear. Is there anything I can get for you?"

"No," Gwen answered quietly. "No, there's nothing." She gave Anabelle a quick, desperate hug. "Please, you go back to bed, I'll be fine."

"All right, dear." Anabelle kissed her brow in a way Gwen recognized from childhood. Satisfied that there was no fever, Anabelle patted her cheek. "Good night, Gwen."

"Good night, Mama," Gwen murmured, watching her disappear down the hall.

Gwen waited until the sound of the closing door had echoed into silence before she let out a shuddering breath. Face it, Gwen, you've been falling for your mother's man. For a moment, she merely stared down at her empty hands. Doing nothing wasn't enough, she reflected. I could have stopped it... I didn't want to stop it. There's nothing to do now but get untangled while I still can. It's time to face things head-on. Lifting her chin, she began to climb the stairs to the third floor.

Without giving herself a chance to think any further, she knocked at Luke's door.

"Yes?" The reply was curt and immediate.

Refusing to give in to the urge to turn and run, Gwen twisted the knob and pushed open Luke's door. He was, as he had been before, seated in the midst of his own disorder. He was hitting the keys of the typewriter in a quick, staccato rhythm, and his eyes were intent and concentrated. Faded, low-slung jeans were his only concession to modesty. The faintest hint of lilac drifted through the air. Moistening her lips, Gwen kept her eyes from the tousled sheets of the bed.

I am in love with him, she realized suddenly, and simultaneously remembered it was impossible for her to be so. I'll have to find a way to fall out of love with him, she told herself, warding off a brief stab of misery. I'll have to start now. Keeping her head high, she closed the door behind her and leaned against it.

"Luke?"

"Hmm?" He glanced up absently, his fingers still working the keys. His expression altered as he focused on her. His hands lay still. "What are you doing here?" There was such sharp impatience in his voice that Gwen bit her lip.

"I'm sorry to interrupt your work. I need to talk to you."

"At this hour of the night?" His tone was politely incredulous. "Run along, Gwen, I'm busy."

Gwen swallowed her pride. "Luke, please. It's important."

"So's my sanity," he muttered, without changing rhythm.

She ran a hand through her hair. *Sanity,* she thought desperately, I must have lost mine the moment he put down that ax and walked toward me. "You're making this very difficult."

"I?" he tossed back furiously. "I make it difficult? Do you know how you look at me? Do you know how many times I've found myself alone with you when you're half-dressed?" Instinctively, Gwen reached for the low neckline of her robe. "Contrary to popular opinion," he continued as he rose and strode to a small table across the room, "I am a mortal man given to normal instincts." There was a decanter of brandy on the table, and he poured himself a hefty glass. "Damn it, I want you. Haven't I made that clear enough?"

His tone was rough. Gwen felt the tears burn in her throat. When she spoke, her voice was thick with them. "I'm sorry, I didn't mean…" She broke off with a helpless shrug.

"For God's sake, don't cry," he said impatiently. "I'm in no mood to give you a few comforting kisses and send you along. If I touch you now, you won't leave here tonight." His eyes met hers. She swallowed even the thought of tears. "I'm not in a civilized mood, Gwen. I told you once that I know my limit. Well, I've reached it." He lifted the decanter and poured again.

Temptation fluttered along her skin. He wanted her, she could almost taste his desire. How easy it would be to take just one small step…to steal a night, a moment. The night would be full and rich. *But the morning would be empty.* Gwen's eyes dropped, and she struggled with her own heart. When his passion was spent, she knew her love would starve. Love has found another fool, she thought resignedly. It's best to do this quickly.

"This isn't easy for me," Gwen told him quietly. Though she fought for calm, her eyes were tragic as they met his. "I need to talk to you about Mama."

Luke turned and walked to the French doors. Tossing them open, he stared out into the night. "What about her?"

"I was wrong to interfere." Gwen shut her eyes tight and struggled to strengthen her voice. "It was wrong of me to come here thinking I had any say in whom my mother becomes involved with."

Luke swore and whirled back to face her. She watched him struggle with temper. "You are an idiot. Anabelle is a beautiful woman—"

"Please," Gwen interrupted swiftly, "let me finish. I need to say this, and it's so difficult. I'd like to say it all at once." She still stood with her back to the door, poised for escape. Luke shrugged, dropped back into his chair and signaled for her to continue. "It isn't up to me to decide what's right for my mother, it's not my right to interfere. You're good for her, I can't deny it." Gwen's breath trembled before she could steady it. "And I can't deny I'm attracted to you, but it's nothing that can't be resolved by a bit of distance. I think—I think if you and I just stay out of each other's way for the rest of my visit, everything will work out."

"Oh, do you?" Luke gave a quick laugh as he set down his glass. "That's an amazing piece of logic." He rubbed the bridge of his nose between his thumb and forefinger. Gwen frowned at the action, finding it somehow out of character.

"I'm leaving next week," Gwen told him. "There's no need for me to stay, and I've left several things undone back in New York." Hurriedly, she turned to the door.

"Gwen." Luke's voice stopped her, but she could not bear to turn and face him again. "Don't waste yourself on Michael."

"I don't intend to," she answered in a choked voice. Blind with tears, she opened the door and plunged into the darkness.

Chapter 12

Gwen dressed with care. She stretched out the process, dawdling over the buttons of her pale lavender blouse. After another sleepless night, Gwen knew she could not survive even a few more days in the same house with Luke. She could not be sophisticated, mature or philosophical about love. She went to her closet and pulled out her suitcase.

When two women love the same man, she mused, one of them has to lose. If it were anyone else, I could fight her. She opened the first case. How does a daughter fight her own mother? Even if she wins, she loses. I haven't really lost, she reflected as she moved to her dresser and pulled open a drawer. You have to have something first to lose it. I never had Luke.

Gwen packed methodically, using the task as a diversion. She refused to speculate on what she would do when she returned to New York. While packing, she had no past and no future, only the present. She would have to face the shambles of her life soon enough.

"Gwen." Anabelle knocked quickly and stuck her head into the room. "I wonder if you've seen… Oh!" She opened the door all the way when she saw Gwen's half-packed cases. "What's this?"

Gwen moistened her lips and strove for casualness. "I've got to get back to New York."

"Oh." There was disappointment in the single syllable. "But you just got here. Are you going back to Michael?"

"No, Mama, I'm not going back to Michael."

"I see." She paused a moment. "Is there some trouble at your office?"

The excuse was so perfect, agreement trembled on Gwen's tongue. Regretably, the lie would not form on her lips. "No."

Anabelle tilted her head at her daughter's tone, then quietly closed the door at her back. "You know I don't like to pry, Gwen, and I know you're a very private person, but..." Anabelle sighed before she walked over to sit on Gwen's bed. "I really think you'd better tell me what this is all about."

"Oh, Mama." Gwen turned away and rested both palms on her dresser. "It's such an awful mess."

"It can't be as bad as all that." Anabelle folded her hands neatly in her lap. "Just tell me straight out, it's the best way."

Gwen took a breath and held it. "I'm in love with Luke," she said quickly, then expelled the breath in one swift whoosh.

"And..." Anabelle prompted.

Gwen's eyes flew to the mirror in search of her mother's. "Mama, I said I was in love with Luke."

"Yes, darling, I heard that part. I'm waiting for the part about the dreadful mess."

"Mama." Gingerly, Gwen turned around. Anabelle smiled patiently. "It's not just an infatuation or a crush, I'm really in love with him."

"Oh, yes, well, that's nice."

"I don't think you understand." Gwen covered her face with her hands for a moment and then dropped them. "I even wanted him to—to make love with me."

Anabelle blushed a soft, gentle pink and brushed at her skirts. "Yes, well...I'm sure that's quite natural. I don't believe you and I ever had a talk about...ah, the birds and the bees."

"Oh, good grief, Mama," Gwen said impatiently. "I don't need a lecture on sex. I know all about that."

"Oh?" Anabelle lifted her brows in maternal censure. "I see."

"No, I don't mean..." Gwen stopped in frustration. How did this conversation get away from me? she wondered. "Mama, please, this is hard enough. I came home to get rid of the man, and before I knew it, I was involved with him. I didn't plan it, I didn't want it. I'd never, never do anything to hurt you, and I was wrong because years don't mean a thing, and no one has the right to choose for anyone else. Now I have to go away because I love you both so terribly, don't you see?" Gwen ended on a note of despair and dropped down at Anabelle's feet.

Anabelle stared down at the tragic face thoughtfully. "Perhaps I will in a minute," she answered, furrowing her brow. "No, actually, I don't think I will. Why don't you try again? Start with the part about your coming here to get rid of Luke. I believe that's where I got confused."

Gwen sniffled and accepted Anabelle's lace hankie. "I wanted to make him go away because I thought it was wrong for you to have an affair with him. But it was none of my—"

"A what?" Anabelle interrupted. Her hand paused on its journey to smooth Gwen's curls. *"An affair?"* she repeated, blinking rapidly. "An affair? Luke and I?" To Gwen's amazement, Anabelle tossed back her head and laughed. It was a young, gay sound. "How delightful! Darling, darling, how flattering. My, my." She smiled into space, her cheeks rosy with pleasure. "Such a handsome young man, too. He must be—" she stopped and fluttered her lashes "—well, a year or two younger than I." She laughed again and clapped her hands together as Gwen looked on. Bending down, she kissed her daughter soundly. "Thank you, sweet, sweet child. I don't know when I've had a nicer present."

"Now *I* don't understand." Gwen wiped a lingering tear from her lashes. "Are you saying you and Luke aren't lovers?"

"Oh, my." Anabelle rolled her eyes. "How very blunt you are."

"Mama, please, I'll go mad in a moment." Briefly, Gwen pressed her fingers to her eyes. Rising, she began to pace the room. "You talked and talked about him in all your letters. You said he'd changed your life. You said he was the most wonderful man you'd ever met. You couldn't get along without him. And just last night you were coming out of his room in the middle of the night. And you've been acting strangely." Gwen whirled around and paced in the other direction. "You can't deny it. Locking your door and practically pushing me out of the house on the flimsiest of excuses."

"Oh, dear." Anabelle clucked her tongue and touched a hand to her hair. "I begin to see. I suppose it was silly of me to keep it a secret." Standing, Anabelle took a blouse from Gwen's suitcase, shook it out and walked to the closet. "Yes, it's obviously my fault. But then, I wanted to surprise you. Poor darling, no wonder you've been so unhappy and confused. I'm afraid I thought you were brooding over Michael, but it wasn't him at all, was it? Luke makes much better sense, I'm sure." Carefully, Anabelle hung up the blouse. "Now, when I think back on it, I can see how you might think so." She moved back to the suitcase while Gwen prayed for patience. "Luke and I aren't having an affair, though I do thank you for the kind thought, dear. We are, however, collaborating in a sense. Why don't you sit down?"

"I think," Gwen said, "I'm going to scream any minute."

"Always so impatient," Anabelle sighed. "Well, this is a bit embarrassing. I feel so foolish." She placed her hands on her cheeks as they grew warm. "Oh, I do hope you won't laugh at me. I'm…I'm writing a book." The confession came out in a swift jumble of words.

"What?" Gwen exclaimed, touching her hand to her ear to check her hearing.

"I've always wanted to, but I never thought I could until Luke encouraged me." Excitement joined the embarrassment in Anabelle's voice. "I've always had such pretty stories in my head, but I never had the courage to write them down. Luke says—" Anabelle lifted her chin and glowed proudly "—he says I have a natural talent."

"Talent?" Gwen echoed as she sank onto the bed.

"Isn't that lovely of him?" Anabelle enthused. She shook out one of Gwen's packed dresses and moved toward the closet. "He's given me so much help, so much time and encouragement! He doesn't even mind if I pop up to his room and try out an idea! Why, just last night he stopped his own work to listen to me."

Remembering the conclusions she had drawn, Gwen shut her eyes. "Oh, good grief! Why didn't you tell me?"

"I wanted to surprise you. And to be honest, I felt you'd think I was being silly." She began neatly to put away Gwen's lingerie. "My, what a pretty chemise. New York has such wonderful shops. Then there's the money."

"Money," Gwen repeated. Opening her eyes, she tried valiantly to follow her mother's winding train of thought. "What money?"

"Luke thinks I should sell the manuscript when I'm finished. It's—well, it's a bit crass, don't you think?"

"Oh, Mama." Gwen could only close her eyes again.

"I am sorry about not telling you and about locking my door so you wouldn't catch me writing. And about shooing you out of the house so that I could finish up. You aren't angry with me, are you?"

"No, no, I'm not angry." Gwen stared up at Anabelle's glowing face and then buried her own in her hands and laughed. "Oh, help! What a fool I've made of myself!" She rose quickly and embraced her mother. "I'm proud of you, Mama. Very proud."

"You haven't read it yet," Anabelle reminded her.

"I don't have to read it to be proud of you. And I don't think you're silly, I think you're marvelous." Drawing away slightly, she studied Anabelle's face. "Luke's right," she said, kissing both of her mother's cheeks. "You are a beautiful woman."

"Did he say that?" Anabelle dimpled. "How sweet." After patting Gwen's shoulder, she moved to the door. "I think we've solved everything nicely. Come down after you're unpacked, and I'll let you read my first chapters."

"Mama." Gwen shook her head. "I can't stay…."

"Oh, Luke." Anabelle beamed as she opened the door. "How lucky. You'll never believe the mess Gwen and I have just straightened out."

"Oh?" Luke looked past Anabelle to Gwen, then studied the open cases on her bed. "Going somewhere?"

"Yes."

"No," Anabelle said simultaneously. "Not anymore. She was going back to New York, but we solved everything nicely."

"Mama," Gwen said warningly, and stepped forward.

"I've confessed all," she told Luke with a bright smile. "Gwen knows all about my secret hobby. The poor darling thought you and I were having a romance."

"Weren't we?" Luke lifted her hand to his lips.

"Oh, you devil." Anabelle patted his cheek, highly pleased. "I must get along now, but I'm sure Luke will want to hear what you told me about being in love with him."

"Mama!" The sharp retort emerged as a tragic whisper.

"I'd close the door," Anabelle suggested to Luke. "Gwen favors her privacy."

"I'll do that," Luke agreed, and kissed her hand again. With a delighted blush and flutter, she disappeared.

"A truly marvelous woman," Luke commented, quietly closing the door and turning the key. He turned it over in his palm a moment, studying it, then slipped it into his pocket. Gwen decided it was better strategy not to comment. "Now, suppose you tell me what you told Anabelle about being in love with me."

Looking into his calm eyes, Gwen knew it wasn't going to be easy. Temper would not work as long as he had the key. It was vital that she remain as calm as he. "I owe you an apology," she said as she casually moved to her closet. Taking the dress Anabelle had just replaced, Gwen folded it and laid it back in the suitcase.

Luke continued to stand by the door, watching her movements. "For what, precisely?"

Gwen bit the underside of her lip hard and moved back to the closet. "For the things I said about you and Mama."

"You're apologizing for believing we were having an affair?" Luke smiled at her for the first time, and although she heard it in his voice, she did not turn to see it. "I took it as a compliment."

Turning slowly, Gwen decided to brazen it out. It was impossible, she decided, to be any more humiliated than she already was. "I'm well aware that I've made a fool of myself. And I know that I deserve to feel every bit as ridiculous as I feel. As I look back, I believe that you decided on the very first day to teach me a lesson. You never admitted you were having an affair with my mother, you simply told me it was none of my business. I felt differently at the time." Gwen paused to catch her breath, and Luke moved into the room to lean comfortably on one of the bedposts. "I was wrong and you were right. It wasn't any of my business, and you succeeded in teaching me a lesson just by letting me draw my own conclusions. These were helped along by Mama's unusual behavior and her affection for you. You could, of course, have saved me a great deal of anxiety and humiliation by explaining things, but you chose to make your point. Point taken, Mr. Powers," she continued as she worked herself up into a temper. "I've been put in my place by an expert. Now, I'd like you to get out of here and leave me alone. If there's one thing I want above all else, it's never to see you again. I can only be thankful we live on opposite ends of the continent."

Luke waited a moment while she tore two skirts out of her closet and heaved them into the case. "Can I get a copy of that speech for my files?"

Gwen whirled, eyes flaming. "You unfeeling, pompous boor! I've done all the groveling I'm going to do. What more do you want?"

"Was that groveling?" he asked, lifting a brow in interest. "Fascinating. What I want," he continued, "is for you to elaborate on the statement Anabelle made before she left the room. I found it very interesting."

"You want it all, don't you?" Gwen snapped, slamming the lid on her first case. "All right, then, I'll give it to you. It makes little difference at this point." She took a breath to help the words come quickly. "I love you. What will you do now that you know?" she demanded, keeping her head high. "Write it into one of your books for comic relief?"

Luke considered a moment and then shrugged. "No. I rather think I'll marry you."

In stunned silence, Gwen stared at him. "I don't think that's very funny."

"No, I doubt marriage is a funny business. I'm sure it has its moments, though. We'll have to find out." Straightening, he walked over and put his hands on her shoulders. "Soon."

"Don't touch me," she whispered, and tried to jerk out of his hold.

"Oh, yes, I'll touch you." He turned Gwen to face him. "I'll do much more than touch you. Idiot," he said roughly when he saw her tear-drenched eyes. "Are you so blind you can't see what you've put me through? I wanted you from the first moment I saw you. You stood there smiling at me, and I felt as though someone had hit me with a blunt instrument. I wanted to teach you a lesson, all right, but I didn't expect to learn one. I didn't expect some skinny kid to tangle herself up in my mind so that I couldn't get her out." He pulled her close as she stared up at him, dry-eyed and fascinated. "I love you to the edge of madness," he murmured before his mouth crushed hers.

It's a dream, Gwen thought dazedly as his mouth roamed her face, teasing her skin. It must be a dream. She threw her arms around his neck and clung, praying never to wake up. "Luke," she managed before her mouth was silenced again. "Tell me you mean it," she begged as he tasted her neck. "Please tell me you mean it."

"Look at me," he ordered, taking her chin in his hand. She did, and found her answer. Joy bubbled inside her and escaped in laughter. Laughing with her, Luke rested his brow against hers. "I believe I've surprised you."

"Oh, Luke." She buried her face in his shoulder, holding him as if she would never let him go. "I'm not surprised, I'm delirious." She sighed, weak from laughter, dizzy with love. "How did this happen?"

"I haven't the faintest idea." He brushed his lips over the top of her head. "Falling in love with you was not in my plans."

"Why not?" she demanded, rubbing her cheek against his. "I'm a very nice person."

"You're a child," he corrected, lost in the scent of her hair. "Do you realize what we were doing when I was your age?" He gave a quick, mystified laugh. "I was working on my second novel, and you were drawing pictures with your Crayolas."

"It's twelve years, not twenty," Gwen countered, slipping her hands under his shirt to feel the warmth of his back. "And you can hardly make an issue out of an age difference, particularly a twelve-year age difference, after all this. You don't have any double standards, do you?" she asked, lifting a brow.

Luke gave her hair a brief tug. "It's not just the years. You're so innocent, so unspoiled. Wanting you was driving me mad, then loving you only made it worse." He kissed her lightly behind the ear, and she shivered with pleasure. "Even up to last night I was determined not to take advantage of that innocence. Part of me still wants to leave you that way."

"I hope the rest of you has more sense," Gwen tossed back her head to look up at him.

"I'm serious."

"So am I." She ran a fingertip along his jawline. "Buy Bradley's portrait, if you want an image."

"I already have." He smiled, caught her fingers in his and kissed them. "You don't think I'd let anyone else have it, do you?"

"Have me, too." Amusement vanished from his face as she pressed against him. "I'm a woman, Luke, not a child or an image. I love you, and I want you." Rising on her toes, she met his mouth. His hands sought her, possessed her, while she trembled with excitement. Her love seemed to expand, surrounding her until there was nothing else. She pressed closer, offering everything. It was he who drew away.

"Gwen." Luke let out a long breath and shook his head. "It's difficult to remember that you're Anabelle's daughter and that she trusts me."

"I'm trying to make it impossible," she countered. She could feel the speed of his heartbeat against hers, and reveled in a new sense of power. "Aren't you going to corrupt me?"

"Undoubtedly," he agreed. Framing her face with his hands, he kissed her nose. "After we're married."

"Oh." Gwen pouted a moment, then shrugged. "That's sensible, I suppose. Michael was always sensible, too."

Luke's eyes narrowed at the mischief in hers. "That," he said distinctly, "was a low blow. Do you know how very near I came to pulling the phone out of the wall last night when I heard you talking to him?"

"Did you?" Gwen's face illuminated at the thought. "Were you jealous?"

"That's one way of putting it," Luke agreed.

"Well," Gwen considered carefully, trying not to smile, "I suppose I can understand that. As I said, he's a very sensible man. It's all right, though, I'm sure you're every bit as sensible as Michael."

Luke studied her carefully, but Gwen managed to keep the smile a mere hint on her lips. "Are you challenging me to kiss you into insensibility?"

"Oh, yes," she agreed, and closed her eyes. "Please do."

"I never could resist a dare," Luke murmured, drawing her into his arms.

* * * * *